CIR
of DAYS

KEN FOLLETT

CIRCLE *of* DAYS

QUERCUS

First published in Great Britain in 2025 by Quercus
Part of John Murray Group

1

Copyright © 2025 Ken Follett

Map artwork by Daren Cook
Book design by Janette Revill
Endpaper image © The Printer Collector / Alamy Stock Photo

A CIP catalogue record for this book is available
from the British Library

HB ISBN 978 1 52944 234 2
TPB ISBN 978 1 52944 235 9
EBOOK ISBN 978 1 52944 236 6

Typeset in Celestia Antiqua by Palimpsest Book Production Ltd,
Falkirk, Stirlingshire

Printed and bound in Great Britain by Clays Ltd, Elcograf S.p.A.

Papers used by Quercus are from well-managed forests and other responsible sources.

Quercus
Carmelite House
50 Victoria Embankment
London EC4Y 0DZ

John Murray Group
Part of Hodder & Stoughton Limited
An Hachette UK company

The authorised representative in the EEA is Hachette Ireland,
8 Castlecourt Centre, Dublin 15, D15 XTP3, Ireland (email: info@hbgi.ie)

CIRCLE
of DAYS

NORTHRIVER
North-West Hills
The Great Plain
OldOak
The Break
East Wood
West Wood
Farmplace
SOUTHRIVER

Stony Valley

North Hills

Scarp

Knap Hill

Huish Hill

Flint Mines

EAST RIVER

The route of the stones

Upriver

Monument

Riverbend

The story begins around
the year 2500 BCE

1

SEFT TRUDGED ACROSS the Great Plain, carrying on his back a wickerwork basket containing flints to be traded. He was with his father and two older brothers. He hated all three of them.

The plain stretched as far as he could see on all sides. The summer-green grass was dotted with yellow buttercups and red clover that merged, in the distance, into a haze of orange and green. Great herds of cattle and sheep, many more than he could count, grazed contentedly. There was no path, but they knew the way, and they could make the journey with time to spare in a long summer day.

The sun was hot on Seft's head. The plain was mostly flat but there were gentle ups and downs that were not so gentle when you were carrying a heavy load. His father, Cog, maintained the same walking pace regardless of the terrain. 'The sooner we get there, the sooner we can rest,' he would say – a stupidly obvious statement that irritated Seft. Flint was the hardest of all stones, and Seft's father had a heart like flint. Grey-haired and grey-faced,

3

he was not big but he was very strong, and when his sons displeased him he punished them with fists like stones.

Everything that had a cutting edge was made of flint, from axes to arrowheads to knives. Everybody needed flints, and they could always be traded for anything else you wanted, food or clothing or livestock. Some people stored them up, knowing they would always be valuable and never deteriorate.

Seft was looking forward to seeing Neen. He had thought about her every day since the Spring Rite. They had met on his last evening, and had sat talking into the night. She had been so warm and friendly that he felt sure she liked him. As he toiled in the pit during the weeks that followed he often pictured her face. In his daydream she was always smiling and leaning forward to say something to him, something nice. She looked lovely when she smiled.

When they parted she had kissed him goodbye.

He had not met many girls, working all day in a hole in the ground, but those he had met had never affected him in this way.

His brothers had seen him with Neen and had guessed that he had fallen for her. Today as they walked they mocked him with vulgar comments. Olf, who was big and stupid, said: 'Are you going to stick your thing in her this time, Seft?' and Cam, who always followed Olf's lead, made thrusting movements with his hips, which made them both laugh, sounding like a pair of crows in a tree. They thought they were witty. They carried on in the same vein for a while, but they soon ran out of jibes. They were not imaginative.

They carried their baskets in their arms, on their shoulders, or on their heads, but Seft had devised a way of strapping his to his back with strips of leather. It was awkward to put on and take off, but once it was fixed it was comfortable. They had made fun of it, and called him a weakling, but he was used to that sort of thing.

He was the baby of the family, and the cleverest, and they resented him for being smart. Their father never intervened; he even seemed to enjoy seeing his sons quarrel and fight. When Seft was bullied, Cog told him to toughen up.

As they progressed Seft began to feel the weight of his basket, despite his contraption. Looking at the others, he thought they were not as weary as he was. That was strange, because he was just as strong as they were. But he found himself dripping with sweat.

It was noon, judging by the sun, when Cog announced a rest, and they stopped under an elm tree and put down their baskets. They drank thirstily from the flasks they carried, stoppered pots in a leather sling. The Great Plain was bounded by rivers to the north, east and south, but across the plain there were few streams or ponds, many of which dried up in summer; wise travellers carried their water.

Cog gave out slices of cold pork and they all ate. Then Seft lay on his back and looked up at the leafy branches of the tree, enjoying the stillness.

All too soon Cog announced that they must move on. Seft turned to pick up his basket, and hesitated, staring at it. Flints from underground seams were deep, shiny black, with a soft white crust. When they were hit with a stone, flakes broke off, and that way they could be shaped. The flints in Seft's basket had been part-finished by his father, bashed into roughly the right shape to become knives or axe heads or scrapers or piercers or other tools. In this form they were a little lighter to carry. They were also worth more to an expert flint-knapper, who would knock them into their final form.

There seemed to be more of them in Seft's basket than there had been when he set out this morning. Was that his imagination? No, he was sure. He looked at his brothers.

Olf was grinning and Cam was sniggering.

Seft realized what had happened. While they were walking, the others had taken flints from their own baskets and surreptitiously added them to his. He recalled, now, that they had come up behind him to make coarse jokes about his romance. That had distracted him from what they were really up to.

No wonder the morning hike had tired him.

He pointed at them. 'You two . . .' he said angrily.

They fell about laughing. Cog laughed, too: he had clearly been in on the prank.

'Wretched pigs,' Seft said bitterly.

Cam said: 'It was just a joke!'

'Very funny.' Seft turned to his father. 'Why didn't you stop them?'

'Don't complain,' his father said. 'Toughen up.'

Olf said: 'You have to carry them the rest of the way, now, because you fell for the trick.'

'Is that what you think?' Seft knelt down and tipped flints out of his basket onto the ground until he again had roughly his original load.

Olf said: 'I'm not picking those up.'

Cam said: 'Me neither.'

Seft lifted his basket, lighter now, and shrugged into it. Then he walked off.

He heard Olf say: 'You come back here.'

Seft ignored him.

'Right, I'm coming after you.'

Seft turned around, walking backwards. Olf was marching towards him.

A year ago Seft would have given in and done what Olf said. But since then he had grown bigger and stronger. He was still scared of Olf, but now he would not yield to his fear. He reached back over his shoulder and took a flint out of his basket. 'Do you want another stone to carry?' he said.

Olf gave an angry roar and broke into a run.

Seft hurled the flint. He had the powerful arms of a young man who spends all day digging, and he threw hard.

The stone hit Olf's leg above the knee. He howled with pain, limped on another two paces, and fell to the ground.

Seft said: 'The next one gets your head, you dumb bullock.' He turned to his father and said: 'Tough enough for you?'

'No more of this nonsense,' Cog said. 'Olf and Cam, lift your loads and get moving.'

Cam said: 'What about the stones Seft has left on the ground?'

'Pick them up, you stupid fool.'

Olf staggered to his feet. Clearly there was no serious damage, except to his pride. He and Cam collected the flints and put them in their baskets. Then they followed Seft and Cog. Olf was limping.

Cam caught up with Seft. 'You shouldn't have done that,' he said.

'It was just a joke,' Seft said.

Cam fell back.

Seft walked on. His heart was beating fast: he had been frightened. But he had come out of it all right – for now.

In the days since the Spring Rite he had made up his mind to leave his family at the first opportunity. But he had not yet figured out how he would make a living alone. Mining was always a team effort, never a solo job. He had to plan his future. It would be too humiliating to have to go back to the family, dispirited and starving, and beg to be allowed to resume his old role.

All he knew for sure was that he wanted Neen to be part of his plan.

A high earth bank surrounded the Monument. The entrance was a gap in the circle that faced north-east. Some distance away was the cluster of houses belonging to the priestesses. No one went inside the Monument today. The Midsummer Rite would be held tomorrow.

People came to the Monument for the quarterly ceremonies, but the gathering of so many people from near and far was an opportunity, and they often brought with them things to trade. Some were now setting out their wares. They knew not to go inside the sacred circle. They favoured the area near the entrance, and stayed clear of the priestesses' houses.

There was a rumble of chatter and a sense of excitement in the air as Seft and his family drew closer. People were arriving from all directions. One group met every year at a hilltop village four days' walk away to the north-east, then followed a well-worn trail, said to be an ancient road, new marchers joining them as they went from village to village, until they arrived, a long column of people and livestock, at the Monument.

Cog stopped next to a couple called Ev and Fee, who made rope out of honeysuckle vines. The miners emptied their baskets, and Cog started to build a pile of the flints.

Cog was interrupted in his work by another miner, Wun, a small man with yellow eyes. Seft had met him before, several times. He was a gregarious type, everybody's friend, and he loved to chat, especially to other miners. He always knew what was going on. Seft thought he was nosy.

Wun shook hands with Cog, using the informal left-to-right handshake. Right-to-right was formal, indicating respect more than friendship. The affectionate handshake was right-to-left and left-to-right at the same time.

Cog was as taciturn as ever, but Wun seemed not to notice. 'All four of you here, I see,' he said. 'No one guarding your pit?'

Cog looked suspiciously at him. 'Anyone who tries to take it over will get his head broken.'

'Good for you,' said Wun, pretending to endorse Cog's belligerence. All the while he was taking a good look at the pile of part-finished flints, assessing their quality. 'By the way,' he said, 'there's a trader here with a huge collection of antlers. Marvellous.'

The antlers of the red deer, almost as hard as stone and with pointed ends, were among the most important of the miners' tools, being used as picks. Olf said to Cam: 'We should see that.'

They were all looking at Wun, and no one was taking any notice of Seft. Seeing his opportunity, he quietly slipped away, quickly disappearing into the crowd.

There was a straight path from the Monument to the nearby village of Riverbend. Livestock grazed either side of the beaten track. Seft did not like cows. When they looked at him he did not know what they were thinking.

Apart from that, he envied the herder folk. All they did was sit around and watch their herds. They did not have to hammer at a flint seam all day, breaking up the hard stone and carrying it up a climbing pole to the surface. Cattle, sheep and pigs reproduced themselves with little help, and the herders got richer all the time.

When he got to Riverbend he stared at the houses, which all looked the same. Each had a low wall of wattle-and-daub – thin branches interwoven and daubed with mud – plus a roof of turves laid over rafters. The doorway was two posts with a lintel lashed to them. In summer everyone cooked outside, but in winter there was a permanent fire in the central hearth. Meat was hung under the rafters to be smoked. Right now a wicker gate half the height of the doorway let in fresh air but kept out stray dogs and all the little creatures that crept about at night looking for food. In winter the doorway could be completely closed with a more substantial hurdle made to fit exactly.

There were a lot of pigs wandering around the village and the surrounding land, searching with their snouts for anything edible.

About half the houses were empty. They were for visitors, who came four times a year. The herder folk took care of their visitors, who brought great wealth by coming to trade.

Rites were held at the autumn equinox, called the halfway; at midwinter; and at the Spring Halfway; and, as now, at midsummer, which was tomorrow. A key function of the priestesses was to keep track of the days of the year, so that they could announce that, for example, the Autumn Halfway would be in six days' time.

Seft stopped a herder woman and asked the way to Neen's house. Most people knew her, because her mother was an important person, an elder, and he got directions and soon found the place. It was clean, tidy and empty. Four people live here, he thought, and they're all away from home! But no doubt they had a lot of work in connection with the Rite.

Impatient, he began to search for Neen. He wandered around the houses, scanning for her smiling round face and her lush dark hair. Many visitors had already moved into the spare houses, he noticed; single people and families with children, a few showing the wide-eyed curiosity of visitors to an unfamiliar place.

He wondered anxiously how Neen would welcome him. It was a quarter of a year since they had spent that night talking together. She had been warm to him then, but she might have cooled off. She was so attractive and likeable that there must be plenty of other men interested in her. There's nothing special about me, he thought. And he was a couple of years younger than Neen. She had not seemed to mind that, but he felt that she was awfully refined.

He came to the riverside, which was always busy, people fetching fresh water from upstream and washing themselves and their clothes downstream. He did not see Neen, but he was relieved to come across her sister, whom he had met at the last Spring Rite. She was a confident girl with a lot of curly hair and a determined chin. He thought she was about thirteen. She would be fourteen tomorrow. The people of the Great Plain reckoned age in midsummers, so everyone would be a year older on Midsummer Day.

What was her name? It came back to him: Joia.

She and two friends seemed to be washing shoes in the river. Their shoes were like everyone else's, flat pieces of hide cut to shape and pierced with holes for drawstrings, which were made of the sinews of cows, and were pulled tight to make the shoes fit closely.

He went up to her and said: 'Remember me? I'm Seft.'

'Of course I remember.' She greeted him formally. 'May the Sun God smile on you.'

'And on you. Why are you washing your shoes?'

She chuckled. 'Because we don't want to have smelly feet.'

Seft had never thought of that. He never washed his shoes. What if Neen smelt his feet? He was embarrassed already. He resolved to wash his shoes at the earliest opportunity.

Joia's two friends were whispering and giggling, as girls sometimes did, unaccountably. Joia looked at them, sighed with irritation, and said loudly: 'I expect you're looking for my sister, Neen.'

'Of course.'

The two friends had expressions that said: So that's it.

Seft went on: 'Your house is empty. Do you know where Neen is?'

'She's helping with the feast. Shall I show you the way?'

That was kind of her, he thought, to offer to leave her friends and help him. 'Yes, please.'

Carrying her wet shoes, she said a cheery goodbye to her

friends. 'The feast is prepared by Chack and Melly and all their kin, sons and daughters and cousins and I don't know what else,' she said chattily. 'It's a big family, which is a good thing, because it's a big feast. There's an open space in the middle of the village and that's where they do it.'

As they walked side by side it occurred to Seft that Joia might be able to tell him how Neen felt about him. He said: 'Can I ask you something?'

'Of course.'

He stopped, and she did the same. He spoke in a lowered voice. 'Tell me honestly, does Neen like me, do you think?'

Joia had lovely hazel eyes that now looked at him candidly. 'I believe she does, though I couldn't say how much.'

That was an unsatisfactory answer. 'Well, does she talk about me, ever?'

Joia nodded thoughtfully. 'Oh, I think she has mentioned you, more than once.'

She was being careful not to give things away, Seft thought with frustration. All the same, he pressed on. 'I really want to know her better. I think she's . . . I don't know how to describe her. Adorable.'

'You should say these things to her, not me.' Joia smiled to soften the reprimand.

He kept trying. 'But will she be glad to hear them?'

'I think she'll be glad to see you, but I can't say more than that. She will speak for herself.'

Seft was two midsummers older than Joia, but he could not persuade her to confide in him. She was a strong character, he realized. He said helplessly: 'I just don't know if Neen feels the way I do.'

'Ask her, and you'll find out,' Joia said, and Seft heard a touch of impatience in her tone. 'What have you got to lose?'

'One more question,' he said. 'Is there someone else she likes?'

'Well . . .'

'So there is.'

'He likes her, for sure. Whether she likes him, I couldn't say.'
Joia sniffed the air. 'Smell that.'

'Roasting meat.' His mouth watered.

'Follow your nose and you'll find Neen.'

'Thank you for your kind advice.'

'Good luck.' She turned and headed back.

He walked on. The two sisters were different, he reflected. Joia
was brisk and bossy; Neen was wise and kind. Both were attractive,
but the one he loved was Neen.

The smell of meat grew stronger and he came to the open space
where several oxen were being roasted on spits. The feast would
not be held until tomorrow evening, but he guessed it took a long
time to cook something so big. No doubt the smaller beasts, the
sheep and pigs, would be roasted tomorrow.

Twenty or so men, women and children were milling about,
tending the fires and turning the spits. After a moment Seft spotted
Neen, sitting cross-legged on the ground, head bent, intent on
some task.

She looked different from his memory of her, but even lovelier.
She was tanned by the summer sun and her dark hair now had
lighter streaks. She frowned over her work, and her frown was
impossibly charming.

She was using a flint scraper to clean the inside of a hide,
doubtless the skin of one of the beasts now being cooked. Seft
recalled that her mother was a leather tanner. The force of her
concentration fascinated him and moved him almost to tears.

All the same, he was going to interrupt her.

He crossed the open space, his tension mounting with each
step. Why am I worried? he asked himself. I should be happy.
And I am happy. But also terrified.

He stopped in front of her, smiling. It took a few moments for her to tear her gaze away from the hide. Then she raised her head and saw him, and over her face there spread a smile so lovely that his heart seemed to stop.

After a moment, she said: 'It's you.'

'Yes,' he said happily. 'Me.'

She put down the scraper and the hide then stood up. 'I'll finish this later,' she said. Taking Seft's arm, and kicking a pig out of the way, she said: 'Let's go somewhere quieter.'

They walked west, away from the river. The ground sloped up, as it usually did near rivers. He wanted to talk to her, but he did not know how to begin. After some thought he said: 'I'm very glad to see you again.'

She smiled. 'I feel the same.'

That was a good start, he thought.

They came to a strange edifice, concentric rings of tree trunks. It was obviously a holy place. They walked around the circle. 'People come here just to be quiet and reflect,' Neen said. 'Or to talk, like us. And the elders meet here.'

'I remember you said your mother was an elder.'

'Yes. She's really good with disputes. She gets people calmed down and thinking logically.'

'My mother was like that. She could get my father to be reasonable, sometimes.'

'You told me she passed away when you were ten midsummers old.'

'Yes. She conceived a baby late in life, and she and the baby died.'

'You must miss her.'

'I can't tell you how much. Before she died, my father had nothing to do with us three boys. Maybe he was scared to pick up a baby, or something. He never touched us, never even talked to us. Then when Mamma died he suddenly had to look after us. I think he hated taking care of children, and hated us for making him do it.'

Neen said quietly: 'That's awful.'

'He still never touches us – except to punish us.'

'He hits you?'

'Yes. And my brothers.'

'Didn't your mother have any kinfolk who could have protected you?'

That was a big part of the problem, Seft knew. A woman's parents, siblings and cousins were supposed to take care of her children if she died. But his mother had had no living relatives. 'No,' he said, 'my mother had no kin.'

'Why don't you just leave your father?'

'I will, one day, soon. But I have to figure out how I can make a living alone. It takes a long time to dig a pit, and I'd starve to death before I came up with any flint to trade.'

'Why don't you just collect flints from streams and fields?'

'That's a different kind of flint. Those nodules have hidden flaws that cause them to break often, either while they're being shaped or when they're in use as tools. We mine the floorstone, which doesn't break. It can be used to make the big axe heads people need for chopping down trees.'

'How do you do that? Dig a pit?'

Seft sat down, and Neen did the same. He patted the grass beside him. 'The earth here is not very deep. When we dig down we soon come to a white rock called chalk. We dig up the chalk with pickaxes made from the antlers of the red deer.'

'It sounds like hard work.'

'Everything to do with flints is hard. We smear clay on the palms of our hands so they don't blister. Then we dig down through the chalk – it can take weeks – and sometimes, eventually, we come to a layer of floorstone.'

'But sometimes you don't?'

'Yes.'

'So you've done all that for nothing.'

'And we have to start again somewhere else and dig a new pit.'

'I never even thought about how people dig for flint.'

Seft could have told her more, but he did not want to talk about mining. He said: 'What was your father like?' She had told him before that her father was dead.

'He was lovely – handsome and kind and clever. But he wasn't cautious, and he was trampled by a maddened cow.'

'Are cows dangerous?' Seft did not tell Neen that he was scared of them.

'They can be dangerous, especially when they have young. It's best to be careful around them. But my dadda just wasn't the careful type.'

Seft did not know what to say.

Neen said: 'I was heartbroken. I cried for a week.'

Seft tried: 'How sad.'

Neen nodded, and he felt he had said the right thing.

'I'm still sad about it,' she said. 'Even after all these years.'

'What about the rest of your family?'

'You should meet them,' Neen said. 'Do you want to come home with me?'

'I'd love to.'

They left the holy place and made their way through the village. Seft had accepted the invitation eagerly, because it was a sign that Neen really liked him, but he worried whether he would give her family a good impression. They were sophisticated village dwellers – they washed their shoes! He lived a rough life with little social contact. His family had never stayed anywhere long: they built a house near the pit they were currently working, and left it behind when they moved on. Now he would have to talk to Neen's mother, clearly a distinguished person. She in turn would be appraising him as a possible father to her grandchildren. What would he say to her?

Outside Neen's family's house a pot nestling in the embers of a fire gave out an aroma of beef and herbs. The woman stirring the pot was an older version of Neen, with lines around her eyes and silver strands in her black hair. She gave Seft a welcoming smile that was just like Neen's, only with more wrinkles.

Neen said: 'Mamma, this is my friend Seft. He's a flint miner.'

Seft said: 'May the Sun God smile on you.'

'And on you,' she said. 'My name is Ani.'

Neen said: 'And this is my little brother, Han.'

Seft saw a fair-haired boy of eight or nine midsummers sitting on the ground beside a sleeping puppy. 'Smile on you, too,' Seft said, using the short form of the greeting.

'And on you,' Han said politely.

There were two other children. A little girl was sitting with Han, stroking the puppy. Neen said: 'And this is Han's friend, Pia.'

Seft did not know what to say to a little girl, but while he was thinking about it she spoke to him, revealing herself to be socially adept beyond her years. 'My kin are farmers,' she said. 'I live in Farmplace. I'm here for the Rite.' She paused then said confidingly: 'My dadda doesn't let me play with herder children, but he isn't here today.' She was smaller than her playmate, Han, but her self-assurance made her seem older. She added: 'I'm looking after my cousin Stam. He's nearly four.'

Stam looked sulky and said nothing.

Ani said interestedly: 'Tell me, Pia, why did your dadda not come to the Rite this year? He usually does.'

'He had to stay behind. All the men did.'

Ani said musingly: 'I wonder why.'

Clearly she saw some significance in this that escaped Seft.

He was distracted from this line of thought by Han, who looked at him with a mixture of awe and curiosity and said: 'Can anyone be a flint miner?'

'Not really,' said Seft. 'It's usually done by families. Young people are taught by their parents. There's a lot to learn.'

Han looked crestfallen. 'That means I have to be a herder.'

Han looked as if he was not too keen on that. He wanted to get away, Seft guessed, and see something of the rest of the world. He would probably grow out of it.

Seft said: 'What's your dog's name?'

'She hasn't got one yet.'

Pia said: 'I think she should be called Pretty.'

'Nice name,' Seft commented.

Without waking, the puppy farted loudly. Han roared with laughter and Pia giggled.

'She doesn't like the name Pretty,' Ani said with a smile. 'Sit down, Seft. Be comfortable.'

Seft and Neen sat on the ground. Seft thought this was going quite well. He had chatted to Neen's mother and her little brother, and had not yet embarrassed himself. He felt they liked him. He liked them, too.

Neen's younger sister, Joia, appeared, carrying her shoes. 'You found Neen, then,' she said to Seft. She put her shoes near the fire to dry.

'Yes – thanks for your help.'

'Do you like being a miner?'

It was a direct question, and Seft decided to give a direct answer. 'No. And I don't like working for my father. I'm going to leave as soon as I can figure out how to make a living on my own.'

Ani said: 'That's interesting, Seft. What might you do instead of mining?'

'That's the problem – I don't know. I'm a good carpenter, so I might make disc shovels, hammers or bows. Do you think I could trade them for food?'

'Certainly,' said Ani, 'especially if they were better than anything people could make for themselves.'

'Oh, they would be that,' Seft said.

Joia commented: 'You're very confident.'

She was a challenging person, Seft noted. But she could also be kind. A person could be both. Thoughtfully, he said: 'Isn't it important to know what you're good at and bad at?'

Joia said mischievously: 'What are you bad at, Seft?'

Neen protested: 'Unfair question!'

'I'm not good at making conversation,' Seft admitted. 'In the pit we hardly say three words all day.'

'You talk very nicely,' Neen said. 'Take no notice of my little sister – she's mean.'

'Dinner is ready,' Ani said, averting a sisterly spat. 'Joia, fetch bowls and spoons.'

The daylight dimmed as they ate. The air became pleasantly mild, and the sky took on the soft grey hue of twilight. It was going to be a warm night.

The food was delicious. The meat had been cooked with wild roots. He tasted silverweed, burdock and pig nut. They had softened and soaked up the flavour of the beef.

Seft reflected on the contrast between this family and his own. Neen's family were all nice to one another. There was no hostility here. Joia was combative, but nothing serious. He felt sure they never hit one another.

He wondered what was going to happen when night fell. Would he have to return to his father and brothers? Or would he be allowed to sleep here – perhaps next to Neen? He hoped that somehow he and Neen would spend the night together.

When they finished supper, Ani told Neen to take the bowls

and spoons to the river and wash them, and Seft naturally went with her. As they dipped the dinnerware into the water, Neen said: 'I think Pretty would be a good name for a puppy.'

Seft said: 'I've never had a dog. But when I was a boy I longed for one, and I wanted to call it Thunder.'

Neen chuckled. 'She's too cute to be called Thunder.'

'Han can say it's because of the way she farts.'

Neen laughed. 'That's perfect! He thinks farting is hilarious – he's at that age.'

'I know. I was that age once. I remember it well.'

Walking back, Seft heard a man's voice from behind say: 'Hello, Neen.' The tone was warm. He turned to see a tall man of about twenty midsummers.

Neen turned and smiled. Seft reluctantly felt obliged to stop too. Neen said: 'Hello, Enwood. Are you all ready for the Rite?'

'Yes, I'll look out for you.' This annoyed Seft. Who was this Enwood, to promise to look out for Neen? Enwood went on: 'I plan to be there early to get a good view. You should do the same.'

Enwood wanted a rendezvous. Neen said: 'If I wake up in time.' It was neither agreement nor refusal. All the same, Seft was bothered by the tone of intimacy he detected in both their voices.

There was a moment of silence, and Neen said: 'Seft has been helping me wash the dinnerware.'

Enwood gave Seft a cool look. 'Nice,' he said. 'See you tomorrow.' He strode away.

Seft was disturbed by the encounter. 'Who was that?' he said as they resumed walking.

'Oh, just a friend.'

Seft suspected that Enwood was the man Joia had referred to when she had said, *He likes her, for sure. Whether she likes him, I couldn't say.* 'He's handsome,' he said.

'Not as handsome as you.'

Seft was surprised. He did not think he was handsome. But he did not really know. He hardly cared about it. He could not remember the last time he had looked at his reflection in a pond.

It was dark now, and the stars were out. Seft felt that Enwood had spoiled his intimacy with Neen. He said: 'Well, what are we going to do now?' It came out more abrupt than he had intended.

She seemed not to notice. 'What would you like to do?'

The answer came to him immediately. 'It's not cold. I'd like to sit with you under the stars, just the two of us. Would that be all right?'

'Yes,' she said.

He smiled. It's all right again, he thought.

They reached the house. Han was inside, tying the dog up for the night. Pia and Stam had gone back to their family. Joia was already asleep. Ani was taking her shoes off.

Neen said to her mother: 'We're going to sleep out tonight.'

'I hope it doesn't get cold,' Ani said.

'We'll be fine.'

'I'm sure you will.'

Neen took Seft's arm and they walked away.

He said: 'Where shall we go?'

'I know a place.'

They went to the river, then turned along the bank until they left the houses behind. They came to a sheltered grove with leafy trees, and Neen said: 'How's this?'

'Perfect.'

They sat down close to a thicket.

Seft said: 'Your life is perfect. All your family love you. You have plenty of food. The herders have so many cattle that no one could count them. You live like gods.'

'You're right,' Neen replied. 'The Sun God smiles on us.' She lay back.

It seemed like an invitation. Seft leaned over and kissed her.

He had not done much kissing and he was a bit vague about what was expected, but she led the way. She put her hands to his head and then kissed his lips and his cheek and his throat, stroking his hair at the same time. It was the most delightful thing that had ever happened to him.

Desperate to touch her body, he put his hand on her knee and moved it slowly up her leg.

He had seen naked women, usually when they were bathing in the river. They did not care about being seen, but it was considered rude to stare. Nevertheless, he had a pretty good idea what they looked like with their tunics off. However, he had never touched a naked woman. Now he did for the first time.

'Gently,' Neen said. 'Stroke it gently.'

She kissed him while he touched her and after a little while he noticed that she was panting. Then she said: 'I can't wait.'

She rolled him onto his back, pushed up the skirt of his tunic, and straddled him. As she sank down on him, he said: 'Oh! It's lovely!'

'It is with the right person,' she said; and after that, neither of them said anything coherent for a while.

It was still dark when Seft woke up. There was no birdsong – it was too early – but he heard the lapping of the nearby river. He felt Neen beside him, her soft warm body pressed against his, with a leg and an arm thrown over him. He was cold, but he did not care. He hugged her.

She stirred and opened her eyes. Looking at him, she stroked his cheek. 'My sister says you look like the Moon Goddess,' she murmured.

He smiled. 'What does the Moon Goddess look like?'

'Pale and beautiful, with a mouth made for love.' She kissed his lips.

He said: 'I suppose we're a couple now.'

She sat upright. 'What do you mean?'

'That we'll live together and raise our children.'

'Wait,' she said, with a little laugh.

He frowned, puzzled. 'But after last night . . .'

'Last night was wonderful, and I adore you,' she said. 'And I want to do it again tonight. But let's not rush into our future.'

He did not understand. 'But you might be pregnant!'

'Probably not, after only one night. Anyway, that's in the hands of the Moon Goddess, who rules over everything to do with women. If she wants us to have children, so be it.'

'But . . .' He was bewildered. 'Does this have something to do with Enwood?'

She stood up. 'Listen. Can you hear what I can hear?'

He stood silent and picked up the sound of a distant crowd of people walking and talking.

'Everyone's getting up,' said Neen. 'They're all going to the Monument.'

Seft was confused, but he did not know what to say, how to get her to unravel the mystery. He followed as she led him to the river, where they drank the cool fresh water and washed quickly. Then they returned to the village and joined the crowd heading west. Everyone was chattering excitedly, looking forward to the big event.

Neen's house was empty: her family had already left. She went inside and came out with two pieces of cold cooked mutton. She gave one to Seft and they chewed on them as they walked.

Seft consoled himself with the thought that she had said they would spend another night together. That meant she was serious about him. And perhaps they would talk some more about becoming a couple, and he might begin to understand her thinking.

Outside the village, everyone followed the straight south-west path. Cattle resentfully moved aside as the crowed spilled over the edges of the beaten track. People talked quietly and trod softly, as if fearful of waking a sleeping god; but all the same, their collective noise sounded like a river tumbling over rocky falls.

The path led straight to the entrance to the Monument. People were sitting inside facing the entrance, the way they had come, which was the direction of the rising sun at this time of year. A priestess was kicking the pigs out.

The circle was filling. In the crowd Seft and Neen could not pick out Ani and Joia and Han. Neen suggested going to the far side and sitting on the ridge of the earth bank, from where they would see everything.

The circle was about a hundred paces across. Just inside the bank was a ring of upright stones, spaced more or less evenly, each a little taller than a tall man. There were too many for Seft to count. Their surfaces had not been shaped or smoothed. The rock had a bluish tinge, and Neen told Seft that they were called bluestones.

In the middle was a wood circle, and this was completely different. Seft looked harder and made out a large ring of tree trunks, taller than the bluestones. The timber uprights were joined together at their tops by lintels, or crossbars, that made a continuous circle that was perfectly level. In contrast to the bluestones, these timber structures had been cut to exact sizes, and the surfaces had been rubbed smooth. The carpenter in Seft admired the work, but wondered how sturdy it was. If a crazed cow charged one of those tree trunks, how much of the circle would fall down? No doubt everyone was careful to keep cows out of the holy place.

Within that circle Seft made out a second, smaller ring, an oval of free-standing pairs, each pair having a crossbar but detached from the others. These were just as carefully made but taller.

He immediately felt that the timber rings were the important ones. By comparison, the outer stone ring seemed haphazard and careless. Seft wondered whether it was older, and had been erected by less skilled folk.

The crowd was now surprisingly quiet, feeling the holiness of the place. Seft sensed a mood of tense anticipation. He had been here before, and had seen the priestesses perform the Spring Rite, but this was clearly a more important occasion, and the crowd was much bigger. Midsummer was the end of the old year and the beginning of the new. Everyone was one midsummer older today.

People knew that everything that kept them alive came from the sun, so they worshipped it.

Most of the crowd were herders – most of the population of the Great Plain were herders. But there were a few farmers, who worked the fertile soil in the river valleys, and could be identified by their tattoos. The women usually had bracelet tattoos on their wrists, and the men neck tattoos. However, he could not see any male farmers, and he recalled Ani's conversation with Pia last night, and the way Ani had looked troubled by the absence of the farmer men.

Also absent were the woodlanders, but Seft knew why. They had gone on their annual pilgrimage, following the deer into the North-West Hills, where there was fresh summer grass.

People were still coming in when dawn broke in the eastern sky. There was no cloud, and as the silver light strengthened it seemed to bless the heads of the multitude.

At last the priestesses appeared, about thirty of them, dancing two by two, wearing leather tunics like everyone else's but longer, down to their ankles. Their feet were bare.

One of them carried a drum, a hollowed-out log that she beat rhythmically with a stick, making a surprisingly loud, clear sound.

They all did the same movements, swaying to the side and back, like tall grass blown by the wind. Seft was fascinated. He had never seen people dancing that way, all moving together like a school of fish.

They sang as they danced. One with white hair, perhaps the high priestess, would sing a line that sounded like a question, and the others would respond all together. They stepped in and out of the outer circle, winding through the posts, weaving like reeds in the hands of a basket-maker. They seemed to address the wooden uprights individually, as if each meant something different. Seft had a feeling they were counting as they sang, but the words they used were not familiar.

The dance was not sexy. Well, not very sexy. Swaying women were always sexy to Seft, but in this dance that was not the main point.

The outer circle of bluestones, which was just inside the earth bank, played no part in the Rite, which took place around the two timber rings: the circle and, within that, the incomplete oval. The priestesses made their way around the circle, then did the same around the oval, the missing part of which was opposite the entrance – again, facing north-east. This was where the dance ended: in the gap.

The priestesses sank to the ground, still in a long line of pairs. They sang louder as the upper rim of the sun inched up over the horizon. Seft was almost directly in line with the sunrise, and he saw that the orb was coming up exactly between two timber uprights of the circle. Clearly the Monument had been carefully designed that way. The uprights and the crossbar formed a frame, and Seft realized, with a feeling of awe, that this was the archway through which the Sun God came into the world.

The crowd went quieter and the priestesses sang louder as the red disc rose in the sky. Although the sun came up every day, here and now its appearance seemed a special event, as the crowd gazed in a holy trance.

The sun was almost completely up. The song of the priestesses grew even louder. The lowest edge of the sun's curve seemed to linger below the horizon, as if reluctant to lose contact; then at last it came free, and a fragment of light appeared between it and the earth. The song reached a climax, then song and drum suddenly stopped. The crowd broke out into a triumphant roar, so loud it might have been heard at the edge of the world.

Then it was all over. The priestesses marched two by two through the gap in the earth bank and disappeared into their houses. The people in the crowd began to stand up, stretch their legs, and chatter to one another as the tension seeped away.

Seft and Neen remained sitting on the grass. He looked at her. 'I feel sort of . . . knocked over,' he said.

She nodded. 'That's how it takes you, especially the first time.'

He looked at the people crowding out through the gap. 'I'd better return to my family – but I'll see you again, won't I?'

She smiled. 'I hope so.'

'Where shall we meet?'

'Would you like to have dinner with my family?'

'Again? Are you sure your mother won't mind?'

'Sure. Herders like to share. It makes meals more fun.'

'Then I accept. Yesterday's dinner was wonderful. I mean, the food was delicious, but most of all I liked that . . .' He hesitated, not sure how to express what he had felt. 'I liked that you all love one another.'

'That's normal in families.'

He shook his head. 'Not in every family.'

'I'm sorry. Escape to us again tonight.'

27

'Thank you.'

They stood up. Seft said reluctantly: 'I'd better hurry.'

'Go on, then.'

He turned and strode away.

He did not know whether to rejoice or not. He had made love with the girl he adored, and it had been wonderful – then she had told him she was not sure she wanted to spend her life with him. Worse, it seemed he had a rival, a tall, confident man called Enwood, who was older than Neen, whereas Seft was younger.

Tomorrow he would have to leave with his family, and would not see her until the Autumn Halfway. Enwood would have a quarter of a year to woo her with no rival in sight.

But tonight Neen would be with Seft, not Enwood. Seft had one more chance to make it permanent.

Outside the Monument, crowds of people were already bargaining, offering their wares and asking for what they wanted, arguing about the relative values of flint axes, flint knives, stone hammers, pots, hides, ropes, bulls, rams, bows and arrows.

He found his family. He expected Olf and Cam to ridicule him about where he had spent the night, making obscene suggestions and trying to turn his love affair into something sordid. But they sat side by side on the ground, looking at him, as if waiting for something to happen.

That was ominous.

His father was turned away, talking to Ev and Fee, the rope-makers, and Seft waited for the conversation to end.

After a few moments Cog turned around and said: 'Where were you last night?'

Seft said: 'All the work was done before I left, wasn't it?'

'As it happens, yes, but I might have needed you.'

'I'm glad you didn't.'

'Anyway, I'm worried about leaving our pit unattended. I don't trust that Wun.'

This was going to be bad news, Seft felt. 'What do you imagine Wun is going to do? He's here.'

'He's got a big family, and he probably left some of them behind.'

'And what will they do – steal our shovels?'

'Don't make jokes, or I'll knock your stupid head off.'

Cam laughed loudly at that, as if it was the funniest thing he had ever heard.

Seft said: 'I'm only wondering what the danger is.'

'The danger is that some of Wun's people spend three days taking flint in a pit they didn't have to dig because we dug it.' He pointed a finger at Seft. 'There, clever boy, you didn't think of that, did you?'

'True.' Seft thought Cog's whole idea was unlikely, but there was no point in arguing with him.

His father said triumphantly: 'That's why you're going back to guard the pit.'

'When?'

'Today. Now. And you can clean it up before I get back. The floor of the pit is filthy.'

Seft took a step back, paused, and said: 'No.'

'Don't you dare say no to me, boy.'

'I've met a girl—'

Cam and Olf jeered.

'Tonight I'm going to her house, and her mother is going to make us dinner. I'm not going to miss that.'

'Oh, yes, you are.'

'Send Olf. He hasn't got a girl here, or anywhere. And he would be better than me at throwing Wun's team out of our pit.'

'I'm sending you.'

'Why?'

'Because I'm head of this family, and I make the decisions.'

'And you refuse to reconsider, even when your decision is stupid.'

His father punched him in the face.

Cog's fists were hard and his punches hurt. Seft staggered back, hand to his face. The blow had struck to the side of his left eye. His vision was blurred.

Olf and Cam cheered and applauded.

Seft was shocked. Although this had happened before, it always surprised him that his own father would be so cruel.

His father drew back his fist again, but this time Seft was ready and he dodged the blow. He felt encouraged: his father was not omnipotent. Seft quickly hit back, wildly, and managed to punch Cog's nose.

It was the first time he had ever struck his father.

Cog's nose spurted blood. He roared indignantly: 'How dare you strike me, boy?' and came at him. This time Seft failed to dodge the punch, which hit the side of his head and knocked him to the ground.

He was dazed for a moment. When he came round he saw that he was lying next to a small pile of flints. He was vaguely aware of a small crowd watching the fight.

He got up and snatched up a stone with which to defend himself.

Cog said: 'Hit me with a stone, would you, you disobedient dog?' He came at Seft again.

Seft raised his right hand with the flint in it.

But the blow was arrested before it made contact. Seft's wrist was seized from behind in a powerful grip, and he dropped the stone. His wrist was released and his two arms were grabbed, pinning him in place. He realized that Olf had grabbed him. He struggled but could not move: Olf was too big and too strong.

As he wriggled helplessly, Cog punched him again, hard; first on his face, then in his belly, then on his face again. He screamed and begged his father to stop. Cog's face came close, with a twisted smile that betrayed pleasure in savagery. Cog said: 'Will you go back to the pit?'

'Yes, yes, anything!'

Olf released him and he collapsed on the ground.

He heard Ev, the rope-maker, say to his father: 'You'll get yourself in trouble.'

Cog was still angry. 'Me? In trouble?' he said aggressively. 'Who with? You?'

Ev was not intimidated. 'With people a lot more important than me.'

Cog gave a contemptuous snort.

Seft was hurting all over and crying. He managed to get to his hands and knees. He crawled away. People stared, which made him feel worse.

He tried to stand. A stranger helped him and he managed to stay upright.

Then he stumbled away.

2

AFTER THE CEREMONY, and before the evening feast, the main occupation of the day was trading livestock. Herders knew the dangers of inbreeding, and were always keen to introduce fresh blood. They acquired new livestock at every Rite, especially bulls, rams and male pigs, generally exchanging them for their existing stock one for one. Herders from far away would go home with males from the Great Plain to improve their own stock.

Ani walked around with two other elders, Keff and Scagga, watching for signs of discord. Bargaining was normally good-natured, but it could turn nasty, and the elders had the job of keeping the peace.

Elders were loosely defined, and people joined and left the group without ceremony. Keff was recognized as leader and called Keeper of the Flints, because he was in charge of the herder folk's reserve of wealth, a stash of part-finished flints in a guarded building in the centre of Riverbend. Scagga belonged because he was the head of a large family and had a forceful personality –

sometimes too forceful, for Ani's taste. Ani herself was generally regarded as wise, though she would have described herself as sensible. She had siblings and cousins, all younger, kinfolk who might serve as elders when she died.

The elders ruled the herder community with a light touch. They had no means of enforcement, except that a person who defied the elders would suffer widespread disapproval, and that could be hard to live with. So their decisions were usually accepted.

Ani believed that the happiness of her children, and of potential grandchildren, depended on the prosperity and smooth running of the community, so her work as an elder was part of her duty to her family.

She had already been pregnant with Han when her fearless man, Olin, had been trampled to death by a cow, leaving her to raise three children alone. People had assumed she would find another man to share her burden and her bed: she had been still young, quite nice-looking, and well-liked all over the Great Plain. There were always plenty of single middle-aged men, because many women died in childbirth, but Ani had rejected all her suitors. After Olin, she could not love again. She pictured him now, striding across the plain, with his bushy blond beard, and the vision brought a tear to her eye. 'I'm a one-man woman,' she sometimes said; 'for me there is only one true love.'

She was pleased about Neen and Seft. He seemed a decent boy, kind-hearted, rough around the edges but smart enough to learn fast. And he was terribly good-looking, with high cheekbones and dark eyes and straight hair, almost black. I'll be very glad if those two give me a grandchild, she thought.

She was not so easy in her mind about Joia. On the surface, Joia was happy with her family and friends, and amiable to others, but underneath she was restless and dissatisfied. She seemed to be searching for something without knowing what it was. Perhaps that was just adolescence.

Han was a cheerful boy, especially now that he had a dog. He liked Pia, but of course they were too young for romance. Childhood friendships did sometimes turn into adult love affairs, but not often, and Ani hoped it would not happen in this case: Pia was a farmer girl, and romance between farmers and herders often caused trouble.

Looking around, she again noticed the lack of farmer men with tattooed necks. Why had they stayed at home? What were they up to? She had asked several of the farmer women, casually, as if making small-talk, but they seemed not to know.

Other than livestock, the goods traded were food, flint tools, leather, pottery, rope, and bows and arrows.

The herders benefited as hosts. Everyone else had to transport their goods, often over long distances. In recognition of this privilege the herders provided a feast at the end of the day.

She spotted little Pia offering goat's cheese, the soft new kind and the hard long-lasting type. Next to Pia was a woman who was probably her mother. Ani greeted Pia and said to the woman: 'I'm Ani, Han's mother. May the Sun God smile on you.'

'And on you,' said the woman. 'I'm Yana. Thank you for feeding Pia and Stam yesterday.'

'Han enjoyed playing with Pia.' Ani did not mention sulky Stam.

'Pia loves Han.'

Pia looked embarrassed and said: 'Mamma! I don't *love* Han. I'm too young for *love*.'

'Of course,' said Yana.

Ani smiled.

Yana said: 'Taste my cheese. No obligation.' She offered Ani a piece of soft white cheese on a leaf.

'Thank you.' The people of the Great Plain did not milk their cows, because cow's milk made them ill. But the farmers knew how to turn goat's milk into cheese, and it was a delicacy. Ani ate it and said: 'Very good. Would you like two pieces of leather big enough to make shoes?'

'Yes. You can have a large measure of cheese for that.'

'I'll send someone with the leather.'

'Good.'

A boy messenger appeared and summoned the three elders to a dispute. He led them to where a potter was offering his wares. A disgruntled man was holding a large pot with water dripping from the bottom.

When the potter saw the three elders he immediately said: 'He made a trade – he can't go back on it!'

The man said: 'The pot leaks!'

'It's perfectly fine for keeping grain or wild turnips. I never said it was for water.'

Ani said to the potter: 'What did you get for the pot?'

'Three arrows.' The potter showed her three arrows with sharp flint flakes embedded in their points.

The arrow-maker said: 'They're perfect.'

Ani noticed that the potter was a short, round man and the arrow-maker was tall and thin. They resembled the things they made. She had to suppress a smile.

She turned to the potter. 'Did you tell him that the pot would not hold water?'

The potter looked guilty. 'I might have. I don't remember.'

The arrow-maker said: 'You never told me. If you'd said it, I wouldn't have given you three good arrows.'

Ani took Keff and Scagga aside for a consultation.

Scagga said: 'That potter is a cheat. He was trying to get rid of a flawed piece of work. He's dishonest.'

Keff said: 'It's bad for our reputation if people get away with trading second-rate goods.'

Ani agreed.

She turned to the potter and said: 'You have to give back the arrows, and he'll return the pot to you.'

'What if I refuse?'

'Then you might as well pack up your goods and go home, because no one will trade with you if you defy our ruling. People would think you were dishonest.'

Scagga put in: 'And they'd be right!'

'Oh, all right,' said the potter. He handed back the arrows and accepted the pot.

Ani said: 'If you want to trade that pot, tell people it's not for fluids, and for that reason they can get it cheap.'

The potter grunted reluctant assent.

Ani was surprised to see Joia appear, looking ruffled. 'Mother, you have to come,' she said. 'And Keff and Scagga. Follow me, please – it's urgent.'

They followed her. Ani said: 'What's wrong?'

'There's been violence.'

There were often disputes at the Rite, but the elders did everything they could to prevent fights.

Joia led them to where half a dozen people stood around a pile of half-finished flints as if waiting to see what would happen. Ani had an unpleasant feeling that this might have something to do with young Seft.

Joia said: 'This is Cog, the father of Seft. I met Seft a few moments ago, heading back to their pit. His face was cut and bruised and swollen and he was walking half bent over from a belly punch. He said his father beat him up.'

Ani said: 'Where is Seft now?'

'He's gone. He felt too ashamed to speak to people.'

Cog said indignantly: 'It's no one else's business how I choose to discipline a disobedient son! And the boy hit me. Look at my nose.' Cog's nose was bloody and bent. 'It was a two-way fight,' he said defiantly.

Two rope-makers, whom Ani knew, were nearby, and now the woman, Fee, laughed scornfully. 'Two-way?' she said. 'The big stupid one held the boy still while the father beat the shit out of him. He was like a mad bull. The boy crawled away on his hands and knees!'

Cog, enraged, moved towards Fee with a fist raised, saying: 'You call me a mad bull again and I'll tear your ugly head off.'

Fee looked at Ani and said: 'I think that proves my point, doesn't it?'

Ani stepped between Cog and Fee and spoke to Cog. 'The spirit of the Monument abhors violence.'

'I don't care about the spirit of anything.'

'Evidently,' she said. 'But you can't come here if you disrespect the spirits of the place.'

'I say I can.'

Ani shook her head. 'You must go somewhere else. And never come back.'

Cog said scornfully: 'You can't make me go.'

'Yes, I can,' said Ani. She turned away and spoke in a low voice to Keff and Scagga. 'If you two go and put out the word, I'll stay nearby and make sure.'

The other two went away. Ani moved to a nearby place from where she could keep an eye on Cog. She sat down with two older folk, Venn and Nomi, who made needles and pins of bone.

Nomi was upset. 'I saw that fight,' she said. 'It was cruel. Have you told people not to do business with that horrible miner?'

'Keff and Scagga are doing that right now.'

They chatted for a while. After a few minutes, a man with a

37

leather tunic over his arm approached Cog. Nomi said: 'He hasn't heard.'

'He will,' said Ani.

Sure enough a bag-maker opposite Cog called to the tunic man and said something to him quietly, and he went away.

No one else came to trade with Cog.

After a long wait, he and his two older sons began to put their flints back in the baskets. Soon afterwards they went away.

Nomi said to Ani: 'Well done.'

Joia loved the evening feast. She liked the poets. They sang about how the world began, when the people first came to the Great Plain, and what the gods did when they interfered in the affairs of humans. The stories transported Joia from the everyday world to the universe of gods and spirits, where anything could happen.

In the beginning, a poet sang, *there was no sun.*

Joia had heard this one before, sung by a different poet. The story was always the same, but each poet told it slightly differently. However, they all included certain repeated phrases.

The only light came from the pale moon and the flickering stars. So people slept all the dark day long, and looked for food at night, and worshipped the pale Moon Goddess. Life was hard, because they could not see well to hunt game or gather wild fruits.

Joia lay down on her back and closed her eyes, the better to imagine the world of long, long ago.

One day the pale Moon Goddess spoke to a brave man whose name was Resk.

Everyone knew that meant trouble. The gods could be kind, but they were easily offended – a bit like the woodlanders.

Brave Resk told the pale Moon Goddess how difficult life was, and said the people needed more light. The pale Moon Goddess was offended and angry because the people said she was too weak.

Strange things began to happen in the sky.

The pale moon got smaller every night until it disappeared altogether, and only the flickering stars gave light. The people moaned and wept. But the pale moon came back as a thin crescent, and got bigger every night until it was round again, and they rejoiced. However, it waned and waxed like that ever after, as a punishment to the people who had said the light of the pale Moon Goddess was weak.

Brave Resk searched for a solution to the problem. He travelled all over the world.

There followed a long account of Resk's adventures in three strange countries: a place where it never rained, a place where the rain never stopped, and one where there was always snow.

Then he went to the edge of the world.

The listeners went quiet. The edge of the world was a scary idea.

He knew it was dangerous, but he would not turn back.

Because it was dark, he fell off.

There were lots of gasps, and one person said: 'Oh, no!'

But an owl flew beneath him and caught him. And then brave Resk saw a bright light shining underneath the world. At first he did not know what the bright light was.

Several people said: 'The kind Sun God!'

Yes, that was where the kind Sun God lived.

The kind Sun God spoke to brave Resk, and asked him why he had come to the edge of the world. Brave Resk explained that the people were blind all the dark day long, and asked the kind Sun God to come above the earth and shine.

The kind Sun God said: 'But the pale Moon Goddess is my sister. I don't want to outshine her.'

'Then just come in the day, and light up our darkness,' said brave Resk. 'Then we can hunt and gather fruits while you are with us, and sleep when you disappear.'

The kind Sun God agreed to that.

Brave Resk said: 'You will come every day, though, won't you?'

'I expect so,' said the kind Sun God.

And the people had to be satisfied with that.

Until she heard this story, Joia had wondered why the moon waxed and waned, and why the sun vanished at night and came back in the morning. And she was fascinated by the idea of the edge of the world. The world had to have an edge, she supposed.

Darkness had fallen during the recitation. Now the children went to sleep. So did some of the adults, but not all. It was time for the revel.

Everybody knew that a baby should ideally be raised by the mother and father, and parental couples normally avoided romantic entanglements with others. But inbreeding was dangerous in humans just as it was in herds. Even the farmers, who normally made women subservient, understood the benefit of new blood. So on the night of Midsummer Day many couples would separate, just for a few hours. It was especially good to make a baby with someone from far away. When that happened, both local couples and visiting couples would raise the child just the same as their other offspring.

The revel was a major attraction.

It got started quickly. Joia guessed that some people had arranged in advance whom they would go with, and now they paired up immediately and eagerly headed out of the village together. Others strolled around, waiting to catch someone's eye. Older people did not look at Joia and her friends: old-young sex was taboo.

Joia was with her cousin Vee and her friend Roni, who were excited. They talked about which boys they liked, and laughed about the unattractive ones. They agreed that they did not want to make babies, and they discussed what caresses they might permit instead.

Joia thought that Roni could probably attract any of the boys. She was the beautiful one of the three, with smooth brown skin and big eyes. Vee might be a bit intimidating: there was a defiant look about the way she stood and the way she walked, as if she was always ready for a quarrel. That could put boys off.

Joia herself was not excited. She supposed she would probably kiss some boy, but she could not work up any enthusiasm for the prospect. She was different from other girls in that way.

She was fascinated by the sun, the moon and the stars, and the different ways they moved in the sky. She thought a lot about the spirits who lived in the rivers and the rocks and the wild creatures, spirits who could be kindly or mischievous or downright mean. She liked numbers. She remembered her mother once saying: 'Your first word was *Mamma*, but your second was *two*.'

At times Joia thought there must be something wrong with her.

The three girls walked around the outskirts of the village in the warm evening air, careful not to tread on people who were already enjoying the freedom of the special night in pairs, threes and fours, some all-male or all-female, some mixed. It was too dark to see exactly what people were doing, but they made passionate noises, sighs and groans and sudden exclamations.

Joia looked out for her sister, Neen. She was eager to know

whether Neen would be with Enwood, now that Seft had gone. But she did not see either Neen or Enwood.

Vee and Roni were eager and at the same time apprehensive, and Joia noticed that their voices rose in pitch. Before long they ran into a group of boys including Vee's brother, Cass, who was sixteen midsummers old. They talked for a minute, joshing, until the most good-looking of the boys, Cass's friend Robbo, put his arm around Roni.

Just like that, Joia thought.

Robbo's move was the cue for Moke, a rather plain boy, to rush to Vee. Joia expected her to reject him. Vee had talked a lot about how she would kiss only really attractive boys. However, she now seemed to forget all that, and she kissed Moke without being asked.

Only Joia was left.

There was a moment of uncertainty, then Cass smiled at her. She liked him. He was friendly and intelligent. Now he said: 'I guess you liked the poem about the Moon Goddess and the Sun God.' He knew what interested her.

Despite that, she had no inclination to kiss him. But she thought she ought to do it.

He seemed hesitant too, and she thought: Let's get this over with. She put her hand on his shoulder, tilted her face up, and kissed him.

She did not know what to do next and, it seemed, nor did he. They stayed like that, mouth on mouth, for several moments. His lips did not excite her. Nothing happened. She neither liked it nor hated it. It seemed pointless, meaningless. She broke away.

He sensed that. 'It didn't make you feel good, did it?' he said. His tone was good-natured: he was not upset.

'No, it didn't,' she said. 'I'm sorry.'

'What would make you feel good – do you know?'

'I have no idea.'

'Well . . . I hope you find out soon.' He kissed her again, briefly, then turned away.

Vee and Roni were still kissing Moke and Robbo. Joia felt unhappy and somehow lost. She left the group and walked on around the outside of the village. What was wrong with her? She was surrounded by people up to all kinds of sexual acts that they seemed to be enjoying hugely, and she was indifferent.

She saw Vee's mother, Kae, coming in the opposite direction, walking arm in arm with Inka, one of the priestesses. Kae was kin: she was the widow of Ani's late brother. Joia liked Kae, who was warm-hearted and generous, with an easygoing smile. On impulse, Joia went up to her and kissed her.

This was different. Kae's lips were full and warm on Joia's. Kae put her arm around Joia's shoulders and hugged her. Her lips moved a little, as if exploring Joia's, then Joia was startled to feel the tip of Kae's tongue.

Joia could have stayed like that for a long time, but Kae broke the embrace with a sigh. 'You're lovely, Joia,' she said. 'But you should really learn about all this kind of thing with people your own age.'

Joia felt let down, and she must have shown it, for Kae said: 'I'm sorry.' She stroked Joia's curly hair. 'But it's no good with an older one teaching a younger.'

Her companion, Inka, said: 'Lovers need to be equal.'

'All right,' said Joia. 'I liked the kiss, anyway.'

'Good luck,' said Kae, and she and Inka moved on.

Joia felt overwhelmed. She needed peace and quiet to think about everything. She headed for home.

Ani was there and so was Neen. They were lying down, but still awake and talking. Joia said to Neen: 'Didn't you go to the revel?'

'No.'

'I thought you might be with Enwood.'

Neen sighed. 'I can't make up my mind. I was planning to see Enwood tonight. Then Seft appeared and I kept thinking about him. But now Seft has gone.'

'Seft thinks you're a goddess.'

'Whereas Enwood is twenty midsummers old, and too grown-up to worship a mere human.'

'You must like one more than the other,' Joia said argumentatively.

'Seft is nicer, but Enwood is here.'

Ani changed the subject. 'You look troubled, Joia. Obviously you didn't enjoy the revel. What happened?'

Joia lay down beside the other two. 'Well,' she said, 'first of all Roni got Robbo.'

'The two best-looking,' Neen said.

Ani said: 'It's often the way.'

'And Vee got Moke. She seemed very keen.'

'Good for her. But what about you?'

'I kissed Vee's brother, Cass.'

'And . . . ?'

'Nothing.' Joia shrugged. 'I didn't feel anything. Just some boy's mouth.'

'Was he annoyed?'

'No, he was nice about it. But it was a waste of time.'

'And then you came home?'

'No.' Joia hesitated, then decided to tell the truth. 'Then I kissed Vee's mother.'

Neen said: 'A woman! That's a surprise. What was it like?'

'Really nice. But then she said I should kiss someone my own age.'

Ani said firmly: 'Quite right.'

'But now I don't know what I want – if anything.'

Ani said: 'Well, you've learned that you're attracted to women, not men.'

'I don't know. I can't imagine kissing Vee or Roni or any of the girls.'

'Don't worry. If you're not driven to have sex, just accept that. It's not compulsory. And you may change.'

'Really?'

'Some people do. When I was your age I knew a boy who always went with boys, never looked twice at a pretty girl. Then, when he was older, he fell in love with a woman. They're still together and they have children. Though I think he still goes with men at the revel.'

'I don't like being different from everyone else,' Joia said unhappily. 'I felt a failure tonight.'

'You are different. I've always known it. But you're not a failure – just the opposite. You're special. Believe me, you will live an interesting life.'

'Will I?'

'Oh, yes,' Ani said confidently. 'You'll see.'

3

SEFT WOKE UP in the house near the pit. His body hurt all over. He had a pain in his belly, his head ached, and when he touched his face he found a swollen, tender patch near his left eye.

But the shame of it was worse than the pain.

All those people had seen him beaten like a bad dog. He had crawled away on his hands and knees. Once upright he had kept his head down and slunk through the crowd trying to avoid attention, but he had been unlucky and had met Joia. Now Neen would know how he had been degraded. How could she possibly respect him after that?

He had gone so quickly from happiness to misery.

He got up and went to the nearby spring, where he drank and dipped his head in the cool water. Back at the house, he found cold pork in a leather bag and ate some for breakfast. It made him feel better.

Then he looked down into the pit. It was a mess. The ground was littered with lumps of chalk and flakes of flint, meat bones, discarded antler picks, broken shovels and worn-out shoes. His father had told him to clean it up. We should just clean up every day, he thought. Then we wouldn't spend our lives wallowing in filth.

He decided he had better get on with it. It was a necessary chore, he had nothing else to do, and he would be in trouble if he disobeyed orders.

He went back to the house to get a basket, but when he looked at the building he saw it was in danger of collapse. The doorway consisted of two posts and a lintel lashed to the posts with leather straps. While the family had been away, the straps had broken and the lintel had shifted. It was still on top of one doorpost but its other end hung loose. He had not noticed this last night because he had been in such distress.

The rafters above the lintel now had no support, and would fall sooner or later, bringing down part of the roof, if not all. It needed to be repaired right away.

The easy way to do it would be to get some new leather straps and re-tie the lintel to the doorposts. However, he did not have any leather straps. And, anyway, that approach seemed unsatisfactory to him. The straps would eventually rot again.

He wanted to take a closer look at the lintel, but it was too high. He gathered some pieces of chalk rubble from the rubbish pile and made a little platform in the doorway. Standing on that he could look down on the lintel.

It was a tree trunk about as thick as his thigh and as long as his arm. He saw that it was rotten with damp, and it would have collapsed soon if the straps had not gone first. So he needed another lintel.

There was a hidden place in the house, a hole in the ground with a wooden lid, covered with a layer of earth, underneath the hide that served as a floor covering. He lifted all the layers and took out a flint axe. Then he hid the hole again.

He searched the territory around the pit and eventually found a young tree of about the right size. Chopping it down and cutting the trunk to length with his flint axe took him the rest of the morning, and he had to sharpen the edge of his axe several times.

At midday he ate some more cold pork, drank at the spring, and lay down to rest for a while. He still hurt all over but the work took his mind off his aches.

He removed the old lintel and replaced it with the new one, but of course it was not stable, and he did not have any straps. However, he wondered if there was another way to attach the lintel to the doorposts.

Perhaps he could use a flint bradawl to dig two holes in the lintel, make matching holes in the tops of the doorposts, and drive a long peg through the lintel and into the doorposts. He did not much like that solution: it would be a lot of work with the bradawl, and the pegs might break.

He thought a bit more and had a better idea.

With a flint chisel he could shave the tops of the doorposts, leaving a bit sticking up in the middle, like a peg. Then he could dig out matching holes in the lintel. It would have to be carefully measured so that when he placed the lintel across the two doorposts, the pegs would fit exactly and firmly into the holes.

He could not see any reason why that would not work.

He spent the afternoon doing it and thinking about Neen.

Recalling his time with her cheered him up. During their night together she had taught him things he had never dreamed of. He smiled as he remembered. In his fantasy, Neen would become a wise and kind mother like Ani. He and Neen would be loving parents, and their happy children would never be hurt.

But she had refused to talk about their future together, which meant – he became more sure of this as he mulled it over – that she was still thinking about Enwood.

He longed to talk to her again. But when would he see her? Did he have the nerve to defy his father again and run away? It was a possibility he could not contemplate while he still hurt all over. And what would she say, next time he showed up outside her house?

The pegs fitted the holes first time. He fixed the loose rafters to the lintel. Their weight would make the peg-and-hole joints even stronger.

He heard a noise and turned to see that his family had arrived home. Cog, Olf and Cam stood at the edge of the pit, looking down. Cog's nose was red and swollen, Seft saw with secret satisfaction.

Cog said: 'You haven't cleaned up!'

Olf said: 'There's loads of rubbish left.'

Cam said: 'You lazy dog!'

'That doesn't matter,' Seft said. 'I've stopped the house falling down.' He stepped off his platform.

'Don't tell me it doesn't matter,' his father said angrily. 'I ordered you to clear up the floor of the pit, and you haven't done it.'

Seft's heart sank. Was Cog really going to pretend that he had done nothing useful? How could he be so stupid? 'The lintel was rotten and it had slipped off one doorpost. The house was about to fall down. But I've made a new lintel.'

Cog was unyielding. 'It's no good. You haven't even strapped the lintel to the doorposts. You've just been shirking hard work, boy. You should have followed my orders. Now get on with clearing up.'

Seft said: 'Aren't you even going to look at how I've done it?'

'No, I'm not. I'm going to cook a piece of beef I got at Upriver.'

Seft was surprised by the reference to Upriver. Cog and the other two must have left the Monument early and gone to Upriver to trade their flints there. He wondered why. Perhaps they had got into trouble over the fight.

Seft hoped so.

Cog went on: 'And you don't get any supper until the pit is clean.'

This was outrageous. 'I'm entitled to that beef. I mined the flints that you gave for it. Are you going to steal it from me now, like a common thief?'

'Not if you finish cleaning the pit.' And with that Cog withdrew from the edge of the pit, and the brothers did the same.

Seft could have wept. But he took a basket and went down the climbing pole, a tree trunk with notches cut in its sides to serve as handholds and footholds. He picked up litter until the basket was full, then climbed the pole to the surface and dumped its contents on the rubbish pile.

Cog, Olf and Cam were now resting on the ground outside the house. They had made a fire and Seft smelt the roasting meat. He went back down the pole and picked up more rubbish.

The next time he climbed the pole he saw that Wun, the nosy flint miner, was there. He was a small man who made quick movements and thought fast. He was asking Cog how he had got on at Upriver.

'Very well,' Cog said briskly. 'I sold everything.'

'Well done,' said Wun.

'I shan't go back to the Monument. No point.'

'I don't suppose they'd have you, anyway,' Wun said. 'They were very cross.'

That annoyed Cog, and Seft saw his mouth turn down at the corners. But Wun was not intimidated. He had no fear of Cog. Seft liked him for that.

Wun said to Cog: 'That beef looks just about ready. Smells good, too.'

'Does it?' said Cog. He was not going to offer Wun any.

Seft dumped the rubbish from the basket and returned to the edge of the pit. Wun caught sight of him and said: 'Here's the cause of all the trouble. I gather you've had a lazy day, Seft.'

Seft wanted someone to acknowledge his achievement. 'If you

want to know how I've spent the day, Wun, look at the lintel over that doorway. It had collapsed, and the house was going to fall down.'

Wun said: 'But you haven't strapped it.'

'Yet it looks sturdy, doesn't it? Give the lintel a push, Wun. See if it moves.'

Wun did so and the lintel did not budge. 'How did you do that?' Wun said.

'The lintel is fixed to the doorposts with pegs.'

Wun was fascinated. 'Who told you how to do that?'

'No one. I was thinking about the problem, here on my own, and I tried out some ideas.'

Wun stared at Seft with his yellow eyes. 'Truly?'

Seft was irritated by Wun's scepticism. 'No one else knows how to do this!' he said indignantly. 'I invented it.'

'Well done.' There was admiration in Wun's expression now. That partly made up for Cog's rejection. Wun turned to Cog and said: 'You must be pleased.'

Cog did not look at Wun. 'I told him to clear up the pit floor.'

Wun laughed and shook his head incredulously. 'That's my friend Cog.' Looking thoughtful, he went on: 'I like your boy and I'd be glad to employ him. Would you let him go?'

'No, thanks,' said Cog.

'Really?' Wun was surprised. 'The way you treat him I thought you'd be glad to get rid of him.'

'That's my business.'

'Of course, Cog, of course it's your business, but I'd make it worth your while.'

'The answer's no,' Cog said obstinately. 'And it's not going to change.'

'Oh, well.' Wun accepted the decision. 'Congratulations, anyway, Seft.' He swept the group with his glance. 'Enjoy your beef. May the Sun God smile on you all.'

'And on you,' said Seft, but the others remained silent.

Seft watched Wun go.

Cog said to him: 'Why are you standing around? That pit isn't clean yet.'

Seft went back down the pole.

Seft carried on after dark, working by starlight. When at last he finished, everyone else had retired, and the gate of the house was in place.

It was the usual basketwork hurdle. He lifted it silently, stepped inside, and replaced it.

Cog, Olf and Cam were asleep, Cog snoring.

Seft was starving. He looked for the beef, but there was only a bone left.

Fury boiled up inside him. He had the flint axe in his hand. He gripped it hard: he could kill them all now. But he relaxed his grip and lay down. Perhaps I'm not the killing kind, he thought, and he closed his eyes.

He was exhausted, but his mind was restless and he did not fall asleep. Wun had changed everything. Cog had rejected Wun's proposal but Seft had not. For some time Seft had been asking himself: How could I make a living if I ran away? Today Wun had answered the question.

Seft felt a surge of hope, but there were snags. Would Wun let Seft join his team against Cog's will? Seft thought he might. Wun was not easily bullied, and did not seem afraid of Cog. He had sons of his own to protect him, and other kin too. He might well defy Cog.

Could Seft get away from here without waking the family?

They were full of beef and fast asleep, and his footsteps would make little noise. But what if one of them woke up? He would murmur something about going outside to piss.

His father would surely come after him. It would be wise to disappear for a day or two. Let them waste time looking for him and get fed up with the search. Then he could go to Wun's pit.

Anyway, now that freedom beckoned he could not say no to it.

He imagined himself telling Neen about it. I just got up and went, he would say.

No more dreams. I'm going to do it, he thought, and he stood up.

Olf grunted, rolled over, and stopped snoring. Seft stood as still as a tree. Olf's eyes did not open. Soon he snored again.

Seft stepped to the doorway and put his hands on the gate.

His father said: 'What are you doing?'

Seft turned and looked. Cog was still half asleep, but his eyes were open.

Seft was inspired. In an angry voice he said: 'Where's the beef for my dinner?'

'All gone,' said Cog. He closed his eyes and turned over.

Seft lifted the gate silently, stepped outside, and replaced the gate. If necessary he was ready to run for it.

No more was said.

He stepped away. The night was warm and the moon had risen. He headed north. When he was too far away for his footsteps to be heard back in the house he turned and looked back.

All was quiet.

'Goodbye, you miserable pigs,' he whispered.

He broke into a run.

Seft went north. He left the plain, entered the hill country, and walked on, taking no chances.

He had explored this area often. His father observed the twelve-day week, with two days of rest, and Seft had liked to get away from his family and wander. Now he came to a valley he remembered from one such trip. It had stuck in his memory because he had seen an aurochs here, one of a species of giant cattle with wide pointed horns. They were rare and he had not seen one before or since. He had been scared and climbed a tree until it wandered away.

Hoping the beast was not still around, he lay down on the ground. He heard an owl hoot, and then he fell asleep.

He woke at dawn. The place was familiar. A few sheep grazed between the trees. Looking around, he saw hundreds of flat stones on the ground, as if scattered there by the gods. Some of them were enormous, as long as four men lying head to toe. He had privately called the place Stony Valley. Somewhere nearby lived a shepherd, the only inhabitant for a long way.

He ate some wild raspberries then returned south to a hill from which he could see the pit and the house in the distance. He stood under a tree whose shadow hid him from view, and watched while his family got up and ate breakfast. Then the three of them set out westwards, undoubtedly heading for Wun's pit.

Seft stayed at his vantage point all day, until he saw Cog, Olf and Cam come back, their bodies slumped and weary with walking and discouragement. They had found Wun's pit, and Seft had not been there.

He would sleep in Stony Valley again tonight. Perhaps the shepherd would give him something to eat.

In the morning he would go to Wun's pit.

4

THE FARMERS' WIVES and children took two days to get home after the Midsummer Rite. They had to walk the length of the plain, from east to west. A healthy adult could do it in a day, but children took longer, as did adults who were carrying children. However, it was a pleasant trip in summer and Pia was happy, walking with a girl of her own age, Mo. Her cousin Stam threw a tantrum and refused to walk and had to be carried all the way by his mother, Katch.

They passed several herder villages. Most were at the edges of the plain, near the three main rivers, the East River, the North River and the South River; but a few were in the middle of the plain, always near a stream or spring. Each had just two or three houses, usually occupied by people from the same family. Pia's mother, Yana, explained that the herders had to keep watch on their livestock, making sure they did not get into trouble or wander away; and after that Pia noticed that near the herd there were always two or three people, men, women and children, keeping watch.

Pia and Mo were frightened of the animals and stayed near the grown-ups.

Pia told Mo about Han and his mother and sisters. 'He's really nice to play with, and he let me pat his dog.'

Mo said: 'Are you his girlfriend, now?'

'No. He says that's silly grown-up stuff.'

Han's mother had been kind, inviting Pia and Stam to stay for dinner. Pia had been surprised to realize that there was no man in the house, something that was not permitted among the farmer folk. In the farmer community every woman belonged to a man.

As they neared farming country she decided to ask her mother about it. 'Why are herder families so different from ours?' she said.

'In what way?' Yana asked.

'When they make dinner, they just share it with everyone who's nearby. We don't do that.'

'That's because a herder doesn't have his own livestock. With so many cattle wandering all over the Great Plain it would be impossible to keep track of who owns which cow. So the beasts belong to the whole community, and everyone's entitled to whatever's cooking. We don't have that system. With us, each man has his own land, farmed by him, his woman and children and no one else. Why should we share our produce with people who haven't helped to grow it?'

'Well, Han's mother hasn't got a man.'

'That's not possible for us. We think every woman belongs to a man, either her father or her partner.'

'Han's father died.'

'If his mother were a farmer woman, she would have to take another man within a year. That's our rule.'

It made sense, but Pia thought Han's mother had seemed to live happily without a man.

She asked a different question. 'The way herder men talk to women is strange. Not like the way Dadda talks to you.'

'We think someone has to be in charge, and among us it's the man who tells the woman what to do.'

Pia thought for a while, then said: 'Why?'

Yana looked away, and Pia wondered whether this was one of those things children should not talk about. But after a moment Yana said: 'Men are strong.'

'Well, if the woman is smart, she should tell the strong man what to do.'

Yana laughed. 'Maybe, but just don't say that in front of our men – they'll get cross.'

That made Pia think her mother did not completely accept the rules of the farmer folk.

Approaching farmer country, they passed into a gap between two woods. Pia knew that the woods were called East Wood and West Wood, and the gap between them was called the Break. Now she noticed that the Break did not look like it had when they left for the Rite. Then the land had been grass. Now it was earth broken up and ready for sowing. She wondered why.

Her mother stopped dead and stared. After a moment she said: 'So that's what they were up to.'

'Who?'

'Our men. While we were away.'

Pia remembered Ani asking why the farmer men had not come to the Rite. At the time Pia had not thought much about it. Ani had made it seem like a casual question, but maybe it was not so casual.

Yana spoke irately, half to herself: 'They wanted to do it while we were at the Midsummer Rite – so we couldn't try to talk them out of it.'

'What has Dadda done?'

'Ploughed up the Break. It was probably all the men, doing what Troon told them to do, whether they liked it or not.'

She was speaking as if this was a big problem. Pia could not see why. Farmers broke up the soil to sow seeds: that was no surprise. She said to her mother: 'Why are you cross?'

'Because the Break was grazing land for the herders, and they're going to be angry with us for changing it to farmland.'

Pia thought for a while. 'So it's like when Stam takes my ball and runs away.'

'Exactly.'

'But I run after him and knock him down and take it back, and he cries.'

'Yes,' said Yana. 'That's what I'm afraid of.'

A friend of Yana's, a broad-shouldered woman called Reen, said: 'The men must have worked day and night to dig up the entire Break so quickly. Men are sneaky. You're never sure what they're up to.'

Yana said: 'My Alno wouldn't have done anything this foolish unless he had to. I'm just hoping there won't be trouble with the herders.'

Some of the others made noises of agreement.

Reen looked grim. 'I don't see how it can be avoided,' she said.

Pia saw two figures approaching across the Break. As they came closer she recognized them. One was Troon, the leader of the farmers, called the Big Man, which was funny, because he was quite small – though he made up for it by shouting bossily. The other was his minion, Shen.

Troon was Stam's father, and Stam ran to him excitedly. Troon patted the boy's head and nodded to Stam's mother, Katch. She was a timid person, Pia thought, perhaps because her man was so domineering.

Stam's mother and Pia's father were sister and brother, which was why Stam and Pia were cousins. She had recently learned what 'cousin' really meant.

Most people were afraid of Troon, but Yana was not. 'What on earth have you done?' she said.

The other women came closer to hear the conversation. Yana was sticking her neck out by criticizing Troon. They would not have dared, but they were pleased to see her standing up to him.

Troon looked offended by her tone but he only said: 'I've created more farmland. We need it.' He looked around the listening circle. 'You women keep having babies. Every year there are more mouths to feed.'

Yana was not satisfied with that answer. 'This land was grazing for the herders. And it's their way through the woods to the river. They'll be outraged.'

'I can't help that. We need it.'

'You've done something reckless. The herders may not take this lying down.'

Pia could see that the women were awestruck by Yana's persistence.

'Leave this to me,' Troon said, and he looked defensive, as if Yana was the leader and he was being reprimanded. 'Don't you worry.'

'I'll worry, and you'll worry too if this starts a war. For every farmer there must be ten herders, at least. We would be wiped out.'

'They'll never attack us. Herders are ruled by their women. They're cowards.'

'I hope you're right,' said Yana.

Ani had been wondering what the farmer men had been up to while absent from the Midsummer Rite, and now she knew.

Urgent messages were often carried by quickrunners, young men and women who could travel the length of the plain in less than half a day. Two days after the Midsummer Rite a quickrunner from the herders in the west arrived in Riverbend with a message for the elders. The farmers had taken over a large area of grazing land and broken up the soil ready for seeding.

The farmers were aggressive. Ani thought it was because their way of life was insecure: they could be wiped out by a single year of bad weather, whereas the herds could survive two or more summers of drought. And young farmer women bore a fat baby every midsummer or two, perhaps because they lived on grain and cheese. Herder women, fed on meat and wild vegetables, were leaner, and that might be why they gave birth less often, about once every four midsummers.

The elders gathered in Riverbend, by the circles of tree trunks, to discuss the news. But they realized quickly that they needed to see for themselves what the farmers had done before they could make any decisions. So they agreed that a delegation would walk to the Break the following day. Keff, Ani and Scagga, the three most active elders, were chosen to go.

It was a long walk, but Ani enjoyed the bright wild flowers and the endless grass and the vast blue sky. Living in a large village next to a river, she was liable to forget the magnificence of the Great Plain. She felt lucky to live there.

The ancestors of the Great Plain people had liked to bury their dead in tombs covered with earth. Such little hills, called barrows, were everywhere, but most of all near the holy Monument. As Ani passed them she wondered why the ancestors had done this and how the practice had died out. Today's people burned their dead. Sometimes they scattered the ashes and sometimes they buried them, but they built no tombs.

Ani's aim on this trip was to avoid a battle and thus prevent the need for many funeral pyres.

They reached the farmer country late in the afternoon, and had enough time and daylight to take a first look at what the farmers had done.

South River formed the southern border of the plain. Parallel with the river was a long, narrow wood. Between river and woodland was fertile soil, which was what made farming possible. In this stretch of woodland was one gap, called the Break. It divided the woodland into East Wood and West Wood. The Break gave the herd access to the river.

Or it had. Now it was farmland.

The farmer men had used scratch ploughs, probably two men to pull each one, to break up the grassy soil. Then they had turned over the sods with wooden shovels. This allowed the seeds to sink into the ground. At this time of year they would probably plant barley, which grew quickly.

As Ani looked she became more worried. This seizure of land by the farmers would outrage many in the herder community. It could lead to something more than a battle. There could be war.

There had been no war on the plain in her lifetime, but she remembered her parents talking in solemn tones about a war that had taken place when they were young, a war between the herders and the woodlanders. The issue had been herders coppicing hazel trees to make them grow the thin, bendy branches to be woven into wattle for house walls. Coppiced hazel produced no nuts, and hazelnuts were a staple in the woodlander diet. The war had ended with a compromise whereby the herders agreed to coppice only the trees on the outer fringes of the woods. But a lot of people had died before peace was made.

'These farmers!' said Scagga. 'They're just thieves! They think they can take whatever they want!' Scagga had bulging eyes that made him seem even more aggressive.

Keff said mildly: 'So it seems.'

Ani said nothing. It was best to let Scagga rave. He might be more reasonable afterwards.

They went to the nearest herder settlement, a hamlet called Old Oak, and spent the night with a young couple, Zad and Biddy, who had a new baby. Living in this remote spot, Zad and Biddy were thrilled to host visitors from the sophisticated east. The elders were woken in the night when the baby had to be fed, but they had all suffered that with their own children, and no one really minded.

In the morning they walked to Farmplace, the village on the north shore of the South River.

The farmers did not work collectively. Each man had a large field, a pasture for a few livestock, a house, and a small store. Now, early in the summer, people were weeding the fields where green shoots of wheat were coming up.

Looking across the water, Ani saw that the farmers had already expanded to the other side of the river. A strip of fertile land there ended in a range of hills. The farmers had cultivated that strip even where it was only a few paces wide. Their hunger for fertile land drove them.

The elders found Troon in the centre of the village, with a group of young men carrying heavy carved wooden clubs, a show of force. Troon had small dark eyes and a permanent scowl. He had been Big Man here for two years. Ani had met him before and found him to be clever, ruthless and angry. Right now he seemed to be suppressing a burning hostility.

A small crowd of villagers watched. Ani saw Pia and Stam, and was about to greet them when she remembered that they were not supposed to play with herder children. She saw Stam gazing at his father with an adoring look. Just don't grow up like your dadda, she thought.

Pia's mother, Yana, was in the crowd. Ani had acquired some of Yana's cheese and liked it. Yana introduced Ani to her husband, Alno, who smiled pleasantly. Ani had seen Yana again later that Midsummer Day, when the revel had begun. Yana had been hand in hand with a handsome herder man a good deal younger than Alno, and they had been heading eagerly for the outskirts. The farmers were keen on the revel, no doubt because their community was so small that everyone was related to everyone else, and inbreeding could be a serious problem.

Ani picked out two other familiar faces in the waiting crowd. One was Katch, Troon's woman, the mother of Stam. She came across as nervous and fearful, as who would not be, stuck with a bully such as Troon? But Ani had talked to her occasionally and got the impression she might have hidden strength.

The other familiar face was that of Shen, Troon's right-hand man, a sly individual with an ingratiating smile and ever-shifting eyes. Ani noticed that Shen was wearing a flint axe attached to a leather belt, in imitation of Troon who had exactly the same.

The elders approached Troon, and Ani tried to set a friendly tone, saying: 'May the Sun God smile on you.'

He did not give the conventional reply. 'What have you come here for?'

Ani smiled. 'You're an intelligent man, Troon.' She spoke in an emollient tone, but her words were uncompromising. 'You know we're here because you're trying to steal grazing land that has been used by the herder community since before any of us were born.'

He was unapologetic. 'That's rich soil, wasted on grazing,' he said. 'It's good farmland and we need it.'

Scagga, standing next to Ani, said angrily: 'You have no right to make that decision. It's always been grassland and you can't change that.'

Behind Troon, little Stam was making a noise. He was shouting: 'I'm a hunter,' and prodding other children with a stick, making them cry. Troon turned and slapped the child's face. It was an open-handed blow, but forceful enough to knock Stam to the ground. He burst into tears. Katch quickly stepped forward, picked him up, and walked away with him in her arms.

Stam was going to have a black eye. Ani believed that children had to be chastised sometimes, but knocking them to the ground was going too far.

Troon resumed the argument as if nothing had happened. 'You herders have plenty of grazing land – almost the entire Great Plain! You don't need the Break – we do.'

Scagga was bursting with indignation. 'You can't steal something simply because you need it!'

'I just did,' said Troon.

Scagga got angrier. 'All right!' he said. 'Plant your seeds. Pull up weeds. Watch your crop grow tall.'

'That's exactly what I'm going to do.'

'And then we will drive the herd across it and trample it all. And when you say to me: "You can't do that!" I'll say: "I just did." Now, what do you say to that?'

Ani guessed that Troon had already thought of this possibility, and she was right. He pointed to the young men, who grinned and shook their weapons. Troon said: 'Any cattle that trample our crops will be slaughtered.'

'You won't be able to kill them all.'

'But at least we'll have plenty of meat.'

Ani saw that this was getting nowhere. She said: 'We're not here to threaten you, Troon. We're just finding out what's happened, so we can report to the other elders and the herder community.'

Scagga added: 'And they're going to be very angry about this.'

Unnecessary, Ani thought, but it makes him feel better.

'Go ahead,' said Troon. 'Be angry. But the Break is farmland now, and it always will be.'

The elders turned away and left, heading for home.

Ani was tired the next day. She supposed it was because she had walked all the way to Farmplace and back in two days. Perhaps I'm getting old, she thought. How many midsummers have I seen? Both hands, both feet, both hands again, and my left hand and my right thumb and one more finger. Shouldn't I be able to walk for two days without feeling tired?

Perhaps not.

The elders met at the circle of tree trunks in Riverbend. It was quiet and still. The trees had been created by the earth, and she sensed that the Earth God was here.

A lot of villagers came to the meeting, whether they were elders or not. This was usual when there was something big to discuss. Many of them just sat and listened, but occasionally they would have a collective reaction, sounds of agreement or doubt, surprise or disgust. This was useful to the elders, because they got an instant public response to what they said.

Ani began by saying: 'Well, the farmers have dug up the entire Break, a large area of pasture that our herds have grazed for as long as anyone can remember. It's also our path to the river, so now if we need to water cattle in the west of the plain we will have to drive them on a long detour, all around the far end of West Wood. But Troon would not listen to our protest.'

Scagga spoke up impatiently. 'We have to start making arrows

– flint-headed arrows. We'll need as many as there are farmers to be killed. More, probably, as archers sometimes miss. And bows.'

'Wait a minute,' said Ani. She knew that Scagga had been born in some faraway place, and had been driven away by a war – a war that in his mind he still wanted to fight. He had to be restrained. 'We haven't decided to go to war, and we won't make that decision if I have anything to do with it.' She saw women in the audience nodding agreement.

Scagga said: 'We outnumber the farmers! There must be ten of us to every one farmer. Maybe more. We can't lose.'

'Perhaps,' Ani said. 'But how many of our people will have their skin pierced by arrows, their heads smashed by clubs, their flesh sliced open by sharp flint knives? How many of us will be killed before we can say we have won?'

Keff intervened. 'Too many,' he said. 'War is a last resort, Scagga, not a first response.'

Good for you, calm Keff, thought Ani, with your black beard and your big belly.

Scagga said: 'If we let them get away with this, they won't stop! How much more land are we willing to lose?'

The young men murmured agreement with that. Young men were quick to anger, Ani had noticed. She hoped her Han would not turn out that way.

Encouraged, Scagga added: 'They won't be satisfied until they've dug up the entire Great Plain!'

There were louder shouts of assent from the young men.

Ani stepped in. 'We should bargain with them. Let them have extra land, as long as they don't block our access to water or pasture, or interfere in any way with our herds.'

'You'd have us all be cowards!' said Scagga.

'I'd have us all alive,' Ani retorted.

The argument raged, with many villagers joining in; but in the end

most people came round to Ani's point of view, and there was no war.
Not yet.

The news reached Farmplace a few days later.

Yana had a she-goat tethered to a post and was milking her, the warm liquid squirting into a shallow pot. Pia was watching, holding the goat's head to keep her still. Troon came striding along, all sneering triumph. 'I told you so!' he said.

Pia had been taught that kind people never said that.

Yana did not look up from her work. 'What did you tell me, Troon?' she said, in a tone of weary tolerance.

'The herders are cowards.'

'And what has happened to make you so sure you're right?'

'A travelling man has come here, one who sings and plays a drum for food and a place to sleep. He was in Riverbend before, and someone told him the whole story of us cultivating the Break, and the herders squealing and threatening war. But they told him they had decided not to have a war. So there!'

'Sensible people. Congratulations.'

'Thank you.'

He was enjoying this, Pia could tell. She said: 'How many enemies do you think we've made?'

'What?'

'I'm asking how many enemies we made with your venture. Too many to count, I suppose, since no one knows how many herders live on the plain.'

'I don't care. They're all cowards.'

'You don't mind being hated?'

Troon grinned, showing uneven teeth. 'Mind?' he said. 'I love it.'

5

THE MIDSUMMER RITE was over, life had returned to normal, and the girls were bored. Joia, Vee and Roni were sitting by the river on a warm morning, idly watching people washing their cookpots, their clothes and themselves. Then something interesting happened. A group of men and women appeared and began to manoeuvre a raft into the water.

Joia recognized Dallo, an old craftsman, much respected though never eager to try new ideas. He was the leader of a group of carpenters and handymen, many of them his kin, who did the craft work people could not do for themselves. They were called cleverhands. The cleverhands coppiced willow trees at the end of winter, cutting the trunk just above ground level so that in spring it would sprout many long, thin, bendy branches suitable for weaving together to form walls and doors and baskets. A cleverhand could build a boat, or a smokehouse, or a roasting spit that could be turned with a handle.

Joia watched with eager curiosity, wondering what project

Dallo and the cleverhands might be engaged upon today. Whatever it was, it would relieve the boredom.

Her curiosity was further piqued when the cleverhands began to load large coils of rope onto the raft. The process of twisting honeysuckle vines into long, strong lengths of rope was slow and tedious. A lot of work had gone into producing these big coils.

A cleverhand called Effi was manhandling a coil with the help of his son, Jero, a boy the same age as Joia and her friends, when Jero stumbled and Effi fell into the water. Everyone laughed: Effi was famously clumsy, and Jero was turning out just like his father.

Soon a crowd began to gather. Whenever something unusual happened, herders would watch. They liked communal experiences, and any event would do. The rope-maker Ev, who was a wit, had once said: 'Herders would form a crowd to watch a pot of water come to the boil.'

When finally the loaded raft set off, it crossed only to the opposite bank. The crowd followed. People who could not swim crossed in their clothes, holding on to bits of wood; the others undressed and swam across, holding their tunics and shoes above the water.

There were a few farms on the far side of the river valley. The crowd followed Dallo to a field recently reaped. Conspicuous in the middle of the field was a large stone, about the size of one of the mysterious bluestones that formed the outer ring of the Monument. It lay flat, one end rounded, the other in a rough point. Joia learned that the farmer, an older man, was fed up with having to work around this useless stone and wanted to get rid of it. He had agreed to give the herders a fine young bull if they would move the stone off the field and dump it at the riverside.

The herders gathered around the stone, eager to see how Dallo would manage this.

He began by instructing his cleverhands to lay ropes across

the stone in straight lines. One end of each rope was then pushed under the stone, the cleverhands using sticks to shove the rope into the soft earth. The other end stretched out on the opposite side.

Next, longer ropes were laid along the length of the stone, then the two sets of ropes were interwoven. Joia saw that Dallo was making a giant version of a familiar object, the string bag that people made with cords of plant fibres twisted together. The round end of the stone would lie at the bottom of the bag, she explained to her friends.

Vee said: 'But how will he get the stone into the bag?'

Joia could not figure that out. Listening to the conversations all around her, she gathered that others were asking Vee's question.

They soon learned the answer.

Five of the strongest men and women stood beside the stone with stout tree branches in their hands, careful not to tread on the long ends of rope. Putting the ends of the branches where the stone met the ground, they shoved together, attempting to roll the stone. On the other side, another five kept pushing the short ends of the ropes under the stone. Inch by inch, the stone moved, rolling onto the short ends and pulling the long ends with it. The stone moved, then stopped; then, with a big effort from the cleverhands, it moved again. They kept it up until the short ends of rope emerged from under the stone on the other side, where they could be joined to the long ends.

The stone was in the bag.

Working quickly, the cleverhands completed the weaving and knotting of the rope bag, joining the two sides then bringing up the long base, so that the entire stone was contained within the bag.

At the open end, Joia now noticed, the ends of the ropes were much longer than it seemed they needed to be. But now she learned why. The long ends were grab lines. All the cleverhands took hold of grab lines, held them hard, and pulled.

The stone did not move.

Dallo stood in front of them, shouting: 'Ready . . . heave!' When nothing happened, he tried again. 'Ready . . . heave!' The cleverhands reddened and perspired, and the muscles of their arms and legs bulged with the effort, but it was not enough.

Some of the crowd joined in, grasping the ropes and pulling when Dallo said: 'Heave!' They seemed ineffectual. More came forward, doubling the original number. They took a few moments to work out what was required. Joia noticed that they quickly learned to set their legs firmly, digging their feet into the ground, and lean forward, putting their weight into it.

When there were about twenty people pulling, the stone at last moved.

It shifted, stopped, and shifted again; and Dallo yelled: 'Keep it going! Keep it going!' Joia guessed that the stubble might be slippery, which would help. This time when the stone moved it did not stop.

Now Dallo had to direct it. Facing the pullers and walking backwards, he gestured with his arms, getting them to move to their right, towards the riverbank.

The field looked flat, but it was not perfectly so, and the stone stopped as it hit a bump. Joia guessed there had been a tree in that spot, and when it was felled, probably long ago, a stump had remained, and then the crops had slowly grown over it. How was Dallo going to deal with this? Perhaps the cleverhands would try to flatten the bump with flint axes and wooden shovels; but then they might come across the remains of the stump, which could be very difficult to dig up.

But the long grab lines gave Dallo room to manoeuvre. He directed all the pullers to move to one side, then got them heaving at an angle, so that the stone would avoid the hump. Once again it took several tries to get the stone to move at all; and once again it continued to move smoothly when it got started. It tracked perilously close to the hump, but Dallo had judged well and it just missed the obstacle.

The last short stretch of the journey was easier, as the ground sloped gently down towards the river. Before the stone reached the bank, Dallo stopped the pullers, and his cleverhands untied the ropes for re-use. Ropes were never to be wasted.

When the bag had been dismantled the stone was rolled down the last few paces to the edge of the water.

The crowd cheered their congratulations.

The ropes were taken back across the river and the bull was brought and forced to swim across. The spectators drifted away. Once again the girls found themselves at a loose end. Sitting on the riverbank, Joia said: 'Let's have an adventure.'

The three girls had had adventures before. One time they had sailed down East River on a log. It had been great fun, with people waving from the banks, until the log came to a stop in the middle of a wide swamp where East River met South River. They had had to tramp through muddy meadows with dangerous ponds, and it had taken them all afternoon to walk home, soaking wet. But now when they talked about it they laughed at their own silly cheek.

On another occasion they had gone into Three Streams Wood to look for the village of the woodlanders. They had got lost, but the woodlanders had rescued them and had shown them the way home.

It was Joia who dreamed up these adventures, and they were always a little bit dangerous – that was part of the fun. Joia was like her father, or so her mother said: he had been a risk-taker.

Now Vee and Roni were keen to hear what Joia had in mind,

but they were also wary. They often resisted an adventure at first, and had to be talked around, each in a different way.

Joia looked at Vee, who was stocky and strong, and had a rebellious air, as if ready to defy the world. If she was approached in the right way, she would hide any anxiety. Joia said to her: 'I'm not sure about it. You might be too scared.'

'I would not,' Vee said immediately.

She was the only girl in a family of boys, and was always in competition with her brothers, proving that she could run fast and shoot arrows and cut a pig's throat just as well as they did. She took pride in being fearless, and could never resist a dare – something Joia liked about her.

'Maybe you wouldn't be scared,' Joia conceded.

Roni said anxiously: 'What's the adventure?'

'I want to spy on the priestesses.'

Roni gasped.

The priestesses allowed people inside the Monument on special days, but most of the time they were secretive, and kept everyone out. They performed a ritual every morning at sunrise, and you could hear their singing. Presumably they were dancing too, but no one seemed to know, and their privacy was respected from a mixture of reverence and fear. The Monument was a sacred place.

Joia wanted to know what they got up to.

The priestesses intrigued her. They always knew exactly when it was Midsummer Day and Midwinter Day, and the Spring Halfway and the Autumn Halfway too. If you asked them questions, they would say things like: 'Midwinter will be in ten days' time.' How did they do that? How did they know these things? Clearly they had secret knowledge that no one else possessed. The thought excited her.

Roni said: 'But their rituals are holy secrets. We might displease the gods.'

'I don't believe the gods would care about three girls peeking – do you?'

Roni was reluctant to concede the point. 'I don't know. You don't know either.'

Vee said: 'I agree with Joia. We wouldn't offend the gods. But the high priestess might be angry with us. And then we could be flogged.'

Grown-ups were never flogged, but children were sometimes, for serious offences: setting fire to a house, tormenting a cow, that sort of thing. Joia had suffered this punishment twice, and it really hurt, but somehow that had not turned her into a rule-keeper. 'If the priestesses see us peeking, we'll run away,' she said. 'They won't know who we are, they don't know us, and they can't run fast in those long tunics.'

Joia and her friends and everyone else wore a simple knee-length tunic, two pieces of leather sewn together with a bone needle, using the sinew of a cow as thread. The stitching left a hole for the head and two holes for the arms. The priestesses also wore leather tunics, but theirs were ankle-length and had sleeves, warm but constricting. Joia had never seen a priestess run.

Roni still looked dubious.

Joia said: 'You don't have to come with us if you don't want to.'

As Joia knew, Roni could not bear to be left out. She was unsure of herself – despite being so beautiful – and she needed the comfort of belonging to a group. 'But I do want to go with you,' she said.

Vee said: 'When shall we do it?'

'Tomorrow,' Joia said immediately.

Roni was dismayed. 'So soon!'

'No point in delaying.' Joia did not want to give her more time to change her mind. 'Let's meet outside Vee's house before dawn. We need to reach the Monument by daybreak or soon after.' The

Monument lay to the south-west of the village, and to walk there took about the time needed to boil a pot of water.

The others nodded assent, and Joia stood up. 'It must be nearly time to eat,' she said. The sun was high and she was hungry for the midday meal.

They left the riverside and went separate ways through the village.

As Joia walked she recalled the adventure of the Three Streams Wood. Looking back, she could see that she had been foolish to suggest it, and the others should not have let her talk them into it.

The woodlanders were normally gentle people. They sometimes came to the Rites, bringing nuts and game to trade. They needed flints – everyone needed flints, which were the only tools with a sharp edge – but there were no flint mines in the woods. They also liked to trade for bracelets and necklaces of beads made from carved bone.

However, people said that the woodlanders were easily offended, and then they could be violent. Joia had forgotten this when she led Vee and Roni into the wood.

At first they did not meet any woodlanders, though Joia saw evidence of their presence in the form of hazelnut bushes carefully pruned and trimmed to yield the maximum harvest – a skill only the woodlanders had.

There were three levels of vegetation, she noticed. The pine trees were highest. Oaks and alders were lower and wider. There was an understory of hazel, elder and birch, and finally moss and lichen at ground level.

She began to feel that she was being watched, hidden eyes peering curiously at her through the foliage. She told herself not to worry. The woodlanders were probably shy. Perhaps they were even afraid of strangers.

The girls did not find a village and soon they were lost.

'We're not lost,' Joia said firmly. 'We just have to walk in a straight line until we come to the edge of the wood.'

A long time later, Vee said: 'We've been here before. I remember that bog. We're going around in circles.'

Roni began to cry.

For once Joia did not know what to do.

Then she saw the woodlanders.

They appeared as if from nowhere, moving silently, surrounding the three girls. The women and children were naked, the men wearing leather loincloths. Joia gave the polite formal greeting: 'May the Sun God smile on you.'

The correct response was: 'And on you.' But a woman replied in the woodlander language, which Joia and her friends did not understand. Joia knew they had their own language, but the ones who came to the Rites had always spoken a few words of the plainspeople's tongue. Now she realized that bilingual woodlanders must be exceptional.

But she could not think what to do, so she tried again: 'We're lost and we want to go home.'

The woodlanders spoke among themselves, as if discussing what to do next. Then suddenly three of the men picked up the three girls and slung them over their shoulders. Vee screamed and Roni sobbed. Joia wriggled fiercely, trying to get free, but the man was too strong for her.

The men carried them through the undergrowth, followed by the rest of the group, all chattering excitedly among themselves. Joia feared what they might be going to do. Will they rape us? she thought. Or even kill us and eat us?

She stopped struggling, too tired to go on with a useless effort.

Soon they emerged from the wood onto a grassy plain.

The three men put the girls down.

Joia looked around and realized that they were in exactly the place where they had entered the wood.

Without speaking, the three girls began to run.

All the woodlanders roared with laughter.

Afterwards, Joia had pretended that she never thought the woodlanders intended any harm. Vee and Roni said they, too, had never really felt in danger. All three of them were lying, Joia realized.

Her reverie was ended by her sister's voice. 'Are you going to walk past me without speaking?'

Joia came back to the present. 'Sorry, Neen,' she said. 'I was daydreaming.'

The sisters were close. Neen had often been tasked with looking after young Joia, so they had spent a lot of time together. Joia now understood that Neen had a strong mothering instinct. She had played games with Joia, told her stories, sung songs, and taught her the good manners that were so important in the community of the Great Plain. Joia in turn had worshipped her big sister, and still loved her for her kindness and wisdom.

'I was remembering that time I got lost in the wood,' Joia explained.

'Oh.'

Joia saw that Neen was distracted, and she guessed why. 'No word from Seft yet?'

'No. I still have no idea what has happened to him.'

Joia remembered Seft limping away from the Midsummer Rite, his handsome face a mass of cuts and bruises and tears. 'Perhaps he just went back to his family.'

Neen said: 'Or he might have kept walking, beyond the borders of the plain, to start a new life somewhere else. Or he might have drowned himself in a river.'

Joia was disappointed for Neen. Seft seemed right for her. Neen wanted to be a mother, and Seft – judging by the easy way he had chatted to young Han – seemed to have the makings of a natural father. He was younger than Neen – sixteen midsummers to her eighteen – and quite shy, but very handsome, with his pale, narrow face, high cheekbones and curved nose. Neen said he was clever, too.

Now she said: 'I don't know if I'll ever see him again.'

'Wait till the Autumn Rite,' Joia said. 'We'll either see Seft there or get word of him.'

'I suppose so.'

At some point, Joia feared, Neen would have to give up hope.

Joia did not have the same aspirations as Neen. She did not think she would be a good mother. And she had never fallen in love with a boy.

There was definitely something wrong with her.

It was still dark when Joia woke up. She immediately remembered the adventure planned for the day. Yesterday she had been all confidence, but now she felt worried. Was it a completely stupid idea? However, she was desperate to learn more about the priestesses. They held the secrets of the sky, and Joia ached to know them.

She listened to the night sounds of her family, lying around her on the hides that covered the earth floor of the house. Neen was breathing evenly, Han was muttering a little in his sleep, and their mother was snoring. The puppy – now called Thunder – sensed that Joia was awake, and wagged optimistically, his tail beating the ground, but it was a familiar noise and did not disturb the sleepers.

Joia wondered how long it would be before daybreak. She was wide awake, so it must be soon. She had to leave, silently.

She felt around, found her shoes, grabbed them, then stood up. She was wearing her tunic – she slept in it, as most people did. Carrying her shoes, treading softly, she lifted the wicker gate, slipped through the doorway, and replaced the gate carefully, making no noise. Thunder gave a disappointed whimper that was almost human: she was tied up, and could not follow Joia. Once again the puppy's noise did not wake anyone. No one else stirred.

Outside, Joia paused for a moment. The chill night air was like a drink of water from a cold stream. There was no moon, but the stars shone in the black sky and showed her the peaked silhouettes of silent neighbouring houses.

She might not be the only early riser, she thought anxiously. She did not want to be seen and recognized. Anyone coming across her would ask, in a friendly way, what she was doing up so early; and the person would casually tell her mother, then the truth would come out.

She looked carefully all around but saw no one.

She walked away across the dewy grass. When she was fifty paces or so from her house she sat on the ground and put on her shoes. They were made of cow hide, like her tunic, and had drawstrings that could be pulled tight.

She saw no one as she made her way to Vee's house and sat on the ground nearby to wait. She wondered whether Vee and Roni would appear. Vee's mother, Kae, might have guessed that something was up. Joia liked Kae, but she was not a rule-breaker and she would not allow her daughter to be one. If she found out what the girls were planning to do today she would put a stop to it without hesitation.

More likely, Vee might just get scared and stay in bed. Joia herself was having second thoughts, so Vee must be too, and the same went for Roni.

Joia wondered what to do if neither of them showed up. It would be dismal to return to the house and go back to sleep, like a hunter coming home with nothing in the basket. If necessary she would go on her own to the Monument, she decided, and alone she would spy on the priestesses and learn their secrets.

She shivered. It would continue cold until the Sun God came to smile on the earth.

A ghostly figure materialized beside her, and after a startled moment she recognized Roni. Neither of them spoke. Roni sat down beside Joia, and Joia squeezed her arm by way of greeting, feeling a thrill of excitement. The adventure was on.

A few moments later Vee stepped silently out of her house. Joia and Roni got to their feet, and the three girls set off.

They soon left the village behind and took the well-worn track that led in a straight south-westerly line from Riverbend to the Monument. When they were safely distant from the houses they all laughed with relief, then linked arms to walk side by side.

Dawn came up behind them, its faint glow spreading across the sky. The Great Plain became more clearly visible. Joia felt a shudder of fear as they passed a burial mound. Her ancestors were in there. What would they think if they knew what she was doing?

She looked away. As far as the eye could see, sheep and cattle bowed their heads to graze. The herds were guarded day and night, and a few herders saw the girls and gave friendly waves.

Joia was dismayed. She had not thought of the danger that they would be seen by herders. But she could not make out their faces in the faint light, and she hoped that meant they could not see hers. 'Don't act guilty,' she said, and waved back cheerily. Vee and Roni did the same.

Everyone worked with the herds, but about half the population also did special tasks, like tanning leather, which was Ani's skill. The main job of a herder was to make sure the beasts did not wander where they should not go – to the woods or swamps, or into houses. Herders had bows and arrows to use against thieves, but theft was rare. From time to time they would move part of the herd to fresh pasture. Older and more experienced people might intervene when a cow was having difficulty calving, or when one was injured or sick. Much of the time the work was not demanding.

People in the community worked for ten days and rested for two, making a twelve-day week, but herders staggered their rest days so that the beasts were never left untended.

The three girls came within sight of the high earth bank that surrounded the Monument. The path they were on led straight to the gap in the bank where there was a ceremonial entrance, so they veered away to approach indirectly, hoping they would not be seen.

Outside the circle a little way to the north was the priestesses' village, a handful of houses and two larger buildings. Some priestesses lived in communal dormitories, and a few couples made their homes in regular houses. Joia could see no activity there, but all the same she led the group on a wide detour that brought them to the Monument from the south. She felt her heart beating hard as they bellied up the grassy bank and peeked over the edge.

Joia had seen other timber and stone circles – there were several on the Great Plain – and they all had a random look, as if no one had planned how many stones or posts there would be, or how they would relate to one another. Now it struck her forcefully that there was nothing random about this circle. Someone had wanted it exactly like this. The design had a purpose, but what? The mystery intrigued and annoyed her.

The priestesses began to emerge from their houses. Joia tensed and lowered her head, pressing her chin into the earth, so that her mouth and nose were below the ridge, and only her eyes and forehead were above it. Her hair was dark. She felt sure she could not be seen at a distance.

Vee and Roni copied her.

The priestesses were naked. As they came through the entrance they began to sing, dancing to the beat of a drum. They paused, waiting. Then a woman with white hair appeared. That would be Soo, the high priestess, Joia guessed.

Suddenly there was a whoop of triumph from right behind them. Shocked, Joia rolled over, wriggling down the slope, and was amazed to see her brother, Han, throw himself down beside her. 'Caught you!' he said, and laughed.

Vee and Roni quickly slithered down from the ridge. Joia pulled Han's leg ungently to bring him down out of sight. 'You idiot!' she hissed. She was furious. She could have killed him. 'You followed us here!' she said, in an outraged whisper. 'Now you've probably given us away!' She was tempted to hit him but that would make him yell again.

He looked pleased with himself. 'I knew you were doing something bad – you sneaked away in the dark.'

Roni said: 'We'd better leave.'

Joia hated the idea, but she thought Roni might be right.

However, the singing had not stopped.

Joia crawled back up the slope and peeped over the ridge again. She was afraid she would see a group of priestesses running towards her, intent on grabbing hold of the spies who had defiled their holy Rite, and she was ready to run, with the others, away from the Monument as fast as they could. But the priestesses were still dancing, none of them looking towards the place where she lay. She studied the scene. They were concentrating on their ritual. 'I don't think anyone heard my stupid little brother,' she said.

'Are you sure?' said Roni.

Joia shrugged. She was not sure. 'They're just carrying on.'

Vee and Roni joined Joia and looked over the ridge. Then Han did the same. Joia said to him: 'Go away!'

'I want to watch.'

'You can't.'

'If you don't let me, I'll tell Mamma what you're doing.'

'And then I'll take you to the river and hold your head under the water for a long, long time.'

'You wouldn't dare!' He looked as if he was going to cry.

Joia gave in. 'Go and find a branch or something to put over your head. Otherwise the priestesses might see your yellow hair.'

Han rolled down the bank and uprooted a small leafy bush. He returned to Joia's side, holding it on his head.

In the east, the edge of the sun appeared over the horizon.

The priestesses, led by Soo, were performing a complicated dance around the posts. Some of them carried pottery discs, about the size of Joia's hand, which they ritually laid down and picked up in front of the timber posts.

It was clear to Joia that their movements had meaning. She could make out some of the words of the song, which mentioned winter and summer, spring and autumn, and other seasonal events: the appearance of new grass, the migration of deer, the falling of leaves. Somehow, Joia guessed, this dance was the way they always knew which day of the year it was, and how many days were left before the next quarterly event.

The priestesses moved out of the timber circle and danced across the grass to the bluestone circle at the edge, fortunately at a spot distant from where the spies lay. They moved from one big standing stone to another purposefully, and once again they seemed to be counting. Joia's curiosity intensified.

They returned to the timber circle and gathered in the inner oval. They all knelt down facing north-east, watching the sun rise. It was now more than three-quarters over the horizon. They began to hum softly, getting louder.

The rite was coming to an end, Joia saw. She was half pleased, half frustrated. She had learned a lot, but much more remained mysterious.

The humming rose dramatically. As the disc of the rising sun detached itself from the edge of the world, the priestesses stopped humming and gave a climactic shout of triumph. After a short silence, they got to their feet and began to walk, slowly and without speaking, back to their houses. The ceremony was over.

The four onlookers pushed themselves down the slope, out of sight. Joia turned over to get up, and was shocked to see three priestesses, all dressed in their long tunics, standing in the way, looking cross. Her heart seemed to falter.

The spies had been caught.

They all stood up. Joia recognized Ello, the second high priestess, Soo's deputy. She was said to have a mean streak, and she had the face to match, with a nose like a flint knife and a thin-lipped mouth.

Han darted away, trying to escape, but Ello was quicker and she grabbed his arm and jerked him back, making him stand at her side.

'You're hurting my arm!' he wailed but she took no notice.

She glared at him and said: 'I suppose you're the one who yelled and gave the game away.'

Han burst into tears.

Joia said: 'Leave my brother alone!'

Ello nodded to the other two priestesses. Moving quickly, they seized Joia, each holding an arm. She was a prisoner.

Ello looked at Vee and Roni and said: 'You two had better come with us, or you'll be in even worse trouble.'

Roni looked ready to run away, but Vee said to her: 'Come on, we can't desert Joia.'

The priestesses marched Joia and Han towards the village, and Vee and Roni followed. Joia felt helpless and fearful. No one knew where they were. Anything could happen and their families would never know.

They reached the village and were pushed into one of the small houses.

Inside, the high priestess sat on a leather mat in the middle of the floor. Seeing her close up for the first time, Joia noticed her piercing blue eyes. Joia had never met a woman that old. She recalled her mother saying that priestesses lived longer than other women because they did not bear children.

Ello sat down next to Soo. Joia had the impression that the two of them dwelt together in this house.

The other two priestesses stood outside. There was no escape.

Joia felt she had to say something in her defence. 'I only . . .' Her throat seemed constricted and her voice trembled. She tried again. 'I only wanted to know how you can tell the number of days left until midsummer, or midwinter.'

Soo looked at her dispassionately. 'So you're the ringleader.'

Joia felt she was justly accused. She nodded miserably.

Soo said: 'The rest of you, go home.'

They hesitated, as if they could not quite believe it. Soo nodded to Ello, who got up and escorted Vee, Roni and Han out. Ello did not come back.

Joia was glad her little brother was being freed, but clearly she herself had been singled out for special punishment, and she wondered fearfully what form it would take.

But first Soo asked her a question. 'Did you notice how many upright posts there are in the outer wooden circle?'

As it happened, Joia had counted them. She answered the

question by holding out both hands, pointing to both feet, and holding out both hands again.

'Correct,' said Soo. 'And that's how many complete weeks there are in a year. Think how many days that is.'

Joia was baffled. She could not count that high. After hands, feet, wrists, elbows, all the way up to the top of the head, she ran out. 'There aren't enough numbers for so many days,' she protested.

'But there are better ways to count, not using your body.'

Joia was surprised. Everyone who could count indicated numbers by fingers, toes, and other parts of the body; everyone except the woodlanders, who could only say, *one, a pair, another one* and *a lot*, which was hardly counting at all. 'What other way is there?'

'I'll show you.' Soo indicated a stack of pottery discs on the floor beside her. Joia had not noticed them before. Now she looked at them and realized they were the discs used in the ritual.

Soo said: 'Count these as I lay them down.' She made a line of discs across the floor, and Joia counted from her left thumb across all her fingers to the right thumb.

Next, Soo picked up a disc similar except that it had a line carved across it. 'Imagine,' she said, 'that this is worth all the discs in that line.' She put down the marked disc and picked up the plain ones. 'Now we carry on.' She put the plain discs back on the floor one by one as Joia counted them with her toes. Then Soo again replaced the plain discs with one marked disc.

But as she was repeating the process a third time, Joia touched the top of her head and said: 'This is the highest number.'

'With discs, you never run out of numbers. And every number has a name. The first thing novice priestesses have to learn is how to name all the numbers.

Joia was fascinated and thrilled. 'So you can count all the days in the year!'

'Yes. You're very quick to understand.' Soo seemed to be enjoying this conversation, and Joia dared to hope that she had forgotten the punishment.

Soo scooped up the plain discs and made a new line with the marked discs. Counting them, Joia went from left thumb to right thumb again. Soo then replaced the discs with one that had a cross engraved on its face. 'This represents all the ones I picked up.'

'So . . .' Joia was rapidly taking all this in. 'So you could go on counting . . . for ever.'

'Exactly.'

Joia was bowled over. She was seeing the world in a whole new light. These were the secrets of the priestesses. And she was being told them.

Her mind leaped forward. 'So when you dance and sing, you're counting the days and weeks.'

'And marking how many have passed since the last solstice or equinox, and how many are left before the next.'

'And the big stones around the edge?'

'Those help us predict eclipses, which is a lot more complicated.'

'Are all stone circles used in this way?'

'Certainly not!' Soo seemed offended and sat upright. Joia remembered nervously that the question of punishment was not yet resolved. Soo said: 'Every other stone circle I have seen does not have the right number of stones for any useful purpose – they're just random. And that goes for wood circles too. Anyway, we priestesses are the only people who know the rituals. Our Monument is unique, and so is our priestesshood.'

'And the songs?'

'Also unique.'

Joia frowned thoughtfully. 'The wood circle is vulnerable. Timber can rot, or fall down in a gale, or be carried away by thieves. The whole Monument ought to be made of stone, not wood.'

Soo nodded. 'You're so right. And one day it will be.'

Soo was too old to be talking about what might happen 'one day', Joia thought. But she did not comment.

Soo said: 'Everything we know about the sun, and the moon, and the days in the year is in our songs. It's our holy duty to teach the songs to the next generation, so that the knowledge will never be lost.'

Joia nodded agreement.

Soo said: 'You're the next generation. You must think about becoming a priestess. You're the perfect age to be a novice.'

This had been a conversation of surprises, but Joia had not expected *that*. For a moment she was lost for words. Then she said: 'But . . . I spied on you.'

Soo shrugged. 'That showed me how interested you are. And in talking to you I've discovered that you're clever too. Even smart people don't usually understand all this as easily as you.'

Joia struggled to imagine leaving her mother and Neen and Han for a new, completely different life. She would still see her family: the priestesses were not isolated. But she would live here, eat and sleep with the priestesses, and sing the songs of the sun and the moon. She would not be there to stop Han falling into the river, or to help Neen raise her children, or to take care of Mamma when she grew old.

Soo saw her thoughtfulness but guessed wrong about its cause. 'You may want to go with boys and have children.'

Joia did not care about that. 'I don't know why they all keep talking about boys and babies,' she said, allowing her irritation to show. 'As if that was the only thing that mattered!'

'That's how I felt at your age.' Soo smiled at the memory, and as she recalled her youth her lined face looked beautiful for a moment. Then she said: 'But you must go home and talk to your mother. What's her name?'

'Ani.'

'The elder?'

'Yes.'

'I know her, of course. She's a very sensible woman. But she will be reluctant to lose you, especially so young. And she'll worry that you may not like the life of a priestess as much as you expect.'

Joia nodded. That would be exactly how Ani would react.

Soo went on: 'Tell her that the Monument is not a prison. Any priestess can leave any time she wants to. If you find that you don't like the life after all, you'll be able to walk away from it.'

In fact Joia was not worrying about that. The life seemed perfect to her. She was reluctant to end her talk with Soo, but she was now eager to tell her mother all about it.

Soo sensed her restlessness. 'It's time you went home for breakfast.'

'Yes.' Joia realized she was very hungry.

'Think about this, and don't hurry. We can talk again – and I'll be glad to speak to Ani, too. Kiss me goodbye.'

Joia bent to kiss Soo's wrinkled lips. The kiss went on a moment or two longer than she expected. Then Soo said: 'You're a special girl, Joia. I hope you decide to join us. May the Sun God smile on you.'

'And on you, High Priestess,' said Joia.

Ani was furious. 'What evil spirit possessed you to do such a thing?' she said. 'Your brother was scared out of his wits!' She was cooking sheep's liver with wild sorrel, and she stirred the pot angrily with a wooden spatula.

This was unusual. She had a round, friendly face framed with gently greying hair. Rage did not suit her.

Joia was sitting on the grass, looking at her warily. 'Han wasn't supposed to be there,' she said. 'He just followed us, the little sneak.'

'You shouldn't have been there either. The priestesses have a right to keep things private if they wish. I hope they gave you a thrashing.'

'No.'

'No? What then?'

'I had a long talk with High Priestess Soo.'

'Is that all?'

'Mamma, I learned so much! She taught me a new way to count, using discs instead of parts of the body. You can keep counting higher and higher and never stop.'

'Oh.'

'She said I was very quick to understand.'

'Oh, yes, you've always been quick. It's ordinary common sense that you lack.' Ani threw a handful of wild grains into the pot.

'No one was hurt, Mamma. Only Han, a little bit, when Ello grabbed his arm. And that was his own fault.'

'Poor child, he pissed all down his leg. I had to wash him.'

Joia wanted to get her mother off the subject of poor Han. 'The priestesses' songs contain everything we know about the sun and the moon. That's why they're so important. They're the only way we can preserve our knowledge from one generation to the next.'

'Is that so?'

Ani was still cross but she was softening, Joia could tell.

Joia took a deep breath. 'That's why I want to be a priestess.'

At first Ani did not take her seriously. 'Well, you've got several years to think about it before you're old enough.'

'Soo said I'm the perfect age to start.'

'That's ridiculous! You've only seen thirteen midsummers!'

'Fourteen.'

'Don't quibble.'

Joia was frustrated. How could she make her mother understand? 'I know what I want!'

'Nobody knows what they want at thirteen. Or fourteen. The high priestess just wants to get you in her clutches before you get pregnant.'

'I'm not going to get pregnant.'

'I said that at your age, and look at me now, cooking for three disobedient children.'

Joia sighed. 'You're very mean this morning.'

'I'm making you breakfast, aren't I?'

'I hate liver.'

They were silent for a while, then Joia said: 'Soo says you're wise.'

'Too wise to give her my daughter.'

That angered Joia. 'You don't own me, and neither does she!'

Ani put down her spatula and came to sit by Joia. 'Seriously,' she said, 'could you be happy, living with a group of women, repeating the same songs and dances?'

'Yes. I'm quite sure I will like it a lot better than herding cattle or making leather.'

'You know that priestesses aren't allowed to have children. If you get pregnant, you have to leave.'

'I don't want children. I never have.'

'Do you realize that many of the priestesses are women who love women?'

'There's nothing wrong with that.'

'Of course not, but are you that type?'

'I don't know what type I am.'

'All the more reason to delay your decision.'

'I won't have to stay if I don't like it. Soo said priestesses can walk away any time.'

That made Ani think. After a moment she said: 'So if you become a priestess—'

'Novice, I suppose.'

'If you become a novice and three weeks later you change your mind, the high priestess will say: "That's fine, don't worry, thank you for trying." Is that what you're telling me?'

'I don't know what she would say, but in any case—'

'I want to know exactly what she would say.'

Joia realized she had moved her mother from No to Perhaps. That was progress. 'So you'll talk to her and ask her?'

'Yes.'

'Good,' said Joia.

6

SEFT REJOICED IN his freedom, but he knew that his father would not accept his escape. There would be a confrontation sooner or later, and he had to be ready for it. Every night he slept with a flint knife close to hand.

He was happy at Wun's pit. His system of mining was superior. Chalk removed by the digging of new tunnels was disposed of in abandoned tunnels, so that it did not have to be laboriously carried up the climbing pole to the surface.

The work was satisfying and the atmosphere even better. The men liked one another. They even seemed to like Seft. He had made a friend his own age: Tem, a nephew of Wun's. They sat together in the evenings, eating the dinner cooked by Wun, who was too old to dig. They all slept in the open, and Seft and Tem generally lay down side by side and talked quietly until they fell asleep.

Some of the miners were single young men such as Seft and Tem; others had families they visited whenever they could. There were no women at the pit. A few women were strong enough for the work, but not many.

Seft's family showed up one evening at suppertime.

He felt a cold hand grip his heart as he saw the three of them approaching: stern Cog, with a face like war; big shambling Olf, always hoping for a fight; and scrawny Cam, looking at Olf to know what to think. The setting sun threw long shadows behind them. They strode across the grassland like an army come to destroy Seft's new life.

For a little while he had lived in a place where there was no hatred. Was that over now?

He put down his dinner bowl and stood up. Tem, beside him, stood too, and Seft was grateful, for that would show Cog that Seft had at least one person on his side.

For the first time, Seft noticed that his family's clothing was grubby. Here at Wun's pit the men took off their tunics in the evening and cleaned the chalk dust off them, using leaves dipped in the stream, and Seft had taken up the practice to be like the rest. Now he felt that his family was just dirty.

Cog looked as determined as a cornered wild boar. Olf swung his arms from the shoulders, limbering up. Cam was trying to look threatening, with little success.

Seft hoped that he himself did not look too scared.

Cog said to him: 'You have to come home with me.'

Seft decided to say nothing.

After a pause, Cog said: 'Pick up your tools and let's go.'

Seft did not move.

He saw Olf clench his fists. Not long now, he thought.

Cog moved menacingly closer. 'Do as you're told, boy, or you'll be the worse for it.'

Seft trembled.

Then he heard Wun say: 'No violence, please, Cog. This is my place and I won't stand for it.' He crossed the space to stand with Seft and Tem.

A thrill passed through Seft. He had friends and supporters. He was no longer at Cog's mercy.

Cog said: 'You keep out of this, Wun. It's a family matter.'

Wun stood his ground. 'Call it what you like, I'm in charge here and I won't have you starting a fight.'

'No fight,' said Cog, trying to sound reasonable, but failing. 'Seft here knows his duty. He's coming back to his family.'

Seft spoke for the first time. 'No, I'm not.'

'You have to, you're my son.'

'You don't want a son, you want a slave. I'm staying here.'

Cog became angry. He could never tolerate defiance. He raised his voice. 'You're coming with me, even if I have to pick you up and carry you.'

Olf and Cam moved closer and stood either side of Cog, ready for action. But Wun's men also moved, six of them surrounding Wun and Seft.

Wun said: 'Give up, Cog. You're not going to get what you want.'

'Oh, yes, I am,' said Cog. 'It may not be today, but I'll get this boy back, and when I do he'll have the thrashing of his life.'

Seft felt cold fear. His face still bore the marks of the last thrashing.

'That's as may be,' said Wun. 'But for now I want you to get away from my place and stay away.' He indicated the men around him. 'If you come back again, we may not be so polite to you.'

Seft could see his father calculating the chances. If his opposition had been herders or farmers, he might have risked the odds of three against six. But the six were miners, just like Cog and his sons, as hard as the flint they dug up. Cog's face showed that he was reluctantly accepting defeat.

Cog found it hard to give in. He stared at Wun with hate, and then at Seft with rage. He seemed to be searching for words. At last he said to Seft: 'The time will come when you'll rue this day with bitter tears – and blood.' And then he turned away.

Olf and Cam looked surprised. They did not often see their father back down. They turned and followed him, trying not to look defeated.

Seft felt weak with relief. His legs seemed about to give way, so he sat down abruptly. He picked up his dinner bowl, realized he was too tense to eat, and put it down again. Now that the clash was over he felt helpless with fear.

Wun said: 'Well done, lad. You stood your ground. Good man.'

Seft said: 'Thank you for defending me.'

'I don't like to see a decent young man bullied.' He returned to his dinner, and the others did the same.

Tem sat beside Seft. 'Your father is horrible,' he said. 'No wonder you ran away.'

'It took me a long time to work up the courage.'

'I can imagine! But it's over now.'

'Perhaps,' said Seft, and he picked up his bowl again.

Night fell, the birds went quiet, and everyone lay down. Seft took from his bag a long-bladed flint knife, well sharpened. After a while the moon rose silently.

Seft thought about Neen. He had a recurring daydream about how he would reunite with her. His departure had been so ignominious that he was determined to return with dignity, as an independent young man with a role to play and the ability to make his own living and one day feed his children. He would be able to do that soon.

He wished he could have got a message to Neen, but there was no way. Most people travelled only for the quarterly Rites. Occasional itinerants arrived, singing poems or offering to trade something small, bone jewellery or magic potions, but they were not trustworthy messengers and, anyway, Seft had not seen one.

So Neen must be in the dark about his intentions. He hoped she might wait a while for him. But she probably saw Enwood every day. How long would it be before she gave up on the vanished Seft?

The men around him fell asleep, but Seft felt sleep was dangerous. His family might not be far away. He planned to stay awake all night.

Tem stayed awake beside him for a long time, and they talked intermittently, but eventually Tem's breathing became regular, and Seft was the only one left awake. He clutched the flint knife in his right hand. He listened to the sounds of the night, the scurry of small creatures and the melancholy moan of the owl as it hunted them. He strained his hearing for human footsteps on the grass, and he wished he had a dog.

Against his will, he fell asleep.

He was awakened by something with a sharp point digging into his neck. He opened his eyes to see his brother Olf straddling him, pressing an antler into his throat. His heart thudded like a drum.

Olf whispered: 'Make a noise and I'll kill you.'

Seft tried to calm his panic and think. Would Olf really kill him? Seft would be no use to his father dead. But this was about pride as much as anything else. Cog could not bear to be disobeyed. Yes, he thought, if I cry out now there is at least a chance that Olf will stick that antler point into my soft throat and I will bleed to death.

So he lay still and silent. But he felt the lump of the flint knife under his thigh, where it had slipped out of his hand during sleep. He would not go quietly. He would not lightly abandon the chance of happiness that had so recently come his way. He might die; others might too.

Olf seemed unsure what to do next. He had not planned his next move in advance, which was typical of him. There was a pause while he figured it out. Then, awkwardly, he contrived to get off Seft without withdrawing the weapon. 'Now get up,' he whispered.

'All right,' Seft murmured. 'All right.'

Tem grunted and turned over, but did not wake.

Seft rolled slightly right, his leg hiding the knife. He got up on one knee, which forced Olf to retreat a few inches. He slid his hand along the ground to the knife.

He would have only one chance.

'I'm coming,' he said, grasping the knife.

He rose to his feet in a fast fluid motion. He used his left arm to knock Olf's antler aside while lifting his right hand high. Then he brought the knife down hard and slashed Olf's face.

He felt the flint connect. There was a sickening sensation as it cut through flesh to bone. Pressing down hard, he drew the blade across Olf's face. He saw fluid burst from Olf's left eyeball. Blood from Olf's cheek spurted over his hand.

Olf screamed.

Cog emerged from the darkness, trailed by Cam. Wun's men, abruptly awakened, got to their feet.

Olf staggered around blindly, hands to his face, yelling: 'My eye! My eye!'

Seft knew he should be horrified by what he had done, but in fact he felt exultant.

Cam screamed at Seft: 'What have you done?'

Wun's voice said loudly: 'No need for violence, calm down, everyone.'

Cog shouted at him: 'Look what this evil boy has done!'

Wun shouted: 'You're to blame, Cog, you fool. You come

slinking into our camp like a thief in the night – what do you expect? A polite welcome? You're lucky you weren't killed.'

Cog turned on Seft. 'You've half blinded your brother!'

Seft found in himself a streak of reckless aggression. 'Let me tell you something, Father,' he said. 'If I ever see Olf again, I'll take his other eye.'

Cog was shocked. 'You've turned into a monster.'

'I've toughened up,' said Seft. 'Just like you told me to.'

Inka was instructing Joia and another novice. Joia had met Inka before, at the revel, when she had been holding hands with Vee's mother, Kae. She was knowledgeable and clever, and Joia soaked up the information she had to offer.

The other novice, Sary, was older than Joia by a couple of midsummers, but she was small and thin and timid. Because of her nervousness she had difficulty understanding and remembering the lessons, so Joia helped her, despite occasionally becoming impatient with her.

Ani had argued stubbornly against Joia's joining the priestesshood. Neen had supported her, saying she did not want to lose her sister. But Joia would not give in, and in the end Ani had said: 'You're going to hate it, but perhaps it's best you find that out for yourself. Go ahead, become a novice. You'll be back home in two weeks.'

Ani had been wrong. Joia was happy.

The lessons were the best part. She had already learned how to name the numbers: you did not have to remember them all, because there was a logical system for making them up. The dance steps, which always involved counting, were not difficult for Joia, and she knew them all already. The songs were more challenging. There were so many of them, and the priestesses never sang the same song two days running. As Soo had told her, on that fateful day when she had spied on the sunrise ceremony, the songs were a storehouse of learning, the treasure of the people of the Great Plain. One day Joia would be able to remember all the words, and then she would know as much as anyone in the world.

For today's lesson they were inside the Monument, sitting on the grass, in front of the wooden arch within which the sun rose on Midsummer Day. 'Look at the upright on the right-hand side,' Inka said. 'When we dance on the day after midsummer, we place two counters at the foot of that upright, to show that it is the second day of the week.'

The counters were the pottery discs that Soo had shown Joia.

Sary came out of her shell far enough to say: 'We must have a lot of counters, for all the days of the year.'

Inka was always patient with Sary. 'Not really, though I can see why you might think that,' she said gently. 'We add a counter every day until we have twelve, and we know that is the last day of the week. On the following day we pick up all the counters and move to the second upright, where we put one down.'

Joia said: 'And there are thirty uprights.'

'Yes. So how many days are there in thirty weeks?'

Joia knew the names of the numbers, but she still could not make difficult calculations. She was humbled. 'I don't know, sorry.'

'Don't worry, it's difficult. The answer is three hundred and sixty. But in a year there are five more days.'

Joia guessed what Inka was going to say next. In the middle of the Monument, surrounded by the thirty uprights with their crossbars, were five stand-alone arches – paired uprights with crossbars but not joined together – forming an incomplete oval shape. They must represent the five extra days.

Inka went on to say exactly that.

'And finally,' she said, 'using this method, we find that after a few years the midsummer sunrise seems to start a little late.'

'But it can't!' Joia protested.

'You're right. The sun's course never alters from year to year. Rather, there's a flaw in our calculations. The true number of days in a year is three hundred and sixty-five and a quarter.'

Joia could not understand how there could be a quarter of a day.

Inka went on: 'So once in every four years we add an extra day. And then the midsummer sun always rises when we expect it to.'

Joia was amazed and thrilled. The priestesses really understood what was happening in the sky. It seemed miraculous.

Inka said: 'Now it's dinnertime. And try to remember everything I've told you, so that you can explain it back to me tomorrow.'

Joia realized that it was midday and she was hungry. She and Sary headed for the building that was the dining hall by day and a dormitory at night. Sary said fearfully: 'I can't remember all that. It's so difficult. She's going to be angry with me tomorrow.'

'Let's go over it early in the morning,' Joia suggested. 'Perhaps we can help each other remember.'

Outside the dining hall Joia saw her older sister, Neen, leaning against the wall, obviously waiting to see her. 'Can I talk to you?' Neen said.

'Is something wrong?'

'In a way, yes.'

Sary went inside. Joia took Neen's arm and they walked around the outside of the earth bank. The plain stretched away into the hazy distance. Joia said: 'What's happened?'

Neen said: 'I'm having a baby.'

Joia smiled broadly. 'How wonderful! A new tiny baby in our family.'

'You've never liked babies much.'

'Well, no, but I'll love *your* baby. And Mamma must be thrilled.'

'Oh, she is.'

'But you're not so happy.' That much was obvious.

Neen looked uncomfortable. She stopped, and Joia did the same. They found themselves looking at a calf suckling from its mother. After a long pause Neen said: 'The father is Seft.'

'Not Enwood.'

'I've never lain with Enwood.'

'Really? I assumed . . .'

'I like Enwood but I love Seft.'

'A while ago you weren't so sure.'

'The longer Seft stays away, the more I love him.'

This was bad news, Joia thought. Neen was in love with a man who had vanished. It was sure to make her unhappy. But what could she do?

They walked on around the circular bank. Joia tried to be practical. 'When you have a baby you'll need a man.'

'That's what Mamma says. I should forget Seft and make up my mind to have Enwood. I know he wants me – he's made that clear. He doesn't know I'm pregnant, but when I tell him he'll be happy to raise a child conceived on midsummer night – it's the tradition.'

'And you still don't know where Seft is.'

Tears came to Neen's eyes. 'I don't even know whether he's alive.' Neen began to cry.

Joia hugged her, thinking hard. When Neen's sobs eased, Joia said: 'You can wait a bit longer.'

'I can. But the longer I wait, the more obvious it becomes that Enwood is my second choice, and I only want him because Seft has disappeared.'

Joia nodded. 'Sooner or later that will put a man off.'

'And the baby makes that worse. Oh, Joia, what am I going to do?'

'You could wait until the Autumn Rite. If Seft doesn't show up for that, you could give up.'

'It can't be many more days until the Autumn Rite.'

'Twenty.'

Neen smiled through her tears. 'You know that sort of thing now, of course – you're a priestess.'

They had walked full circle around the outside of the Monument and had come to the start of the track that led to Riverbend. 'I should go home,' Neen said.

'I'll walk with you.'

On the way Joia tried to cheer Neen up. 'Would you prefer a boy or a girl?' she said.

'Oh, I don't mind. I'd love a little baby girl. But boys are sweet too, when they're little. I adored baby Han. I still adore him.'

'Mamma will help you when the baby comes. She knows all about it.'

'She should, she's had three.'

Neen's tears had dried by the time they reached the house. Ani was outside, stirring a pot, but she looked worried. Joia said: 'What's the matter, Mamma?'

'It may be nothing,' she said. 'I went looking for Scagga, to speak to him about a matter to do with the elders, but I couldn't find him. His mother told me he was off somewhere making birch tar.' Birch tar was a glue. 'I saw his sister Jara, and asked her where I could find him, and she said: "Oh, he's around here somewhere." But she was lying, I could tell.'

She took the spatula out of the pot and stared at it as if it could reveal secrets. 'Scagga has vanished,' she said.

Pia woke up in the middle of the night and said: 'What's that smell?'

There was an instant of silence, then her father jerked upright. 'Smoke,' he said. He snatched up his tunic and ran out of the house.

That frightened Pia.

Her mother came awake and said: 'What is it?'

'Dadda says it's smoke,' Pia said.

'I smell it.' Yana pulled on her tunic and shoes, and Pia did the same. She followed her mother out of the house, but then Mamma began to run, and Pia could not keep up.

In the moonlight Pia saw men, women and children all running in the same direction. The smell got stronger as they ran. Pia heard the word 'fire' several times. Of course, she thought, something must be burning – but what?

A few moments later she found out. It was the Break. The bean crop had sprouted and was now as high as Pia's waist, and it was burning. She could see that the fire had started at the far end of the Break and spread south. But she did not understand how the leaves could be burning. Normally only dry things burned.

Her father was naked and trying to put out the flames by smothering them with his leather tunic. Other men and women were doing the same. Yana said to Pia: 'Stay well back!' Then she stripped off her tunic and joined those fighting the fire. Others had taken leafy branches from the wood and were using them to swipe at the flames. Everyone was coughing in the smoke.

Troon was walking up and down, angrily shouting orders, telling people to fetch leather mats or bring water from the river, and to run, run, run.

Someone brought a large pot of water and threw it on the blaze, but it was too little to make a difference.

Pia's friend Mo came and stood beside her. Mo's parents were in the field, fighting the fire. Mo was crying, and Pia put an arm around her.

Soon everyone in the village was there, attacking the flames with whatever came to hand. Pia thought they would never put it out, but after a while she saw, with relief, that they had stopped its advance. In the next few minutes the flames began to die down. Mo stopped crying.

Pia saw that about half the bean crop had been destroyed.

Only smouldering ashes were left in the north half of the Break. Everyone withdrew from the field. Pia's father, Alno, was coughing.

Someone said: 'How could a fire start in a field in the middle of the night? There was no lightning, was there?'

Troon said: 'It was done deliberately.'

His wife, Katch, said: 'You can't know that.'

The people standing around contemplated that thoughtfully.

Pia's mother, Yana, walked to the far end of the field, where the ashy remains bordered the herders' pasture. The cattle had gone, frightened by the flames. She came back holding some shards of pottery. She stood squarely in front of Troon as if she was about to fight him. Others came closer to see what was going to happen.

Troon pretended not to care. He said: 'What's that?'

'A broken pot,' said Yana.

Pia wondered why that was important. Pots broke from time to time: it was normal.

Yana wiped the inside of a curved piece, sniffed her finger, then made a disgusted face, as if the smell was bad. She handed the shard to Troon.

Troon did the same. Then he said: 'Birch tar.'

'Exactly,' said Yana.

There was a murmur from the crowd. Pia knew why: birch tar caught fire easily.

Yana said: 'Someone brought birch tar here in pots in the middle of the night. They threw the tar on the crops and set fire to them. And you know who they were, don't you, Troon?'

'Of course. It was the herders.'

'And you know why they did it.'

Pia was mystified. Why would the herders want to do that?

Her mother answered her unspoken question. 'They did it because we ploughed up the Break.' She raised her voice in anger. 'I warned you!' She pointed a finger at his chest. 'You have brought this down on our heads. It's the herders' revenge.'

Troon said: 'I'll show them revenge.'

Wun's team came to the end of the seam of flint they had been mining for the past year or so. It was worked out in every direction. Before leaving, Wun and his miners performed an important ceremony. They had violated the ground, digging a big hole and taking away the flints, and now they needed to placate the Earth God.

They began by shovelling back all the chalk they had removed, together with broken antlers and other rubbish, meat bones and wood ash and worn-out shoes. Then they spread earth over the lot, so that the grass could grow again in the spring, and the plain would not be disfigured.

When it was all done they stood together, holding hands, and solemnly sang a prayer they all knew that thanked the spirit of the pit for what it had given them.

The balance was restored.

Wun and his miners would now move on and dig another pit. Seft decided to go back to Riverbend. He was thrilled and terrified: thrilled at the prospect of seeing Neen again, terrified that she might no longer love him.

Tem asked to go with him, just to see Riverbend – he had never travelled away from the mining country. Wun kindly gave permission. 'Come back and work for me any time you like,' he said to Seft.

Seft and Tem set off early in the morning on the day after the pit ceremony. During the long walk across the Great Plain, Seft reflected on how much he had achieved since Cog had beaten him up outside the Monument. He had escaped from his family. He had invented a way of joining pieces of wood without straps. He had fought off an attempt to kidnap him, and he had given Olf a wound he would never forget. He had established himself as a useful member of a working team. In Tem he had found a friend, something he had never had before. And he had made his living.

He was ready to face Neen again.

As he and Tem walked they talked amicably, and he ended up telling Tem the whole story of himself and Neen. Tem was fascinated. He had not yet had a love affair. Embarrassingly, he treated Seft as an expert on everything to do with women. When Seft said he was no such thing, Tem thought he was being modest.

Seft liked Tem's quick mind and cheerful disposition. He found himself regretting that their ways would soon part.

They reached Riverbend in the late afternoon. Summer was coming to an end and the air was cool. As they made their way through the village, Seft was seized by fear. What if he got to the house to find Enwood ensconced there, with a proprietorial arm around Neen? Then all his great achievements would turn to ashes.

Before they got there, they were spotted by eight-year-old Han. 'It's Seft – he's back!' he yelled delightedly to no one in particular, then he raced away towards his house, repeating the cry. It was a good sign, but Han was not Neen.

By the time Seft and Tem got there, Neen was standing outside the house waiting for him.

One look at her told Seft he need not have worried. A lovely smile spread over her face, the same smile that had gladdened his heart on the day before the Midsummer Rite, when he had found her scraping a hide; a smile that seemed to occupy her whole face from forehead to chin. All his fears had been unfounded.

He stared at her, drinking her in, and slowly walked up to her. She threw her arms around him and kissed him. It was all worth it, he thought, everything; worth it for this. The hug went on for a long time, but neither of them wanted to quit, until at last he heard Ani's voice saying: 'You'd better stop soon so that you can talk to us.'

Seft let Neen go and turned to Ani. 'May the Sun God smile on you.'

'And on you, Seft. How wonderful to have you back here with us!' Her welcome was warm but he sensed that she was distracted. She went on: 'But perhaps you should introduce your companion.'

'This is Tem, my friend. We've been working together at his uncle's pit.' Then he had to tell the whole story of how he had left Cog and his family and taken refuge with Wun. They all sat on the grass in a ring as he did so, and Neen held his hand, which thrilled him because it told the world they were a couple.

When he had finished his tale Ani said: 'How marvellous! And dinner will be ready soon.'

Seft said to Neen: 'Could we go to that timber circle, just to talk quietly for a while?'

'Of course,' she said, and got to her feet.

They strolled hand in hand through the village. Seft said: 'Is your mother worried about something?'

'She's angry,' Neen said. 'Scagga and some of his family went to Farmplace and set fire to the crop on some land called the Break, which the farmers stole from us.'

'To me that sounds justified,' said Seft.

'The elders decided to take no action. Scagga's an elder but he defied his colleagues.'

'I see that.'

'Mamma says that revenge always leads to reprisals, and that's how people end up at war.'

Seft did not know what to think about that and, anyway, he had something more important on his mind. They came to the concentric circles of tree trunks. They sat close together and kissed for a while.

Then Seft said: 'Are there rules about people joining the herder community?'

'Well,' she said, 'yes, I suppose there are. I mean, you have to work. Strangers can't just come and move into a house and eat beef and lie around all day.'

'So I could join.'

'Yes. You could be a herder. We'd teach you.'

'I'd be glad to learn. But what I'm really good at is carpentry. I could make bows, and shovels, and chests for keeping precious things. And I've worked out how to make a doorway without straps.'

'You could do that. Like my mother makes leather.'

'There's something really important, the most important of all.'

'Go on.'

'I want a family like yours, where everyone loves each other, and there's no beating.'

'That's what I want, too.'

'Last time we were together you said you weren't ready to make a baby.'

'True.'

'When do you think you might be ready?'

She took his hand. 'I'm already pregnant.'

He was shocked, and his heart seemed to thud. 'From just that one night?'

She smiled. 'From just that one night.'

Seft was filled with joy. 'Well, then,' he said, 'everything is perfect.'

Joia was awakened by the sound of two women having sex. It would be a couple of novices, she guessed, too in love and excited to care who heard them. She wondered whether to tell them to hush, but someone else said it first, and they giggled and carried on, not quite in silence.

In the relative quiet Joia heard a strange, muffled noise. It sounded like carpenters at work some distance away, hammering and sawing, chopping and chiselling. They were up early. Was it dawn already? She looked across the room at the doorway. She could see the edge of the moon, silver against a deep black sky.

This is the middle of the night, she thought; no carpenters are working now.

She stood up, pulled her long tunic over her head, and laced her shoes. As she crossed the room in the dark she stumbled over the drum used in some of the ceremonies, and it fell with a resonant boom. Several sleepy voices told her to hush. She picked up the drum and its stick and put them by the door, in the moonlight.

She stood by the wicker gate and leaned out. She could hear the carpentry noise better, but it still seemed muffled. She lifted the gate, stepped outside, and replaced the gate.

Once she was out of the building she could tell which direction the sound was coming from. It seemed to be at or near the Monument.

She hurried across the stretch of grassland that separated the priestesses' village from the Monument, and as she did so the sound got louder. It was coming either from the far side of the Monument, or from actually inside the circle.

She began to be fearful. On impulse, she returned to the house and picked up the drum and stick. She had a worrying feeling that she might need to raise an alarm.

Retracing her steps, she became convinced that the noise came from inside the earth circle. She broke into a run.

Rather than go through the entrance, she raced up the side of the earth bank, for a better view and perhaps for her own safety. She reached the top and stood looking down at a scene of devastation. The wood Monument was wrecked. The noise that had sounded like carpentry was in fact destruction. Ten or fifteen men were using stones and axes and clubs to destroy the wooden structures, pulling them down and smashing the timbers. For a moment Joia stood frozen, horrified. Then she felt an impulse to run down the bank and attack the men. Suppressing that, she began to beat the drum.

The attackers stopped what they were doing and looked at her. They had blackened their faces with ash and mud so that they could not be recognized, but she was struck by the fact that they had also blackened their necks, undoubtedly to hide their typical farmer neck tattoos.

One man ran in her direction. She instantly made up her mind to hit him over the head with the drum as he came up the slope towards her. But another man called out to him – Joia did not quite hear the name – and the man turned around.

Behind her she heard the voices of priestesses awakened by the drum and coming out of their houses. She guessed she was clearly visible by moonlight, standing as she was on the ridge of the earth circle, and a glance over her shoulder showed the women running towards her.

The farmers all turned away. As if at a signal, they ran across the circle, away from Joia and the priestesses. They went up the far bank and disappeared down the other side. They would head across the plain, Joia was in no doubt, and soon be out of sight.

She walked slowly down the slope and stared at the damage.

There was nothing but scrap timber. The Monument was gone.

She began to cry.

By sunrise a crowd had gathered, standing around the wreckage, many weeping. Soo and all the priestesses were there, plus the elders, and Dallo and some of his cleverhands, with many villagers including Neen and Seft.

Dallo, inspecting the ruins, said: 'A lot of this wood was already deteriorating. I see brown rot, powder-post beetles that lay their eggs in the wood, and damp in the postholes. The Monument might not have lasted much longer even without being vandalized by the farmers.'

Soo, the high priestess, said: 'So if we rebuild, it will rot again.'

Dallo shrugged. 'Sooner or later.'

Soo seemed to stand more upright, and speak with regal authority. 'Then we must rebuild in stone.'

There was a murmur from the crowd. Joia thought their reaction mixed surprise and approval. Joia herself was thrilled: she wanted this. Could there be anyone who did not want it?

Dallo looked dubious. 'Let me get this clear. You're talking about a stone Monument that exactly copies the old wooden one?'

'That would be essential. The Monument was carefully designed to fulfil very specific purposes. The layout cannot be changed.'

Dallo shook his head sceptically. 'Stones of that size are very difficult to transport, perhaps impossible.'

Soo pointed to the ancient ring of stones just inside the earth bank. 'The bluestones were brought here.'

'Do you know where they originated?'

'Our song says they came from a place six days' journey north-west of here, a quarry by the sea.'

Dallo's face showed that he did not have much faith in an old song, but he said: 'And how were they transported?'

'By water.'

'Ah. If only that were possible. Many years ago the East River may have been deeper and wider, but today a raft broad enough to support a bluestone could not navigate the bends and the narrows.'

Soo persisted. 'There are stones all over the Great Plain.'

'That's true. But most of them are not large enough to replace your timber uprights. And those that are would have to be dragged from however far away they are for many days to get here.'

Joia had noticed that Seft was listening intently to the conversation, and he now interrupted it. 'There's a place where there are many large stones – more than would be needed to rebuild the Monument.'

Everyone looked at him.

Soo and Dallo simultaneously said: 'Where?'

'In the North Hills, a little way beyond the pit my family mines. I know the place well. I call it Stony Valley.'

There was a thoughtful silence.

Seft said: 'I could take you there.'

Seft led the group with Neen by his side. Dallo took five of his cleverhands. Soo could not manage the long walk, so her deputy, Ello, came, bringing Inka and Joia. Elders Ani, Keff and Scagga joined the group. A dozen or so villagers went along out of curiosity.

It was a full day's walk, and the sun had risen before they set out, so it was getting dark by the time they reached Stony Valley. Seft had wanted them to be astonished by the sight of all the stones, but in the twilight they could see only a few, and their arrival was an anticlimax.

They lit fires and ate some of the smoked meat they had brought with them, then they settled down to sleep in their tunics. The summer was almost over, and the night air was cool. Seft and Neen lay together. Tired by the walk, they fell asleep immediately.

It was light when Seft woke. Some of the others were already walking about, gazing at the stones, marvelling at their size and smoothness. There were hundreds of them, some piled one on top of another. Perhaps long ago they had all lain on a level field, Seft imagined, and the Earth God had raised the sides of the field, causing the stones to tumble into the middle, leaving the hillsides free for the sheep to graze.

And what stones! Some of them must have been as heavy as a herd of cows. They were grey in colour, though partly covered with moss and lichen.

Neen's sister, Joia, was visibly excited. 'These are magnificent!' she said. 'The biggest stones I've ever seen.'

'Me, too,' said Seft.

'The new Monument *must* be built of these!'

'That's what I think,' said Seft. 'But we have to convince Dallo.'

They looked around and spotted Dallo staring thoughtfully at one of the larger stones. They went to his side. The stone was the length of four men and as wide as one man was tall. He said: 'I want to know how thick it is.'

The stone was partly sunk into the ground. Seft said: 'We'll need to excavate around it.' He had got into the habit of carrying a bag with a few essential tools. Now he took from the bag the shoulder blade of an ox, useful for digging. He knelt and began to loosen the earth around the stone. Joia picked up a stick and did the same. Several others joined in.

With a dozen or so people working, it did not take long to find the depth of the stone. It was about half as thick as it was wide.

Now that the full size was visible, Seft felt overwhelmed. Surely it was not possible to move this all the way to the Monument?

Dallo was feeling the same, for he said: 'Well, now that we're here, let's see whether we can even tilt it up on its side. Everyone, cut yourself a stout branch to use as a lever. We're going to try to raise this monster.'

Seft used his flint axe to chop down a small tree. It was not a quick job, and the sun was high by the time he had a usable lever. Others were taking even longer, and he spent some time helping them. He noticed that Dallo had accumulated a pile of narrow logs, and he wondered what their purpose was.

When everyone was ready, they needed to undercut one long side of the stone so that the levers could get underneath. Seft got down on his knees and again deployed the shoulder blade to dig away the earth. When he had finished, everyone with a lever lined up alongside the stone. There were about twenty-five people, he guessed.

They all pushed the thinner ends of their levers into the soft earth under the stone. Dallo said: 'In as deep as they'll go, or you won't get any leverage.' When he judged the levers were well set in ready, he said: 'Ready . . . heave!'

Seft put all his strength into pushing his lever inwards and upwards. He heard others grunt with the strain. The stone did not move. The people stopped pushing and breathed hard.

Dallo said: 'This time, the moment I tell you to heave you must throw all your weight into it instantly.' He gave them a few moments to reset, then said: 'Ready . . . heave!'

The stone moved. Its edge was lifted about the width of a man's hand. Immediately, Dallo thrust a long, narrow log under the stone to stop it collapsing. He added a second log then said: 'And . . . rest.'

The people relaxed. There was a crushing sound as Dallo's narrow logs took the weight. The gap shortened, but not by much, and the logs held up the stone at the slight angle it had reached.

They went on in that way. Eventually the stone was standing at a wide angle, with upright logs supporting its weight. Seft saw that from now on the levers would be less effective and it would be increasingly difficult, and finally impossible, to raise the stone farther. Dallo clearly reasoned the same way, for he said that was enough.

It was late afternoon. Dallo moved away from the stone and asked everyone to sit on the ground around him. Seft felt sure he was going to give them a message of pessimism. He said to Neen: 'I think your poor sister is going to be disappointed.'

Neen nodded agreement. 'She always has such high hopes,' she commented.

Dallo began by saying: 'Remember the stone we moved for the farmer across the river?' Several people nodded. Seft was not one of them. This must have taken place before he returned to Riverbend. But he saw from Joia's expression that she had been there.

Dallo went on: 'Recall how we got the stone into the bag: we laid the ropes down and rolled it. We've just spent a day proving that we can't roll the giant stones we see here in this valley. We can't even get this one upright.'

Joia said: 'There might be a way.'

Dallo pretended to be interested. 'And what is that?'

'I don't know,' she said, looking foolish. 'But there might be one.'

'In any case, that's not our only problem,' Dallo said. 'Once the farmer's stone was in the bag, it took twenty people to move it. This stone is ten times the size of the farmer's one, so ten times twenty people will be needed to move it. I can't count that high but it would be impossible to assemble so many people.'

Joia could count very high, Seft knew, and he looked at her, but she kept stubbornly silent.

Dallo said: 'It took us all morning to move that farmer's stone across a field and down to the river. Yet now we're talking about moving this giant stone a distance that takes all day to walk, up and down hills and over uneven fields. How many days, or weeks, or perhaps even years would that take?' He glanced over at the stone and said: 'Best not to mess about with that, Jero.' Seft saw that Jero, the son of Effi, was studying the stone and touching the props keeping it upright.

Dallo turned back to his audience. 'All this time we've been talking about just one stone,' he said. 'But how many of these giant stones would be needed for a new Monument? The inner oval of the wooden Monument has five arches, making fifteen wooden parts, which would mean fifteen stones. But that's the smaller part. The outer circle would require many more than that, more than I can count.'

There was a bang, and they all looked to see that Jero had dislodged one of the main props and brought the stone down with a crash. He seemed unhurt: he must have got out of the way quickly.

Dallo said: 'And we haven't even talked about accidents caused by foolish people that would delay the process still further.'

Jero looked embarrassed and walked away.

Dallo said: 'So what I've learned today, friends and neighbours, is that the project of the stone Monument is impossible. Completely out of the question. It was a wonderful idea, but it will never happen.' He looked at Joia. 'I'm sorry,' he said, 'but I must tell the truth.'

Seft looked at Joia's face, which was set in an expression of stubborn determination. He whispered to Neen: 'She hasn't given up.'

Neen shook her head and said: 'She never will.'

Ten midwinters pass

7

JOIA WAS WALKING on the Great Plain just outside Riverbend with her brother, Han. They both studied the landscape anxiously. Last year's hot, dry summer had been followed by a cold, dry winter, and spring was looking no better. Streams crossing the plain often dried up in summer then were replenished by winter rain: there was a name for such a stream, a winterbourne. But this year the winterbournes had stayed dry. The vast green plain had become a brown desert occupied by thin cattle and scraggy sheep. Fewer females were giving birth, and fewer young lived to adulthood.

The herd was resilient. Some died, and some survived. It was saddening to see bony carcasses lying on the dusty ground, but some beasts – younger, stronger, luckier – still cropped the few shoots that sprang up in the morning, then sought shade in which to hide from the noonday sun.

The herders butchered the dead ones and boiled their scanty meat. People hunted alternative food – deer, beaver, and the wild cattle called aurochs – but these were scarce for they, too, were dying of thirst. The wild vegetables and fruit that gave variety to the herders' diet in good times were now hard to find. Half-starved children ate worms, and adults looked speculatively at their neighbours' dogs.

'What can we do?' said Han.

'Nothing,' Joia replied.

Han had grown up. He had seen seventeen midsummers, and soon it would be eighteen. He had enormous feet. He made himself special shoes, with the stitching along the top, instead of at the side like everyone else, saying his way was more comfortable. His friends called him Bigfoot.

He was tall, handsome and charming, reminding Joia of their father, Olin. He even had a blond beard. He also had Olin's fearlessness. He had never seen a tree he could not climb, a river he could not swim, a wild boar he could not kill before it killed him. Their mother worried about him, and so did Joia.

His dog, Thunder, was at his heels. Joia remembered Thunder as a puppy. Han had tried to teach the pup to sit, lie down, wait, and come running, but she had refused to learn anything. Remarkably, she had grown into a loyal and obedient dog. She went everywhere with him.

Han worked as a herder. He was too restless to tan leather, like his mother and Neen, or make rope, pots, flint tools or any of the other things people needed. He liked being out on the open plain, even in bad weather, striding around and keeping the beasts out of trouble.

Thunder was a herder, too. When Han was moving the cattle, or trying to stop them moving where they should not go, Thunder deduced his intentions from his movements and ran ahead of him, turning the beasts the way Han wanted. She was not unusual. Dogs seemed to be born with some instinctive understanding of herding.

Han said: 'How is it for the priestesses?'

Joia hesitated. 'Well, we have enough to eat – but, in a way, that's the problem. People have begun to resent us. They ask why they need priestesses. The spirit has left the Monument, they say, and the priestesses can't bring it back. They make it sound as if the drought is our fault.'

Han was scornful. 'What do they want you to do – jump in the river and drown yourselves, just to save a few bowls of beef per day?'

Joia shrugged. 'Perhaps. They're desperate.'

Han said tentatively: 'They don't like Ello, you know.'

This was not news to Joia. The second high priestess was not lovable. 'She has a rough tongue. She makes enemies unnecessarily.'

'This is not a good time to make enemies.'

He was right, but Ello would never change. Joia said: 'The drought will break. We just don't know when.'

'It had better be soon.'

Han was right. Joia had already seen that older people were dying, not of starvation exactly, but of the illnesses that came with an inadequate diet. And more babies were dying before they reached their second midsummer. They suffered the usual baby illnesses that most would normally have survived. Soon it would be the middle-aged and the children, and eventually everyone.

'It's worse for the farmers,' Han said. 'They're expecting a second bad harvest. And their women have almost stopped conceiving.'

Joia said: 'And the woodlanders are in trouble too. The younger hazelnut bushes have all died. Only the old-established plants survive, and they're giving less fruit.'

There was a silence, then Han said: 'Is it possible that the entire plain community could disappear?'

'Yes,' Joia said. 'I wouldn't say this to anyone else, because I don't want people to panic, but the truth is that if our beasts die, we die.'

'And then the Great Plain will be left to the birds.'

Joia thought over their conversation, then said: 'You know a lot about the farmers.'

'Do I?' He offered no explanation.

'At the Midwinter Rite I saw you talking to a farmer girl.'

'Pia. She's an old friend. We used to play together when we were children.'

Joia recalled a self-assured little girl. At the Midwinter Rite she had seen a young woman, poised and graceful, with an authoritative look, surprising in someone of Han's age. 'I remember,' she said. 'She had a horrid little cousin.'

'Stam, yes.'

'So that's how you know all about the farmers.'

'I suppose so.'

Joia pictured Han and Pia as she had seen them at the Rite. He had been chatting amiably, and the girl had been looking up at him with an expression of deep interest. Joia said: 'Will you see her tomorrow?' The Spring Rite would take place then.

'I hope so.'

This looked like a romance – which was bad news. Joia said: 'Don't fall in love with her.'

Straight away she wished she had not blurted it out. Why couldn't she have said it tactfully? Too late now.

Han was offended. 'I don't see why not, and I don't know why you think you have the right to give such instructions.'

That response told her that her advice was too late. If Han had not been in love with Pia, he would have laughed and told Joia she had nothing to worry about. The evasive *Why not?* meant he had already fallen.

Now that she had started this conversation she had to finish it. 'The farmer folk are different from us,' she said. 'There, every woman is the property of a man, first her father, then the father of her children. You would never feel at ease in farmer society.'

'Pia could join the herder folk.'

'The farmers hate it when that happens. They feel that something has been stolen from them. They cause trouble, trying to make the woman return to them.'

'Yet it happens.'

Joia shrugged. He was fearless to the point of recklessness, like his father. 'I'm just warning you. Trouble lies ahead.'

'Thank you,' Han said surprisingly. 'You're rude, but you speak from love.'

She put an arm around his waist and gave him a brief hug.

A moment later she heard the lowing of a cow in distress. They were herders and they instinctively followed the sound. They came across two people arguing about a cow.

The two were near a tall tree. From a stout branch, a young cow hung upside-down, its hind legs tied to the branch with a rope made of honeysuckle vines. Joia could see by its small udders that it was a heifer, a cow that had not yet calved.

Directly under its head was a large pottery jar with a wide mouth. A tall man stood next to the jug, holding in his hand a large flint knife. The scene was commonplace: he was about to slaughter the cow, and the jug was to catch the nourishing blood.

The man looked familiar, and in a moment Joia placed him. He was handsome Robbo, who had been part of her adolescent circle and was now the partner of beautiful Roni. He looked angry.

The other person was a priestess: Inka, once Joia's teacher, a middle-aged woman with a warm heart. She stood with her long legs apart and one hand on her hip, looking aggressive. She had a heavy stick in the other hand and seemed about ready to hit Robbo with it.

Joia said: 'What's going on?' She had to raise her voice over the noise the cow was making.

Robbo said: 'None of your business, so just creep off.'

Han said: 'Speak to my sister with respect, Robbo.'

Joia said: 'There's no need for a fight.'

Robbo said: 'I don't want a fight.' He pointed at Inka. 'She's the one with a weapon.'

Inka said: 'And you're holding a knife.'

'To cut the cow's throat, obviously.'

'Which is the problem.' Inka turned to Joia. 'This young fool wants to slaughter a heifer that's young and healthy enough to calve. It's a terrible waste, when the plain is dotted with beasts that have died of thirst. I'm not going to let him do it.'

Robbo said: 'She has no right to stop me.'

Unfortunately, he was right. There was no rule about who could slaughter cattle or when. People killed a beast when they needed to eat. In times of plenty this worked well. All through Joia's childhood there had never been arguments about meat. But the good times were over, and Joia was seeing more and more quarrels.

Robbo had not finished. 'Anyway, she's a priestess,' he said. 'She does no work, but expects to be fed by the rest of us. The gods have given us no rain, and who is to blame for that if not the priestesses?'

Joia asked herself what her mother would do in this situation. Ani would gently talk Robbo round, probably. So Joia now said: 'Robbo, be reasonable.'

Robbo said angrily: 'I've got two children and a pregnant woman at home and they need meat. Don't tell me to be reasonable.'

Joia said: 'You should butcher a carcass – there are many on the plain.'

'Children should have good meat.'

'But what will they eat when the cattle are all gone?'

'That's in the hands of the gods.'

Han said quietly to Joia: 'If you want me to knock him down, just give the word.'

'He's got a knife.'

'I can take him.'

Joia was not certain who would take whom. Han thought he was invincible, but Robbo was almost as big. Anyway, she had her mother's aversion to violence as a solution. 'We're going to resolve this question peaceably,' she said, and she could hear the desperation in her own voice.

Inka stepped closer to Robbo and the cow. Han moved in too. Joia was losing control. She said: 'Robbo, if you put down the knife she'll drop her stick. Then we can talk sensibly.'

It was useless, she saw. Robbo's expression hardened. He grabbed the cow's horn and stretched its neck.

Inka screamed.

Robbo cut the cow's throat with one strong stroke of the flint knife. The plaintive lowing was abruptly silenced. Blood splashed into the pot.

Inka, enraged, hit Robbo over the head with her stick. It was a stout tree branch, and Robbo staggered.

Joia yelled: 'Stop it!'

Inka was maddened and she hit Robbo again, catching his left shoulder.

Thunder barked hysterically.

Inka raised her stick for the third time.

Han jumped into the fray, seizing Inka from behind to restrain her.

Robbo stepped closer to Inka, who could not dodge him because Han was holding her. He slashed with the knife in a wide left-to-right arc, cutting Inka's throat as he had the cow's. For a second time in a few short moments, blood spurted.

There was a horrified silence.

Inka slumped in Han's arms, and he tightened his grip to hold her upright. The blood ran down the front of her leather priestess tunic.

Robbo was aghast and frightened at what he had done. 'She tried to kill me!' he said, making his excuse although no one had accused him.

Han said: 'There was no need! I had her pinned!'

Joia bent over and threw up on the ground.

Han gently laid Inka's body down. The bleeding stopped. Her eyes stared lifelessly up at the cloudless blue sky.

Joia stood upright. She was shocked to her core. She had never known a murder among the herder folk. There had not been one in her lifetime. And the killing of a priestess was sacrilege. Horror paralysed her thinking. She did not know what to do or say.

Thunder sniffed her vomit.

That brought her down to earth and she pulled herself together. Inka's body had to be taken to the Monument. The herder community must be told what had happened. And it must never happen again. This was a first, yes, but it arose from the crisis, the drought. Unless the situation changed, there would be more rows and more killings.

Something had to be done.

Ani was tanning leather beside the river. First she built a fire. While it was burning up, she pushed tree bark into her largest pot until it was half full, then filled it to the top with clean river water from upstream. She set the pot into the embers at the edge of her fire. She stirred the mixture with a stick as it was heating.

While she waited she thought about her family. She remembered how worried she had used to get when Joia was a restless adolescent. Now Joia had found her destiny. She loved being a priestess, and was wholly absorbed by the work of keeping track of the days of the year.

Neen, too, was happy. She and Seft had three children, the joy of Ani's life.

Han had not settled down yet, but he was a fine young man and one day he would give Ani more grandchildren.

She herself was healthy, and thanked the gods for it. She had seen more summers than she could count, and had given birth five times, including two babies who had not lived beyond a year, but she did not feel old, not yet.

Occasionally she missed having a man. She had loved the intimacy, and the sex, and the feeling of having a friend she could always rely on. But when she thought about men she knew she could not love any of them. She did not want 'a man', she wanted Olin. No one else would do.

Her only worry was the drought. The plain had known droughts before, and Ani remembered a severe one from her childhood. She had survived, but some of her friends had died. And when it ended it had left people very cautious, averse to any change. The plain had taken years to recover its prosperity.

The pot was boiling merrily. Beside her was a second large pot with a basketwork sieve over its mouth. Using two thick leather pads to protect her hands, she picked up the boiling pot and poured the liquid through the sieve into the second pot, pausing when she needed to clear fragments of bark from the sieve.

She now had a pot of tanning solution.

She picked up the hide of a cow that had been prepared for tanning – bits of flesh removed from the inside, the hair scraped off the outside – and stuffed it into the pot of tanning solution.

It would remain there for three twelve-day weeks, being stirred every day to make sure the solution reached every part. The process of tanning could not be rushed: the solution had to penetrate right through the thickness of the hide. The purpose of tanning was to arrest the natural process by which the hide, like most parts of animal cadavers, would break down and rot, whereupon someone's tunic would become smelly and gradually fall apart.

She had several hides ready, and she was about to start on the next when Joia appeared.

Joia had not been a noticeably pretty girl, but she had grown into a beautiful woman. Ani believed that beauty came from the inside. When someone was doing work they hated or was partnered with someone they disliked, or was possessed by a deep resentment or a terrible failure or an ancient enmity, they looked ugly. People whose lives were in harmony looked attractive, and Joia was like that. It was not the colour of her hazel eyes, it was the way they twinkled; her mouth was lovely because she smiled so much; her body was slim and supple because she danced every day and enjoyed it; her speech sounded musical because she spent so much time singing. But then, Ani thought wryly, perhaps I'm biased.

As Joia came closer, Ani realized that she was in a serious mood; no, more than that, she had suffered a shock. Ani was immediately worried. 'What's happened?' she said.

'Robbo killed a priestess, Inka.'

Ani was horrified. 'Killed? How did that happen?'

'Robbo was trying to slaughter a heifer. We all told him it was wrong, but he took no notice, so Inka hit him with a club.'

'Herders don't kill each other!' Ani said.

'It just escalated.' Joia was close to tears. 'I couldn't stop them. Nor could Han.'

'He was there too?'

Joia nodded. 'He tried to intervene, but it didn't work. Robbo put his knife to the cow's throat, so Inka tried to stop him, but she failed. He cut the cow's throat, and—' Joia sobbed, then went on: 'And he cut Inka's throat.'

'Oh!' Ani put her hand over her mouth.

'What do we do? I mean, what does the community do, when there is a murder?'

'I've only known one,' Ani said. 'I was young, about fifteen midsummers. There was a man, a very bad-tempered man, who had a row with another man about which of them owned a certain flint axe. The bad-tempered man killed the other with the axe.'

'But what did the community do?'

'Well, when the story got around, no one would speak to the killer. Whenever they saw him they walked away. They wouldn't let their children play with his children. They didn't share meat with him. One day he and his family walked away from Riverbend across the Great Plain and were never seen again.'

'It doesn't seem much of a punishment.'

'It's the best we've got. In the farmer community, the murderer is killed, usually by the victim's family. But sometimes they get the wrong person. And sometimes the killer's family takes revenge, and so the killing goes on. In the long run our system is better.'

'What do the woodlanders do?'

'I don't know.'

'So Robbo and Roni and their children will just have to move away, out of the Great Plain.'

'Probably, yes.'

'I wonder what Robbo is saying to people about what happened.'

'That's a good question. Let's find out.'

Ani quickly tidied her work materials and they left the riverside, heading for Robbo's house. Robbo was outside, butchering the heifer, watched by Roni and their children and a small crowd. He was telling the story.

Joia was about to speak to him when Ani held her back and, with a finger to her lips, told her to keep quiet and listen. At first Robbo did not see Joia, and he went on with what he was saying. 'She hit me twice with her damned club,' he said indignantly. 'I thought that mad priestess was going to kill me.'

Joia spoke up. 'It wasn't quite like that, was it, Robbo?' she said. She stepped forward so that everyone could see her. 'I was there,' she said. 'My brother, Han, was actually holding Inka, restraining her, preventing her from hitting you, and then – when she was quite helpless – in your rage you cut her throat with your flint knife.'

There was a murmur of surprise from the crowd. Clearly Robbo had been telling people a different story.

'It was a fight,' he said. 'I don't recall the exact details, except that she started it.'

'I remember everything clearly,' Joia said firmly. 'Inka was no danger to you once my brother had hold of her. She was helpless. The violence should have ended there, but you killed her in your rage.'

'That's not how it was. You're just saying that because Inka was a priestess.'

'I'm saying what I saw. You were killing a heifer, which was foolish and wrong. Inka wasn't innocent – she should not have hit you with her club. But your life was never in danger.'

Keff, one of the elders, was in the crowd, and now he said: 'This beast was a heifer?'

Robbo said: 'No, it wasn't.'

Ani looked at the carcass and saw that it had been disembowelled and the underside was gone, so it was not possible to be certain whether it was a heifer. Robbo must have done it on the plain, before dragging it here. He had given some thought to how he would pretend innocence.

Joia said: 'Of course it was a heifer. That was why Inka tried to stop you killing it.'

'You're just making excuses for your brother's part in this.'

'My brother tried to save you.'

'I don't have to answer to you.'

'That's true,' Joia said. 'You don't have to answer to me. You've murdered a priestess. You will answer to the gods.' She turned around and walked away.

Ani caught up with Joia and said: 'Robbo is being very sly about this.'

'I'm going back to the Monument,' Joia said. 'I have to speak to the priestesses.'

'I'll talk to the other elders,' Ani said, and they parted company.

Joia's mind was spinning. After talking to Ani she had felt satisfied that Robbo's offence would be recognized by the community. She did not want him to be killed, as in the farmer custom, but she wanted the herder folk to acknowledge that he had done something terribly wrong. The murder of a priestess should not be lightly passed over. But Robbo was putting out a story in which he and Inka had been equally guilty.

As she strode from the village to the Monument, she saw many strangers, and she remembered that tomorrow was the Spring Halfway, and hundreds of people would be here for the Spring Rite. That opened up a possibility. The priestesses would have a chance to speak to the entire community of the Great Plain about the murder of Inka.

But the more she thought about it, the more she felt that it would not be a matter of logical argument. Robbo had an answer for everything and he was clever enough to confuse people. In the end, how people saw this issue would depend on how they felt, about the priestesses and about Robbo.

Tomorrow would be an opportunity, but not for a speech.

The glimmer of an alternative formed in her mind.

As soon as she reached the Monument she sought out Soo, the high priestess. She was sitting on the ground outside her house, enjoying the mild air of spring. In the last ten years Joia had come to see her as a friend and mentor.

Joia sat down without ceremony.

Soo said: 'This is a terrible thing that has happened. Poor Inka. The novices are washing her body now.'

'Robbo is putting out a false story,' Joia said, without preamble. Soo liked people to get straight to the point. 'He's saying that Inka tried to kill him and he had to defend himself.'

'But that's not true,' Soo said. 'I've spoken to your brother, Han, who carried the body here, bless his soul.'

'Robbo is trying to persuade people that what happened was a fight, not a murder. But I want Robbo's crime to be acknowledged.'

'So do I,' said Soo. 'I'm guessing that you have something in mind.'

'I think we should cremate Inka's body here tomorrow as part of the Spring Rite.' Cremation was the usual method of disposing of the dead. The ashes were scattered. 'It will give everyone the sense that something holy has been lost.'

Soo nodded slowly. 'We have a very sad song for the death of a priestess.'

'I know it,' Joia said. She knew them all.

'Then you can lead the singing,' said Soo.

Pia was looking for Han. She adored him and waited impatiently from one Rite to the next to see him. In between she pictured him every day, with his blond beard and his big shoes; and in the daydream he leaned close to her and whispered in her ear, so that she could feel his warm breath as he told her he loved her.

She smiled when she looked back at herself, not quite eight midsummers old, asking him if she could be his girlfriend; and his embarrassed answer: 'No, that's silly grown-up stuff.' She had felt sure that in his heart he really wanted her to be his girlfriend, but was too shy to admit it. So she had not minded his refusal, in fact she had cherished his words.

A few years later, when she had started thinking about boys in a different way, she had forgotten him for a while. She had flirted with farmer boys, and kissed them, and discovered her power to make them groan and spurt. Then she had talked to Han at a Rite, and the old bond between them had come back in a new form.

It was surprising how the enmity between herders and farmers had faded. It was not gone, not completely, but the two groups met frequently at Rites, watching silently as the priestesses danced and sang, and afterwards did business amiably enough.

She found Han coming out of the priestesses' village. He looked stressed, and she was shocked to see blood on his cheek. 'Han!' she said. 'What happened?'

'Murder,' he said. 'It was awful. I'm very glad to see you.'

She hugged him. She could not help being thrilled that she was the one he wanted when he needed comfort.

She took his hand and led him away from the village. They sat on the outside slope of the earth bank. 'Tell me all about it,' she said.

'There was an argument between a priestess called Inka and a herder called Robbo, and it turned violent. She hit him over the head, twice. I grabbed her to restrain her, and while she was helpless he slit her throat with a flint knife and she died.'

Pia gasped. 'So you saw everything!'

'I was part of it. It might even be my fault she died.'

'No,' she said immediately. 'Robbo held the knife. You were just trying to stop the fight.'

'That's what I keep telling myself.'

'You've got blood on your face.' She pulled up a handful of grass, wetted it with her saliva, and scrubbed the stain off his cheek. 'That's better,' she said.

'Thank you. There was such a lot of blood, all of a sudden, then it stopped, and she died in my arms.'

'Who was with you?'

'My sister Joia. She was terribly upset. She's a priestess, as Inka was.'

'Where's the body now?'

'I carried it here. The priestesses have it.'

'You should eat something. It will make you feel better.' Pia took from her bag some goat's cheese wrapped in leaves. 'Here, eat this. My mother makes it. It's delicious.'

He hesitated. 'Is this your supper?'

'Don't worry, I'll get something. Eat it, please, it will do you good.'

He unwrapped the leaves and ate the cheese. 'I didn't know I was hungry,' he said, through a mouthful. 'You're right, it's delicious.'

When he had finished she said: 'Now you can kiss me.'

'It may be a rather cheesy kiss.'

'It will taste delicious.'

They kissed for a long time, then she said: 'Let's go and see your mother. Does she know about the murder?'

'Joia has probably told her.'

'She'll want to see you, to make sure you're all right.'

He looked at her thoughtfully. 'You're very considerate,' he said. 'You think about people's feelings – first mine, then my mother's.'

She did not know what to say to that.

He said: 'I think you're wonderful.'

She did not see herself as wonderful, but she was thrilled that he thought she was.

They got to their feet and headed across the plain towards Riverbend. When they reached the village he took her hand.

That means I belong to him, she thought, and he belongs to me.

And he wants everyone to know it.

The drum sounded so slowly that Seft found himself waiting, almost anxiously, for the next beat. This was not how the Spring Rite normally began. He stood in the crowd as the dawn light filled the sky. The spectators were quiet. Neen and the two older children stood beside him. He was carrying the baby, who was asleep.

As he waited he had a chance to admire his work. He had rebuilt the Monument in wood using the peg-and-hole joints he had devised ten midsummers ago. With the crossbars firmly attached to the uprights, the big circle was neater and steadier. It would survive very severe weather, and if the farmers attacked it again – which he asked the gods to forbid – it would prove much more difficult to destroy. Though not impossible, he thought; that would require a stone Monument.

The song began when the priestesses were still outside, so that the music seemed eerily to come from nowhere. It was a sad tune that spoke of regret and loss. It made Seft look to make sure his children were all right.

When the priestesses appeared they were led by Soo and Joia, who were side by side. The song followed the familiar pattern of a line sung by one person and answered by the whole choir.

After Soo and Joia came six priestesses carrying, at shoulder level, a wickerwork bier on which rested the body of Inka. She was naked except for some foliage, leafy branches interspersed with wild flowers. Her skin seemed white in the early light. She looked soft and vulnerable, as if still alive, except for the cruel gash across her throat.

Each of the priestesses following the bier had painted a white line across her own throat, probably with chalk. People in the crowd gasped to see the repeated vivid reminder of how Inka had died. Seft heard Neen mutter a shocked oath. He noticed that the two older children, standing either side of her, were both holding hands with their mother. He began to wonder if he and Neen had been wrong to bring the children to this.

At the back of the procession, two novices held blazing torches.

The song was unbearably melancholy. Joia's voice soared as Seft had never heard it before, seeming to fill the earth circle with sound, and the priestesses responded in unison like mournful thunder. As the pale cold body was slowly carried around, Seft heard people in the audience begin to cry.

The sun started to rise as they completed their circle. Now Seft saw that a funeral pyre had been built in the inner oval. People craned their necks to see between the posts. It was a low bed of dry leaves and twigs with logs on top: it would catch alight immediately and burn hot.

The priestesses laid the bier gently on top of the pyre.

Soo, the high priestess, bent and picked up a jar previously hidden behind a post. Tipping it, she poured an oil that Seft guessed was birch tar over the body of Inka, holding the jar upside-down until it was empty. Then she nodded at the novices with the torches.

The two girls came forward. One was weeping uncontrollably and barely able to stand. They went to the two ends of the pyre, knelt down, and held the torches to the dry tinder. The wood blazed up. The priestesses knelt and sang a song of the sun, a ball that itself seemed aflame as it rose on the eastern horizon.

Many watchers turned away as the body of Inka blackened in the heat and began to be consumed. Her soul rose in smoke, drifted and thinned in the air, and then was no more.

On the following night, under cover of darkness, Robbo and his family, carrying a few possessions, quietly crept out of Riverbend onto the Great Plain, and turned south.

8

THE EAST RIVER was still flowing, but it was shallow. Seft studied it with Tem. Seft had been head of the cleverhands since Dallo died, and Tem was his right-hand man.

When Tem had accompanied Seft to Riverbend, all those years ago, he had intended to go back to work for his uncle, Wun, in the flint mine. Then he had fallen in love with Joia's friend Vee. Now they were a couple with a house in Riverbend and two children.

Seft and Tem were the first people to be consulted about any problem of carpentry or landscape. They knew little about living things, the ailments of cattle or trees or human beings, but they had a reputation for clever solutions to problems of inanimate objects such as houses and axes and rafts.

They worked together comfortably, and the two families often spent the evenings together. Seft sometimes thought that Tem was what a brother was supposed to be like.

The communal life of the herders suited them well. It was a

collective effort, where everyone worked together and got fed and shared the rewards, if there were any – just like a flint mine.

Today they were south of Riverbend by a distance that could be walked in the time it took for a pot to boil. Here livestock often came to drink. But in the drought, as the beasts had encroached on the riverbed in reaching for a shrinking stream of water, they had trodden down the banks, and instead of a river there was a field of mud. The continuation of the river downstream was no more than a trickle.

Tem said: 'We have to rebuild the banks.'

Seft nodded. 'We need to drive stakes into the ground along the paths of the old banks, then secure the stakes with rocks on the inside and earth on the outside. If a few bushes grow in the earth, so much the better – their roots will strengthen the new banks.'

'The new waterway needs to be narrower than the old, so that the water runs high enough for the beasts to drink without stepping in,' said Tem.

'We can judge by the natural banks upstream.'

Seft had anticipated something like this, and had brought a dozen cleverhands with him. Now he set them to cutting stakes, hammering them into the mud, and piling stones and earth at either side.

With enough people the work went quickly, but still it would take a few days. Soon everyone was covered in mud, but no one minded. The spring sunshine kept them warm, and they would wash in the river at the end of the day.

Seft was marking the line of the new bank on the far side when a herder man passing by stopped to speak to him. 'Someone was looking for you, Seft,' he said. 'I didn't know where you were.'

'Who was it?'

'He didn't say his name.'

'What did he look like?'

'Big chap. One eye and a big scar down his face.'

Seft's heart sank. It was his brother Olf. 'What did he say?'

'Just that he was looking for you.'

'Thank you,' Seft said.

The man nodded and went away.

Tem had heard the interchange, and now said: 'Bad news.'

'I haven't seen Olf for ten midsummers and I'd be happy not to see him for another ten.'

Tem nodded. 'As I recall, the last words you said to him were that if you ever saw him again you'd take his other eye.'

It was a different Seft who had made the threat. That young man had been terrified but defiant. Seft was no longer frightened of Olf. Big stupid men were not so difficult to deal with when you were surrounded by a large, supportive family and a host of good neighbours.

But what on earth had brought Olf here after all these years?

Seft sighed. He had better find out.

Tem read his mind. 'Go on,' he said. 'I can handle this. Go home and deal with your brother.'

'Thanks.'

Walking home, Seft reflected on how his life had changed. He had longed to be with Neen, his wish had come true, and they still loved each other after ten midwinters. He had vowed to have a family different from the one he had grown up in, and that wish had come true too. He and Neen had three children, they loved them all, and no one was derided or tormented or beaten.

And he was no longer the mistreated runt of the litter. He was an honoured person among the herder folk, someone they consulted about problems and turned to in trouble. Everyone knew him, and he was greeted deferentially by people he hardly knew.

For a long time he had thought that this life would carry on unchanged until the end of his days. But the drought had changed that. The herder community was not invulnerable. It might be wiped out just by the weather. He felt a new burden, the responsibility of protecting the herder folk and their way of life. He admired Ani for her dedication to the welfare of her people.

After the murder of Inka, Ani had devised a rationing system to prevent waste and avoid quarrels about meat. It had been adopted, though not easily. People hated it, but respected individuals, such as Keff and Joia and Seft, had championed it, and eventually most herders saw the sense of it.

Peace returned, and there were no more fights over food. But if the drought persisted there would be more trouble.

Olf was not a threat to the herder society, but he was a disrupter, and his arrival felt menacing. Seft was not fearful, but wary, as he neared his home.

Olf and Cam were sitting on the ground outside the house, eating hare's ears. Game was not included in the rationing scheme, and Neen had been given a hare by someone whose house Seft had repaired. The ears had to be boiled all day then roasted, and even then they were chewy, but Olf and Cam were tearing and chomping like starving men. They looked starved, too. Olf was half the size he used to be, and Cam was as thin as a stick. They were also dirty and their clothes were ragged. Olf had no shoes and Cam's tunic was ripped. They were in some kind of trouble, clearly. And that would be why they were here.

He looked at Neen, who was standing with her arms folded, looking guardedly at Olf and Cam, as if they were strange dogs who might not be fully housebroken. Recalling the events of ten years ago, he realized that she had never met his brothers. But she knew about the beating he had suffered that day and, over the years, he had told her all about his childhood.

She had asked him once or twice about his mother. He rarely spoke about her, and did not like to remember her death, but when Neen asked he had felt the need to explain. The way he recalled it, his mother had been kind and generous, and when she died there was no one who loved him. When he said this to Neen, his childish grief and bewilderment rolled over him like a stampeding herd and knocked him flat, and he had astonished himself by bursting into tears.

Now Neen was visibly relieved to see Seft. Her body relaxed and she smiled. The older children were staring at the bedraggled newcomers. Ilian, the eldest at nine, seemed to be struggling to come to grips with the idea that such creatures were part of his family. Denno, the elder girl, five years old, just gazed at Olf's disfigured face. Seft decided not to tell the children that he was the one who had done that damage. Olf himself might tell them, though. He had never had a sense of tact and Seft doubted he had learned one.

Anina, a year old, was lying on her belly, waving her arms and legs, trying to crawl, oblivious of the strange visitors.

This was not like a family reunion. In other houses Seft had seen them hugging and back-slapping, joking and laughing, bursting with memories and anecdotes. Here the atmosphere was tense, no one saying much, little noise except for the hares' ears being loudly consumed.

Seft did not sit down. Looking at Olf and Cam, he said: 'What has brought you here, after ten midwinters?'

Olf continued chewing while he spoke. 'Our father is dead,' he said.

Seft's immediate reaction was incomprehension. What did that mean? How could it be? Father, dead? Then common sense returned. His father had been old – Seft did not know how old – and now he was dead.

The world was better off without him, Seft thought. 'He was a cruel and brutal man,' he said. 'I'm glad he's gone.'

Olf said: 'I'm not.'

Cam swallowed what remained of his hare's ear and said: 'Nor me.'

Seft said: 'I hated him.' But there was an unexpected tear in his eye. He brushed it away impatiently. 'I hated him with good reason.'

Neen said: 'But, Seft, he was your father.'

That was it. Cog's malice and violence were not everything. He had filled the space in Seft's soul marked 'father', and now the space was empty, and would remain so for evermore. A sense of loss took hold of Seft. This is bereavement, he thought. This is grief.

He said: 'How did he die?'

'He died working,' said Olf.

'That's right,' said Cam. 'He carried a basket of flints up the climbing pole to the surface, and put them down. Then he stood upright and said: "I think I need a rest," and fell flat on the ground. By the time we got to him he had stopped breathing.'

Seft said: 'When was this?'

Cam answered. 'About a year ago.'

So, Seft thought, you didn't come here to give me the news. Something else has happened. He was about to ask when Neen said: 'Let's have something to eat.' The sun was high: it was time for the midday meal. 'There's not a lot,' she said.

Ilian fetched bowls and spoons. Neen doled out small portions from the pot on the fire.

Olf said: 'Is this all?'

'Yes,' Seft said firmly.

'It's not enough for me.'

'If you're dissatisfied, go and get your dinner somewhere else.'

Neen said: 'We have a rationing system here. Each family gets only what it needs. So we're sharing our rations with you.'

Olf shut up and began to eat. He disposed of his share in a few mouthfuls and looked sulky.

Cam explained: 'We haven't had a decent meal for weeks. We've no food and nothing to trade.' He scraped his bowl with his spoon.

'And why is that?' Seft asked. 'You're miners, and people will still give food for the flints they need.'

Cam put down his empty bowl. 'After Dadda died, we carried on in the pit, until the seam ran out.'

'And then you dug another pit, I presume.'

'Yes, but it was a dud. No flint seam. So we dug another pit. Same result.'

Seft said: 'Did Dadda never show you how to find a flint-bearing seam?'

Cam shook his head from side to side.

How did I learn? Seft wondered. I think I just watched as my father looked at locations and chose one, and perhaps I heard him muttering to himself as he did so. Anyway, it's quite simple. But clearly these two paid no attention until it was too late.

He said: 'You could work for another miner – like Wun, for example.'

'We asked him. He refused. We tried others, too, but they seemed to be prejudiced against us.'

They know what you're like, Seft thought. The mining community is small and word gets around.

Cam said: 'We need you to help us.'

So that's it, Seft thought. He said: 'In the name of the gods, why should I help people who terrorized and persecuted me for years?'

Olf adopted a threatening tone. 'You have to save us. You're our brother.'

Seft said sharply: 'I don't *have* to do anything for you, Olf, so you'd better drop that attitude right now.'

Olf looked away and said no more.

Neen told the children to take the bowls to the river and wash them. Seft stood up and said to Neen: 'Come and talk with me.' They stepped away from Olf and Cam and stood where they could not be overheard.

Seft said: 'They just need me to teach them how to find a seam of flint.'

'I think it's outrageous. After all they put you through.'

'You don't think I have a duty to help them?'

'Certainly not! They haven't even said they're sorry.'

'They may starve to death. Or they may try to steal one of our cattle, and get shot by a herder with a bow.'

'Would you care?'

Seft hesitated, feeling again the sense of loss at his father's death. 'I don't know,' he said. 'They're vile, but they are my brothers.'

Neen was thoughtful for a few moments, then said: 'I would never try to stop you doing something you saw as your duty.'

Was it his duty? He was clear about his duty to Neen and his children, but not to his brothers. He needed time to think.

He returned to the brothers and said: 'Go away and don't come back until sundown. We'll give you a small supper and you can sleep in the house tonight. I'll tell you my decision in the morning.'

Olf said: 'Where are we supposed to go all afternoon?'

Seft said impatiently: 'I don't care. Go and look at the Monument. Just stay away from my house until suppertime.'

They got up grumpily and walked away.

Seft said to Neen: 'I'll go and see how Tem is getting on.'

'Thanks for getting rid of those two,' she said. 'I'm not comfortable with them hanging around.'

'They'll leave tomorrow, with or without me.'

'Good.'

Seft left her and walked to the river. The cleverhands had stopped to eat their midday dinner, but they were getting on well, and they might finish in another two or three days. He sat beside Tem and said: 'I may have to go away for a few days.'

'Why? Where?'

Seft told him the story of the destitute brothers.

'Well,' Tem said, 'not many people would be so forgiving. Half of me admires you and the other half thinks you're a fool.'

'I haven't made up my mind yet.'

'Yes, you have,' said Tem.

It took them a day to walk to the northern edge of the plain. On the following morning Seft told them how to find a flint seam.

'You're looking for three things,' he said. 'First, a steep hill or bluff. It doesn't have to be very high, but it must be steep. A gradual slope's no good. Second, a stream running along the foot of the hill.'

Cam said: 'All the streams are dry.'

'If it has a trickle of water it may suffice, as long as it has the third thing you're looking for, a few loose flints in the streambed.'

'Someone might have taken the flints.'

'Perhaps. But a miner would know they are a sign of a rich seam nearby.'

They came across a streambed that was almost dry, with just an intermittent trickle of water. Seft followed it to a low cliff. 'Look at this,' he said. Water was seeping out of the side of the cliff into the streambed. 'That's called a springline. Water gathers in any place where two layers of different rock meet. It might be chalk and clay, in which case it's no good to you, but we're hoping it's chalk and flint.'

Cam said indignantly: 'You mean we can't be sure?'

'Yes. Dadda made that mistake sometimes, don't you remember? We'd dig through chalk for weeks and come to a bed of useless clay.'

'But there are flints in this stream. Only a few.'

'Which is a good sign. The place to start digging will be a little way beyond the edge of the cliff. Let's go up and look.'

The three brothers scrambled up the hill and crossed its peak. 'Well, we were right,' said Seft. There was already a pit at the spot. He saw a hill of excavated chalk and a stack of new flints. They went to the edge of the pit and looked down. There was a climbing pole, and five miners were energetically breaking up the seam of flint at the bottom of the hole.

Olf said: 'Well, that was a waste of time.'

'Was it?' said Seft. 'Haven't you learned what to look for when you're trying to decide where to dig? And wasn't that what you needed me to teach you?'

Olf grunted.

They walked along the top of the rise, passing three more pits, each being worked by a different family, before the ground sloped down again. They had started in the most thoroughly exploited area, and Seft realized they would have to go farther west to find unexplored territory. Olf and Cam, never patient, became irritated with the number of times they found good flint terrain that was already being dug. But, Seft reflected, they were becoming better at identifying promising sites.

Around mid-afternoon they came across a hill with a springline and found no one digging. Seft said: 'Look at the whole length of the spring, and decide where the middle is. That should be the centre of the seam. Walk straight up the hill, not wandering left or right.'

He showed them and they followed.

'We start the pit a few paces from the summit.' He used a sharp stick to scratch a rough circle in the earth.

Olf said: 'Let's rest now.'

'Good idea,' said Seft. 'We've walked a long way today.' They ate some of the food they had brought with them, then lay down. The weather was warm and there was no sign of rain – sadly – so they slept comfortably in the open.

Next morning Seft took his leave.

Olf said: 'Aren't you going to help us dig?'

'No,' he said. 'I'm going back to my family.'

Cam said: 'What are we going to eat?'

'I don't know,' said Seft. He guessed they would survive on roots and leaves, and perhaps kill a hare or a squirrel occasionally. In any case he had done all he could for them.

'Good luck,' he said, and walked away.

'You're abandoning us!' Cam said plaintively.

Seft shook his head bemusedly and walked on.

He had not told anyone, but he wanted to take another look at Stony Valley.

All those years ago, Dallo had laid out very clearly why it was impossible to rebuild the Monument from stone. Yet even then Seft had thought Dallo gave up too soon. The problems Dallo had described might have solutions. Seft knew that Joia thought as he did, that Dallo had been too pessimistic.

Now, when the community was in a profound crisis, Seft knew something was needed to reunite them. The murder of Inka had been a warning. The collective spirit of the herder folk was ebbing away. The rebuilding of the Monument could bring everyone together again.

He crossed the North River and reached a steep hill called the Scarp, then followed it east until it became no more than a series of hills. His eye for landscape had been sharpened by the search for signs of a flint seam. Eventually he recognized the territory through which he was passing, and he turned north.

He began to examine the terrain with a view to dragging giant stones through it. At first glance he was dismayed. The area was hilly and there was nothing that could be done about that. He remembered Dallo saying how difficult it had been to move a stone across a field. Now Seft thought about how hard it would be to move even bigger stones up and down these hills, through woods and across fields; and he felt discouraged.

He reached Stony Valley at mid-afternoon and sat with his back to a tree, thinking about the problem. The first thing to do, he decided, would be to find the least difficult route.

The sheep that grazed the valley were presumably owned by someone, but Seft had not met a shepherd on his two previous visits. However, this time a man in a sheepskin tunic appeared. He smelt very bad, and Seft guessed that, not living near a river, he never washed.

The shepherd gave him a slab of raw mutton.

Seft was surprised to be given food in the drought. 'This is a generous gift,' he said.

'Ah, well,' said the shepherd, 'it's so you don't feel tempted to kill one of my sheep for your supper.'

That was shrewd. But Seft said: 'All the same, I appreciate your kindness.'

'My name is Hol,' said the shepherd.

'And I'm Seft, a herder.'

The shepherd nodded and went back the way he had come.

Seft made a fire and roasted the meat. He ate some and saved the rest for tomorrow. He woke early and set off right away, chewing mutton. As far as possible, the stones should follow the valleys. But they would have to avoid swamps, woods and rocky ground. And those pulling would get thirsty, so they needed always to be near water.

From Stony Valley the stones would have to go south-west up a rise, a challenging start on rough ground. But from then on it was mostly downhill. He saw how to avoid two steep hills by passing between them.

Soon after that he came down into the north-east corner of the Great Plain, uneven but grassy. By then he thought he had covered about a quarter of the distance. The plain was not flat but rose and fell gently. A large herd browsed what little growth there was.

He talked to a man called Dab and a pregnant woman called Revo, both carrying long, flexible herding sticks. 'We moved the herd here a few days ago,' Revo said. 'There's always some spring growth here, although this year it's not much. How long will this drought go on?'

Seft did not know.

He reached the East River shortly before coming to the village of Upriver, and now he reckoned he was halfway home. Beside the river was a large meadow, and he sat there to rest and eat his remaining mutton. The villagers were not unfriendly, but no one questioned him about what he was doing or where he was going. Perhaps they saw a lot of travellers.

East River ran more or less straight from Upriver to Riverbend. The easy way to transport the giant stones would have been to float them downriver on rafts. But he saw immediately that East River was too narrow and bendy. Any raft big enough to carry the enormous weight would be wider than some stretches of the river.

He had never walked the entire distance, but he knew that a pathway ran alongside the river. A riverside path was bound to be flat, and he guessed that would be the best route for the second half of the journey.

Moving on, he encountered several other travellers, and he concluded that he was on a much-used route.

However, he saw that in some places the path was narrow, much too narrow for a giant stone. It would have to be widened by felling trees and clearing bushes. Also, they might have to dig into the adjoining slopes to make room.

It would be a lot of work, but he saw no obstacles that could not be removed.

When he got back to Riverbend he felt he had probably found the best route.

Neen welcomed him with hugs and kisses. 'I was afraid those two would kill you,' she said.

'I found them a pit,' he said. 'It should keep them busy for many years.'

'Thank the gods for that.'

Seft was bursting with what he had learned that day, and wanted to share it. 'I'd like to invite your sister, Joia, for supper,' he said.

'I'd be delighted – especially if she could bring something to put in the pot.'

'Good,' Seft said. 'I've got a lot to tell her.'

9

SOUTH RIVER WAS running low and slow. The hot sun gleamed off the precious water. Pia dipped into it a large waterproof leather bag and let it fill. She lifted it out, now much heavier than before. Then she stood upright and began to walk.

She did this all day, every day.

Her father's farm was mercifully close to the river, but his fields stretched a long way upward to the edge of East Wood. Her shoulder hurt and her breath came in gasps, but she had to carry on. She passed her mother coming back with an empty bag, and then her father doing the same. Dadda was ill, coughing all the time. He refused to rest, but he would only half fill his bag at the river, being too weak to carry a full one. This was supposed to be a secret, but Pia had figured it out.

Everyone among the farmer folk was doing the same: men, women and children. People who normally spent some of their time building scratch ploughs, making pots or baskets, knapping flints or producing bows and arrows, all had dropped their tools to irrigate the parched fields. There had been little rain in the winter and none since, and now the seeds urgently needed water before they could sprout green above the ground. As the spirits of the clouds were refusing to do their duty, the people had to bring the water themselves.

Pia went to the farthermost edge of the farm. The scratch plough made shallow furrows that all ran parallel to the river, a pattern that retained rainwater when there was any. Pia walked along a row, sloshing the water from her bag until it was empty. The thirsty earth sucked it in and turned dusty again. She rested briefly, luxuriating in the moment; but as she stood looking across the area of land that needed to be wetted she felt dispirited. It was a never-ending task; or, rather, it would not end until the rain came, and there was no sign of that.

Pia's family were lucky to have goats. Those creatures ate almost anything: brambles, thistles, tree bark. It was one of Pia's duties to bring leafy branches from West Wood to feed them. Her mother made cheese most days. Often it was all the family had to eat.

She hoisted the empty bag onto her shoulder and walked down the slope. As she went she pulled any weeds that caught her eye, but that hardly occupied her mind, so she thought about Han. Something big had happened at the Spring Rite. They had both come to feel that their love was a permanent thing. His mother had sensed it, and Pia had felt that Ani was pleased with Han's choice.

But they had a problem. There was always trouble when a farmer and a herder fell in love.

The farming folk were all descended from Alkry the Great, a herder who had despised the slack herder way of life and had founded Farmplace with his wife and children. That meant they were all kin. They brought new blood into the community in the form of babies sired by unknown strangers at the revel, but otherwise they did not like outsiders.

They did not want their young people to go away and set up home with herders. The farms needed their youthful strength for weeding and watering, reaping and binding, threshing and grinding. Farming was work, work, work, and no one could be spared. It was just as bad when a herder came to live with the farmers. Herders were lazy and disobedient. The idea that they should do hard labour from dawn to dusk was incomprehensible to them. They would say things like: 'Don't worry, the crops will grow, they always do, don't they?' which drove the farmers mad.

Pia was determined that she and Han would overcome these obstacles, even though she did not yet know how.

As she approached the river she saw a scene that puzzled and troubled her. Her father seemed to be lying in the riverside mud. Her mother was kneeling beside him, speaking to him. Pia put down her bag and ran to them.

She said: 'What's the matter, Mamma?'

Pia knelt down. Her father's eyes were open. His lips moved and he mumbled: 'I'm all right.'

Yana said: 'Don't leave me, Alno, please, not yet.'

Pia was shocked. Mamma thought Dadda might die. Pia had known he was ill but had not imagined it could be this bad. The thought bewildered her. It had always been the three of them. Pia had known nothing else. Life without her loving, kind-hearted dadda was unimaginable.

And he was young! She was not sure of his exact age, but his hair was dark brown with no grey, and his face was unwrinkled.

Yana said: 'We have to take him to the house. Help me get him up.'

She grasped him under the shoulders. Pia bent to help and they lifted him to his feet. He clearly could not stand unaided. Mamma said: 'Hold him upright for a moment, and I'll get him over my shoulder.'

Pia took his weight, and was startled by how light he was. He had got thin without her noticing. She held him effortlessly. Yana bent down, grasped him around the thighs, and lifted. Pia let him fall forward over Yana's shoulder.

Yana turned and headed up the rise. Pia followed, crying.

When they reached the house Yana took him inside. Pia helped her lay him down on the leather mat. As she did so he said quietly: 'Water.'

There was a jar in the house, keeping relatively cool in the shade. Pia dipped a bowl in the jar then knelt beside him. She lifted his shoulders until he was sitting upright and held the bowl to his lips. He drank thirstily.

Pia was caring for him as if he was a child. It was the wrong way round.

He said: 'Enough.'

Yana said: 'I'll stay with him. You'd better carry on.'

Pia resumed her work. What was going to happen? Might he get better? Or was it certain that he would get worse and die?

She trudged back up the hill with her load, splashed it in the furrows, then took a diversion from her downhill route to go by the house. Stepping in, she heard her mother speaking in a quiet monotone, apparently not expecting her father to reply, for she did not pause. 'You'll rest, and I'll lie beside you at night, and bring you porridge in the morning, and slowly you'll recover, and eventually be yourself again, strong and ready for anything—'

Pia interrupted her. 'Is there anything you need? Can I help?'

Yana replied without looking away from Alno. 'He's sleepy now. In a few moments he'll drop off. Just carry on with your work.'

Pia did as she was told.

She carried her bag down to the river. As she was filling it, a voice said: 'What's this?'

She turned to see Shen, right-hand man to Troon. She disliked him. He was a thin man with a long bent nose – bent from sticking it where he shouldn't, people said. He reported everything to Troon, they said. He looked at her with arrogant dark eyes. 'On your own?' he said.

Pia saw no point in answering stupid questions.

'Where are your parents?'

'House,' she said, then hoisted her bag to her shoulder.

Shen turned and surveyed the fields, then spotted the house and headed for it.

Pia decided she needed to be present at the meeting. Shen was sly and malicious, and any visit from him meant trouble. She put down her bag and followed him. She had to hurry to keep up with his long strides.

When he entered the house she was right behind him.

Shen said: 'What's happening on this farm? Two people in the house and all the work being done by one little girl?'

Yana said: 'My man's unwell. A minor thing. He'll be better shortly.'

Pia said: 'And I'm not a little girl. I'm a woman, and I can carry a bag as well as anyone.'

Shen ignored her. 'You can't just stop work, Yana,' he said. 'You can't afford it in this drought. You know Troon doesn't like anyone to slack off.'

'I'm not slacking off!' Yana said indignantly. 'I'm tending a sick man and I'll be back at work in no time. And so will he, and then he will want to talk to you about barging into his house and trying to bully his womenfolk.'

'I'll inform Troon. What you say had better be true.' Shen left, ducking his head to pass through the doorway.

Pia said: 'I hate that man.'

'He is vile. But a servant generally does what he's told. His master, Troon, is the one you should hate.'

Pia thought about that as she returned to her drudgery.

She worked on until it got too dark, then returned to the house with her bag. Her father was asleep. Her mother had put together a meagre supper. There was porridge made with last year's grains, some cheese, and a bowl of mixed leaves: mallow, chickweed and bracken fronds.

They lay down, and Pia, exhausted physically and emotionally, fell asleep immediately.

She was awakened by her mother sobbing.

She sat up. The cool light of early day came in through the open top half of the doorway. Yana was lying beside Alno, half on top of him, her arm thrown across his chest, her knee on his leg. Her sobs seemed wrenched from the heart. Pia said: 'What's happened?' Yana did not reply, but Pia knew the answer. 'He's dead, isn't he?' she cried. She thumped the floor rhythmically with her fist. 'He's dead, he's dead, he's dead.'

Her distress penetrated Yana's misery. She stopped crying, wiped her face with her hands, and stood up. Her sudden transformation calmed Pia, who realized it was stupid to bang the floor. She got up, and mother and daughter hugged for a long time. At least I've still got Mamma, Pia thought, and she felt grateful.

Eventually Yana broke the hug and said: 'We have duties to perform.'

They washed the body using a piece of soft leather, then dressed him again ready for his funeral. They went outside to look for a suitable place by the river, and agreed on a spot in the shade of an oak tree. As they stood thinking that this would be the last place where he would lie down, Shen appeared.

'What are you doing?' he said, then answered his own question. 'Deciding where to cremate him. I'm not surprised. When I saw him yesterday I knew it wouldn't be long. You'll be busy today, but get back to work tomorrow, without fail.'

Yana said: 'You'd better tell Katch. She's his sister, and she'll tell the other relatives.' Katch was Troon's woman. That was how Pia came to be cousin to the unpleasant Stam. Katch herself was likeable, though under Troon's thumb. Yana continued: 'That will save me time, and I might even be able to return to watering this afternoon. I expect Troon would like that, wouldn't he, Shen?'

Shen did not like to be told what to do. 'I'll tell her if I see her,' he said, and he went off.

Yana and Pia went to the wood and picked up armfuls of dry twigs for the pyre. They carried them down to the oak tree, but they needed more. Next time they arrived at the tree two other people were there. One was Katch. The other was a boy a few years older than Pia called Duff, who said: 'My deepest sympathy, Pia and Yana.'

'And mine,' said Katch.

'Thank you.'

Katch and Duff helped to collect dry logs and the job was soon done.

Yana, Pia and Katch went back to the house and picked up Alno's corpse. Walking side by side, holding the body in their arms, they carried him to the pyre. Pia scattered wild flowers on the corpse.

It was midday. People began to arrive, Alno's kin and Yana's, Pia's friend Mo, and a surprising number of others, all women.

Yana nodded to Katch, who lit a torch.

Yana stood up and spoke to her dead man. 'We should have had many more years. We should have grown old and grey with one another for company. If you had died in old age, I could have said I was lucky to have had you for so long. But now I have to go on without you.' Her voice broke down, and she said in a whisper: 'Without you.'

She took the torch from Katch and held it to the pyre. The dry wood caught quickly and blazed up. Someone began the funeral song, and everyone joined in. Then they all sat quietly around the pyre, remembering the kind man with the ready smile, as the body slowly burned to ash and fragments of bone.

Katch opened a small basket and produced cakes she had made with grain and milk, and they ate.

When at last the fire went out Katch, who had thought of everything, produced a wooden shovel and handed it to Yana. The mourners began the song of the dead, asking the spirit of the river to welcome the ashes of their loved one. Yana picked up some of the remains and scattered them in the river. She handed the shovel to Pia, who did the same, hardly able to see through her tears. One by one, each of the crowd performed the ritual, until a light breeze blew the remaining ashes away, and the song came to an end.

The sun began to set. In the sad half-light of dusk the mourners separated, moving away, each with their own thoughts about life and death, and returned to their homes for the little death that is sleep.

Next day Pia and Yana returned to watering. Pia thought about the cremation while she did the tedious work. She had been surprised at how many people showed up. She had not known that her father was so well-liked. But perhaps they had come for her mother's sake. Yana was popular among farmer women for the way she stood up to Troon.

At mid-morning Pia noticed two men apparently surveying their fields. She screwed up her eyes against the sun and said: 'The shorter one is Troon.'

Yana nodded. 'And the tall one is Stam.'

Pia was surprised. 'How he's sprouted!' She had not seen him for a while. 'He's only seen thirteen midsummers.'

'Boys do that at a certain age. It doesn't make them men.'

'I wonder what they want.'

'Oh, I know,' said Yana.

'What?'

'You'll see.'

The two women put down their pots and walked across the fields to where the visitors stood in the shade of an elm tree. Although Troon was short he was wiry, and looked menacingly strong. Stam was taller by a head and neck. He had only one ear, the other apparently having been violently cut off, leaving a hole surrounded by the lumpy remains. People said Troon had cut off his son's ear as a punishment for some misbehaviour, but Pia did not know whether that was true, and could hardly believe it, even of Troon.

Troon said: 'My deepest sympathy to you both.'

Stam added mechanically: 'And mine.'

Yana said briskly: 'My man died after breathing smoke from the fire on the Break — a fire caused by your foolish feud with the herders. If you want to make amends, stop fighting the herders.'

'Never mind about that. I've come to tell you that you must find another man immediately.'

Among the farmer folk a woman could not own property, so Yana could not inherit Alno's farm. It was a widow's duty to find another man to run the farm with her. Pia's mind had been so possessed by grief that she had not thought of this.

Now she recalled that if a widow failed to find a man within a year, the Big Man would choose one for her.

Yana said: 'I'm aware of that, Troon, and I thank you for the reminder. However, according to custom I have a year to look for the right man.'

'Normally, yes.'

Yana stiffened. 'What do you mean, *normally*?'

'There's a drought. We're starving. We can't allow a good farm such as this, right near the water, to be run by a woman and a child when we so badly need its crops.'

'Pia and I can run the farm perfectly well.'

'I came here this morning to have a good look. This farm is too big for you. You must have a man.'

'And I will, within a year.'

He shook his head. 'I can't risk this summer's harvest.'

Yana was indignant. 'You don't have the right to make that decision!'

'Of course I do, in an emergency.'

'No, no. There's no precedent. No previous Big Man has claimed emergency powers in my lifetime.'

'Nor in mine. But there has not been a drought this bad in our lifetimes. You have seven days to get a man.'

Yana was shocked. 'I can't team up with a man for life in such a short time!'

'If you don't, I will choose someone for you.'

'This is wrong, and you know it.'

Troon ignored that. 'And don't think of running away,' he said. 'We'll come and get you, wherever you go. So you'd better start looking today.' With that he turned and walked away, and Stam followed him.

Pia said: 'This is outrageous. He can't do it.'

Yana said: 'The trouble is, I think he can.'

Bort's farm was some distance from the river, on the new land in the Break that had been ploughed ten years ago. The farm was small but Bort also had half a dozen cattle. His woman had died and he now farmed with his son, Deg. Yana and Pia found father and son bringing water from the river, like every other farmer.

It was six days since Troon's ultimatum. Yana, with the help of Pia and Katch, had considered every family in the farmer community. Many men were left single when a woman died in childbirth, but they did not remain single for long. Duff was single, but he had his hands full running his aunt Uda's farm. Yana had found only one possibility, and with great reluctance she had settled on Bort.

He was neither tall nor short, neither handsome nor ugly. He had thinning brown hair and a wispy beard. There was nothing at all to admire about him, Pia thought dismally: he was not charming, or intelligent, or even just likeable. Yana would never love him. But she would have him. She had to.

He was surprised to see them, but quite pleased, which Pia thought was a good sign.

Yana began by saying: 'It's a hard pull from the river to your farm.'

'That's the truth,' Bort said.

'A lot less at my place.'

Bort looked disapproving, and Pia realized her mother had made a mistake. The farm was not Yana's. Bort reminded her of that by saying: 'I was sorry to hear that Alno died.'

'Thank you.'

'I suppose that's why you've come to see me.'

Yana did not answer directly. 'Shall we sit down?' They moved into the shade of a hawthorn tree in pale-pink blossom. They sat. Clearly Bort was not going to offer them so much as a drink of water.

Yana pointed to Bort's son, Deg, who had not said a word so far. She said: 'Deg must have seen twenty midsummers.'

'Twenty-one come this midsummer,' Bort said, stating the obvious.

'Soon he'll want to settle with a woman, and together they will run this farm. But it doesn't need three. Now, my Pia's younger than Deg, but it won't be long before she wants a man and a place of her own. So there's an empty space for a man on my farm.'

Bort said: 'You're offering this to me.'

'Yes. It's good land, close to the river, and when the drought ends it will give rich harvests. It can be yours.'

'And sex too, I presume?'

'If you wish.'

'You don't sound enthusiastic.'

Pia almost laughed. Who could be enthusiastic about sex with this mediocrity?

Yana said to Bort: 'I'd be guided by what you want.'

'A good principle for a woman to follow.'

Pia almost hoped he would refuse Yana. Her mother could never even like this man, let alone love him. But she needed him.

Bort said: 'I'd say I'm flattered but, thinking about it, there isn't really another man available, is there?'

There was not, but Yana tactfully did not say so.

Bort said: 'Deg, what do you think?'

Pia began to worry. Bort had not eagerly jumped at the opportunity he was being offered. In itself that was surprising. A bigger and better farm, plus an attractive woman younger than him by about ten midsummers: what did he need to think about?

Deg pondered for a while then said: 'It's up to you, really, Father.'

Bort turned to Pia. 'And what about you, young woman? Do you have an opinion about this?'

'I hope you accept, Bort,' she said. 'I won't be living with Mamma

for ever, and when I leave I'll be glad you're there to look after her.'
She had never in her life uttered such an insincere sentence.

'Well, then, I must decide,' said Bort.

Pia realized that Bort was enjoying this. Perhaps it was nice to
be in demand.

He paused, then at last said: 'I'm saying no.'

Pia did not know whether to be glad or sorry. Her mother
looked equally ambivalent.

Bort went on: 'I don't want a different farm and a new woman,
or any other changes in my life. I plan to work on this farm until
Deg brings home a woman, and then I'll continue to work here
but not so hard.'

It could be a long time before the milk-and-water Deg brought
a woman home, Pia guessed.

'I don't know how old I am, but in any case I'm ready for a
rest,' Bort went on. 'So I'll stay here.'

Yana got to her feet, and Pia did the same. Both put a brave
face on their rejection. Yana said: 'Thank you for listening to me,
Bort, and I wish you and Deg well for the future.' She turned and
left, and Pia followed.

When they were out of earshot, Yana said: 'What a humiliation,
to be rejected by someone so unattractive!'

Pia felt that too, but she was thinking about the consequences.
'He was the only prospect,' she said. 'So what happens next?'

'I don't know,' said Yana.

They went to see Troon on the day of the deadline.

He lived in a house built of the same materials as an ordinary
house but larger. He had a lot of possessions, Pia noticed: a

basketful of hazelnuts, a stack of firewood, pots with unknown contents, and shearling winter coats – made from sheepskins that had been tanned with the hair left on – hanging from wooden pegs. He had no farm, so everything he ate or wore came from others. If he asked you for something, it was dangerous to say no.

He was there with Stam, sitting on one of several leather floor mats. Yana and Pia sat facing them, and Troon's woman, Katch, offered them cool water in pottery bowls. She had an anxious, embarrassed look. Pia guessed she was sympathetic to Yana but scared to defy Troon.

Yana said: 'I have done my best to meet your demand. I proposed to Bort.'

'A good choice,' said Troon.

'No doubt,' said Yana, 'but he turned me down. And as far as I can see he is the only available man. So you have two options, Troon. You could order Bort to take me—'

'Not possible,' said Troon.

'But you ordered me to take someone.'

'You're a woman. That's different.'

'In that case we have to wait until another man becomes available. It may not be long. People are dying because of the drought.'

Pia thought this would be the best possible outcome. Her mother was still obliged to take a man, but at least there was a chance that it would be someone she liked. Troon would not be pleased, but what could he do?

However, Troon did not look like a man who had been defeated. He should have been angry – it did not take much to anger him. Not getting his way always did it.

This worried Pia. Could he possibly have another plan?

He did. Troon said: 'You say Bort is the only available man. But you're wrong.'

Yana looked startled, but said nothing.

Pia felt a chill. She did not think she and her mother – and several friends and neighbours who had helped – could have overlooked anyone.

But Troon was smugly confident. 'He's sitting right here,' he said. 'My son, Stam.'

Yana's reaction was explosive. 'Stam?' she shouted. 'Stam? Don't be stupid!'

Troon looked thunderous. 'I am not stupid. Stam is an available man, and you are going to partner with him whether you like it or not.'

'He's not an available man because he's not a man! He hasn't yet seen fourteen midsummers. He's a child!'

Stam was also Yana's nephew, Pia thought; but only by marriage, so Yana could not argue that the relationship would be incestuous.

Troon said: 'He's big and strong, and a hard worker. He will surely become Big Man when I die. You should feel lucky that he wants you.'

'He's too young even for my daughter.'

Pia said: 'And too ugly.'

Troon turned a look of hate on Pia. But he swung back and spoke to Yana. 'Go to your farm now and get back to work. Shen will sit outside your house tonight, to keep you safe.'

To keep us imprisoned, Pia thought.

'Stam will come to you tomorrow at suppertime.' Troon paused for emphasis, looking directly at Yana. 'And he will spend the night with you.'

Pia was enraged, but she forced herself to stay silent.

Troon went on: 'And if you're thinking of running away, think again. I will find you, wherever you go, and when I do, I will make you very, very sorry.'

It was the second time he had made this threat, and it turned Pia cold. He never made empty threats. She knew he meant it.

His vengeance would be terrible.

Walking home, Yana said to Pia: 'Sometimes a Big Man can be made to change his mind.'

'I've never known it,' said Pia in surprise.

'The last Big Man did, once or twice, but you might not have realized. It doesn't happen often, but it's not unknown.'

'When it does happen, what persuades him?'

'A cry of outrage from the people.'

'I'd like to see that.'

'Remember when he got the men to plough up the Break? He waited until all the women had gone to the Midsummer Rite. Why would he trouble to hide what he was doing? He was afraid there would be an outcry. And there was a good deal of indignation, but by then it was too late, the ploughing had been done.'

'And you think there might be an outcry now?'

'We must make sure of it.'

'How?'

'I'm going to talk to the women. They must realize that if he gets away with it this time it could happen again, and one of them would be the victim.'

'I'll help you.'

'Good. In that case I want you to talk to Duff. He likes you.'

Pia had not registered this. 'Does he?'

'It's obvious, but not to you, because your mind is on Han.'

'Anyway, what do you want me to say to Duff, my overlooked admirer?'

'Ask him to talk to the men. He may be able to persuade at least some of them that what Troon is doing is wrong.'

Pia was dubious, but willing to try. 'I'll do my best.'

They split up. Pia headed for Duff's place, at the far eastern end of the farming country. As she walked she tried to decide what to say, but she found herself distracted by Yana's revelation. Duff was always pleasant and friendly, but it had never occurred to her that he might be romantically interested in her. Yana had said Pia was too involved with Han to notice, and that was probably right.

Anyway, Duff would be keen to help.

The stream that normally ran from the wood through Duff's fields down to South River was now dry, Pia saw with dismay.

Duff's farm was one of the oldest. He had inherited it from an uncle. The uncle's woman was still alive and energetic, a small, wiry woman called Uda. Pia found them at the edge of the wood, having a break and eating smoked pork, taking advantage of the shade of the trees. Duff offered Pia some of his meat, and she took a small piece.

Duff was wiry like his aunt, and a contrast to Han, who was something of a giant. Duff's frame was compact and neat. The farm was neat, too: the furrows straight, the house in good repair, and a well-behaved yellow dog sitting next to Duff, hoping for some pork.

Pia sat down with them and told the story of Troon and Stam. Duff and his aunt Uda were gratifyingly indignant. Uda said: 'Women are sometimes bullied into accepting a man they don't love, but normally the man is more or less suitable. Stam is no more than a boy!'

'Thirteen midsummers,' Pia said. 'My mother is approaching . . .' She showed her hands, pointed to her feet, then repeated both gestures.

Duff said: 'And Stam is a thug. He gets into fights. The girls are frightened of him.'

Pia said: 'My mother is going round the farms, speaking to the women, telling them what has happened. She's hoping they will protest, knowing they could be next.'

Uda said: 'I wish her luck.' She sounded neither hopeful nor pessimistic.

Pia said: 'Duff, would you talk to the men? See if any of them think this is wrong.'

Duff nodded. 'I will, gladly. I don't know how much sympathy I'll find.'

'Concentrate on men who have daughters. Point out that this could happen to them.'

'That's a good strategy,' Duff said, with a touch of admiration. 'A man who's fond of his daughter would hate to see her forced to partner with a young bully.'

Pia said: 'We have until tomorrow evening. That's when Stam is coming to . . . take possession.'

'In that case I'd better get started.' Duff got to his feet and wiped his hands on a leaf. 'I'll begin with my next-door neighbour.'

'Thank you,' said Pia. 'You're very kind.'

A crowd gathered outside Yana and Pia's house the following afternoon. Most of the people were women. One of them was Pia's friend Mo, and Pia quietly asked her: 'What are they saying?'

'They're outraged, naturally. But some of them are scared, too. They're here, but they don't want to offend Troon too much. Others are more robust.'

Mo was among the robust ones, Pia could guess. She was a stocky

figure, with dark hair and freckles, and she was not easily intimidated.
Pia said: 'I suppose the really frightened ones have stayed at home.'

'Exactly.'

Shen was there, sharp-eyed, noting who was present and who
was not. Troon would have a complete list tonight.

Pia noticed Bort and Deg in the crowd. They did not look the
least bit embarrassed. Did they not realize the part they had played
in this crisis? Of course not, she thought.

There were more men present than she had expected, and she
said so to Duff.

He was cautious. 'I rounded up a few supporters, but some of
these here I never spoke to, and I'm not sure whose side they're
on. They might have come to back Troon.'

Pia nodded. That was what she had been afraid of. The outcome
was in doubt, she realized. She was tortured by anxiety, but there
was nothing more she could do.

Just as the lower edge of the sun's disc touched the western
horizon, Troon and Stam appeared across the fields. Conversation
in the crowd faded to whispers as they came close.

Stam was wearing a new tunic and a bowl-shaped leather cap.
Pia guessed that Katch, his mother, had made the cap. He seemed
pleased with himself, but in truth the little cap on his big head
made him look foolish.

As father and son approached the crowd, Troon said loudly:
'Clear the way, clear the way.'

Pia felt the crowd hesitate. This was a key moment. Would
they defy Troon and stand in his way?

One or two moved back, and others followed suit. Those who
had not moved looked very exposed, and in ones and twos they,
too, retreated. It was not immediate obedience, but it was very far
from defiance, and in a few moments there was a clear passage
through the crowd open to Troon and Stam.

Pia and Yana stood side by side in front of the house door. Troon and Stam walked up to them.

Troon said to Yana: 'Here is your new man.'

She said: 'I don't love this boy and I don't want him.'

Troon said: 'All the same, you must have him.'

A woman in the crowd shouted: 'This is not right!' Pia thought she recognized the voice of Mo.

Troon spun around, looking for the source of the shout, but he could not pick one woman out of fifty. He shouted: 'It's right because I say it's right.'

A man's voice said: 'Can't the boy speak for himself?' That sounded like Duff.

Once again Troon tried and failed to identify the speaker.

Stam was stung into speaking at last. 'She's my woman, because my father says so.'

It made him seem even less grown-up, and there was a scatter of laughter.

But, Pia noted with dismay, no one was willing to stand up to Troon openly.

Stam did not like to be laughed at, and he looked cross. He said to Yana: 'We're going inside.' He took hold of her upper arm.

'One moment,' she said, and he let go. Pia thought that was a heartening sign. It meant that her mother was not going to lose all control.

The crowd went quiet, and Yana spoke to Stam in a clear voice, so that everyone could hear and understand. 'You will never, ever strike me. For if you do – just once – know that afterwards you will not sleep, not that night or any subsequent night. You will live without sleep. Because you will be sure that if you close your eyes, and fall asleep, then' – her voice rose to a cry – 'when you're in your deepest, most unconscious sleep, I will take a flint bradawl – the kind that bores little holes in wood – and I will pierce both your eyes with it, so quickly that you will wake up blind, not knowing what has happened to you; and you will never be able to strike a woman again.'

The crowd was silent and Stam was pale.

Then Yana said: 'Now you can come inside.'

And the two of them disappeared into the house.

10

BEZ WAS WALKING through West Wood with a young woman called Lali. He was fond of her. People said she looked like him, with a wide mouth and a flat nose. She was probably his daughter, though the woodlanders were not able to be exact about such things. They believed that a woman who had sex with several different men would have stronger babies.

Anyway, he liked to teach Lali, and she loved to learn. Bez was one of the few woodlanders who spoke a little of the herder language, and he was teaching it to Lali. Suddenly he stopped and said: 'Look at that.'

She said: 'What?'

He pointed to a dead pine tree.

'It's a dead tree,' she said.

'There's a hole, at about the level of a tall man's head. What do you see?'

'Oh!' she said. 'Bees – lots of them. Going in and out. Hey, let's run! We might get stung.'

'Just hold on,' Bez said calmly. 'They're not interested in us – yet. And if that changes, the pond is only a few steps that way.' He pointed. The big pond in the middle of the wood had not yet dried up. Bez thought it must be fed by a spring, rather than rainfall – which was lucky for the woodlanders. 'Jump into the water and the bees can't get at you.'

'All right,' she said doubtfully.

'Don't you want some honey?'

Lali licked her lips. The woodlanders were living on spring fruits and vegetables. The deer were shyer and more elusive than ever, and they had not had venison all winter. And it was too early in the year for hazelnuts. Everyone was hungry.

Bez said: 'Go back to the village and bring me some fire, please, and I'll show you something.' There were always cooking fires going in the village, regardless of the weather.

Lali hurried off, glad to get away from the bees.

Bez started collecting fuel for a smoky fire: damp moss from around the pond, the grey lichen called old man's beard, green pine needles, fresh shoots. To start the fire he picked up old dried-up twigs and dead leaves and piled them at the base of the dead pine. As soon as Lali got back he lit the dry tinder. Then, when it was burning well, he put the other fuel on top. Thick smoke rose and visibly irritated the bees.

Lali said: 'I don't like this.'

'Go home, if you like,' Bez said. 'I can do this on my own, but I thought maybe you'd like to learn how it's done.'

'All right,' she said.

'Now, can you see a large-leaf lime tree nearby?'

They both looked around. Such trees were common. 'Over there,' said Lali.

The tree had heart-shaped leaves bigger than a man's hand. 'Fetch me some big leaves,' said Bez.

She did so.

'Now,' he said, 'get ready to run.'

Using two of the leaves as protection for his hands, he picked up the smouldering fire in its entirety and stuffed it through the entrance hole to the bees' nest. 'Ow, that hurt!' he said, shaking his hands. Then he said: 'To the pond!'

As he ran he felt a sting on the back of his neck. He heard Lali say: 'Ouch!' The bees knew who had violated their nest.

Lali beat him to the pond. They went in but the water was shallow. They both sank down as far as they could, then dipped their heads. When he could hold his breath no longer, Bez put his head up. He was stung again. He saw Lali surface. Quickly, he scooped up handfuls of mud and spread it over her head and neck while she gasped for breath. Then they both submerged again.

Next time they came up, the bees had gone.

Bez had several stings but Lali had only two or three.

They came out of the pond and washed off most of the protective mud. 'Now,' said Bez, 'let's have a look at that nest.'

They returned to the dead pine. The bees were swarming around the nest entrance, which was partly blocked by the still-smouldering fire. But the insects moved slowly and uncertainly, as if dazed.

Bez used a couple of sticks of dead wood to remove the remains of the fire. The cavity was still full of smoke. The bees flew around aimlessly. Their nest was right in front of them but they did not recognize it.

Tentatively, Bez put his hand inside, ready to jerk it out instantly. But he was not stung. He felt around, then touched what he was searching for: a sticky mass. He pulled it out. 'Look at that!' he said triumphantly to Lali. It was a honeycomb, dark in colour but dripping with yellow honey. 'Do you want a taste? Take some!'

She dipped her fingers into the liquid and put them into her mouth. She swallowed and said: 'Oh, my, it's so good!'

'Take the comb,' he said, handing it to her. 'Put it on a lime leaf so the honey doesn't drip to the ground and go to waste.' Then he reached inside and brought out two more. 'Three,' he said. 'We were lucky.' He stacked his two on another leaf.

'We have to share,' said Lali, in a wistful tone.

'Of course we do.'

They made their way to the village, a cluster of houses close to a stream – which had now dried up. Lali offered honey to some children and soon had a crowd around her.

Bez looked into the hut where he usually slept. His brother, Fell, was there, a younger, shorter, better-looking version of Bez. He was with Gida, a warm and sexy woman they both liked.

Fell and Gida were lying on their backs, side by side, looking pleased with themselves. Bez guessed they had just made love. He said: 'I've been walking with Lali.' Gida was Lali's mother. 'We raided a bees' nest.'

They both dipped their fingers into the honey, then made ecstatic faces.

Bez went outside and began offering the honey to everyone.

It was a lucky day.

A few days later, Lali was in floods of tears. Gida, her mother, had her arm around Lali, comforting her. The reason for her distress lay on the ground in front of them. A puppy had been killed and mostly eaten.

There were several dogs in the village. They warned of strangers and joined enthusiastically in any hunt. A dog did not belong to anyone in particular, but sometimes a dog would attach itself to an individual. Fell had one that followed him around. Bez had noticed that girls of Lali's age liked to befriend a particular pup.

Gida confirmed his guess. 'She was fond of that little dog.'

Bez said: 'I wonder what killed it.' Wolves rarely came near human habitations. It might have been a boar, a highly aggressive wild pig, but they were so dangerous that the woodlanders would immediately chase and kill any that entered the wood. Bez guessed it had been killed by a merlin, a small falcon that might hunt in the woods.

Then he noticed something unusual on the ground nearby. It appeared to be the droppings of a big animal. There were four large brown turds, too big to belong to a wolf or a boar.

Bez felt hopeful. If his guess was right, the woodlanders were in luck.

Lali stopped sobbing. 'What is it?' she said.

'I think it's a bear,' said Bez.

'I've never seen a bear.'

'Nor have I,' said Gida.

Bez picked up a turd and broke it in half. He could see undigested leaves and the stalks of berries. 'A bear that hasn't eaten much meat lately,' he said.

'Like us,' said Gida.

Lali said: 'Did a bear kill my favourite puppy?'

'I think so,' said Bez. He looked around for more signs. A few paces away there was a fallen tree, the bark of which had been mostly stripped off. 'It's definitely a bear,' Bez said. 'Look at this.'

Lali said: 'It's just a dead tree.' Then, remembering how she had been wrong about the dead pine tree that contained honey, she added: 'But perhaps it's more than that.'

Bez smiled. 'The bear stripped the bark,' he said, 'with its claws.'

'Why?' Lali wondered. She had recovered from her grief.

'There are usually bugs under the bark of a dead tree. Bears like to eat them.'

They walked on. Gida said: 'The bear has probably been living in some place that ran out of water, and it moved to this wood in desperation. It obviously drinks from our pond.'

Lali said: 'I'm never going to that pond again.'

Bez said: 'Let's take a look.'

When they got there they studied the mud at the edge of the water, looking for prints. Gida showed Lali the marks of deer and fox. Then she said: 'Aha! Here it is.'

The print of the bear paw in the mud was not unlike that of a rather broad human foot, with five toes. But in front of the toe marks were small, distinctive claw marks.

Bez frowned. 'The wide foot suggests a full-grown animal, but the print is not deep. He's not very heavy, probably because he isn't getting enough to eat.'

Gida said: 'He's lost a claw, look.'

Lali bent down. 'Oh, yes! The little toe on the left foot.'

'Probably in a fight, or maybe just an accident.'

Lali was surprised. 'What creature fights a bear?'

'Another bear sometimes – in a quarrel over a female, perhaps. Or it could have been a boar. Those creatures will fight anything.'

Bez said: 'We have to tell the others.'

'Yes,' said Gida. 'Let's ask everyone to come together at suppertime to discuss this.'

Lali said: 'What are we going to discuss?'

'How to catch this bear and kill it,' said Bez.

The hunt took place on the following day.

The entire population got up at dawn. Bez could not count them – woodlanders were not good at numbers – but they were surely enough to kill a bear. Bez was eager. A big bear could feed the village for a week – if they could catch it. It could also kill someone with one sweep of its massive paw.

The village was near the Break. The pond was west of the village. The dead puppy had been farther west again. That made sense. The bear would choose to stay away from humans, and would want to get to water without passing the village.

They had agreed their plan the previous evening. It was based on the way they organized a deer hunt. They spread out across the width of the wood: men, women, children and dogs, all both excited and scared. Bez and Fell were close to the centre of the line, Gida and Lali with them. Two experienced hunters, Omun and Arav, were on the wings, the ends of the line.

Woodlander society had no leaders. There were no elders, no Big Man; no one had the right to give orders to anyone else. But there were always strong personalities. Bez and Gida told people what to do only when asked – but that happened quite a lot.

Fell's dog was with them. All dogs looked like small wolves, but Fell's was larger than most, with a heavy coat of fur. The herders named their dogs, but woodlanders did not: they thought it was silly.

The hunting party moved forward at a steady pace, unhesitating despite the danger. Everyone could see at least one other hunter, so they were able to stay roughly in line. This was also reassuring. No one wanted to be alone when they saw the bear.

They moved as quietly as they could, and the dogs were trained not to bark until they scented prey. The quarry would hear them coming, of course – animals had good ears – but the later the better.

Bez and Fell and many other hunters had bows and arrows. Others had clubs and axes. The children would throw stones.

They passed the pond, and Lali proudly pointed out the paw prints to Fell. A little farther they saw the droppings and the dead tree with its bark stripped. The bear was a presence now, somewhere in their wood, lurking, threatening.

As they pressed on Bez kept his eyes open for other signs. He stopped at an aspen tree and pointed out that many leaves had been torn away. 'The bear came this way,' he said. 'It ate the leaves.' They must be getting closer, he thought.

Not long afterwards, Fell's dog became agitated. It did not bark, but it started to run from side to side and sniff energetically.

Fell said: 'He's scented the bear.'

They picked up their pace.

Bez saw a flattened fern. 'The bear's running from us now. Look, he squashed that fern in his hurry.' He felt the tension of upcoming peril, perhaps just moments away.

He heard distant barking that seemed to come from both left and right. The dogs that had been at the ends of the line had now scented the bear, he guessed, and were moving towards it. The people would be following the dogs' lead.

They were closing in.

Bez came to an area of low bushes leading to a dense grove of young beech trees growing close together, competing for the sunlight. He gestured to the others to stop. The bear was in the grove. It had tried to smash its way through, but the trees were too thick, and it was stalled.

The creature was dark brown, almost black. It was medium size: if it stood on its hind legs it would be about as tall as Lali. Its fur seemed loose on its body, as if it was starved. It was panting after running, saliva dripping from its open mouth, its sharp canine teeth like flint arrowheads, designed to kill. It turned and looked at Bez and growled, a deep, guttural noise that seemed to vibrate in Bez's heart. It was as if the bear hated him.

Fell's dog barked, but did not move forward.

Lali threw a stone, and it fell short. Gida said: 'Wait till we're closer.'

Then dogs came into the clearing from left and right, barking madly. One leaped at the bear, flying through the air with its teeth bared and its clawed forelegs extended. The bear swiped with a paw as big as a man's head, shockingly fast for such a big creature; the dog crashed to the ground and lay still.

The other dogs backed away.

'That was quick,' said Lali in a shaky voice.

The dogs formed a rough half-circle, pinning the bear in place with its back to the beech grove. They began to work as a team. Three or four would run at the bear from the left, then back off before it could reach them. Meanwhile others would attack from the right, running in and biting it then running away again before it had time to turn to them. The bear barked, a sound much deeper than a dog's woof, and it seemed to settle down to fight for its life.

Bez's arrows were having ominously little effect, and the same was true of the other archers. Points that hit the bear's head or chest broke through the fur and skin but seemed to bounce away without doing serious harm. The bear pulled out the ones that penetrated the flesh of its four legs. Its back would have been a good target, but most of the time the bear was upright, facing its assailants. The ideal now was a serious wound to the throat or belly, but so far it had not happened.

Eventually the bear would tire, but the dogs might tire first.

Bez moved closer, and others did the same. The arrowheads began to bite deeper. The bear bled from several wounds but continued to fight, and soon a handful of dogs lay on the ground, dead or dying. However, Bez thought, loss of blood must weaken it soon.

The bear may have figured this out. It was smart. Bez's father, long dead now, had said that the bear was the most intelligent of all the animals. But what could it do?

A moment later, Bez found out.

The bear dropped onto all fours, put down its head, and charged.

It began by jumping with all four legs, covering a lot of ground and picking up speed, then it began to gallop. The dogs chased it. It raced towards Bez and his companions. Without thinking he picked up Lali with one hand and dashed out of its way. Out of the corner of his eye he saw Fell and Gida leap in the opposite direction.

He smelt a powerful stink as the bear went by.

It did not attack anyone; it was bent on escape.

Surely, Bez thought in dismay, the beast cannot elude us now?

It crashed through the undergrowth, dodging trees and flattening everything else in its path. The dogs went after it and the people followed. The vegetation slowed the bear, and the dogs caught up with it and attacked from behind as it ran, biting its hind legs.

The noise it made now was a loud wail, like the cry of a giant baby.

The hunters came close enough to shoot arrows again, and several struck in the creature's broad back. It slowed. It was nearing its end, Bez thought hopefully.

It stood, turned, and made a weak effort to bat away the dogs. Fell's big dog leaped for the neck, slipping between the front paws, and sank its teeth into the bear's throat. The bear clawed at the dog, striping bloody cuts in its shaggy coat. But the dog's jaws were clamped and it held on. The bear went down on all fours and shook itself violently, but could not get rid of the dog. Blood poured from its throat, around the dog's muzzle and onto the trampled vegetation. The struggle went on for long moments. Then at last the bear faltered. One foreleg bent and collapsed, then the other, and it lay prone.

The dogs rushed in to eat, and the hunters quickly stepped in and kicked them away before they could spoil the carcass.

Both the bear and Fell's dog were dead.

Bez was overwhelmed with relief.

The hunters studied their kill. It was not a fat bear. Fell produced a flint knife and slit its belly. He pulled out the entrails and threw them to the dogs: their reward. They fell on the guts, tearing and eating.

Then Fell began to skin the carcass, peeling the fur back, using the knife delicately to separate the hide from the meat. The resulting coat would keep some lucky person warm next winter.

When that was done everyone could see that they had killed a skinny bear. They would cook it tonight, and there would be meat for everyone, but none left over. By tomorrow they would be hungry again.

Next morning Bez, Gida and Fell sat on the ground in the middle of the village. It was a sign that they wanted a conference. The rest of the inhabitants joined them in twos and threes, not hurrying, for woodlanders rarely hurried. They sat or lay on the ground, talking among themselves, content to wait.

When they were gathered Bez said: 'The migration of the deer could save us from starvation.'

Every spring the deer in the Great Plain went to the North-West Hills for the fresh spring grass. That meant they had to leave the shelter of the woods and cross open ground. They travelled at night, making it difficult to hunt them. However, the woodlanders would anticipate their movements and lie in wait.

Bez went on: 'But last year we did not see the usual signs warning us that the migration was about to start, and this year may be the same.'

Success depended on knowing when the deer would move. The usual indication was the appearance of new grass ripening here on the plain, but last year that had not happened – no doubt because of the drought – and the woodlanders had missed the opportunity.

'I have been told that the priestesses at the Monument know all the days of the year, and can foretell when sheep will bear lambs and when there will be berries or apples or roots to gather.'

He noticed people nodding. They had heard similar things. The priestesses were supernatural beings. Omun, the accomplished hunter, said: 'One of us should ask them.'

Bez nodded.

Omun said: 'It must be someone who speaks the herder tongue.'

Bez nodded again. Omun was making his argument for him, which was fine.

'It must be you, Bez.'

Bez said: 'I will consult the priestesses if you wish.'

Several people said: 'Yes!'

'I will go with my brother, Fell, to keep me company. He also speaks a little of the herder tongue.'

No one objected to that.

Bez said: 'It's settled, then.'

Gida said: 'Be careful.'

11

MANY FRAIL OLD people fell ill in the drought, and one of them was Soo, the high priestess. The poor diet that weakened everyone could be fatal to the elderly.

Soo stayed in her house, and Ello took her food to her. The priestesses noticed that her diet changed from the usual meat to soups and soft berries, indicating that she could no longer eat regular food, and that made them think she might be dying.

Joia was sad. Soo had seen into her heart, and had quickly recognized her need to lead a life different from the norm. Ani, Joia's mother, understood her, but Soo went farther: she accepted her.

Others felt similarly. Soo was wise and kind. There was no one quite like her in the priestess community.

One morning she asked to speak to them all, and they gathered outside her house. Joia sat with Sary, who had once been a faint-hearted novice and was now a confident woman who gathered herbs for healing potions.

Ello came out of Soo's house carrying a log, which she placed in front of the doorway. She had the confident air of one who knew her destiny.

Ello brought Soo out and helped her sit on the log. Joia was shocked by Soo's appearance. Most of her hair was gone, and her shoulders were bony. Joia could see that the other priestesses were equally upset.

'I've been here for almost sixty midsummers,' Soo began.

Her voice was faint, and they all moved closer.

She went on: 'I've survived several droughts, but I think this one will be my last.'

There was a murmur of protest. No one wanted her to go.

'I never achieved my great ambition, to rebuild the Monument in stone,' she said. 'But perhaps someone who comes after me will do that.'

She stopped and coughed, a hard, echoey cough that came from deep inside. Joia thought it had a doom-like sound, something a person might not recover from. She looked at Sary, who nodded discreetly: she, too, had sensed the seriousness of that cough.

'As for the question of who comes after me, you must decide that. Remember that you must have a consensus. A high priestess needs to begin with the wholehearted support of everyone.'

Joia was daunted by the thought of getting them all to agree. Right now there were twenty-eight priestesses, not including novices, who had no say in the choice of a high priestess.

Then Soo said: 'But it must be obvious to all of you that there is only one serious candidate: Ello, who is already second high priestess.'

Joia was dismayed. Ello was unkind. She would change the atmosphere of the Monument. She would be a tyrant.

Soo was wrong: it was not obvious that Ello should succeed her. And a dying high priestess did not have the right to choose her successor.

'I strongly recommend—' Soo started to cough again. This time it went on. Eventually she made a gesture to Ello, who helped her back inside.

The priestesses immediately broke into conversation. Sary said to Joia: 'I'm not sure there's only one suitable candidate.'

Joia was glad someone else had had the same reaction as she had. 'Ello has put Soo up to this.'

'Ello and Soo have been lovers since before you and I were born. Perhaps Ello was once cheerful and kind, and Soo still adores the girl Ello used to be. Anyway, Soo wants to bequeath the position of high priestess to her lifelong darling. It's sweet, but we don't have to go along with it.'

'True.' Joia wanted to think more about this before getting into any discussions. There was, in fact, a second obvious candidate, and it was Joia herself. The question was what she should do about it.

For her, the issue was not just who would be high priestess. It was about rebuilding the Monument in stone. It was now almost ten midsummers since Dallo had persuaded everyone that the task was impossible. Now was the time to try again.

She needed to talk to Seft.

She found him harvesting timber. He had felled an ash tree, its hard wood preferred for construction, and was now trimming it, using a long-handled axe with a large shiny blade of black floorstone flint. With him was his eldest child, Ilian, soon to see his tenth midsummer. He was using a flint knife to cut thin, leafy branches from the felled tree to be used as fodder for cattle. Ilian was strong for his age, and already shaping up to be a good carpenter, as Seft would say proudly to anyone who would listen.

Seft stopped work when Joia approached. She greeted him and said: 'The high priestess is dying.'

'Soo? I'm sorry to hear that.'

'This could be the moment to revive the project of a stone

Monument. If Ello becomes high priestess, it won't happen. If I'm chosen, it will.'

'Good!' said Seft. 'What must we do?'

'We need to convince the priestesses that now is the time. If they accept that, they'll want me as their leader.'

Seft put down his axe and sat on the trunk of the ash tree. Joia sat beside him. Seft said: 'We can tell them that I've determined the best route for transporting the stones from Stony Valley to the Monument.'

'And that's important.'

'But what if they ask where we will find the people to drag the stones?'

'I've been thinking about that. The population of Riverbend is about four hundred, but if we take away the children, the old, those who are sick or away at the time, and the disabled, it comes to fewer than two hundred, which is not enough. So we need people from elsewhere.'

'How would we manage that?'

'Four times a year we have a huge influx of outsiders, for the Rites. The most popular is the Midsummer Rite, when we sometimes have a thousand.'

'I don't understand these priestess numbers.'

'A thousand is far more than we need to pull a stone.'

'But how would we persuade them to help us?' Seft was a master of inanimate objects such as trees and rivers, but he could not manipulate people.

However, Joia could. 'I'll speak to them after the Rite. I'll tell them that this is a holy mission, something the gods want us to do. I'll say it's an extension of the Rite and of the celebrations that go with the Rite, including the revel. I'll tell them that we're going to sing and dance as we march to Stony Valley. They'll love the idea, especially the young ones.'

Seft nodded. 'I can imagine.'

'We could do it every year, after the Midsummer Rite, a few stones a year until we have enough.'

'People might look forward to the march the way they look forward to the Rite.'

'I'm sure they will.'

Seft nodded. 'So,' he said, 'we have to put this to the priestesses?'

'Yes.'

'When?'

'Let's keep it to ourselves while Soo is alive. Then, after her funeral, when the priestesses start to think seriously about her successor, we'll speak to them together.'

'Very good,' said Seft.

Joia left him, feeling bucked, and headed back to the Monument.

Duna was waiting for her. A promising novice, she was a jolly girl with a lovely singing voice. Today Joia had to teach her about eclipses. She put everything else out of her mind.

'Eclipses of the sun and moon are portents,' Joia said. 'They herald floods, plagues and earthquakes. A year of no eclipses is a peaceful one. A year with many is dangerous. So we need to know what dangerous years are coming.'

Instead of entering the central timber circle, Joia led Duna to the outer circle of bluestones that stood just inside the bank. Each stone was taller than a tall man. Duna said: 'How did these big stones get here? They must be awfully heavy.'

'No one really knows,' said Joia. 'Perhaps they came upriver on boats.'

'Then they had to be brought from the river to here.'

'It happened long before anyone alive today was born. But the stones must have been dragged across the ground, presumably with ropes.'

'It sounds very difficult.'

'Certainly.' This was an interesting discussion, but Joia had a lesson to teach. 'Did you notice how many bluestones there are?'

'Yes,' Duna said eagerly. 'Fifty-six.'

'Well done.'

'We were told we had to know the number of everything we see,' Duna admitted.

'A good principle for a priestess. Now, most of our dances take place around the timber circle, and they tell us about the sun. And bluestones numbers twenty-eight and fifty-six are in line with the rising sun on Midsummer Day. But, despite that, the circle is mostly about the moon. And the number fifty-six is very important in the study of the moon.'

Joia did not know why the Moon Goddess had picked that special number. Fifty-six was twice twenty-eight, and a lot of people vaguely thought that twenty-eight days was a lunar month, but that was not quite right: the cycle from one new moon to the next was twenty-nine and a half days.

Nevertheless, the people who had performed the giant task of bringing the bluestones to the Monument had known the goddess's secret numbers, and Joia was now going to explain them to Duna.

'You see that a large pottery disc has been placed at the foot of some of the stones.'

'Six of the stones,' Duna said.

'Well done. Can you figure out the arrangement of discs?'

'Yes,' Duna said eagerly. 'There's a disc at every ninth stone. No, every tenth! No . . .'

Joia put her out of her misery. 'The intervals are nine, nine, ten, nine, nine, ten. If you add them up, it comes to fifty-six.'

'Oh!'

'We move each disc backwards one place every year. It's a special dance that's always done at night, to the full moon.'

Duna nodded. She understood, Joia could see, but she was wondering what was the point of it all.

Joia said: 'Whenever there is a disc at stone number twenty-eight or stone number fifty-six, there will be a year of eclipse, certainly of the moon and perhaps of the sun.'

Duna was impressed. 'But what can we do? We can't stop floods or prevent plagues.'

'We tell people to be cautious. Don't start a war, don't move to a new house, don't voyage across water. Don't take unnecessary risks. They appreciate the advice.'

Duna looked hesitant, then said: 'Can I ask you about something else?'

This often happened. The novices Joia taught would ask her for advice on personal problems, assuming she was an expert on those too. 'Let's sit down,' she said, and she led the way to the bank. 'What's on your mind?'

'It's Ello.'

Joia groaned inwardly. She knew what was coming. 'Go on.'

'She came to me at bedtime and asked me to go to the empty house with her.'

Most people did not care if they were observed making love, unless they were doing something shameful – such as seducing young people. Ello would not care to be watched by disapproving eyes. It would spoil her pleasure. So she contrived to keep one house empty for her trysts.

Making the situation perfectly clear, Duna said: 'Ello wants to have sex with me.'

'You're a very attractive girl.'

Tears came to Duna's eyes. 'I'm sorry, but I don't like her.'

'Don't worry.' Joia patted her shoulder. 'You don't have to have sex with her if you don't want to.'

'Don't I?' Duna found this hard to believe.

'Absolutely not.'

'She's insistent. She grabbed my hand and pulled. It hurt.'

'Oh dear.' This was a pattern with Ello. About once a year she would develop a crush on a novice, then use her position as second high priestess to intimidate the poor girl. A few novices had left, giving no very strong reason, and Joia suspected they had done it to escape Ello.

Joia had complained to Soo about this, but Soo had done nothing. Formidable though Soo was, she would forgive Ello anything.

Joia said: 'If she asks again, tell her you've spoken to me, and I've said you can refuse her.'

'Will that stop her?'

'It has in the past. But if she continues to pester you, tell me, and I'll speak to her myself.'

'Thank you so much.'

I can't let Ello become the high priestess, Joia thought. She would be even more powerful. She would bully more youngsters. I have to do something about this, regardless of what happens about the stone Monument.

Duna said: 'You're so kind. And smart, too. You should be high priestess.'

'People would think I'm a bit young,' Joia said, with false modesty.

Duna shook her head. 'All the novices love you. You're so beautiful.'

Joia smiled. She did not think she was beautiful.

Duna said: 'Any of us would have sex with you if you wanted.'

Joia's heart sank. She knew what was coming next. She had had this conversation before, more than once. Duna was about to declare her love.

She acted quickly to divert the conversation. 'Let me tell you something,' she said. Duna's hand had wandered to her knee, and she gently took it off. 'My mother has been a widow for seventeen midsummers. When my father, Olin, died, everyone told her she should look around for another man she could love. She never did.'

'Why not? It's what most women would do.'

'She says that some of us love only one person in a lifetime. My father was that one, for her. She can't bring herself to want anyone else. Another man would always be a disappointment, no matter how lovable he was, just because he wouldn't be Olin. So she has remained single – even on the night of the revel.'

'Such love!'

'She says she's a one-man woman. I'm like her. I'm not sure if it's a man or a woman I'm waiting for, but I know I haven't yet met the one for me. And when I do, I'll be happy.'

Bez and Fell set out with high hopes. With the help of the priestesses they might save the tribe.

Fell was wearing a necklace he had made from the teeth of the bear they had killed. The four huge curved fangs were particularly striking.

Bez had made the trip across the Great Plain twice before. He always marvelled at how the herders worked all the time, men and women and children too. The farmers were worse. What was the point, when there were deer in the woods and nuts on the trees?

The deer and nuts were scarce now, but the herders and farmers were no better off than the woodlanders. Bez was shocked to see the skinny corpses of cattle that had died of thirst or starvation dotting the Great Plain, casualties of the battle with the weather.

'Herders have all kinds of rules about sex,' Bez said conversationally, as they walked. 'They can't go with their aunt or their half-sister or their brother.'

'What's the point of such rules? Why don't they just go with any willing man or woman, as we do? What's the harm?'

Bez shook his head. 'You know, sometimes herder women want to have sex with woodlanders.'

'Oh! Disgusting! They're so ugly, with their pointy noses and their pale eyes.'

'And they have skinny legs like deer.'

They both laughed.

On the first evening they did what Bez had done on previous trips: they walked into one of the little herder settlements, looked for someone who was cooking, and sat down by their fire. Sooner or later, Bez expected, they would be handed bowls just as if they belonged there.

That had never worked with the farmers and now, they found, it no longer worked with herders. The man cooking explained to him: 'It's the drought. We have rations, only just enough for ourselves. If we share, we go hungry. I'm sorry.'

Next morning they found some wild onions, which they ate while walking. In the evening Fell's new dog killed a month-old roe deer fawn and dragged it proudly to him. They cooked it that night and shared it with the dog.

Woodlanders rarely hurried, and it was noon on the third day when they reached the Monument.

At the times of the Rites the place was busy, with people trading outside the earth bank, but now it seemed deserted. Probably everyone was at the nearby village of Riverbend, the largest settlement on the plain. But the priestesses should be here. Bez led the way to the village where they lived.

He felt nervous. This would be such an important conversation, and he had to make himself understood in the herder language. No one among the herders or farmers could speak the woodlander tongue. He knew that the most important of the priestesses was called the high priestess, and he decided he would speak to her.

The priestesses were not in their houses – few people lived inside in warm weather, houses were for winter – and Bez and Fell found a cluster of women sitting on the ground in the middle of the little settlement. All were wearing the long tunics that marked them as priestesses. Bez and Fell were wearing the short tunics that most herders and farmers wore. They had put them on for the trip: in summer they normally wore nothing but a leather loincloth.

Bez was glad to have found the women so quickly.

They went quiet when they saw the woodlanders. One woman sitting with her back to Bez and Fell turned around and screamed with fright; but the others laughed at her, and after a moment she joined in the merriment.

They quietened down, and a small but confident woman said: 'Hello. Do you need something?'

Bez said carefully: 'May the Sun God smile on you.'

'And on you,' she replied.

'Are you the high priestess?'

They all laughed.

'I'm not the high priestess, no. My name is Sary.'

'I'm Bez and this is my brother, Fell. Can you take us to the high priestess? It's very urgent.'

'The high priestess is old and very ill. I'm afraid she won't be able to talk to you.'

This was a setback. Fell spoke to Bez in the woodlander language. 'What did she say? I didn't understand.'

'The high priestess is too ill to talk to us.'

'Then we must talk to someone else.'

Bez turned back to the woman called Sary. 'Is there someone else? We need to know about the migration of the deer.'

The women talked among themselves, and Bez understood one of them to say: 'Ello knows everything.'

The others seemed to agree, and the one who had become their spokesperson said: 'The second high priestess might help you. Her name is Ello.'

'Can you take us to her?'

'Of course.'

Bez was relieved.

Sary led them to one of the small houses. She looked inside and said: 'Two woodlanders called Bez and Fell are here, asking to speak to you.'

Bez could not hear the reply, and worried that it might have been negative. He poked his head inside. He saw a very old woman lying down, and a middle-aged woman beside her. The younger of the two must be Ello, he guessed. She got up, and he stepped back.

Ello came out. Bez saw right away that she did not have a kind face. He said: 'May the Sun God smile on you.'

She ignored that. 'What do you want?'

'We're from the place you call West Wood. Our tribe is starving because of the drought and—'

Ello interrupted him. 'It's the same for everyone. You're wasting your time here. We can't give you food.'

Bez was offended that she assumed he was a beggar. He stood straight and looked her in the eye. 'We're not here to ask for food. We will be able to feed ourselves when the deer migrate, which should be soon. But we can't tell exactly when. You priestesses know all the days of the year, I've been told. Is that true? Can you tell when the deer will start on their journey to the North-West Hills?'

The woman's face hardened. 'We're not here to serve you.' The way she said it was disdainful. 'The herders feed us, and we give them information, but you people give us nothing. I'm not obliged to help you. I've got enough to do.' She turned her back.

Bez abandoned his pride. 'Please,' he said. 'We're starving and all we're asking for is information.'

Ello went inside and blocked the doorway with a hurdle.

Sary looked embarrassed. 'I'm sorry,' she said, and she walked away.

Bez was distraught. They had come all this way just to meet with a flat refusal. He dreaded the thought of going home and reporting failure.

Fell said: 'What shall we do now?'

'I don't know.' It must be nice to be the younger brother, Bez thought. In a crisis you ask what you should do and wait for the answer. 'I suppose we'd better go to Riverbend.'

'They won't feed us – we know that.'

Bez scratched his head. 'They might trade, though.'

'We've got nothing to trade.'

Bez looked at Fell's throat.

Fell touched the necklace of bear's teeth. 'No.'

'If it's that or starve?'

Fell looked as if he might weep, but he nodded assent.

'Let's go.'

They headed along the path that led from the Monument to Riverbend. They walked with heads bowed. They were disheartened and very hungry.

Bez was contemplating theft. If he saw a way of stealing food without getting caught, he would do it, he decided. His brother loved that necklace.

Last time he visited Riverbend it had had a bustling, prosperous air, with well-fed men and women cheerfully making pots and tools and leather. There had been pigs everywhere, he recalled, noisy and smelly. Now the village had a shrivelled look. People were skinny and seemed tired. In places they were waiting with bowls and pots to receive a measured quantity of meat.

Bez went up to a man who was doling it out. 'May the Sun God smile on you,' he said.

'You can't have any of this,' said the man. 'Sorry.'

'Would you trade?' Bez persisted. 'We can offer my brother's necklace.'

The man laughed, though not unkindly. 'I can't eat a necklace,' he said.

Bez looked at the people in line. 'Anyone?' he said. 'A necklace of bear's teeth for some meat?'

No one wanted to trade. Bez felt completely dispirited.

A passer-by who had been watching spoke to Bez. He was a tall young man with big feet in shoes that were sewn differently from what was usual. 'You men are really in trouble, aren't you?' he said quietly.

Bez nodded.

'Come with me. I may be able to help.'

As they walked he said: 'My sister sometimes gets game – hares, squirrels, pigeons – that aren't covered by rationing. People give them to her man. She might be able to feed you something without taking it from her children's rations.'

He led them to a house outside which a woman who faintly resembled him was cooking. Bez greeted her politely and gave his name and Fell's. She was called Neen, and her kind-hearted brother was Han.

When Han told her about the woodlanders trying to trade a necklace for food, she said: 'I'm making a stew of a small hare. There's not much meat, but you are welcome to some.'

They both nodded eagerly.

She gave them each a spoon and filled two bowls. They drank the fatty broth and chewed the morsels of meat. Bez felt better, until he remembered how he had failed in his mission.

Han asked where they were from, and when they told him, he said: 'You came all this way to trade a necklace?'

'No,' Bez said. 'We're hoping to hunt deer when they begin their migration, but we can't figure out when they will move. You have to be ready for them, otherwise you can miss them. We thought the priestesses would be able to tell us.'

'I'm sure they could. That's just the kind of thing they know.'

'Well, they wouldn't help us.'

Han looked as though he did not believe them. 'But that's what they're there for – to tell people the days of the year.'

'She would not advise us because woodlanders do not give the priestesses food.'

'That's silly. Which priestess did you see?'

'Her name was Ello.'

'Oh, now I understand,' said Han. 'That woman has a mean streak.'

'I can believe it.'

'Listen, don't give up hope. I have another sister, who is a priestess. Her name is Joia.'

Bez brightened. 'Do you think she would advise us?'

'She'll help you if she can, I know it. She's not like Ello.'

Bez said fervently: 'Please take us to her!'

'Come on.'

They stood up. Bez thanked Neen for the stew. He knew that the herders were keen on small courtesies.

Bez and Fell walked with Han through the village and on to the pathway that led back to the Monument. The woodlanders had to hurry to keep up with Han's long-legged stride. That was how the herders were, always in a rush even when there was no reason.

They reached the priestesses' village and Han quickly found his sister. Bez immediately liked the look of Joia. She had a lot of curly dark hair and a lovely smile. He felt she must be a generous person.

Han said: 'Bez and Fell have something to ask you.'

Bez explained: 'Every year in the spring we hunt the deer as they go on their annual migration to the North-West Hills. It's important to have prior knowledge of when they're going to move, so that we can lie in wait. Usually we know by the spring grass on the plain, but that sign is no longer reliable, because of the drought. However, people say that priestesses know all the days of the year. Do you know when the deer will move?'

'I think so,' said Joia.

Bez did not understand that. Either she knew or she did not.

She sensed his bewilderment and explained: 'We have a song about all the natural things that happen in a year: the summer berries, the green beetles, the mushrooms, the birds flying south, the spring flowers, the birds' eggs . . . I know the deer are in there somewhere.'

Han said impatiently: 'Well, can you remember, or not?' It was what Bez had wanted to say, but he was too polite.

Joia said: 'I'll have to sing the song. Come with me.'

They followed her into the Monument. Her song began with Midsummer Day, the first day of the year. Although she was small in stature, her voice seemed to carry all around the circle. As she sang, she danced around the Monument, touching the timber uprights, passing through the narrow gaps between them. Bez was rapt. She sang of summer, autumn and winter. At last she came to the season he was interested in, spring. He waited in suspense, then she sang:

Forty-eight days from the Spring Halfway, the deer go north to the hills,

Two days sooner if the spring is fine, two days later if the weather's bad

She stopped there.

Bez said in frustration: 'I understood everything except the first word.'

'Forty-eight?'

Han said: 'I didn't get that one either.'

'Forty-eight days is four herder weeks,' Joia said. That satisfied Han but Bez was still in exasperated ignorance. He had the answer and he could not understand it.

'I can simplify it for you,' Joia said to Bez. 'Forty-eight days from the Spring Rite is five days from now. The drought is very bad weather, so we add two days, making it seven.'

Bez was still baffled. 'We don't have those number words,' he said. It was maddening. She had the information he needed but they could not communicate.

Joia said patiently: 'Shall I show you how to count on your fingers?'

Bez nodded. That was how herders counted, he knew, on their fingers and toes and other parts of their bodies. Woodlanders never seemed to need that skill – but now he did.

'Give me your hands. Make fists, gently.' She pulled his left thumb and four fingers straight, then added two fingers of his right hand. Touching them in turn, she said: 'Tomorrow. The next day. The day after that. Another day. Another day. Another day. And then . . .' Holding the seventh finger, she said: 'This day you hunt.'

Bez repeated what she had said. Then he showed his hands to Fell, saying: 'Remember this, in case I forget,' and he again repeated what Joia had said.

Fell made the same shapes with his own hands and repeated the words. Then he said: 'I'll remember.'

They were elated. They had the answer to their question. Their trip was not a failure after all.

Joia said: 'One more thing. The sun and the moon aren't fickle – they always rise and set when we expect it – but the animals and plants are not so reliable. My date for the deer is likely to be right, but it's not as certain as tomorrow's sunrise.'

Bez understood. A deer might come to drink at a pond every night for a week and then, the night you lay in wait to kill it, it would not appear. He was prepared for disappointment.

He said: 'I thank you, Priestess Joia, and all my tribe thank you, too.'

Joia said: 'I wish you luck.'

Soo died that night.

Ello came and woke the other priestesses before dawn, but she would not let anyone help her wash the body for cremation. She wept constantly, inconsolably.

The priestesses built a funeral pyre inside the oval. At dawn six of them made a cradle with their linked hands and carried the body from the house to the pyre, laying Soo down with her head towards the east, while everyone sang to the Sun God.

Ello put a torch to the pyre.

Then they stood in solemn silence. Joia thought anxiously about what lay ahead. Soo had been high priestess for all of Joia's time here – nearly ten midsummers. This would be a big change. The most important thing, for Joia and for the people of the Great Plain, was that the knowledge of the days of the year should be preserved for future generations. That must happen whether the new high priestess was Joia or Ello or someone else. The more they knew, the better they would be able to manage the crises that life threw at them.

Many priestesses wept now, as smoke rose and the flames devoured the corpse. When the edge of the sun peeped over the horizon, the priestesses began a new song, asking the spirit of the wind to cherish the ashes of the high priestess. Soon there was little left, and the sun was up. The funeral was over.

Ello returned to her house, still weeping. The others went to the large rectangular building that served as a dining hall. The novices put out smoked pork and a salad of chickweed leaves. Everyone sat on the floor to eat and discuss who should be the next high priestess.

The younger priestesses favoured Joia. Others said tactfully that a high priestess needed the wisdom that comes with age. The humbler among them felt that they should obey the dying wish of Soo.

Then Seft came in.

The conversation went quiet, and everyone looked at Joia. They knew that Seft was her sister's man, as well as the leader of the cleverhands.

Joia said: 'I asked Seft to come here this morning for a special reason. If, after long discussion, you should decide to ask me to be high priestess, I would want to rebuild the Monument in stone. If I could not do that, I would not want to be high priestess.'

She paused to let them take that in.

She resumed: 'Ten years ago we were persuaded, by Dallo, that it was impossible. But Seft is not Dallo, and he and I think it is possible to build a stone Monument. If you wish, we will tell you why.'

Some looked dubious but everyone was curious.

Joia noticed one of the older priestesses slipping out, and guessed she had gone to tell Ello what was happening.

Seft said: 'I've surveyed the territory between Stony Valley and here, and I believe I've found the best route for transporting the stones. Stony Valley is in the North Hills, and we would have to cope with some ups and downs, but we can avoid the steeper hills. After that there is a stretch of the plain, then we come to Upriver. From there we travel along the bank of East River, which is flat. Just before Riverbend we turn onto the plain for the last stretch.'

This practical talk made the project seem real and possible.

Joia then said: 'We estimate that it will take two hundred people to move one of the giant sarsen stones in Stony Valley. Seft naturally asked me where we would get the people.'

At that point Ello walked in.

Joia said smoothly: 'I'm so glad you've joined us, Second High Priestess. I was about to explain where we would find the necessary people to drag the giant stones for the rebuilding of the Monument.'

'I'd be most interested to know,' said Ello, with a hint of sarcasm.

'It's simple,' Joia said. 'We recruit the visitors who come to the Midsummer Rite. We tell them this is a holy mission – which it is – and that the celebrations, including the revel, are being extended for a few more days. They will love the idea. It will appeal particularly to the young – and strong.'

It appealed to the priestesses, too. People liked any kind of expedition. They talked excitedly among themselves for a few moments, then Ello interrupted. 'May I say something?' she said. She did not need permission, of course, but she was pretending to feel usurped.

She waited for a reply, so Joia said: 'We're eager to hear what you have to say, as always.' She could be sarcastic too.

Ello said: 'I'm remembering the day, ten years ago or more,

when Dallo and the cleverhands moved a big stone for the farmer on the other side of the East River.'

Joia remembered it too. Her calculations about moving giant stones from Stony Valley were mostly based on what had happened that day.

Ello went on: 'I think I heard you say that the Midsummer Rite festivities would be extended for a few days.'

'Yes.'

'I'm wondering whether a few days will be long enough. It took twenty men all afternoon to move that stone from the middle of the field to the riverbank – about the distance of an arrow's flight.'

Joia nodded. That was right.

Ello said: 'The Stony Valley stones are much bigger, but you hope to have two hundred people to move each one. For the moment, leave aside the question of whether you really can muster two hundred volunteers. Assume that you will move your giant stone at about the same speed as the twenty people moved the farmer's stone the distance of an arrow shot. Now, how many arrow shots are there between here and Stony Valley? A hundred? Two hundred? It's a key question, because the number of arrow shots is the number of afternoons. A hundred arrow shots would take a hundred afternoons, or fifty days.'

Joia had not done this calculation and she was floored. Could she persuade volunteers to give up fifty days?

But Ello had not finished. 'Everyone here knows that the outer timber circle of the Monument consists of thirty upright posts and thirty crossbars. The inner oval is five triliths, which is another fifteen timbers. You are talking about bringing seventy-five giant stones from Stony Valley to the Monument.'

She paused. 'You can all do arithmetic, but that calculation may be hard for you, so I'll tell you. If your two hundred volunteers work non-stop, it will take them three thousand seven hundred and fifty days, or a little more than ten years.'

Joia knew then that she had lost. If it took fifty days to bring one stone, the Monument would never be rebuilt in stone. And now that everyone knew that, she would not be made high priestess.

The conversation continued among the priestesses, but the issue had been settled. Ello left the building, looking dignified, probably concealing great delight that she had squashed Joia. Soon after that, a defeated Seft took his leave.

Joia spent the rest of the day quietly, doing chores, not talking much, getting used to her downfall. But she continued to worry about how Ello would behave as high priestess. That problem had not gone away. She decided she would speak to her, and she thought hard about what she could say.

She went to Ello's house in the late afternoon. Ello was sitting on the leather mat, her eyes red with tears. Joia said: 'This is a sad day for all of us.'

Ello said: 'What do you want?'

'You're going to be the high priestess.'

'Yes.'

'But there's a problem.'

'What – that you want the position?'

'The problem is your relations with young novices, and what you do in the empty house.'

Ello's response was indignant. 'How dare you?'

Joia shot back: 'How dare *you*?'

They stared at one another. Ello was the first to look away.

Joia said: 'We should care for our young people, not use them for our pleasure. When you are high priestess you cannot use the power and prestige of the office to seduce and coerce youngsters. It's just wrong.'

Ello looked both angry and guilty. 'What do you want me to say?'

'I want you to solemnly promise that you will cease your ways.'

'Oh, very well, if you insist.'

'Don't say it lightly. I shall hold you to it. From now on, every novice is going to know that she is not obliged to have sex with anyone, even the high priestess. I am going to move into the empty house, so there will be nowhere for you to indulge your obsession. And if you ever break your promise I will reveal it to everyone and hold a meeting to decide what to do about it.' Joia knew that she could do such a thing, even though she held no official rank: she was still sufficiently popular and revered to wield personal authority.

Ello was furious. 'You wicked woman.'

Joia went on remorselessly: 'There will be nowhere for you to hide, Ello.'

Ello began to cry. 'I'm an ugly old woman,' she sobbed. 'No one will love me, now that Soo's gone.'

Joia did not know what to say to this collapse. She could fight with Ello, but could not sympathize with her. She might tell Ello that people would love her if she was nice to them, but that would do no good. Ello had been set in her ways for decades, and she was not going to change just because Joia told her to.

She said: 'I hope I've made myself clear.'

'Get out,' said Ello. 'I wish you were dead.'

Gida gave instructions for the hunt. 'We're going to lie up in the gap between Little Wood and Alder Wood. The deer always cross that gap because it's the shortest way from one wood to the other.

There's a dip where, if we lie down, we will be invisible to the herd as it approaches. Now, some of you have not taken part in this hunt before, so let me remind you how we do it. No talking! Deer can hear well. And, most important of all, no pissing or shitting. A deer can smell a fart a mile away. If you need to go, walk to North Wood. It's not far, but the vegetation will keep the stink in.'

They laughed at that. Gida had a nice touch, Bez thought. She gave orders in a tone that suggested she was just being helpful.

Gida went on: 'When the deer come towards us, wait. If you show yourself too soon, they may turn back, and then we won't get any venison. We've got people both sides of Little Wood, ready to get behind the deer and scare them. When that happens, you'll hear the hoofbeats as they run, heading for the sanctuary of North Wood. But we'll be waiting for them.'

A young man piped up: 'When do we kill them?'

'Leave it as late as possible. When you stand up, the deer will try to veer around you. If you show yourself too soon, they will succeed. The ideal is that they pass you so close that you have a perfect chance to bring them down with an axe or a hammer. Are we ready?'

They were ready.

'And let's go quietly, please.'

They set off, heading north out of West Wood as the sun sank towards the western edge of the Great Plain, and reached the place where they would hide in the time it took to boil a pot of water.

On Gida's instructions they spread out in a loose line. Soon it was twilight, the moment the deer would break cover – if Joia's forecast was right and they were now on the move. If not, nothing would happen.

Bez and his tribe were all very hungry – so hungry that they were talking of eating fish, considered disgusting by herders and farmers as well as woodlanders.

Or they would die. Death was not so bad. It happened to everyone sooner or later. Better not to waste your life worrying about it, as farmers and herders did. Enjoy life while it's good and accept the end when it comes.

So thought Bez, except when he saw hungry children. Among the woodlanders, the responsibility for taking care of a child belonged to every adult in the tribe. Each child was your child, which was sensible as men never knew for sure which children they had sired. It was one of the very few obligations a woodlander had, and to fail at it brought shame.

Bez was lying flat, staring at the distant wood in the shadowy dusk. Was Joia right? Were the deer on the move today? Soon he would know.

He thought he saw movement, and a few moments later several deer emerged. Bez knew immediately that they were the small roe deer, not the giant red deer. They were not much taller than a big dog, and their antlers were small, usually straight with one or two tines. Bez's identification was confirmed when one turned around and showed a white rump patch. The red deer did not have that.

Roe deer did not form large herds, preferring to live in small family groups, but Bez could see eight or nine, and he guessed that three families had come together, perhaps by accident, for the migration. This was good enough, and better than nothing by far.

It might have been a problem if another tribe had arrived to share the location. Nine roe deer would provide a feast for one tribe, but a meagre dinner for two.

The deer seemed to hesitate, then decide they were on the right track, and they set off across the plain towards where the tribe was hiding.

Someone said: 'Here they come!'

Bez hissed: 'Quiet!'

Once the beasts got started they walked briskly, not stopping to graze the sparse brown grass. More so than the red deer, they were uncomfortable in open country and preferred dense cover.

As they came nearer, Bez felt the tension in the group, and hoped the deer could not sense it.

Then he heard the dogs, distant but unmistakable. The deer heard them too, and began to trot, mildly worried but not panicking. They knew they could run faster than dogs.

The beasts were lean, but there was meat on them.

Bez put an arrow to his bow. Just a few moments to go.

As the dogs came closer, the deer began to run.

'Not yet, not yet,' Bez whispered, though no one could hear him.

The hooves were pounding now.

Over to Bez's left, someone jumped up too early: an adolescent boy, he saw out of the corner of his eye. The boy shot an arrow that did not hit anything. It was nervousness, Bez knew; it often happened. He stood up and quickly scanned the group of deer. They had divided, some heading to one side of the boy, some to the other. The mistake was not fatal; the deer were still moving forward.

Everyone was up now, and the deer were almost on them. Hunters on the wings of the line ran to the middle, trying to form a circular trap. A buck tried to pass by Bez, who saw his chance and shot an arrow at close quarters into the animal's throat. It ran on a few paces then fell.

There was no time to put it out of its misery because another beast, this one a doe, was coming straight at him, head lowered. There was an arrow stuck in its rump that did not seem to be slowing it. Too late to shoot another arrow, Bez drew a club from his belt and struck, aiming to break the beast's foreleg. The deer stumbled and fell.

And then it was over. The deer were dead or dying, all but one, which had got through the killing line and was now galloping alone into Alder Wood.

There were eight deer on the ground, enough to feed the entire tribe with more left over for tomorrow. Bez felt a glow of satisfaction. The tribe was saved.

Tomorrow they would continue north-west, hurrying to get ahead of the deer so that they could lie in wait again. In this leapfrogging way they would go on to the North-West Hills, where the deer would graze the new grass and the tribe would eat the deer.

He saw Gida gazing at the beasts, no doubt thinking what he was thinking, and he went up to her and put his arm around her shoulders. She looked up at him and smiled, and he kissed her.

People started to make fires, using dry twigs and branches from Alder Wood, lighting them by striking a spark with flint against the yellowish firestone. They cleaned and skinned the deer, and before long the livers were being toasted on sticks, a special treat for the children. The aroma made Bez's mouth water.

He sat by Fell and Gida while waiting for the meat to roast. Fell said: 'We owe a lot to that priestess, Joia. She told us true.'

Bez said: 'I think we're beholden to the brother, Han, the one with the big shoes. He saw us in trouble and helped us. It's the kind of behaviour you expect from one of your tribe. You don't often get it from a stranger.'

Gida nodded. 'He acted like a tribesman.'

Bez said: 'He's one of us.'

12

PIA HAD HOPED she might get used to living with Stam, but a few days had shown her that it would never happen.

He was a hard worker, and he was able to bring water from the river to the fields twice as fast as Yana and Pia. He did so willingly, happy to demonstrate his superiority. His and their efforts were being rewarded: green shoots were appearing in the furrows, and they had had to get a dog to chase off the hares and other creatures that would eat the crop before it had fully grown.

Stam was also a good shot. He brought down birds using a club-headed arrow that did not damage the meat, and they often had lapwing, swan, heron and fat little woodcocks to supplement their meagre diet.

So far Stam had heeded Yana's warning against violence. She had been very scary at that moment. People still talked about it, the men with outrage, the women with awestruck admiration. Stam had not forgotten it. He was almost subdued when Yana spoke to him, and he never disagreed or argued with her.

Perhaps he was used to taking orders, having been brought up by Troon.

That was the good side.

He was greedy, eating as much as he wanted, then leaving the rest for the women. He was big and clumsy, always bumping into people and things. And he smelt bad.

Every night Pia heard him having sex with her mother. Yana was silent, but Stam made a lot of noise, grunting and groaning. It had been different with Pia's father. They had murmured words, Yana giggling and Alno chuckling. The two had been equally enthusiastic. With Stam the pleasure was clearly all on one side.

Worse, he made a pass at Pia every chance he got. He had not forced the issue, and now she avoided being alone with him; but she was afraid that one day he would catch her unprotected, hold her down and rape her.

When she felt unhappy she turned her thoughts to Han. Soon she would see him at the Midsummer Rite, with his fair hair and his enormous shoes. It would be only two or three days, but it would be like a rehearsal for the rest of their lives. They would eat together and sleep together, and if she became pregnant she would be even happier.

When they became a couple she would leave Farmplace. She was firmly resolved. Troon would be furious, but she was not a prisoner. And she longed to get away from the farmer community. Since Troon became Big Man it had got more rigid. And in the drought people were too afraid of losing their livelihoods to resist him.

Her only regret would be leaving her mother. But she cherished a hope that perhaps one day Yana, too, would flee from Farmplace, leaving Stam behind.

One evening Stam went to shoot woodcocks, which came out at dusk to eat beetles and worms in the fields. Pia and Yana were milking the goats when they were approached by Mo.

She looked scared. Pia said: 'Hello, Mo, what's the matter?' and Mo burst into tears.

This was uncharacteristic. She managed to say: 'Troon is a pig.'

'What has he done?'

'He says I have to partner with Deg.'

Deg was Bort's milk-and-water son. Pia was shocked. 'But the rule only applies to widows!'

Yana said: 'That's the way it's always been. But Troon is changing the rules.'

'I can't partner with Deg,' Mo said in despair. 'He's an empty space that should have been filled with a man.'

Yana said: 'When I proposed to Bort he turned me down.'

'Lucky you,' Mo said bitterly. Anger began to take over from tears. 'Unfortunately, Deg is willing.'

'What are you going to do?'

'I don't know. That's why I've come here. Yana, tell me honestly, what's it like being with someone you don't like and never could?'

Yana hesitated, looked at Pia, looked away again, and said: 'I'm going to tell you the truth.'

Pia wondered what was coming.

Yana said: 'I hate my life.'

Pia was shocked. Although Yana had made no secret about her dislike of Stam, she had put on a brave face and tried to live a normal life without complaining. Now Pia realized it had all been an act.

Mo looked grim. 'That's what I'm afraid of.'

Yana went on: 'He's a boy, and a very unpleasant one. At night he puts his tongue in my mouth and his cock in my cunt, and doesn't speak until he's spurted inside me. Then he goes to sleep. I don't think he really cares who he's in bed with. If I didn't have Pia, I'd jump in the river and drown. There, Mo, now you know.'

Pia was horrified. This was much worse than she had known.

Mo was downcast. 'I was afraid it would be like that. I'm sure I could hardly bear to have sex with Deg.'

'It might not be very often.'

Mo shook her head. 'I have to run away.'

'Troon will go after you.'

'I can evade him. I'll travel by night and sleep in the woods by day. The Great Plain is a big place – he can't search all of it.'

Yana said practically: 'Is there someone who might help you?'

Mo nodded. 'Last year at the Midsummer Rite I spent the night with a herder called Yaran. I talked to him this year at the Spring Rite. He likes me.'

'Don't tell anyone else his name.'

'Good point. I'm no good at deceit. I'm in the habit of saying what I think.'

'Then don't speak to people,' Yana said. 'You've confided in us, but don't tell anyone else.'

'I'm going to go tonight. I'll head through the wood.' She looked thoughtful. 'I wish I had a way of laying a false trail, so that he'd look for me in the wrong place.'

'I've got an idea,' said Pia.

'Go on.'

'The boat.'

The farming community had one boat, made of wickerwork covered with oiled hides, tightly fitted. It was kept at the riverside near Troon's house. Though it was communal property, they had to ask Troon's permission to use it.

Pia went on: 'I could take it while everyone's asleep, sail it downstream, leave it somewhere, and be back before dawn. When they realize it's missing, and you're missing too, they'll assume you sailed away.'

'And Troon will start looking for me wherever you leave the boat.'

'Exactly.'

'Clever girl! I'll come back here when everyone's asleep, to let you know I'm on my way. And then I'll trust you to do your part.' She kissed Pia. 'Thank you.'

Pia said: 'I'll be waiting for you.'

In fact she fell asleep. When Mo shook her awake she thought it must be morning. She suffered a sudden panic, thinking she had slept through the night and let her friend down. Then everything became clear.

Stam was asleep and snoring. Yana was wide awake, but kept silent.

Pia got up quietly and went outside with Mo. There was a moon to relieve the darkness. When they were out of earshot of the house Pia said: 'I'm sorry. I fell asleep.'

'It's all right,' said Mo. 'You're awake now. Are you still willing to lay a false trail for me?'

Pia had not thought very hard when she offered to help Mo. Now that the scheme was about to go ahead, she felt she had been rash. What if someone happened to be awake, and saw her taking the boat? How could she explain her actions? She tried to think how to tell Mo she had changed her mind. She stopped and turned to her.

Mo said: 'Thank you so much for this.' The moonlight glinted off tears in her eyes. 'I'll never forget it.' She hugged Pia hard.

Pia realized with dismay that she could not back out now.

They parted company, Mo heading up the sloping field towards the wood, Pia going down to the riverside.

She walked along the bank, looking around fearfully, but no

one was about. In the days before the drought, the river had sometimes spread its waters wide, so everyone lived farther up, where the river never reached.

Nonetheless, she heard an alert dog bark as she passed one house, which gave her a heart-stopping moment of alarm; but no one appeared, and she imagined sleeping people turning over, realizing the dog had stopped barking, and going back to sleep.

At last she saw the boat.

It was upside-down on the bank and tied to a rock.

She looked around in the moonlight. Nothing moved. There were a few houses in sight, none within earshot.

She untied the rope and turned the boat upright. It was surprisingly light. Underneath she found a paddle and a large wooden bowl. She wondered what the bowl was for.

She pulled the canoe across the dried mud and into the water. It made little noise. She was not used to boats and she clambered inside awkwardly, losing her balance and dropping to her knees, grabbing the sides to avoid a fall.

She snatched up the paddle and tried to steer the boat into midstream. It took her several strokes to get the hang of paddling, but once she knew what she was doing she began to control the boat better.

She looked back. No one was watching.

She noticed water pooling in the bottom of the boat, and realized what the bowl was for. She bailed out until most of it was gone, but it started to seep back right away. She realized that bailing had to be a constant process. On the up-side, she was sailing with the current, so she used the paddle only to keep the boat in midstream, and clear of obstacles.

How far should she go? She had to be back before dawn. Stam slept heavily all night, but he did not linger in bed in the morning.

It was quiet, the water was calm, and the moonlight was dim. She worried that she might go to sleep. She splashed cool river water on her face to keep her awake.

The farmland on her left narrowed: the wood was closer to the water here. Eventually there was no farmland, and the vegetation grew all the way to the water's edge. Anywhere here, Mo might have felt she was free of the farming folk, and safe to go on land. But Pia sailed on, wanting to make Troon waste as much time as possible following this false trail.

But soon she began to worry about the walk back. She was not sure how long she had been on the water. She noticed that the moon had set, and she feared she might have fallen into a light doze for an unknown length of time.

She thought of beaching the boat, then had a better idea. She paddled to the north shore, dropped the paddle in the boat, got out, then pushed the boat back into midstream. It would float along, perhaps just for a few moments, perhaps for a long while, making Troon waste even more time.

By starlight she watched the boat drift out of sight then turned and headed back along the riverside.

It seemed a long time before she found herself back in farmland. She kept looking over her shoulder, fearing she might see the first light of dawn in the night sky. She began to feel tired, and occasionally stumbled over a stone.

The woods retreated and the farmland widened. She passed houses: no one was about. She was almost home, but it was still possible that some early riser would see her and say: 'Hello! What are you doing, wandering around in the dark?'

She reached her farm and walked up to the door of the house. It was silent within. She stepped in noiselessly. Stam was still fast asleep. She lay down beside her mother. Yana reached out and squeezed her arm gently.

Pia closed her eyes.

All was well.

Next morning early, a rumour ran from field to field that Mo had taken the boat and sailed away.

At mid-morning Shen appeared and told Stam to go to his father.

At noon Stam went past, heading downriver, with a handful of his friends, whom the farmers called the Young Dogs. 'The search party,' Yana said to Pia, and they continued watering and weeding. Pia was pleased: Stam was following her false trail.

The Young Dogs came back along the riverside at dusk, tired and frustrated, Narod and Pilic arguing rancorously about why they had failed to find Mo. When Stam came home for supper he said: 'My father doesn't believe Mo even took that boat. He thinks it just got loose somehow and floated downstream. He's furious.'

Troon was not imaginative, Pia reflected. It had not occurred to him that the boat might have been a deliberate decoy. She was relieved.

She said disingenuously to Stam: 'I wonder where Mo could have gone?'

'My father thinks she went to Riverbend. She'll imagine we can't touch her there. She's going to find out differently.'

Stam was clearly repeating things his father had said. Pia wanted to find out how much Troon knew. She said: 'Mo might have someone at Riverbend to protect her.'

'Oh, she's got a man there, we know that.'

Pia went cold. How had they found out? Then she reasoned. Mo had gone with Yaran at the last Midsummer Rite. Then, at a subsequent Rite, she had talked to him long enough to find out that he liked her. Many people would have noticed a relationship developing. And someone had told Troon about it.

Pia said to Stam: 'Who is this man?'

'We don't know. Shen is going there tomorrow to find out.'

Sly Shen would probably learn the name of Mo's protector – and where he lived. And Mo would not be far away. This was not going well.

Shen disappeared early next morning. He returned at the end of the following day. On the morning after that, Troon set off with Stam and the Young Dogs, heading east.

Pia was fearful for Mo.

The herders did not consider women to be property, but they knew that was the farmers' belief, and they were always reluctant to get involved in a quarrel. They would be angry if Yaran was attacked but, if Mo was kidnapped and Yaran was left more or less unhurt, the herders might take no action.

The worst happened. Two days later the Young Dogs came back with Mo. She was marched along the riverside, not the shortest route but the most public. There was a rope around her neck and Pilic was holding the end of it, as if she was a dog. She had a black eye and bruises on her arms and legs, and she walked with a limp. Her hands were tied behind her back. Troon wanted everyone to see what happened to runaway women. A crowd followed her, and Pia and Yana joined them.

Pia was horrified. She realized that if she left to live with Han she would risk suffering the same treatment.

Mo was taken directly to Bort's place. When Deg saw her he looked appalled. Troon threw her to the ground in front of him.

There was rage in the crowd, particularly among the women, but there was fear, too, Pia sensed, and the fear outweighed the rage.

Troon spoke to the crowd. 'Take a good look,' he said, loudly enough for everyone to hear. 'This is what happens to women who betray our community.'

He looked all around the crowd slowly, as if trying to meet everyone's eye in turn.

'From now on,' he continued, 'no woman will go to the Rites at the Monument, or leave the farmland for any other reason.'

Pia almost shouted a protest. This meant she could not see Han at the Midsummer Rite. Or at any time, she realized.

Never again.

That night Pia lay awake. She had to find a way to see Han, but how? They would never meet by accident. He lived in Riverbend and she was at the other end of the Great Plain. She could not leave Farmplace, and if Han tried to visit her then Troon would immediately be alerted to their romance.

And how would they ever get to live together? If she ran away, she would be brought back like Mo. If Han came to live in farmer country he would be miserable – and so would she, for she longed to get away.

After a sleepless night she got up at dawn. Her mother and Stam were not stirring. She took a basket and went to forage in the wood for strawberries and edible leaves. Mornings were warm now; it was almost midsummer.

She ate the first few berries she found, then began to fill her basket.

She saw woodlanders, usually doing the same as her. They would smile and say a few words in their own language. She would smile back and reply in her language. Only the smiles were understood, but they were enough. It seemed never to occur to woodlanders to claim that the fruits of the forest were theirs, and no one else's. They were the opposite of the farmers, who believed that everything had to belong to someone.

In the drought the forest fruits were not plentiful, and her search took her all the way to the northern limit of the wood, where it met the plain. Looking out across the dry, brown grassland, she saw the usual herd, now scrawny. Not far away a herder was sitting on the ground. He was a young man perhaps ten midsummers older than herself. He noticed her and gave a friendly wave.

She was going to turn back into the wood, but he got up off the ground and walked towards her.

She decided to talk to him.

When he came close she said: 'May the Sun God smile on you.'

'And on you. I'm Zad.'

'Pia.'

Zad had an attractive grin and the confidence of people who know they are charming. He looked into her basket. 'You didn't get much.'

'Everything's dried up. How are your cattle doing?'

'Poorly. I drive them west to the river, so they get water, but there's little for them to eat, and they get thinner every day.'

'That's sad.'

'How are things at Farmplace?'

'Bad. The women have been banned from going to the Rites at the Monument.'

'And they're going to obey the ban?'

She smiled. Only a herder would ask that question. 'We're not like your women. We have to do what we're told.'

'That's a shame. Midsummer is the best day of the year. Food, and poets telling tales, then the revel . . .'

'Are you going?'

'Yes.'

She was thinking, and he noticed her expression. 'What is it?'

'I have a boyfriend.'

'And I have a woman. And a child.'

That was a misunderstanding: he had thought she was warning him off. She tried to disillusion him. 'I'm sorry, I didn't mean . . .' It was too embarrassing to explain, so she just said: 'Do you know a herder called Han?'

'Bigfoot? Of course I do. Those shoes!'

'Could you take a message from me to him and give it to him when you go to the Rite? He's sure to be there.'

He grinned charmingly. 'Yes, why not?'

She became excited. She had found a way to communicate with Han. She said: 'If for some reason you don't see Han, speak to his mother, Ani. She's an elder.'

'I know Ani. She stayed a night in my house, a long time ago.'

'Did she? How strange!'

'Not really. It was after the farmers ploughed up the Break. Some elders came hoping to reason with Troon.'

'A doomed enterprise.'

'So it was.'

'Will you deliver my message?' She wanted confirmation.

'Yes.'

'Thank you. It means such a lot to me.'

'What should I say?'

`She thought for a few moments, then decided that simplicity was best. 'Please tell him I love him.'

Han could hardly wait for Pia to arrive for the Midsummer Rite. Herding cattle on the plain between Riverbend and the Monument, he kept looking west, hoping to see her approaching. He was so distracted that the other herders had to keep an eye on him, and alert him to cows that were wandering away. A wolf cub, young and foolish, probably having lost its mother, crept into the herd and Han knew nothing about it until a fellow herder shot it with an arrow.

He talked about Pia all the time. His mother, Ani, listened tolerantly. His sister, Neen, told him to shut up. His dog, Thunder, was fascinated by everything he said.

Most visitors arrived on the day before the Rite. He spent much of that day helping his mother, carrying the tanned hides of sheep and cattle to the area outside the Monument where people sat to trade. He expected Pia at any moment, probably bringing some of her mother's goat's-milk cheese.

It was going to be a quiet Midsummer Day. Most people wanted nothing but food, and would not trade what they had. But there were some things they could hardly do without: sharp flint tools, for example, to slaughter livestock and butcher the meat.

As the sun went down that afternoon Han began to fear that she would not come. Perhaps she had lost interest in him. She might have fallen for another man. There was a young farmer called Duff who was obviously keen on her. There might be others. A girl could change her mind.

Some farmers turned up. He recognized Troon, the Big Man, and his son, Stam, who – unlike his father – really was big. And there was a slimy character called Shen, who had been here a few days back, asking about Yaran. Han was fairly sure Shen had been looking for Mo, a farmer woman who had come to live with Yaran; and sure enough Mo had vanished.

The herders had talked a lot about the incident. No one had

witnessed it. The kidnappers must have been very silent, and have come in the middle of the night. Yaran said he had been fast asleep when someone had stuffed a gag into his mouth so that he could not cry out, then had tied his hands. At the same time Mo, too, had been silenced before she was awake. Then the intruders had carried Mo off.

Scagga had wanted to take an armed party to Farmplace and get Mo back. Others had argued that she was a farmer woman and they should not get involved. Then Yaran had said he was not the fighting type and would not join a rescue party, and that had pretty much settled the issue.

By sundown Han felt sure Pia was not coming. No farmer women were here, just men, which was unusual. Pia's absence might not be a decision of her own but a ban imposed on all women. Just the same, Han feared the worst.

His mother thought there had been some kind of clampdown. 'Troon may have ordered them to stay at home so that they can't fall in love with herder men.'

Han was not soothed by the possibility that Pia had been kept at home against her will. The thought made him even more agitated.

On the following morning Pia was not at the sunrise ceremony. That settled it. She was not coming.

When the ritual was over, Han stood by Ani's pile of hides while she patrolled with the elders. He knew what his mother needed in exchange for her hides: a new cooking pot, a basket and some bone needles. He enjoyed trading, but not today. He would normally chat about the virtues of particular hides, praising a thick one because it would be hard-wearing and a thin one because it was soft. He enjoyed talking to people who had come from beyond the plain. He liked the coastal people from the south, who offered costly salt, which – they told him – they got by boiling sea water until the water was gone and a crust of salt was left in the bowl.

He had no inclination for any of that now. He was just unhappy.

A man a little older than himself approached. He seemed familiar, but almost everyone in the herder community was at least vaguely familiar. The man looked at Han's feet and said: 'You're Han.'

'Yes. Would you like to trade for a hide?' Han tried to summon up some enthusiasm. 'My mother tans them and she does it thoroughly. No weak spots—'

'No,' the man interrupted. 'I have a message for you.'

Han's hopes rose immediately. 'Who from?'

'My name is Zad. I'm a herder from the far western end of the plain—'

'Who is the message from?'

The man grinned appealingly and said: 'Someone called Pia.'

'Thank the gods – what does she say?'

'Not much.' Zad paused. 'Only that she loves you.'

Han was elated. 'Thank you!' He felt weak with relief: Pia had not lost interest in him. She had not decided that Duff was more alluring. She had not found someone else. She still loved Han.

He wanted to know more – he wanted to know everything. 'How did she look?'

'Thin, like most of us. But beautiful.'

'How did you meet her?'

'She'd been gathering strawberries in East Wood – she hadn't found many, though.'

That news hurt Han. He wanted to be with Pia and help her find berries. She was going hungry and he could do nothing to help. It was maddening.

Zad went on: 'I saw her come out of the north side of the wood and look around. I talked to her, and she asked me to seek you out at the Monument.'

'Did she say why she couldn't come herself?'

'Yes. It seems the Big Man has ruled that women can't leave the farmer territory.'

Han felt cold with fear. 'For how long?'

Zad shrugged. 'Indefinitely, it seems.'

'That could mean for ever.'

'I suppose.'

Han's euphoria was dampened. She still loved him, but she had been banned from meeting him. This was a catastrophe. 'My mother was right,' he said bitterly. 'This has been done because of Mo, the farmer woman who came to live with Yaran. The farmers kidnapped her and took her back against her will.'

Zad was indignant. 'They had no right!'

'People here have argued about that. In the end Yaran wasn't willing to fight for her, so nothing was done.'

'I'm guessing you'll fight for your Pia.'

'I'll fight like a wild boar.' Han frowned. 'But right now I don't know just how to go about it.'

'Well, I'll help you if I can,' said Zad. 'I spoke to her for only a few moments, but she's clearly a special girl.'

'Thank you.'

Zad gave that grin again. 'Goodbye, and good luck.' He went away.

Han mulled over the news for the rest of the day, doing a poor job of trading Ani's hides. He was never going to give Pia up and he would fight for her, but how would he do it? He thought about kidnapping her, the way the farmers had kidnapped Mo. He would have to do that on his own, for unlike Stam he did not have a band of thuggish friends who would do his bidding. And if he succeeded, that would not be the end of it, for the farmers would come after her.

His courage and strength on their own were not enough. He needed to be smart too.

Pia had been in suspense ever since meeting Zad. Would he go to the Rite, or would something happen to make him cancel his trip? Would he forget about finding Han? Would he get the message wrong?

And how would Han react? Would the message please him? Would he have forgotten her? Would he meet someone new at the revel?

Stam had come back disappointed. The festival had been quiet, with few people exchanging goods. 'Everyone wanted food but no one was offering any,' he said. 'We wanted meat, not ropes or shoes or baskets. The herders were unfriendly – they kept talking about Mo, saying we had kidnapped her, even though she belongs to us!'

Pia said: 'How strange.'

Stam missed the sarcasm. 'The feast was skimpy. The revel was all right, though. There was a girl who wanted two boys at the same time, and—'

'Spare us the details,' Yana had said.

'All right, I will,' Stam had said, annoyed, and he had gone off to see his mother.

Soon afterwards Mo arrived. Yana asked her how she was finding life with Deg.

'Absolutely foul,' Mo said.

Pia was not surprised. Yana had an ability to make the best of things; Mo did not.

Mo said: 'He only ever speaks to give me orders. Weed the far field, cook these hares, go and find some raspberries, lie down and spread your legs.'

Yana said: 'Does he want sex often?'

'Once a year would be too often for me.'

It was sad, but Mo's way of telling it made Pia laugh.

Yana said: 'How are your crops looking?'

'Not bad, now that there are three of us to carry the water up from the river. Not that it matters much. We're all going to starve eventually.'

As Yana and Mo chatted, Pia's mind wandered. What was Han doing now? Probably herding cattle. How was he feeling about her? She wished she had asked Zad to bring back a reply to her message.

When Mo had gone, Pia talked to her mother. 'Now that I've sent him a message, I don't know what to do next. I need to know how he feels but I can't go to him.'

'You must talk to Zad,' said Yana.

That was a point.

Yana went on: 'He would know how Han received the message, whether Han was happy to hear from you.'

'True. He might even have brought me a reply, though I stupidly didn't ask for one.'

'Will you be able to find Zad?'

'Well, I can look in the place where I encountered him. If he's not there, I'll have to think of something else.'

She felt hopeful as she lay down to sleep. Tomorrow she would at least find out where matters stood. The news might be good or bad, but this awful uncertainty would end.

She woke at first light and set off with her basket. Her pretext, if anyone asked, was that she was gathering forest food, and on her way through the forest she plucked some berries, rather small and shrivelled but better than nothing.

The vegetation was parched. She wondered whether the woodlanders were doing better in the hills. They would certainly be hungry if they had stayed here.

She emerged onto the plain. In front of her a herd of cattle was trying to find sustenance from the dry ground. She looked around. A herder was walking among the cattle, but sadly it was not Zad. This man was too tall. In fact he looked . . .

In fact he looked like Han.

It was impossible, but his tall figure and fair beard were unmistakable. Forgetting all about the need for caution and discretion, she yelled his name.

He spun round fast and saw her. He smiled broadly, stepped towards her, then broke into a run. She did the same. They met and she threw herself into his arms.

She hugged him hard and buried her face in his neck and smelt his skin. She could hardly believe her good fortune. He kissed her lips hard. She broke the kiss to stare at his face. She said: 'I was hoping for a message from you, and I got you!' She kissed him again.

Eventually they calmed down. She had dropped her basket and scattered the berries. She bent down to pick them up, and he helped her.

'How long will you be here for?'

He shrugged. 'No limit.'

She was thrilled. 'We could meet every day!'

'Or every night.'

She considered. Could she manage that secretly?

He noticed her hesitation. 'Can you get away at night?'

'My mother won't mind. But she's been forced to partner with Stam, the son of Troon.'

'That thug! Is he a light sleeper?'

'The opposite.' She recalled stealing the boat. She had been out all night without Stam noticing. He never woke before dawn. 'But if one night he should wake, and notice my absence, what would I say?'

'Say you have a lover.'

Actually, that was a good idea. There was generally a certain amount of romantic movement at night in Farmplace. It would not occur to the unimaginative Stam that her lover might be a herder.

Which raised a question. 'Where will we meet?'

'In the wood,' said Han. 'The weather is warm enough. When autumn comes we may have to think again.'

Autumn! she thought. That gives us a quarter of a year of seeing one another every night. Bliss! 'We need to choose a place.'

'I can't leave the herd. In fact, look at that stupid heifer wandering into the wood. She'll get her leg caught in a tree root and die there if I don't rescue her.'

'I'll look for somewhere.'

'And how will I find you?'

'I'll meet you here and take you there.'

'When?'

'I'll come as soon as Stam is asleep.'

'I'll be waiting.'

'Now go and catch that wandering heifer.'

They kissed again, and parted.

In the middle of a thicket there was a space big enough for two to lie down. She saw the white flowers of yarrow among the bushes, and smelt its characteristic scent of fresh-cut herbs. The ground there was covered with soft dry leaves. A passer-by would not see them – not that there was likely to be a passer-by in daytime or night.

The blue sky was visible above.

She hoped Han would like it.

Of course he would like it. What was she worrying about? It was a nice place to lie down with someone you loved, and that was all that mattered.

She got home with a few berries and Stam ate them all.

She carried water and pulled weeds all day. At suppertime she was too tense to eat, despite being hungry. Her mother noticed and raised an eyebrow, but said nothing.

After supper Stam went to see his mother. Pia suspected she gave him a second supper. He came home at nightfall, had sex with Yana, and went to sleep.

Pia waited a little longer, to make sure he was fast asleep, then she got up. Her mother watched silently. Pia lifted the wickerwork gate that stood in the doorway, stepped outside, and replaced it carefully, making almost no noise.

Stam did not stir.

She looked around the fields in the starlight and saw no one. She headed up the slope to the wood.

Han was where he had said he would be, on the far side of the wood, sitting on the ground. He leaped up and kissed her.

They held hands as they walked through the trees to the thicket she had chosen. She showed him the space in the middle.

He smiled. 'This is perfect,' he said. 'The aroma of crushed grass.'

They pushed through the shrubbery and sat down in the middle. They could see each other by starlight. Pia felt that to the rest of the world they were invisible.

She said: 'How did you do it? How is it that you're here? Tell me everything.'

'Well, Zad thrilled me with your message, then brought me

down to earth by telling me that the farmer women have been banned from the Rites. I didn't know what to do but I had to talk to you. So I asked to be assigned to Zad's team of herders.'

'How clever of you!'

'To tell the truth, it was my mother's idea.'

'She's so wise.'

'Anyway, I spoke to Keff and asked him if I could move here, and he said yes. In fact he was glad, because Zad needed another hand. He has to keep driving the herd to the river for water, and it's a long journey since Troon ploughed up the Break.'

'How did it happen so quickly?'

'Zad gave me the message after the Midsummer Rite. He and I walked here the next day. I started work with the herd today and you appeared this morning.'

'And you can stay here indefinitely.'

'As long as you want me.'

She smiled. She wanted him for ever. But she did not say so. They had known one another since childhood, and their romance had been going on since the Midwinter Rite, but in that half year they had actually spent little time together. She felt that she knew him intimately, but did she really? She wanted to talk about how she would escape, and where they would live, and the children they would have, but it seemed too soon to assume they would be together for ever.

Now she felt awkward, as if she had brought a stranger to this lovers' nest. What should she do now? Should she just kiss him? She wanted to, but hesitated.

He saw her discomfort, and said: 'What's the matter?'

'I don't know. I'm nervous. Are you?'

'A bit.'

'I've done things with boys, always at the revel, and I was never nervous, but I am now.'

'I'm glad,' he said.

She was surprised. 'Why?'

'Because it means that to you I'm special.'

She nodded. 'You're right. I didn't care what the others thought.'

'But you care what I think.'

'Yes. I'm worried that you'll be disappointed.' She had not thought about that: it just came out.

He smiled. 'I don't think that will happen.'

'And you? What are you nervous about?'

'Oh, I don't know. Embarrassment.'

She was intrigued. 'Why? What have you got to be embarrassed about?'

'Could I tell you later? I can't wait to kiss you.'

She agreed eagerly. They kissed for a while, then lay down side by side and kissed some more. The tip of his tongue touched her lips, and she opened her mouth a little. She had learned about this kind of kissing at the revel, and she liked it.

He touched her breasts, but she knew he could not feel much through her leather tunic, and she really wanted his hands on her skin, so she sat upright and pulled the garment off over her head. When Han saw her naked body he gave a little gasp. She was pleased. Evidently he was not disappointed.

However, he did not reciprocate by taking off his own tunic, which surprised her. She guessed that it hid whatever he was embarrassed about. Some people had markings on their skin that were harmless but unsightly. Some men had extra nipples, she had heard.

They kissed some more and he touched her all over, with light fingers that seemed to relish everything they found. She wanted to explore his body, too, and she slid her hand up his thigh under the tunic. She touched his balls, which were covered in hair. She knew not to squeeze them: she had made that mistake once before.

She found his penis and was startled. 'Han!' she said. 'It's so big.'

'I know,' he said. 'That's what I'm embarrassed about.'

So that was it. 'Don't be embarrassed,' she said. 'You've got big hands and feet, it's natural you should have a big prick. Anyway, it feels lovely, soft skin and hard inside. And it's warm.'

He touched her vagina. 'I don't know if it will go in.'

Pia remembered a boy who had put in one finger, then two, then three, then four. He had wanted to put his hand in but she had stopped him.

She said to Han: 'Let's try.'

'All right.'

'Lie on your back.'

He did so. His pubic hair was fair, she saw.

She stroked his penis and kissed it, and she could have carried on doing that much longer, but he said: 'If you don't put it in now, it will soon be too late.'

She straddled him. 'Lie still,' she said. 'Leave this to me.' She put the end in place then paused. It did seem too big. Rocking a little, she sank down on it. 'It feels nice,' she said, to reassure him. The end slipped inside.

Han cried out, and she felt him spurting inside her.

'I couldn't wait any longer,' he said. 'Sorry.'

'Don't be sorry,' she said. She lay on his chest with his penis still inside her. 'It was exciting.'

They were quiet for a few moments.

'Aren't you troubled?' Han said. 'That it didn't even go all the way in?'

'It will next time,' she said. 'Don't worry.' Her vagina would stretch: it had to, because one day a baby's head might have to pass through it. Her main worry was his reaction. He might become discouraged and lose desire. She would have to make sure that did not happen.

He put his arms around her and held her close. His body was warm.

She said: 'Remember when I asked if I could be your girlfriend?'

'You never did.'

She laughed. 'You've forgotten.'

'When was it?'

'We were seven midsummers old. Nearly eight.'

'Of course I don't remember. What did I say?'

'You said no. I was distraught.'

He laughed. 'Well, you can be my girlfriend now, if you like.'

'Yes, please.'

She closed her eyes.

After a while he said musingly: 'You're so confident.'

'Mmm.'

A few moments later she fell asleep.

13

'I'M GOING TO have a baby,' said Pia.

'A baby,' said Han.

It was daybreak, and she could see his face. He was happy: a child was what he wanted. She kissed him.

Her pregnancy was hardly surprising. They had made love here, in the thicket, almost every night for a quarter of a year. The grassy scent of yarrow would mean sex to Pia for the rest of her life.

The woodlanders, back from their summer migration, had looked at them suspiciously at first, but had quickly realized they were harmless and left them alone.

Stam had become suspicious. Twice he had woken in the night and seen that Pia was not at home. The first time he had been ill with a fever, and by morning he was not sure what he had seen and what he had dreamed. But the second occasion had been different. Frantic barking from the dog had alerted him and Yana, and in the moonlight they had seen a family of wild boars in the field, a mother and three young, eating the crop. It was dangerous to get close to boars, so Stam had shot arrows at them and Yana had thrown stones, making them run away, the mother with two arrows sticking in her back. One of the young had been left behind, fatally wounded by an arrow, and when Pia got home Yana was cooking it.

And Stam wanted to know where Pia had been.

She had adopted Han's suggestion and said she had a lover. Now he was desperate to know who it was. 'Ask your friends,' Pia had said. 'One of them knows.' That made him even more curious and steered him away from the truth.

All the same, she was anxious. Stam was dumb but his father, Troon, was not. She feared that the secret might come out somehow. And the baby just underlined the precariousness of her position.

She said to Han: 'It's time for us to make some decisions.'

'I'll become a farmer,' Han said immediately. 'I'm big and strong, they'll be glad to have me. I don't know anything about farming, but I'll be happy to learn.'

Pia was dead against this. 'Three snags with that,' she said. She had foreseen this conversation and she knew what she wanted to say. 'First, you would hate being a farmer. Men, women and children work from sunrise to sunset every day of the year.'

'No rest days?'

'No. Herders who join the farmer community can't get used to it and get a reputation for being lazy and unreliable.'

'I'm not lazy.'

'Not by herder standards, no. By farmer standards you do virtually no work.'

'Hmm.'

'Second, women are property here. They have to do what men tell them. If we had a daughter, that's how she would be treated. You're not used to that. It would offend you.'

'It does offend me.' Han was looking uneasy.

Pia went on: 'But the most important reason is the third. I hate it here. I'm desperate to leave. I want a herder family, with everyone being kind and loving to one another.'

Han frowned, thinking. Pia listened to the morning chatter of the birds. Eventually Han said: 'That settles it. We'll have to go to Riverbend.'

Pia shook her head. 'They would try to kidnap me, as they did Mo.'

Han looked angry. 'They'd have to kill me first.'

'But they might do that. And whatever happened would be violent. It's hard to predict how things would end up. Your mother's an elder: if the farmers killed you, the herders might go to war. I don't want our love to be the cause of a war.'

'Nor do I, but there's nowhere else to go.'

'On the contrary, there are many places: north, south, east and west.'

'You mean we should leave the Great Plain?'

'Yes.'

'But we hardly know what there is beyond the plain.'

'We know that the woodlanders spend every summer in the North-West Hills. There's an established path that they use, so we could find our way easily.'

'What would we do for food? The deer have already returned to the plain.'

'We could take a cow.'

'You mean steal one?'

'Would that be necessary? If you took Zad into your confidence, might he not feel that as a herder you're entitled to one cow?'

Han grinned. 'I think you're probably right.' He turned serious. 'But winter in the hills . . .'

She nodded. It was already getting colder here on the plain. 'We'd have to build a house. I'm sure we could manage that.'

'Yes.' He looked thoughtful. 'You and me and a cow . . .'

'And a baby.'

'It sounds cosy.'

Pia nodded. It sounded cosy to her too. She knew there would be difficulties and struggles, but the joy of being together and being free would give them the strength to cope with problems. Just the thought of it made her happy.

There was one big drawback. 'I'll miss my mother, though.'

Han clearly had not thought about Yana. 'Can't she come with us?'

'I've talked to her about it. She refuses. She says she's too old. She can no longer walk very far or very fast – the carrying of water all summer has worn her out. She's afraid she would slow us down, and we'd all be caught.'

'I don't know . . .'

'She won't change her mind.'

Han nodded. It made sense to him. But he said: 'It may be a long while until you see her. Do you imagine we'll live in the North-West Hills indefinitely?'

'No. In a year or two we can return to the plain. Tempers will have cooled and a lot of people will have forgotten about us. We'll have a baby, and that will change everything. If Troon tried to take a mother and baby away from the father, the herders might well go to war, and Troon would know that.'

Han said: 'Anyway, that's a long time in the future.'

Not so long, she thought, but she did not say it. 'We'll have to take some necessities. A cookpot, two bowls and two spoons, some flints, and a big leather bag to put them in.'

'And my bow and arrows. When shall we go?'

'Tomorrow night.'

'So soon!'

'Listen. It's the Autumn Rite in four days. We should leave tomorrow, but not go far, and hide in West Wood. Next day they'll search the farmer country, and the woods, and visit herder settlements nearby. Not finding us, they'll think we've gone to Riverbend. The following day they'll go to the Monument for the Rite and search for us there. Next day, after the Rite, they'll come back here. That gives us four clear days to get ahead of them. They'll never catch us.'

'No,' he said. 'As long as the Sun God smiles on us.'

The next day it rained.

There had been a few paltry showers as the summer cooled down, but this was a real storm. Farmers stood in the fields looking up, their mouths open to catch the pure water. Everyone got soaking wet and no one minded.

The dry streambeds filled again. That solved a problem for Pia and Han: they would not have to search for water on their flight.

As night fell the wind grew strong and the rain came down harder. Pia considered putting off their departure to another night, but she could not bear to. She was too close to freedom to postpone it. Anyway, the weather would make it more difficult for anyone to follow them.

As usual she lay down and pretended to sleep. The wind seemed to disturb Stam for a while, but at last his breathing became regular.

Like most people, Pia had a shearling coat that she wore over her tunic in cold weather. It hung from a peg in a rafter, and now she took it down and shrugged it on.

She knelt by her mother's bed and kissed her. Yana stroked her face and whispered: 'May the Sun God smile on you.'

'And on you, my beloved mother,' Pia breathed.

Then she got up and left. She wondered whether she would ever see her mother again.

She laboured up the slope to the wood, bending forward into the rain and struggling to maintain a steady path as the wind buffeted her sideways. Soon her coat was heavy with water.

She reached the wood and was grateful for the shelter of the trees. She passed all the way through and found Han on the other side at his usual place. He, too, was soaking wet, as was Thunder.

The cattle had huddled in a close mass, sheltering each other and their calves.

Han said: 'This wood is the first place they'll look. We need to cross the Break and find a place to hide in West Wood.'

Pia agreed.

They moved along the north side of the tree line, gaining a little shelter from overhanging branches, heading west. In a flash of lightning they saw a herder, who waved amiably. They reached the Break and started across.

The cultivated field offered no shelter at all. Twice the wind almost knocked Pia off her feet, and from then on she clung to Han. At last they reached West Wood and entered with relief.

'We're free,' Pia said. She was elated. There were hazards ahead, but she had at last broken away from the farmer folk.

Han said: 'Wet, but free.'

They looked first for shelter. The trees still had most of their leaves, and the travellers found a spreading oak that kept off the worst of the rain. They sat with their backs against the broad trunk and rested.

Han said: 'This won't do as a hiding place, but they won't come looking for us before daylight.'

'I'm trying to think what kind of hideout we might find,' Pia said, frowning. She had not considered this question when she planned the escape.

Han said: 'Up or down. Up in a tree, or lying on the ground in some thick shrubbery.'

Neither sounded secure to Pia, but she could think of nothing better. Perhaps when they looked around they would come across something she had not thought of. She began to worry. How dreadful it would be if they were caught when they had got no farther than this.

They moved close together, and Thunder lay against Han's side. Pia spread her sodden coat across their legs. They were cold and wet. As the night drew on they dozed, waking frequently. The rain did not stop.

At first light they stood up. Back in Farmplace, Stam would be waking up and would see that Pia was not there. At first he would assume that she had gone to forage in East Wood, but soon he would wonder why she was gone so long. He would remember her previous night-time disappearances. He would interrogate Yana, who would claim mystified ignorance, which he would not believe. The fact that Yana was not weeping anguished tears would confirm to him that Pia's disappearance was not unexpected, but in fact planned.

Soon he would tell his father of his suspicions. Troon, quicker thinking than his son, would immediately organize a search party. So Pia and Han had to hide as soon as possible.

They heard dogs, and Thunder barked back. This was too soon to be Troon's search party, so Pia guessed the dogs belonged to the woodlanders.

Then two woodlanders appeared from nowhere and stood in front of them, holding clubs. Pia told herself to be calm. Woodlanders were friendly, nearly always.

The shorter of the two was handsome, and probably vain, for he wore a necklace of some kind of teeth. He said something in the woodlander tongue.

Han spread his arms out, palms upward to show he held no weapons, and said: 'We come in peace.'

The second woodlander said: 'I know you. You're Han.'

Han stared at him for a long moment, then said: 'Are you Bez?'

'Yes.'

'And this is your brother, Fell.'

Fell heard his own name and smiled broadly, nodding.

'I should have known by the necklace,' Han said.

Pia was looking at Han in surprise.

Han said: 'You told me you came from West Wood. I remember now.'

Bez said: 'You were kind to me and my brother when we were hungry and destitute. You behaved to us as a member of our tribe would. So now I welcome you as a fellow tribesman.' He looked at Pia. 'And your companion.'

Pia said: 'Thank you.'

Fell looked hard at their clothes and said: 'You need to get dry. Come with us.'

We should be looking for a hiding place, Pia thought nervously. But perhaps these woodlander friends of Han can help us with that, too.

She and Han followed Bez and Fell through the wood to a clearing where there were seven huts. A woman came out of the middle one, and Bez introduced her as Gida. She was attractive and middle-aged, and something in Bez's tone made Pia think Gida was special to him.

Gida invited them into the hut. At least eight people were lying on the floor around a fire. The air was stuffy and the smell of unwashed bodies was ripe, but Pia did not care, because the warmth was blissful.

Gida spoke to the inhabitants, and Pia heard the note of authority in her voice. She was no doubt telling them who the visitors were, and they smiled and nodded, evidently accepting her view that Han should be treated as a member of the tribe. They made room near the fire, and Pia and Han sat down. Soon steam was rising from Pia's coat. She slipped it off and let the heat of the fire warm her bare arms.

Bez and Fell sat with them, and Gida ladled soup from the pot on the fire into four bowls and handed them round. Pia drank it without thinking what might be in it.

When she had finished the soup she spoke to Bez. 'We're running away,' she said. 'The farmers will come chasing us to take us back to Farmplace.'

Bez nodded, understanding.

'We need a place to hide.'

'This is the best place to hide,' he said. 'Lie down here among the others with your back to the door. We won't let them come in. They will just look through the door and see a lot of woodlanders.'

'What if they insist on coming in?'

'They won't. We have clubs.'

Pia looked at Han. 'What do you think?'

'It makes sense to me. And while we are here we have allies, should things go wrong.'

Pia was not much reassured, but guessed this was their best chance. She nodded. 'Thank you, Bez.'

The rain continued heavy, and no one left the hut. Han fell asleep on the floor and Pia did the same soon afterwards, despite her anxiety.

They were awakened by a commotion: dogs barking, men

shouting, people running around outside. Thunder stood up, the hair sticking up on the back of his neck. Two woodlanders stood at the door of the hut, holding clubs.

Pia peeped out through a hole in the wattle-and-daub wall. Coming into the clearing were Stam and four of his Young Dogs, all with bows slung over their shoulders and quivers of arrows hanging from their belts. Rain was pouring down their faces and they had lost their customary swagger – in fact they looked scared. They were outnumbered by woodlanders. They could not throw their weight around here.

Pia bit her lip. She had known that something like this might happen. She could not tell how it might end. She only knew that she would rather die here and now than return to Farmplace.

Stam said: 'We're searching for a wicked farmer girl who murdered her brother and ran away. Have you seen anyone?'

They had invented the murder story in the hope of gaining sympathy. They did not know about Han, it seemed.

'We haven't seen any strangers,' said Bez, who had evidently gone outside to deal with the visitors. 'Perhaps she drowned in the rain.'

Stam did not see the joke. 'We need to look around.'

'You can look, but you can't enter our huts. People are sleeping.'

Stam did not like that, but he did not make an issue of it. He said to his men: 'Stay outside, but take a good hard look into every hut.'

Gida said to Pia and Han: 'Quickly, lie down at the back.' Pia picked up her coat. Han lay on the ground facing the wall. He was surrounded by woodlanders, men and women and children. She draped her coat over his head and shoulders, to hide his fair hair and his bulk. Then she lay beside him, front to front. She thought she was hidden by his body.

She heard footsteps splashing nearer, and held her breath. Then she heard Stam's voice: 'Phew, what a stink.' There was a long silence. Then the footsteps moved away.

She waited in suspense. Would Stam be satisfied with this superficial search? She heard his voice, too low for her to make out what he was saying, but in a tone that sounded wearily irritated. Then he spoke more loudly. 'They're not here. Let's move on.'

She lay motionless, still scared.

A few moments later she heard footsteps approaching the doorway, and Bez said: 'They've gone.'

Pia breathed easier.

She and Han sat up. 'Thank you,' Pia said to Bez. 'You saved us.'

Bez said: 'I don't like the boy with one ear. He has a mean face.'

Pia said: 'He has a mean heart, too.'

'I've sent someone to follow them,' Bez said. 'We'll know if they decide to come back.'

'Thank you.'

Bez left the hut. Some time later he returned and said: 'They've left the wood.'

Pia said to Han: 'I'd like to get away from here as soon as possible.'

Han was not in so much of a hurry. 'Let's think about that,' he said reasonably. 'We may be seen by a stray farmer. It may be safer to stay here until dusk.'

Pia was burning to get away, but she saw Han's point. 'And then get on the path to the hills?' she said.

'First we should go to Old Oak and get Zad to give us a cow.'

He was right about that too. She controlled her impatience. 'Very well.'

Around midday the storm seemed to blow itself out. Pia and Han left the hut and stood outside. The rain-washed air was cool and refreshing. Han looked up and said: 'See that? Blue sky. Do you know what that means?'

'No more rain?' she tried.

'It means we can travel at night. If I can see the North Star, I can find my way.'

Pia was impressed. Farmers did not travel much, and had no need of night-time navigation, so she had never learned it. She said: 'I'd be glad to travel at night, at least for a while. We should be a long way from farmer country before we show ourselves in daylight.'

Han nodded agreement.

'In which case we should start tonight, after we've visited Zad.'

'Yes.'

They went back inside the hut and lay down to rest. If they were going to walk all night they needed their strength.

Pia did not think she would sleep, but she did. She was in a deep slumber when Gida gently shook her awake. At first she thought she was in the yarrow thicket, and it was time to leave Han and go back to her home; then she realized she had escaped, and immediately felt energized.

She got to her feet and looked outside. She could not see the sun, because of the trees, but she guessed by the light that it was setting. She put on her coat. It had dried in the warmth of the hut.

They thanked Bez, Gida and Fell, then took their leave. It was dusk when they emerged from the wood onto the Great Plain. They looked around in the dim light: no one was in sight. Stam and his search party had undoubtedly given up a long time ago. By now Troon would have concluded that Pia had gone to Riverbend.

Han led the way to the hamlet of Old Oak, where he had been living for a quarter of a year – at least in theory: he had spent most nights in the wood with Pia. The thought made her smile.

They found Zad and Biddy and their child, Dini, just finishing supper. Han explained how they had hidden with the woodlanders while Stam searched. 'Now they will think Pia has gone to Riverbend,' he said. 'Which gives us a few days to get clear of the plain and into the hills.'

'Good,' said Zad.

Han took a breath then said: 'I've been a herder since I was eight years old. Do you think I deserve a cow to take with me on this journey?'

Zad smiled. 'Yes, I do,' he said. 'Come on, let's choose one before we lose the light.'

Pia stayed and talked to Biddy. She was a dark-eyed, dark-haired woman with an oval face. Pia thought she was quite beautiful. Biddy said: 'Why are the farmers chasing you? Why don't they just let you go?'

Clearly she knew little about the farmer way of life. Pia wondered how to put an entire way of life into a few words. 'They need strong young people to cultivate the earth,' she said. 'And they consider that women belong to men.'

'Belong to them?'

'Yes.'

Biddy was shocked. 'Now I understand why you're running away . . . even though you're having a baby.'

Pia smiled. 'Does it show already?'

Biddy nodded. 'If you know what to look for. I think you've been pregnant for a quarter of a year. The baby will come soon after the Spring Rite.' She gave a modest smile. 'I was the eldest of six children, so I watched my mother through five pregnancies.'

Pia had not had that experience. She was the youngest of three children, two of whom had died young, so she had always been an only child. She was fascinated by what Biddy had to say, and they talked about pregnancy and childbirth until the men returned.

Pia went outside to look at the cow. She was a young female, thin but strong. Han said: 'Can you also let me have a piece of rope, so that I can tether her at night?'

'Of course.' Zad went into the house and came back with a length of rope, which he tied around the cow's neck.

Pia was on edge now, eager to get away. She said: 'Let's go.'

Zad said: 'I'm going to walk you to the path the woodlanders use. It's north of here, not far. Then you'll be on the right track all the way into the hills.'

'Thank you,' said Pia.

They said goodbye to Biddy and Dini and set off. The moon rose while they were walking, and the night was brightly lit. Wherever there was a stream the cows had gathered. Zad said: 'I won't have to drive them to the river, at least not for the next few days.'

Han said: 'I wonder if the drought has finally broken.'

'Let's all hope so.'

Thunder was a herder dog, and stayed with the cow, making sure she did not fall behind or stray to either side.

Before long they came to a wide beaten path, muddy from the storm. 'Here it is,' said Zad. 'May the Sun God smile on you.'

Han said: 'I'll never forget your kindness, Zad.'

Pia said: 'You brought Han to me, then you helped us escape. You're wonderful.'

'I hope you'll come back one day.'

So do I, Pia thought.

Zad turned and walked back the way they had come.

Pia and Han looked at the moonlit path ahead. Never in their lives before had either of them left the Great Plain.

Pia said: 'Our new life has begun.'

She took Han's hand and together they walked on.

The Autumn Rite at the Monument was a small affair, with nothing like the crowds that came at midsummer. This one, Ani thought, was even quieter than usual. People were trading flints and food, but no one wanted tanned hides.

The cloudburst of two days ago had been a hopeful sign, but the Great Plain needed a lot more rain before it could return to normal.

Zad came to the Rite. Ani had heard nothing about Han since the day he had left, heading for the western end of the plain and Pia. Now Zad told her, speaking quietly so that no one else could hear, how Pia had escaped from Farmplace and, with Han, had headed for the North-West Hills. Ani was both thrilled and worried. She was glad they were out of Troon's control, but she fretted about how they would survive winter in the hills. The woodlanders always came back at the end of the summer.

A contingent of a dozen or so farmers had come to the Autumn Rite, she noticed as she walked around: all men, no women. They did not seem to have much to trade, and Ani wondered if they were here on some other mission. She saw Joia's childhood friend Vee talking to a thin man with a bent nose, and she recognized Shen, the henchman of Troon. Vee looked as if she would rather not speak to the man. When the conversation ended and Troon walked away, Ani went to Vee and said: 'What did that sly villain want?'

'He's looking for Pia. I told him I haven't seen her for a long time. Which is true.'

Ani was not really surprised, but all the same her heart missed a beat. Troon wanted to take Pia back, undoubtedly. He was nothing if not vengeful. Han would of course try to keep her from Troon. Ani just hoped there would be no violence. She said to Vee: 'Did he ask you anything else?'

'He wanted to know if Pia had any friends here. I told him she used to play with Han when they were children but she hasn't had friends here since then.'

Ani heard that with dismay. She wished Vee had not mentioned Han's name. However, she did not say so. Vee had meant no harm.

A little later Shen reappeared and approached Ani. 'Always a pleasure to see you, Ani,' he said.

Ani said: 'What are these farmers doing here? They have practically nothing to trade.'

'Oh, well, in these times every little bit helps, doesn't it? By the way, what's happened to your son, Han? I don't see him anywhere.'

Shen was following up on Vee's indiscretion, Ani realized. He had guessed that the childhood friends might have become grown-up lovers. 'Oh, Han's here somewhere,' Ani lied. 'You'll bump into him sooner or later.'

'He's hard to miss, being so tall,' Shen said insinuatingly. 'Only someone said he's gone to work at the western end of the plain.'

'No, he works here. What business do you have with my son?'

'Oh, nothing particular. I just noticed his absence.' Shen moved away.

Ani was disturbed. Shen was dogged. He might work out Han's secret.

As Shen melted into the crowd, Vee's mother, Kae, appeared. 'I hate these farmers,' she said.

'What have they been doing now?'

'They're such bullies! They're questioning my family, saying we must know where Han has gone with his farmer girl.'

Ani was angry. She had to put a stop to this. 'I'm glad you've told me, Kae. We can't tolerate such behaviour. I'll deal with it right away.'

'Thank you.'

If herders had acted that way in Farmplace, the farmers would have reacted with instant violence. They needed to understand that the herders could be decisive too. She sought out Scagga, who was talking to the rope-makers, Ev and Fee. She took him aside and told him what Kae had reported.

'We'll beat up the lot of them,' Scagga said immediately. 'Break a few bones and crack a few heads. That'll teach them.'

'I'd like to scare them off without actual violence,' Ani said. 'Let's bear in mind our reputation for peaceful gatherings here at the Monument.'

'I suppose you're right,' Scagga said reluctantly.

'There's a large empty house over by the river.'

'I know it. No one sleeps there because the roof leaks.'

'Can you round up twenty strong men and women with stone hammers and suchlike, and put them in that house?'

'Easily.'

'Tell them they probably won't have to fight, just look mean.'

Scagga grinned. 'You want to give the farmers a fright.'

'Exactly.'

'I'll get it organized.'

It was not much later when Scagga returned and said: 'All ready. Twenty strong youngsters, all armed.'

'Right.' Now Ani would see whether her scheme would work.

She sought out Troon. He was with a dozen other farmers, including his son, Stam. They were gathered around a fire where an enterprising herder was roasting split cattle bones so that the delicious marrow could be scooped out and eaten. In exchange the farmers gave him cakes made of grains and cheese, their usual travelling food.

Ani took Troon aside. 'I've found your Pia,' she said.

He looked sceptical. 'Really?'

'If you want, I'll take you to her.'

He said suspiciously: 'Why would you do a thing like that?'

She had anticipated the question and she had an answer ready. 'Because your search is distressing my people and we herders hate conflict.'

He feared a trap. 'I'm not coming on my own.'

'Bring your men. Bring all of them.'

He looked reassured. 'I will.'

The farmers finished off their split bones, wiped their hands on their tunics, and followed Ani. They went from the Monument to Riverbend, then through the village to the big house by the river. Scagga stood by the door and said: 'She's in here.'

Ani said: 'This way,' and walked in ahead.

She was pleased with what Scagga had arranged. The place was dark but for the light from a small fire in a central hearth. Behind Ani, Troon said: 'I can't see a thing. Where's Pia?'

The door closed with a bang.

Ani said: 'Let's have some light.'

A dark figure stooped over the fire, lighting a torch. It blazed into flame and the man held it high.

The farmers gasped and grunted with shock. Twenty young herders stood just the other side of the fire, all holding weapons, staring in silence. After a moment's shocked hesitation the farmers turned to run. But the door would not open. Scagga had barred it from the outside.

Troon turned, scared and angry. He looked at Ani and said: 'You're going to murder us all.'

'No one is going to be murdered today,' she replied. 'But I will not have you and your thugs intimidating the people of Riverbend. You will leave now and go home. If ever you come back, you will behave peaceably while you're here. And if you break my rules again, you will be killed. Listen to me. There will be no second chance.'

She raised her voice. 'Open up, Scagga!'

The door opened.

The farmers hurried away.

There was a burst of laughter and conversation among the young herders as the tension was released. Ani said: 'Thank you, everyone. I hope we've put a stop to their nonsense.'

She felt relieved. Only now did she realize how anxious the performance had made her. She stepped out of the building and walked slowly back towards the Monument. She was still worried about Han, but she thought she had stymied Troon's investigation.

When she reached the Monument she again ran into Zad, who said he had been looking for her. 'Something I forgot to tell you,' he said. 'Pia is expecting a baby. Han's going to be a father.'

Ani was thrilled. She would have another grandchild. 'How wonderful! When?'

'Next spring, my Biddy says. It will be born in the North-West Hills.'

Ani looked around, but no one was within hearing distance. 'Please don't mention their destination to anyone else.'

'No, of course not,' said Zad, but Ani noticed a slight frown.

She said: 'You haven't told anyone, have you?'

'No. Well, only someone who is a real friend of his.'

Ani's heart sank.

Zad went on: 'This friend was very worried about Han, and asked me if he was all right, and would he be murdered by the farmers for stealing one of their women. He was so concerned and distressed that I thought it would do no harm to tell him that Han and Pia were fine and safe, and heading for the North-West Hills.'

'The friend who was so worried,' Ani said fearfully. 'Did he tell you his name?'

'Yes,' said Zad. 'He's called Shen.'

By the third day Han and Pia were in the hills. Their progress was not fast, mainly because they had to stop and let the cow graze. Meanwhile they foraged for nuts and crab apples. Thunder caught a squirrel, but they let him eat it all.

They were searching all the time for a place where they could build a shelter. They needed to be hidden from pathways in case the farmers came after them. They also hoped to find a place where they could hunt and gather food. The cow would not last for ever. They would be living like woodlanders, going out in the morning to find the evening's supper.

The path led alongside a river. At a place where the river broadened, they came to a derelict house close to a short muddy beach. There was a small stone circle halfway up a hill. Pia thought it might be some kind of holy place, though now it was clearly deserted.

They could not use the house as their shelter because it was too visible, right on the path. However, there was a small island in the middle of the river. Han said: 'Shall we cross the river and take a look?'

Pia said: 'Yes, definitely.'

It took a little organizing. Both Han and Pia had been raised near rivers, so they could swim. Cows and dogs could swim too, but the challenge would be keeping the party together. Han untied the rope from the cow's neck and re-tied it firmly. 'I'll keep hold of the cow, you watch Thunder,' he said.

They folded their coats on the riverbank. They would have to come back for those.

They stepped into the water. The river was not fast-flowing.

The cow was happy to be led in, but Thunder was reluctant. However, he did not want to be left behind so, after a few moments of dithering, he plunged in and swam vigorously.

The cow was inclined to go with the current, so Han had to keep pulling it back at the same time as keeping his own head above water. Pia saw that Thunder was all right and went to help Han. When they both pulled on the rope, the cow came their way.

Soon they reached the island and scrambled ashore.

Pia saw that the vegetation was lush. There had been a drought here too, of course, but the roots must be watered by the river. She stood up, looked around, and immediately sensed a feeling of peace.

Thunder shook himself, sending a shower like rain over Pia and Han, making them laugh. The cow saw green grass and immediately started to graze.

Han swam back to the mainland and returned with both their coats held above his head. They shrugged the coats on, then Han said: 'We should explore.'

Pia looked at the cow and the nearby river.

'She won't swim back,' Han said. 'The grazing is better here.'

Pia accepted that. Han was the herder.

They set off around the island. It was small, and they got back to their starting point in the time it took to boil a pot of water. There were no signs of human habitation, and Pia guessed that for most people the river, and the need to cross it to go anywhere, would have spoiled the island as a home.

But for two fugitives it was perfect.

There were no deer, but there were pigeons in the air, squirrels in the trees and hares under the bushes. There were also hazel trees, heavy with nuts at this time of year, nuts that would keep through the winter.

They found a spot in the middle of the island where they could build a roof up against the wide trunk of an oak tree. Han said: 'I'll get some timber from that derelict house.'

'Do it tomorrow,' Pia said. 'The main thing we need today is fire.'

Together they collected dry twigs and dead leaves for tinder, then some larger pieces of dead wood. Han found an abandoned wasps' nest that would blaze up in no time. They struck a spark and started the fire.

Thunder caught a hare. They cleaned it and skinned it and roasted it over the fire. They gave the bones to the dog.

When evening came they built up the fire for the night, then lay down together. They made love in the dusk, firelight painting their bodies, and it seemed especially exciting because this was the first time Pia had done it in freedom.

Afterwards they pulled their coats over themselves to keep warm, and soon they fell asleep.

Stam turned up at Yana's house after a long absence. He was weary and disgruntled. She knew where he had been: everyone did. He had been looking for Pia.

As soon as Yana saw him she knew he had failed to find her. His expression was defiantly sulky. She felt relief and triumph in waves. Hiding her feelings, she said: 'What happened?'

He said: 'Give me something to eat.'

She put soft cheese in a big bowl and mixed it with chopped crab apple. He ate rapidly and became less irritable.

Yana wanted to know more about Stam's search. She said: 'Why did you go alone? I would have thought you'd take some of the Young Dogs with you.'

'They make too much noise,' he said. 'It would give warning that they're coming. On my own I can be silent.'

'But you still didn't find anyone.'

'I know where Pia and Han are,' he said, sounding defensive. 'Roughly where they are, anyway.'

She suppressed her loathing to talk to him. She wanted more details. 'How did you manage that?' she said. 'No one can find them.' She knew he would be flattered.

He looked smug. 'I followed the cow pats. No one takes cattle to the hills, especially at this time of year. And anyway there were only enough pats for one cow. They must be in the area where the pats ran out. I searched, but I couldn't find them.'

They had hidden themselves well, Yana thought. Good for them.

'I ran out of food,' Stam said. 'I killed a pigeon, but I couldn't cook it, because I forgot to take a firestone. Raw pigeon meat is really sickening. I had to give up.'

'What did your father say?'

'He was displeased. He's always displeased.'

'Well, we can forget about them now. They've gone, and that's the end of it.'

'No, it's not,' he said spiritedly. 'Next spring, when the weather gets warmer, I'm going again. I haven't given up.' His expression became cruel. 'Pia thinks she can defy my father's authority and outwit me. But she can't. She's just a little girl who needs to be taught a lesson. I'm going to find her, and I'm going to show her who is the master.'

14

SHORTLY BEFORE THE Midwinter Rite, Joia and Seft went to Stony Valley. The weather was mild, and there was little rain: the drought still had not broken. They arrived in the early dusk of a winter afternoon.

They were both still determined to rebuild the Monument in stone. They understood the difficulties; they just refused to believe the problems were insoluble.

Joia was surprised to see several houses where there had been none last time she visited. Seft's second-in-command, Tem, was living there with his partner, Vee, who was Joia's old friend. Several other cleverhands had moved there with their families, bringing half a dozen cattle and a few pigs to feed everyone. The place was now a small village. Joia had not been aware of this. Seft had done it quietly.

Joia and Seft ate with Tem and family, sitting around a blazing fire. Vee said that Hol, the smelly shepherd at the top of the hill, was grateful to them for burning so much dead wood, saying it allowed more grass to grow for his sheep to graze.

They ate pork stewed with crab apples. Joia said to Seft: 'I'm worried about how long it would take to move one stone to the Monument – fifty days, if Ello is right, and I can't see any flaw in her argument.'

'I've been thinking about that too,' he said.

'We might be able to muster two or three teams of volunteers, who could work more or less at the same time.'

'That would reduce the problem.'

Joia frowned. 'I'm just not sure I could persuade people to volunteer for fifty days. That's not so much a celebration, more like a punishment.'

Seft nodded. 'We've been working on some new ideas here. I'll show you a few things tomorrow morning. I think we can find a way.'

Joia went to sleep full of pork and hope.

She woke up and went outside to a morning of low grey winter clouds, and she saw something she had not perceived yesterday in the dusk. A hundred or so logs, each about as long as two men, had been laid side by side, forming a kind of path. At one end was a small sarsen stone already encompassed in a rope bag.

Seft appeared as she was staring at it. 'Ello is against us, but her pessimism is useful,' he said. 'When she talked about how long it took to move the farmer's stone, she drew my attention to the heart of the problem. It's the unevenness of the ground. A dragged stone would constantly be stopped when its front edge hit a dip or a bump, or a rock or a puddle, and the front would have to be lifted to get over the obstacle, which would be difficult and take a long time. So I've been thinking of ways to make the ground more even, so that the stone can move faster and not be stopped by minor obstructions.'

The cleverhands appeared in ones and twos and stood around.

Joia realized with a thrill that all these people were committed to building the stone Monument.

Seft said: 'By the way, the logs don't roll. They're hammered into the soil, to make the pathway stable.'

One of the cleverhands, Jero, said: 'Shall we show her, Seft?' Jero did not have Seft's patience. He was always in a hurry. His father, Effi, had been the same.

But there was no reason to delay, so Seft said: 'Yes, go ahead.'

The cleverhands picked up the rope grab lines and got ready to drag the stone. Joia thought it was about a tenth of the size of the big monoliths, so about the same size as the farmer's stone. The wives and older children of the cleverhands appeared to help, and in the end there were about twenty people.

Joia remembered the moving of the farmer's stone, when she had seen only fourteen midsummers. The farmer's field had been smoothed out by many years of cultivation, but even so there had been at least one obstacle.

Tem led the pulling team, and they quickly got the stone moving. Joia was astonished by how smoothly it ran along the path of logs. Twice it hit a log that had risen slightly higher than the others, and both times it slowed briefly then crushed the raised edge and went on. The cleverhands pulled the stone to the end of the path.

'That's wonderful!' Joia said to Seft. 'You've solved the problem.'

He shook his head. 'This is useful only for short distances. To build a road of logs from here to the Monument would use up all the trees in the Great Plain. Just chopping them down would take years.'

'Couldn't you use a smaller number of logs, and bring those from behind to the front as the stone was moving?'

'We tried that.' Seft smiled. 'The men were exhausted, carrying the logs, working in pairs, running from the back to the front.

But the real problem is that when the logs are laid in front of the moving stone they're not embedded securely, so the stone pushes them out of the way.'

Joia's euphoria went as quickly as it had come. 'So we're back where we started.'

'Not quite.' At the end of the log path there was a different kind of path, made of branches of all sizes plus loose earth. 'This is much easier to put in place, and we could lay something like it all the way to the Monument in a few weeks. But it's too flimsy.' He nodded to Tem, who got the hands pulling again.

Joia saw the problem immediately. Where the stone had pushed the logs farther into the ground, here it just shoved the branches aside. The path quickly became disarranged and the stone's progress was constantly interrupted and stopped. 'It's better than nothing,' Seft said, 'but not much.'

'So you would plan to use both kinds of path . . .'

'But that still wouldn't be enough to reduce fifty days to five.'

'You don't look completely defeated. You've got something else in mind.'

'You know me too well. I've got one more thing to show you. Come with me.'

He led her to a rough shelter that was clearly his workshop. Inside were flint tools of all kinds, antlers for pressure-sharpening blades, a quern for sanding and polishing, and ropes. Four of the cleverhands went behind the workshop and returned carrying something Joia did not recognize.

It was made from the entire trunk of a tall tree, a flat piece of wood longer than the largest stone in Stony Valley. It was as wide across as a man's arm was long, and thick. It was dead straight from one end almost to the other. Its most noticeable feature was that at one end – undoubtedly the end that had been the base of the tree trunk – it curved upwards like the front end of a wickerwork boat. It had been polished and oiled, so that it gleamed in the weak winter sunshine.

Seft said: 'Instead of trying to make the ground more even, we're going to make the stone more flat.'

Joia did not understand that. 'What is it?' she said.

'It's a runner.'

'Do you put the stone on top of it?'

'Sort of. This is just part of what we're going to construct. There will be two runners, joined by cross struts to form the base of a sled. The base will support a low platform on which the stone will sit. It all has to be put together very soundly with peg-and-hole joints, using short, thick pieces of wood so that the entire thing doesn't collapse under the weight. The curved ends of the runners will enable the sled to be pulled over minor obstructions without stopping.'

'If this works . . .'

'We should be able to move a stone from here to the Monument in two or three days.'

Joia did not dare to believe it. It would be very unusual for Seft to make promises he could not keep, but this seemed too good to be true. She said: 'I can hardly wait to see the finished thing.'

'You'll be the first. But you may have to wait a while.'

Their conversation was interrupted by a striking-looking woman who came down the slope from the shepherd's house. 'I brought you some mutton,' she said cheerfully as she approached, and Joia saw that she had a basket piled with meat.

Joia stared at her. She had a wide mouth that seemed to smile from ear to ear, and her light-brown hair was a mass of curls that shook as she walked. She was about Joia's age, much too young to be old Hol's woman.

Seft said: 'Thank you, Dee. It's very kind of your grandfather to send us meat for breakfast.'

So, Joia thought, she's Hol's granddaughter, and her name is Dee.

Dee said: 'Grandadda says if you ever feel like giving him a piglet he'd be most willing to accept. Pork makes such a nice change from mutton.'

Joia could not keep her eyes off Dee. She seemed to overflow with vivacity and warmth.

'I'll send him one today,' said Seft. It was important to make friends with the old shepherd. They had invaded his valley and they needed him to see their presence as a benefit, not a nuisance. 'By the way,' Seft went on, 'this is Joia, one of our priestesses.'

Dee gave the formal handshake and said: 'What an honour, to meet a priestess.'

Joia said: 'I've been here before but I've never met you. I didn't know Hol had a granddaughter living with him.'

'That's because I don't live with him,' Dee said. 'He's too smelly. I have a flock in the next valley with my brother and his wife. I just come over the hill to check on Grandadda now and again.'

'Well, I'm very glad to meet you,' Joia said.

'Likewise.' She put down the basket. 'Enjoy the meat,' she said, and she turned and strode away.

'My goodness,' Joia said quietly. 'Isn't she wonderful?'

Seft gave her an odd look and said: 'Let's cook this mutton.'

15

THAT WINTER WAS the happiest time of Pia's life.

She had Han, and they loved each other more every day. She was free: no one could tell her what to do, and every morning she had the delicious independence to decide how to spend the day. They had enough to eat: they had butchered the cow in the autumn, when the wild creatures hid away and many of the birds flew south. They had smoked most of the meat, hanging it under the roof where the fumes from the fire gathered. They were warm and dry, even when it snowed. Han had built the shelter well, and covered the roof with many layers of ferns from the riverside. They slept close together, covered by their shearling coats, blissfully comfortable.

She missed her mother, but she believed they would be reunited one day.

Han was unsentimental. He did not seem to miss his family. He showed no sadness about being separated from his mother or his two sisters, Joia and Neen. He spoke lovingly of Neen's children, two nieces and a nephew, but he did not say that he longed to see them and talk to them. He did not express regrets.

When the beef ran low it was spring. The trees were in bud and soon there would be new sources of food, young hares and squirrels, birds' eggs and fresh leaves.

Pia's baby was coming soon. Her belly was huge, the skin taut, and often now she felt movement. As she lay awake, there was a sudden bulge in the dome of her belly as the baby stretched its legs, pushing against its confinement. She wanted it to come now. She was tired all the time, and just standing up in the morning was an effort. Soon she would no longer be pregnant – she would have her baby in her arms.

Life was wonderful, but in her heart she knew it was unreal, like a dream, or a story. Summer would be fine, but beyond that the future was uncertain. She did not know how they would live through next winter. They would not get another cow. Hungry mothers produced weak milk, everyone knew that; and weak milk made for a sickly child.

One thing at a time, she told herself. First, the birth. Then, the summer. And after that they would have to think again.

She felt Han stir beside her. It must be first light. He kissed her then got up.

Han liked to hunt early. He took a drink of water from the wooden jar he had carved, then picked up his bow and arrows. When he stepped out of the shelter there was a hint of grey in the eastern sky. He did not put his shoes on: he needed to walk softly.

He took a familiar route through the wood to a small clearing. He lay down carefully, soundlessly, beside a thorny bramble just coming into leaf. The creatures of the wild had not yet crept out of their night-time hideaways. He lay still and silent, his bow in his left hand and half a dozen arrows close to his right, only his eyes moving. This was the finest moment of the day: the air fresh and cold, the woods damp with dew, silence and peace.

Two pigeons appeared and did a mating dance in a tree. A squirrel scampered along a branch. A hare leaped across the clearing, too fast for him to shoot. It was time to kill.

Moving softly, he put an arrow to his bow and carefully pulled the string. If he was lucky, a duck would come waddling out of the undergrowth and into the clearing, plump and slow and an easy target.

Suddenly there were three hares nibbling the grass. He took slow aim and shot one, then quickly sent off a second arrow and a third. The second found its target, but the third hare bounded away unhurt. The squirrel vanished and the pigeons flew away.

Satisfied, Han stood and picked up his two hares by the ears. He collected the arrows for re-use.

The sun rose. On his way back he scanned the ground, looking for early vegetables. He found a patch of spring onions, picked them all, and washed the earth off them in the river.

He returned to the shelter and showed Pia his harvest. She put a pot of water on the fire to boil. Han skinned the hares then cleaned them and gave the guts to Thunder. When the water was boiling, Pia chopped the onions and put them into the pot, then Han dropped the hares in.

He scraped the skins carefully, thinking of how his mother, Ani, cleaned cattle hides. 'These will make warm clothes for the baby,' he said. 'I wish I could tan them, as my mother does, but I don't have what's necessary.'

'We'll keep the baby warm,' she said.

'Later I'll go and raid some nests. The birds might be laying.' Struck by a thought, he said: 'Can babies eat eggs?'

'I don't know,' said Pia. 'I wish I could ask my mother.'

The weather was warming up, and the inhabitants of West Wood were preparing to leave for the hills. Bez had again consulted Joia, the friendly second high priestess, and they expected the deer to migrate in two days' time. They were making arrows for the hunt and sharpening flints for the butchering, and putting cooking pots, wooden bowls and other necessities into leather carrying bags that could be slung over their shoulders. Excitement was in the air: people talked in loud voices and laughed a lot. The trip was an adventure, even to those who had done it many times. The dogs knew what was happening and ran around impatiently, getting under people's feet.

Bez and Fell were in a hut, discussing the first hunt. Fell's new dog, distinguished by a white patch on his muzzle, lay sleeping beside them. 'Last year's choice of a killing field was successful,' said Bez. 'We should go to the same place this year.'

Fell shook his head. 'The deer will remember and avoid it.'

'Don't be silly. Only one deer escaped last year – and, anyway, they can't warn one another. They have no speech.'

'I'm not so sure,' said Fell. 'They have ways.'

No one knew the truth, Bez thought, so there was no point in arguing. 'Well, then, think of a better place,' he said.

Then they both noticed that the village had gone quiet.

'Trouble,' said Bez, and they went out.

Everyone was looking in the same direction. Bez followed their gaze and saw Stam, armed with a bow and arrows. He was alone this time. He recognized Bez and said: 'You. You can speak like a human. Come here.'

Bez stayed where he was. 'You are welcome, Stam, if you come in peace.'

'You know why I'm here.'

'Perhaps you're looking for that runaway girl again. She wasn't here last year, and she's not here now.'

'She isn't a runaway. A herder has stolen a farmer girl.' Stam became boastful. 'We have discovered who he is. His name is Han. He is tall, with fair hair and big feet.'

'He's not here. Nor are his feet.'

The villagers chuckled, but Stam did not get the joke. 'I believe they were here when I came looking for them last autumn – but you concealed them. You could be killed for that.'

The woodlanders shifted restively. They were being threatened, and they resented it.

Bez said emolliently: 'Best not to talk of killing, Stam, when there's a whole lot of us and only one of you.'

His response was disdainful. 'I'm not afraid of you.'

'You have nothing to be afraid of, as long as you don't speak of killing. And now I think you should leave, before you talk yourself into serious trouble.'

'I'm going,' said Stam. 'But remember this: when I find out who's hiding here, it won't be mere talk of killing.'

Han cocked his head and said: 'What's that sound?'

Pia listened and said: 'It's like a crowd of people walking and talking.'

'It's coming from the north side of the river,' said Han. 'I'm going to look.'

'I'll come.' She struggled to her feet. She was fearful. People meant danger.

They went to the shore and peeped through the vegetation, staying out of sight. Thunder joined them.

On the north shore were woodlanders, too many to count, walking past the derelict house and the muddy beach, taking no notice of the stone circle on the hill. Some carried small children, most had shoulder bags. They walked at the moderate pace of people who have a long way to go.

Thunder growled at their dogs, and Han said sharply: 'Silent!' Thunder hushed.

Pia said: 'This is their migration. They're following the deer. But you and I didn't notice the deer passing.'

'Deer move silently. I could have shot one if we'd heard them. Which is probably why they're so quiet. Which the woodlanders are not. They can be silent, when they want, but now they're noisy.'

'It's because they're enjoying themselves. I've noticed that. When people go on a journey in a large group, they have a good time, see strange places, maybe fall in love.'

They watched the procession for a while, then returned to the shelter. Han said the woodlanders posed no threat, but Pia remained concerned.

Han had shot three fat pigeons, and a mouth-watering fragrance was coming from the boiling pot. He lifted a pigeon breast from the water, using a pointed stick. 'Almost cooked,' he said. He was always hungry, but he divided everything in half, even though he was bigger, because Pia was eating for the baby too.

Suddenly Thunder barked.

'Hush!' said Han.

The dog's ears were up and he was staring north, in the direction of the migrating woodlanders. Han stood up and headed the way Thunder's nose pointed, and Pia followed. When they came to the shore they saw two men in the river. Woodlanders were not great swimmers, and they were holding on to a log and kicking their legs behind them. Following them, swimming effortlessly, was a dog with a white patch on its nose.

Pia said: 'Oh, no! They've found us.'

'It's all right,' Han said. 'They're friends.'

Pia looked harder and said: 'So they are – Bez and Fell!'

As the woodlanders approached the shore, Han knelt down and helped them out of the water. There was ironic cheering from the other side as they stood up on dry land. Han pulled the log out of the water for their return journey.

Pia hurried them into the interior of the island so that they would be out of sight. She did not like so many people seeing where she and Han were. Once they were hidden, they greeted one another warmly, and the dogs sniffed each other warily.

They sat on the ground outside the shelter, and Pia said: 'How did you find us?'

'We saw the smoke from a fire,' said Bez. 'We guessed it might be you.'

Pia disliked the sound of that. 'Someone else might reason the same way.'

'I'm afraid you're right,' said Bez. 'We had a visit from Stam before we left. He's still looking for you. He knows you're with Han, but he doesn't know where you are. He thought you might be with us in West Wood.'

'We're in danger, though,' Pia said.

'I'm here to protect you,' said Han. 'But you're right, we need to be vigilant.'

Fell smiled at Pia and said: 'Your baby is coming soon.'

'I hope so.' She checked the pigeon stew and found that the meat was cooked. 'Would you like something to eat?'

They accepted eagerly.

Pia had only two bowls, so she and Han shared one while Bez and Fell had the other. The woodlanders did not use spoons but slurped from the bowl then picked up the meat with their fingers.

It all disappeared quickly.

Bez said: 'You are woodlanders now!' He grinned.

They were, Pia thought: no herd, no farm. She said: 'But we have no tribe.'

Bez said: 'Our tribe is your tribe.'

Pia considered that. Could they live with Bez's people in West Wood? They would be no worse off than they were here, and they would have the protection of the tribe. But Pia thought she would not like their way of life, especially the way the women had sex with lots of men.

Han said: 'What's happening on the Great Plain?'

Bez shook his head gloomily. 'There was that storm in the autumn, and it snowed at midwinter, but now there has been no rain for many days. We're hoping there will be some good grass in the hills.'

'So the drought continues. This will be the third year.'

'Many people will not see the fourth.'

'Have you talked to my sister Joia?'

'Yes. Once again she told us when to expect the deer to migrate. I hope she's right again.'

'How is she?'

'The same, though she speaks a lot about moving giant stones. I don't understand why.'

Han nodded. 'I do. She wants to build a stone Monument.'

'Will that end the drought?'

'Who knows?'

Bez stood up. 'We have to go. It's another half a day's walk to our usual camping ground. Thank you for sharing your food. If we have good hunting, we will bring you venison.'

Pia said: 'That would be much appreciated.'

They returned to the shore and the woodlanders crossed the river, again using the log.

Pia said: 'Help me gather some fresh ferns, please.'

'Of course,' he said. 'But why?'

'Childbirth can be messy.'

He was startled. 'Is it happening?'

'Yes. I felt a pain earlier, and now it's getting worse. Don't worry, pain is normal. I've watched women giving birth. Pain is what we give in exchange for love.'

'Right,' he said, making an effort to remain calm; and Pia recalled that he was the youngest child in his family, and probably had not witnessed a birth. He began to gather armfuls of the ferns that grew in the damp soil beside the river.

When they returned to the shelter she took off her tunic, to avoid getting it soiled. 'Lay the ferns on the ground inside the house,' she told him. 'I'll need the fire to keep me and the baby warm, especially if this goes on into the night.'

'That long?'

'Let's hope not.'

As soon as he had spread the ferns, Pia lay down on her side. Han knelt beside her and said: 'What can I do?'

'Just stay with me, and don't worry if I yell.'

At first she just groaned at intervals. Han patted her arm in a consoling way, but felt foolish, and stopped. She said: 'Keep doing that, it helps.'

Thunder was agitated. He would come into the shelter, sniff Pia, and go out again, as if seeking an explanation.

Pia began to cry out instead of groaning. She was vaguely aware of time passing, the warmth of midday and the decline of the afternoon. When the pains became severe she knew the baby was ready to be born. She rolled over and got onto her hands and knees. 'Kneel down behind me,' she said to Han.

He did so. She heard his exclamation of shock. 'Oh!' he said. 'I can see the baby's head – but it's too big, much too big!'

'Don't worry, just get ready to hold the baby when it comes,' she said, then yelled in pain again.

She felt the head emerge, and she knew the worst pain was past, although the birth was not yet over.

'I've got it, I've got it,' Han said triumphantly.

She felt the shoulders pass through painfully, then the rest of the baby less so. She collapsed face down, breathing hard, as if she had been running. A moment later the baby wailed. She turned over, carefully lifting her leg over the cord that still connected her to her child. She smiled at Han, who was holding the tiny body in both arms and staring in wonderment.

'Well,' she said, 'is it a boy or a girl?'

'I can't tell,' he said. 'Oh, of course I can. It's a boy. How about that? A boy!'

Everything seemed like a miracle at this moment, she knew. She sat upright, and Han gave the boy into her arms.

He stopped wailing immediately, and his lips worked, as if sucking. Pia put his mouth to her nipple, and he began to suckle with surprising energy.

Pia said: 'Get two long, thin shoots, and tie two knots around the cord. Then cut between the knots with a flint.'

Han looked glad to be able to do something useful. He stepped outside and quickly returned with suitable shoots. Pia said: 'Tie them close to the belly.' He tied tight knots then cut the cord.

The baby stopped sucking and fell asleep. Pia handed him to Han. 'I'm so tired,' she said, and she lay down.

Han picked up one of the hare skins and wrapped it around the baby's shoulders. 'What shall we name him?' he said.

'I don't know.'

'My father's name was Olin.'

'I like that,' said Pia. 'Olin.'

Han hugged the baby to his chest. Olin probably needed to be washed, but that could wait. He wiped the little face as gently as he could with his big hand. 'Olin,' he said. 'How do you like your name, Olin?' The child slept on. 'Well, he doesn't seem to object to it.'

Pia was thinking of a reply but fell asleep.

Olin changed a lot in the first few weeks of his life. He opened his eyes, and appeared to pay attention when he saw Pia's face or Han's. Sometimes he seemed to smile. He slept less in the day and longer at night. He cried angrily when hungry, he grizzled monotonously if he was uncomfortable, and he murmured contentedly as he closed his eyes to sleep. Each day he felt a little heavier in Pia's arms.

Han sang to him. He told Pia that he had suddenly remembered dozens of ditties from his childhood, and he deduced that Ani must have sung them to him. They were simple tunes, often using nonsense words, and Olin would look at him as if marvelling at the sound. Pia knew some of the songs and often joined in.

She wished she could show Olin to her mother. Yana would be so thrilled, and so proud of her daughter and her first grandchild. Yana would see Olin one day, but when? And in the meantime she was missing the thrill of watching him grow and learn.

The weather warmed towards summer, and there was no rain.

One day while Pia was nursing Olin outside the house, and Han was sewing the skins of hares to make a baby blanket, she screwed up her nerve and said to Han: 'I'd like to go to Riverbend before winter.'

He was startled. 'I think it's too soon,' he said. 'Troon surely hasn't forgotten you yet. When he hears that you're back, he'll try to kidnap you.'

'I know,' she said. 'But if we stay here I'm afraid all three of us will starve.'

'We've managed so far.'

'But last winter we had a cow.'

'Perhaps we could get another.'

She shook her head. 'You've left the herder community. Zad won't give you another. And if you steal one you might get shot by a herder's arrow.'

'A deer, then. A red deer would last us all winter – it has as much meat as a cow.'

'You've never hunted deer. They're hard to catch and hard to kill. When the woodlanders hunt them it takes the whole tribe.'

He looked wounded at her lack of faith in him.

She tried to soften her argument. 'Look, if it was just the two of us, as it was last winter, I'd say let's take the chance, and if we die, we die together. But we can't think only of ourselves now. If we starve, Olin starves, and I'm not willing to risk that – are you?'

There was only one answer to that. 'No, of course not,' said Han, but he looked cross.

Olin grizzled, and Pia moved him to the other breast.

Han said: 'We could move into West Wood, and live as part of Bez's tribe. He more or less said that.'

'I've thought about it.' She decided not to mention the woodlanders' distinctive sexual arrangements, but she had another objection. 'West Wood is dangerously close to Farmplace and Troon.'

Han nodded. 'Well, we don't have to make the decision yet. We've got the summer ahead of us. We don't know what might happen.' He brightened. 'Troon might die!'

'All right,' she said. 'Let's stay until the Autumn Halfway, when the night is as long as the day. If at that point we haven't got enough food to last us through to spring, we'll leave.'

'Agreed.'

Thunder stood up and growled softly. Someone was coming, but he did not consider the visitor dangerous. He was looking north, so it was probably someone crossing the river. Han picked up his bow and arrows and went to look. Pia stayed with Olin.

To Pia's astonishment, Han returned with Fell. This was the first time Pia had seen him without his brother. However, the dog with the white patch was with him.

Fell was carrying over his left shoulder the carcass of a roe deer, gutted but not skinned. In his belt was a large flint axe with a bloodstained blade, clearly having been used on the deer. He lowered the beast to the ground with a sigh of relief. 'For you,' he said.

'This is a wonderful gift!' Pia said. She was not sure how much Fell understood of the herder language. Bez usually did most of the talking.

'Very generous,' Han said. 'Thank you.'

'Sit down,' said Pia. 'Will you drink some water?'

Fell nodded, and Han brought water in a wooden bowl.

Pia said: 'How is Bez, your brother?'

'Bez is well,' he said. 'And Bez is happy, for he has Gida and I am gone.' He laughed, as if his remark was not to be taken too seriously.

But Pia was curious. 'So you and your brother share Gida?'

He smiled. 'She loves us both. We are lucky.'

Clearly Fell was content with the arrangement, but Pia did not think she could ever get used to that kind of thing.

Thunder barked. He was pointing in the same direction, north, but clearly this arrival had him worried.

Han said: 'Could this be Bez?'

'No,' said Fell. 'He's in the high hills.' He pointed to the carcass. 'Hunting these.'

'Could someone else be following you?'

'I don't know.'

Pia was suddenly frightened.

Han picked up his bow and arrows and headed for the shore, followed by Thunder.

Pia watched him pass behind a screen of shrubs, then heard a strange noise, a twang and a whistle like an arrow being shot, then a grunt, then a thump as if something had fallen. She said: 'What has Han shot?'

Thunder started barking hysterically, then suddenly went silent. Pia got to her feet, still holding Olin, and called: 'Han? Are you all right, Han?' Scarily, there was no reply.

Fell drew his axe from his belt and stood with one foot on the deer, as if afraid a thief might try to drag it away.

'Han?' Pia hurried past the shrubbery, her agitation growing. Behind the bushes was a tall elm. In the shadow of the tree she saw Han lying flat on his back. There was an arrow in his neck, and blood poured out of his throat.

For a long moment she was paralysed. She could not take in the picture she was looking at. It was impossible.

Then Olin started to cry.

Pia wanted to scream, but she feared she would frighten Olin. She suppressed her terror and knelt beside Han. He was hardly moving. 'Talk to me, Han!' she said, in a voice that was half spoken, half screeched. It seemed he could not speak. She stared at the arrow, feeling helpless. She thought she would vomit, and swallowed hard. Then she forced herself to be calm. As gently as she could, she pulled the arrow out of his neck. The blood flowed faster. 'No!' she said. 'No, no, no!'

Beside Han, Thunder lay with an arrow in his back. He was alive, breathing, but otherwise motionless. How sad and angry Han would be when he saw that!

She looked up. Through her tears she saw Stam, standing a few yards away, fitting another arrow to his bowstring. 'You did this!' she screamed.

She looked at Han again and tried to staunch the blood with her free hand. It made no difference. She knew it was hopeless but she pressed harder. Olin was now crying loudly, a wail of distress. She clung to him as she bent over Han. 'Don't die, my love, don't die!'

The gush of blood slowed. This was a bad sign. She had seen animals slaughtered, and she knew that when the blood stopped flowing the beast was dead. But she could not accept it. 'I'll make you better, I will, I will!' But a part of her mind that remained rational told her that Han would never get better.

She looked up again and saw Stam taking aim – not at her, but at something behind her. She turned and saw Fell, holding his axe high. He threw it just as Stam shot his arrow. She saw the axe graze Stam's shoulder, and she turned again to see the arrow pierce Fell's belly.

Fell screamed in agony and went down on his knees.

His dog ran away.

Stam clapped a hand to his shoulder. With his face screwed up in pain, he strode towards the wounded Fell, dropping his bow and taking a knife from his belt. Pia knew instinctively that he intended to finish Fell off. Still holding Olin, she threw herself at Stam, hitting him with her free hand.

He cursed and slapped her face. He was strong and his hand was hard. She went dizzy and her eyesight became blurred. He did it again, and she staggered, her entire head hurting. The third slap knocked her to the floor, and she lost her grip on Olin. She snatched him up quickly, holding him tightly to her chest, then looked at the others.

Stam turned on Fell, who – incredibly – had managed to rise to his feet and grapple with his attacker. They swayed to and fro for several moments, but Fell was fatally wounded and it was an uneven contest. Stam threw Fell to the ground, bent down, and cut his throat with the flint knife.

Pia stood up. Olin was yelling but she could tell that he was not in pain, just frightened. The carnage around was bewildering. Only moments ago Han and she had been talking, making plans, welcoming a guest; how could he be lying there still and silent? Would he never speak to her again? And kind-hearted Fell next to him.

She began to believe that what she was looking at was reality. Han was gone. Han was dead. The horror of her loss consumed her, and she was possessed by rage. She snatched up the arrow she had taken from Han's neck and dashed at Stam, determined to kill him, screaming: 'You killed my Han, you monster, you animal, you mad wild boar!' Stam put up a defensive hand and parried the arrow, but its sharp flint head dug a groove in his forearm, and he gave a shout of pain and anger.

She drew her arm back for a fatal blow. But he was too quick. Instead of attacking her, he snatched Olin from her. Holding the baby by one ankle, he lifted his flint knife, still red with Fell's blood, and held it next to the soft skin of the naked child.

Pia went weak. 'No, please, don't hurt him,' she cried. Her voice had lost all anger and aggression and had nothing in it but desperate supplication. She moved towards him to take Olin back, but he held the flint closer to the baby and said: 'Stay where you are or I'll cut him.'

She went down on her knees. 'Give him back to me, please.'

'Understand something,' he said. 'I'm taking you back to Farmplace, as that's what my father wants, but I doubt whether he cares what happens to your baby. However, I'll let you keep the brat as long as you behave yourself and do what I say. Any more trouble and I'll throw him into the river and watch him drown.'

The threat made her burst into fresh tears. 'I'll be good, I promise,' she sobbed. 'I'll do anything you ask, please give him to me.'

'And you won't try to run away from me.'

'No, I swear it.'

Still holding Olin by the ankle, he passed him to Pia. She took him and held him to her body, rocking him, murmuring in his ear: 'It's all right now, it's all right now.' His crying became less hysterical.

Stam said: 'Go and get some big flat leaves and some vines. I've got two bleeding wounds, and one of them is your doing. Just put the baby down and leave him here. I'm not giving you the chance to swim the river and escape.'

She hesitated. She could hardly bear to leave Olin.

Stam said: 'Just a moment ago you promised to do anything I asked.'

She saw that he would do no harm to Olin, for he could use Olin to control her. She laid the baby down gently and went to get what he needed.

When she came back Olin was fine.

As she dressed Stam's wounds she felt the rage rise in her again. Here she was, bandaging the wounds of the man who had murdered Han. She had lost everything to Stam. Han was dead and she was going back to Farmplace, back to the harsh farmer society. Everything she hoped for was dust. Were it not for Olin she would drown herself. But she had to suppress her rage. It boiled inside her, as if she had eaten foul poison, but she had to hide her feelings.

When she had bound up Stam's wounds he said: 'Now make me food. I'm hungry.'

She was on the point of saying they should do something about the bodies, but she decided not to argue. She put Olin down while she cut some cold meat from a cooked duck and chopped some meadowsweet she had found by the river. She put the food in a bowl and took it to Stam.

He ate the meal with his fingers.

When he had finished he said: 'It's not long past midday. We can cover a good distance this afternoon. Let's get going.'

She screwed up her courage. 'Surely we should cremate the dead.'

'No time,' he said.

'Then at least let me put them inside the shelter!'

'Be quick.'

She went to Han's body. The sight made her sob so hard she had trouble bending down and taking hold of his ankles. Still weeping, she dragged him across the ground. It seemed a cruel and disrespectful way to move him, but she knew she could not lift him off the ground. He was far too heavy, and she could not ask for help from the murderer.

She took Han into the shelter and arranged his body neatly, his legs straight, his feet together, his arms crossed on his chest. He was dressed in his tunic and his big shoes.

Still weeping, she repeated the process with Fell, who was a lot lighter. The two men lay side by side.

Finally she dragged in Thunder, who had bled to death. She put him beside Han.

She picked up Olin and sang the song of the Earth God. It seemed to soothe the baby. She was afraid Stam would interrupt and drag her away, but he did nothing and she was able to finish the song.

It seemed wrong to leave Han and Fell there, but she could do nothing more.

She stepped outside, then looked back at the shelter. It had been her home for more than half a year. It had witnessed the best time of her life, and the worst.

Stam said: 'Ready at last.'

She nodded.

'Then let's go.'

They walked away.

16

THE WOODLANDERS WERE hunting in the North-West Hills. It was better than the last two summers, which had been dire. The winter snow had refreshed the springs in the hills. There had been new grass when they arrived and, although it was mostly gone now, they had killed some deer and eaten well.

Bez, Gida, Lali and their companions were flat on their bellies, upwind of a herd of red deer, big and meaty. The red deer had an extra attraction: spreading antlers that made invaluable tools. It was a hot day, so the women were naked, and the men wore only their leather loincloths. They crawled forward, needing to get close enough to deploy bows and arrows without spooking the beasts. They kept a disciplined silence: deer had good hearing.

Bez thought they were almost there when the whole herd suddenly became nervous. Some looked up, some stepped sideways, some gave a little jump. Had they scented something? Then he saw a dog trotting across the hill. The deer moved away, getting ready to run. The hunters stood up, and some shot arrows, but they were too far away, and the herd fled.

The dog that had caused the trouble looked weary and dispirited. Some of the woodlanders yelled at it angrily for ruining the hunt, but it seemed too tired to care. Lali, who had a youngster's keen eyesight, said: 'That's Fell's dog.'

Bez saw the white patch on its muzzle. Lali was right.

The dog spotted Bez, gave a pleased bark, and ran to him. He patted it, but he had a cold feeling in his heart.

Gida said: 'What's it doing here, without its master?'

'That's what I'm wondering,' said Bez grimly.

'Something bad has happened.'

Bez nodded. He had the same foreboding. He said: 'Yesterday Fell went to take a roe deer to Han and Pia, as a present.'

'So the first place to look for him is probably that island.'

'Yes.'

'I'm coming with you,' Gida said, in a firm tone that discouraged argument.

Bez looked at the sky. 'We can't get there before dark. Let's start at first light.'

Next day at noon they reached the derelict house on the riverbank. They found a log and put it into the water, then Fell's dog began to behave strangely. It whined, lay down and got up again, approached the water and backed off, all as if scared of something.

Bez and Gida decided to leave it there. If it changed its mind it could swim across and find them.

Bez was full of apprehension as they crossed, but he was not sure exactly what he feared. The woodlanders had no enemies in the hills. The area was thinly populated, mostly by shepherds with small flocks. Was it possible that one of them had killed Fell for the venison he was carrying?

They clambered out of the river onto dry land. No one appeared to greet them, and Bez had a premonition of tragedy.

They made their way through the vegetation to the little shelter. All was quiet and still. Bez concluded there was no one there.

The carcass of the deer lay on the ground, much nibbled by birds and little carnivores. So Fell had been here. But the gift lay on the ground as if spurned, and there was no sign of the giver or the recipients.

Then he looked into the shelter.

Bez gave an involuntary sob as he recognized his brother. At the same moment, Gida wailed: 'Oh, Fell, my Fell, my lovely Fell!'

At first they looked peaceful, two men lying on their backs, their hands folded on their chests, with a dog alongside them. Then Bez was struck by the early signs of decay: the skin grey, with purplish patches; the bellies swollen; and a faint odour of rot.

A moment later he was horrified to notice that the wild creatures had already been at the bodies. The eyes had been pecked out, the lips eaten, the hands bitten.

He turned away, and Gida did the same. Facing each other, they embraced, both weeping, for a long moment. At last Gida spoke through her tears. 'Pia's not here.'

'Perhaps she got away.'

Gida shook her head. 'She's either heavily pregnant or carrying a baby. Either way, it's unlikely she escaped when Han and Fell couldn't. I think the murderer took her.'

'Then it's Stam.'

'It must be.'

They gathered firewood together, and the physical effort relieved the intolerable pressure of grief. They made a double-wide pyre. By the time they had finished they were no longer boiling with grief and rage, but simply tired and desperately sad.

Bez took the band of bear's teeth from around Fell's neck. He wanted to show it to the tribe when he told them that Fell was dead.

They picked up the body, Bez lifting the shoulders and Gida the thighs. They carried him carefully to the pyre and laid him down on one side of it.

Next Bez took off Han's distinctive shoes. They bore patches of dark-red stain, undoubtedly blood. Like the necklace, they would serve as proof of what Bez had seen. Han was bigger and heavier than Fell, and they struggled to lift him, but they managed to get him to the pyre and lay him beside Fell.

Finally Bez picked up the corpse of Han's dog and laid it at its master's feet.

They stood up and lit the fire, and Gida sang a woodlander song of sadness and loss.

As it burned, they sat together beside the pyre and talked about Fell. Gida recalled Fell making the necklace, painstakingly drilling the holes for the string with a narrow flint bradawl. 'And when it was finished he was so proud! He walked around with it on, waiting for people to notice and comment.'

Bez remembered when he was born. His mother had said: 'A little brother for you – you must look after him.' Now Bez said to Gida: 'I tried, I really did, but I failed.'

As the bodies turned to ashes, Bez said: 'We both loved him.'

Gida nodded. 'Yes, we both loved him.'

Leaving the smouldering remains behind, they left the island.

The dog was waiting patiently outside the derelict house. Bez said: 'I suppose you'll be my dog now.' As they set off, heading back to the camp, the dog walked close to Bez's heels.

They arrived back as people were finishing the evening meal. The woodlanders all stopped what they were doing and gathered around Bez and Gida to find out what had happened. Gida told the story while Bez showed Fell's necklace and Han's shoes.

They were angry. Fell had been born into the tribe and Han was an honorary member. Two of their own had been murdered. 'And we know who did it!' said one of the men, Omun, an accomplished hunter. 'We know that Stam was looking for Pia and Han, and we heard him say he would kill anyone who hid them. It's obvious. He came to kidnap Pia and now he's taken her home.'

Bez was not so sure. He would have liked proof. But this was not the moment to say so.

Bez said to Gida: 'Would you wear Fell's necklace?'

'No,' she said. 'You must wear it.'

Bez hesitated. Then he realized he would always have a part of his brother with him. 'Yes,' he said. 'I want to wear it.'

She stood behind him and put the necklace over his head. The bear's teeth felt cold against his skin. Gida stroked them with her fingertips, and a tear ran down her cheek.

Bez turned to the crowd. 'We will always remember Fell. Always.'

Several people repeated the word: 'Always!'

Omun shouted: 'There must be a balance!'

There were shouts of agreement.

'Oh, yes,' said Bez. 'The gods demand a balance. A blow must be returned. That which is stolen must be replaced. A lie demands a truth. And a murder requires a death. There will be a balance. There will.'

Pia was back at Farmplace, on her mother's farm, carrying water from the river to the fields all day, every day, just as she had done before, only now she had Olin on her hip all the time. Her back ached and her shoulder hurt and she was utterly miserable.

She felt she could not put Olin down while she worked. It was too dangerous. The creatures of the wild were hungry. A farmer baby had been attacked by a boar only days ago, and much of the poor mite's thigh had been eaten before its mother came running in response to its screams.

Olin was the bright spot in her life. He was a quarter of a year old now. He smiled a lot and even laughed sometimes. He would turn his head to look at the source of a new voice. He grabbed at everything in reach: a spoon, a flower, his mother's hair – although he often missed. She wished she had more time to simply play with him, sing to him, and kiss his soft skin.

Yana was thrilled with her first grandchild. She held him at every chance she got. She pulled funny faces that made him chuckle. She, too, wished she could spend more time with him.

But the drought continued. Since the winter snow there had been nothing more than a few brief showers. Green shoots were appearing in the fields, but only because the farmers irrigated the land with river water. So they had to continue.

One evening after supper, when Stam had gone out and Yana and Pia were playing with Olin, they were visited by Katch, Stam's mother. Pia was never sure how to react to her. Her man, Troon, was evil, and her son, Stam, was a monster. But that might not be her fault. And Katch was also Pia's aunt, so perhaps she had some loyalty to her niece.

Yana offered water from the jar, and Katch accepted it and sat down. She always seemed timid, but Yana said there was strength behind that. Perhaps she had to be strong, to endure life with Troon.

Olin was on the mat, lying on his tummy, waving his arms and legs. He lifted his head and looked uncertainly at Katch, knowing she was unfamiliar. She leaned forwards and stroked him under his chin. She said: 'You know I'm a stranger, don't you? But I'm a nice stranger, so don't worry.' He was not much reassured.

She sat back, sipped her water, and said: 'You must have noticed that Stam is spending more nights at my house.'

'Yes,' said Yana. 'He says it's because Olin's crying wakes him in the night.'

Katch shook her head. 'That's not the reason. He sleeps through anything. A baby's crying wouldn't wake him.'

'What, then?'

Katch looked at Pia. 'He's scared of you.'

Pia was incredulous. 'He is scared of me?'

'He says you glare hatred at him all the time.'

Pia thought that was probably true. If so, she was not going to stop.

Katch said: 'He's afraid you'll cut his throat in the night.' She glanced at Yana, doubtless remembering that Yana had once made such a threat.

Pia said: 'Well, if I glare at him, it's hardly surprising. He murdered my man, the father of my child, the love of my life.' She started to cry. 'What do you expect?'

'Murder?' said Katch. 'I expect there was a fight—'

Pia became indignant. 'There was no fight! I was there. Stam shot him with an arrow in cold blood. It penetrated Han's throat and he bled to death quickly. If my hatred is Stam's only punishment, he's getting off lightly.'

'An accident, perhaps . . .'

Pia made a scornful noise. 'Stam also shot an innocent woodlander. And a dog. And he picked up baby Olin by the foot and threatened to cut him with a knife.'

Yana gasped with horror. Pia had not told her that part of the story.

Katch winced. As a mother herself she could hardly help

reacting to talk of hurting babies. But she said: 'You can't live with hatred in the air. Can't you put this behind you? Forgive him and start again.'

'What?' Pia could hardly contain her incredulity. She was momentarily silenced.

Yana spoke. 'Katch, did Troon ask you to come here and talk to us about this?'

Katch looked embarrassed. 'Yes, he did.'

'And he told you to ask us to forgive Stam?'

'Yes.'

That explained it, Pia thought. Katch was not expressing her own thoughts or feelings: she was saying what Troon had ordered her to say.

Katch said: 'Troon's awfully cross.'

Pia felt a pang of pity for the woman, living with that horrible man.

Yana said: 'Look, Katch, why don't you go home and tell Troon that we listened to you attentively and we promised to think very hard about what you said?'

Katch brightened. 'Yes, I think he might be mollified by that.'

Pia gave her mother a glance of admiration. That had been very diplomatic.

Katch stood up. 'May I say to Stam that you would welcome him if he wanted to come home for the night?'

Certainly not, Pia thought, but she left it to her mother to reply.

Yana said: 'Best perhaps not to say anything along those lines. Words can be so easily misunderstood.'

'All right,' said Katch. 'Anyway, thank you for listening. May the Sun God smile on you.'

'And on you,' said Pia and Yana together; and Katch left.

Pia stepped outside and watched her walk across the fields. It was full dark, but the nights were usually bright, nowadays, because the stars were rarely hidden by clouds. When Katch was out of sight, a voice close to Pia shocked her. 'It is I, Bez. Don't be afraid.'

She spun around. It was him. 'You surprised me,' she said.

'May I enter your house?'

'Yes, of course.'

'Thank you.'

Yana greeted Bez and got him some water. Pia wondered whether Bez knew that his brother, Fell, had been killed. She might have to give him the news. She was not sure how to put it. Clumsily, she said: 'About Fell . . .'

'I know,' he said. 'Gida and I found the bodies.'

Yana said: 'Oh, how terrible.'

'We burned them and Gida sang a song.'

'I'm so glad,' said Pia. 'Stam wouldn't let me.'

'I guessed so. But it must have been you who laid them out so beautifully in the shelter.'

'It was all I was allowed to do.'

'I was comforted to see that my brother's body had been treated with respect, and I thank you.'

Pia was glad that she had done something right in the midst of horror.

Bez said: 'I placed the dog on the pyre at Han's feet.'

Pia was crying. 'Thank you,' she said.

'But I know only the end of the story. You must tell me the beginning. I need to understand.'

'Of course.' Pia wiped her tears with her hands and tried to marshal her thoughts. 'Fell brought us a deer – such a generous gift. We were sitting down, talking, when Thunder barked and we knew a stranger was coming. Han went to see who it was. I felt that something was wrong and I followed him. I found him lying on the ground with an arrow in his neck, bleeding to death. I'm sorry, I can't stop crying.'

'I'm so sorry to make you cry,' said Bez. 'But I must know what happened. What else did you see?'

'Stam, standing there, putting another arrow to his bow.'

'So the killer was Stam?'

'Yes.'

'No one else was there?'

'No. That second arrow wounded Fell, and then Stam cut poor Fell's throat with a knife.'

Bez nodded. 'We thought it must have been Stam, but I needed to hear it from you.'

Yana said shrewdly: 'Is there some reason, Bez, why you need to be absolutely sure who did this?'

'Yes,' he said solemnly. 'The gods demand a balance. When there is a blow, it must be returned. And where there is a murder, the murderer must die. The hammer of the gods must fall upon the head of the guilty.'

On the day before the Midsummer Rite, the priestesses rehearsed their ritual. The dance and the song that went with it were performed only once a year, so they needed to practise. Joia took them through it, prompting them with the words and guiding them as they wove in and out of the timber posts. They did it a second time. After the third she was satisfied, and they went into the dining hall for the midday meal.

They sat on the floor in neat rows, waiting, until High Priestess Ello came in; then dinner was served, a stew of cow's brains and dandelions. Their numbers were reduced, because three older priestesses had died in the winter.

Conversationally, Joia said: 'Perhaps we should recruit more novices. The Midsummer Rite is a good opportunity – people see us at our best.'

Ello observed sourly: 'More priestesses mean we need more food.'

'But we have to preserve the knowledge that's in our songs. If the priestesshood should die out, the knowledge would be lost for ever.'

'I know that, Joia. Kindly refrain from instructing me.'

Joia persisted. 'We should at least replace priestesses who die.'

'It would be wise to wait until the crisis is over.'

That was typical. Ello always had a reason for doing nothing. Joia said: 'But—'

Ello interrupted. 'No novices will be recruited until the drought has come to an end. That is my decision.'

Joia knew just how bad the crisis was. Before the drought, she had devised a way of estimating how many cattle the herder community had. The exercise had needed the highest of the new numbers Soo had taught her ten midwinters ago.

She had imagined an oblong with its corners at the Monument, the village of Riverbend, a riverside hamlet called Watermeadow, and Three Streams Wood. She had walked the sides of the oblong counting every cow she could see. Guessing that she had probably been unable to see half of them, she doubled the number and got ninety-six, which she rounded up to a hundred. Then she guessed that the Great Plain probably encompassed about twenty oblongs, so the entire herd was two thousand cattle.

That had been before the drought. She had repeated the exercise a few days ago and arrived at a total of five hundred.

It was a frightening change. How soon would the number fall to nothing?

When dinner was over, and they all went outside, Joia saw her sister, Neen, waiting for her. She was always glad to see Neen. Although their lives had gone in different directions, they still had the old affectionate relationship, in which Neen was the wise older sister and Joia the youngster who needed to be looked after.

They both loved Seft, but in different ways. Joia spent a lot of time with him and they shared a dream. Neen admitted that this had bothered her, once. She had talked to their mother about it. Ani had said: 'A woman knows when a man loves her, and she knows when he stops.'

'Seft hasn't stopped loving me.'

'Then don't worry. He's fond of Joia in a different way.'

Neen had related that conversation to Joia, who thought their mother was absolutely right, as she usually was.

Now Joia looked at her sister's round face and lush hair and felt a surge of affection. Then she noticed that Neen was not wearing her habitual broad smile. 'Is something wrong?' she said.

'You must come to Mamma's house,' said Neen. 'There's a woodlander there, insisting on talking to all three of us.'

'It's probably Bez,' said Joia. 'I wonder what he's doing here? He should be hunting deer in the North-West Hills.'

They walked quickly to Ani's house. Bez was outside, looking solemn. Neen's two girls, Denno and Anina, were staring at him with a mixture of curiosity and fear. Denno had seen six midsummers; Anina was still a toddler. The eldest child, Ilian, was away with Seft.

Bez held in his hands a small package wrapped in leather.

They all sat down, and Bez unwrapped the package. It contained an old pair of shoes, very large and laced on top. 'Those are Han's shoes,' said Ani, grimly.

Joia gasped, fearful, and Neen put an arm around her shoulders, hugging her.

Bez passed the shoes to Ani. Her voice was shaky as she said: 'What is this stain? It looks like blood.'

Bez said: 'I have come to tell you that Han is dead.'

Joia cried: 'No!' Tears flooded her eyes. 'He can't be dead!'

'I'm sorry,' Bez said. 'He was killed by an arrow.'

Joia turned her head into Neen's shoulder. 'He can't be dead, he's my brother,' she said. Neen was crying too.

Ani's voice was unsteady, but she had questions. 'Was it an accident?'

'Not an accident.'

'Who shot the arrow?'

'Stam, the son of Troon.'

Joia looked up. 'I knew it!' she said, through her tears. 'They killed Han because Pia loved him.'

Bez said: 'They would say he stole Pia from them.'

'As if she was their property.'

'That's the way they think.'

Neen took the shoes from Ani and pressed them to her chest. 'Oh, poor Han, our Han, our great big little brother.'

Denno, the elder girl, said: 'Mamma, why are you crying?'

'Because Uncle Han has died.'

Denno was uncomprehending. 'Why? Why did he die?'

'A bad man shot him with an arrow.'

Denno said: 'That must have hurt!' and she began to cry.

Joia was overwhelmed by a wave of grief. She had lost her brother. So had Neen. Ani had lost her only son, Denno had lost her uncle, and Pia had lost her man. She cried harder. She felt that she would never stop crying; a rainstorm of tears would never be enough.

Bez waited a while, then said: 'Fortunately, Pia is all right. And the baby.'

'The baby!' Ani said. 'Of course – it must have been born this spring.'

'A little boy,' said Bez.

'A grandson for me,' she said. 'Do you know what they named him?'

'He is called Olin.'

'My late man's name.' She looked thoughtful. 'Olin fathered Han, then Olin died; and Han fathered Olin, and Han died.' Her voice became bitter. 'Is this the way the gods toy with us?'

Bez said nothing to that.

'Olin,' said Ani. 'Olin.'

She was quiet for a while, and then she said: 'I wonder if I'll ever see him.'

Bez waited until the rest of the woodlanders returned from the hills, then he put his plan into motion. It was a good plan, though not without risks.

First he had to capture the guilty man.

Three evenings running he left West Wood and went to East Wood. It was occupied by a different tribe, but woodland tribes living on the Great Plain were not hostile to one another. They had different languages, but managed to communicate – especially when they all went to the hills – in a pidgin that included words from the herder tongue. The East Wood tribes knew he was on their territory, but they left him alone.

He sat behind the shelter of the greenery and patiently watched. Farmers worked even more than herders, he noted. They ploughed the fields and sowed seeds, carried water and pulled weeds, yet in the end they were no better off, in good times or bad. What possessed these people to waste their lives in toil?

Mostly he concentrated on the house where Pia lived with her mother, the baby and Stam. The three adults laboured all day, Pia carrying the baby. Each evening they ate supper together, then – to judge by the sounds coming from the house – Stam had sex with Yana. Soon afterwards, by which time it was dark or nearly so, Stam left the house and did not return until daylight.

It seemed to be a regular pattern. That was very useful.

On the fourth evening Bez returned with three strong woodlander men. The four had smeared wood ash on their faces, hands, legs and feet, so that they would be hard to see in the dark. Bez carried some lengths of strong cord made from the sinews of slaughtered deer, and a small piece of thin leather that bundled up to about the size of his fist. They waited in the wood, watching the house as the evening darkened. They were silent and still whenever anyone walked near their hiding place.

When they heard the sound of sex it was time to move.

Bez scanned the darkening landscape. There was no one in the fields, down by the river, or on the far side of the water. 'Let us go,' he said.

They came out of the wood walking softly. As quickly as they could, they crossed the field to a point where there was a slight dip, just deep enough to hide a man lying flat. Then they spread out across the route Stam usually took.

Soon he emerged, and this was the moment of highest risk. Would he spot them in the starlight, as they lay motionless on the dark field? If he fled, would they be able to catch him? Would the four woodlanders be able to overpower a young man so big and strong?

Stam came closer. He seemed all unsuspecting. If he saw them early enough, he might be able to run to the nearest house and shout for help, then they would have to abandon their plan and bolt.

Bez would have to think of another plan, and a second kidnap attempt would be more difficult because Stam would be on his guard.

A moment before Bez was ready to jump, Stam stopped and grunted an exclamation.

Bez leaped to his feet, and the other three did the same.

Stam turned to run, but he was a moment too late, and they were on him.

Bez quickly stuffed the leather bundle into Stam's mouth to stop him crying out. Then they threw him to the ground and held him down. He grunted, but not loud enough; and he struggled, but he could not escape.

Bez lifted his gaze and looked at Pia's house. There was no movement. Pia and Yana had not heard anything. That was good. Tomorrow they would be questioned about Stam's disappearance, but they would know nothing.

Bez tied a cord around Stam's neck that went into his mouth and secured the gag.

They took off his shoes, then – with some difficulty – wrestled him out of his tunic. They tied his hands behind his back and stood him up.

The plan was working, so far.

They marched him naked into the wood, one man either side of him holding his arms tightly, one man in front, and Bez behind. Stam did not try to escape.

They paused there, at the edge of the wood. Looking back, Bez scanned the fields. No one was about. No one had witnessed the kidnap. He took Stam's tunic and his shoes and walked quickly back across the fields and down to the river. He folded the tunic, set it on the ground near the water, and placed the shoes neatly on top. Then he returned to the wood.

They took Stam through the wood. Then they had to cross the Break, where there was a clear view across the fields, but no one was up. Farmers slept heavily.

At last they reached West Wood, and gratefully entered the concealing vegetation.

There, close to the village, they had dug a hole about as long and wide as Stam.

Now, watched by woodlanders who had awakened and emerged from their huts, they tied his feet and made sure the cords on his wrists were secured. Bez decided to re-tie the gag to ensure Stam's silence. He untied the cord and pulled the gag out of Stam's mouth.

Stam gasped: 'Water, please.'

Bez said: 'Did you give my brother water when he was bleeding to death?' Then he stuffed the leather back into Stam's mouth and tied the gag again.

Finally they lowered Stam into the hole in the ground.

He strained against his bonds and grunted through his gag. Bez guessed he was terrified that he would be buried alive. In fact the death Bez had planned for him was worse than that.

They piled branches on top of him. A heavy one landed on his chest, making him grunt again. He probably had a broken rib. The branches left space for air, ensuring that Stam could breathe.

Over the branches they laid leaves and ferns, so that he could not be seen. His grunts were now inaudible. They raised the heap above the ground and made a roughly circular mound, so that the result looked just like a random pile of foliage.

Bez noticed that people looked at him strangely, and quickly averted their gaze. He knew that his face was as rigid as stone. He was doing something terribly cruel but he was determined to go through with it. He would not show emotion, and he would not back down.

He lay down beside the pile to guard it, and the others went to their houses.

Then they all slept.

Troon came to Pia and Yana's house early in the morning. Looking in, he said: 'I see that Stam isn't here.'

Yana said: 'Isn't he at your house?'

'If he was, I wouldn't be looking for him, would I?'

'Well, he left here at the normal time, and I don't see how he could have got lost between here and there.'

Pia wondered what was going on. Had someone killed Stam? If so, they had not forewarned her or Yana. Which was probably wise.

Troon said: 'Did he tell you where he was going?'

'He said goodnight as usual, and headed off in the direction of your place.'

Troon looked at Pia. 'If I find that your herder friends have killed him . . .'

She was scared. Was she going to be blamed for something she had not done? But she would not show fear to Troon. 'I hope someone has killed him,' she said spiritedly. 'He murdered two people – he deserves to die.'

Troon did not argue with that – he was focused on his questions. 'Have you spoken to any herders lately?'

'No.'

'Or even seen any?'

'No.'

He shrugged. 'Anyway, it's unlikely. Those people haven't got the guts for revenge.'

Troon's minion, Shen, appeared behind him. 'We've found something,' he said. 'Some clothes near the river. A tunic and a pair of shoes. The right size for Stam.'

'By the river?'

'On the edge.'

'Right,' said Troon. 'Search the banks on both sides, upriver and down. And, remember, he might not be alive. So look for a body.'

Troon arrived at Bez's village that evening.

The woodlanders were eating supper. Every one of them knew where Stam was, but they managed to look normal, sharing their food with their children, throwing scraps to the dogs.

Behind Troon emerged a handful of young men, all armed with bows. The woodlanders got up from their supper and picked up their own weapons. But Bez felt sure the farmers would not attack, being outnumbered several times over.

Troon said: 'Where is he?'

Bez was the only one who had more than a smattering of the herder language. He said: 'Who have you lost?'

Troon gritted his teeth. He hated to admit weakness. He said: 'My son, Stam.'

'Stam the murderer,' Bez replied. 'We are the ones who should be looking for him. He killed our fellow tribesmen.'

'If you've killed him in revenge . . .'

Troon's men hefted their bows, and the woodlanders tensed.

Bez said: 'No, we have not killed him.' That was true, although it was only a matter of time. 'And if we did kill him, it would restore the balance.'

'We're going to search for him.'

The woodlanders bristled, but Bez said: 'Let them search. It's the quickest way to get rid of them.'

The farmers looked in all the houses and the surrounding

wood. One of them poked the foliage pile with an arrow, and Bez tensed; but the man moved on.

Troon said to Bez: 'I'm going to search the entire wood. If he's here, I'll hold you responsible.'

'Go ahead, waste your time.'

As they left, Bez pointed to Omun and Arav, two light-footed hunters. 'Follow them. Let us know when they give up and leave the wood.'

The two went after the farmers, who would never know how closely they had been watched.

Those remaining finished their suppers and cleared up, then gathered around for the balance ceremony. Bez had already selected a suitable tree, and a coil of rope lay at the foot of its trunk.

The woodlanders were quiet, awestruck, and Bez realized that most of them had never witnessed an execution. Such things were rare on the Great Plain.

It was getting dark when Omun and Arav returned and reported that the farmers had gone home.

Bez nodded. 'Get him out of the ground.'

The vegetation was removed and Stam was brought out. His eyes were red with crying and he shook with fear. Bez removed his gag.

Stam began to beg. 'Spare me, please,' he said. 'I don't want to die, I'm too young. Have some mercy.'

Bez pointed to the tree he had picked out. 'Tie him to that branch,' he said. 'Upside-down.'

Stam wriggled desperately, but he could not resist, and soon his ankles were tied to the branch, leaving his head above ground by the length of a person's arm.

Bez began to sing a song of mourning, and the tribe joined in, the massed voices sounding through the wood.

He collected some dry leaves and dead twigs and made a little pile under Stam. Then he took a brand from one of the cooking fires.

Stam saw what was going to happen. 'No!' he screamed. 'No, please, no!'

Bez set light to the tinder. It caught quickly, and he added dry wood. The fire blazed up.

Bez spoke loudly, for the whole tribe to hear. 'Fell's ashes are far away, but we mourn him here in his home.'

Stam cried out as the fire began to scorch his head and his naked shoulders. Desperately, he began to swing from side to side. Every time he took himself out of the heat, he swung back in, but it gave him some moments of relief. Bez watched patiently, knowing Stam could not keep it up for long.

At last he stopped, exhausted. The fire was blazing high now, and he began to cry out. Fat under the skin of his head liquefied and came out like sweat. The same happened to his face. Drops fell on the fire and blazed briefly.

Bez put more wood on.

Stam's hair caught fire, and he began to scream. The flames surrounded his head and face, burning off his skin, turning his face black. When the flames receded, his eyes were visible and his teeth showed where his lips had gone. But he was still breathing.

The mourning song continued, soft and low, the sound of sadness and loss.

The screaming stopped but Stam did not die. There came from his awful mouth a low groaning, the sound of a soul in Hell.

At last his brain cooked and his body became completely limp.

Bez checked and found that he was no longer breathing.

He built up the fire again, and some of the men untied the rope so that the entire corpse collapsed into the flames. Stam turned to ash.

Bez spoke to the watching tribe. 'We can sleep now,' he said. 'The balance has been restored.'

17

THE SUMMER GREW hotter and drier. There was no relief even as the Autumn Halfway approached. Pia wondered whether the sweat she produced contained more water than the bag she carried. As well as the bag, she had Olin strapped to her back.

She paused in her work to ease her aching body. The fields stretched as far as she could see along the bank of the river, upstream and downstream, a vista of scorched earth and stunted crops, a landscape broken only by bent, weary figures doing the same grinding toil.

But their efforts were being rewarded. The many pots she and others had lugged up from the river had had an effect. There was a crop growing from the parched ground. The shoots were stunted and feeble but they had come up green and were now turning golden yellow. There would be grain. Her breast milk would be nourishing, and Olin would be healthy.

Poor Olin. He would never know his father. He would not

remember the big man who had sung to him. He would have no songs to sing to his own children.

Pia missed Han every moment of the day. She knew she would never have a love like that again. Why not? Because another man might have all the qualities a woman would want, but still he would not be Han.

She tried to remember reasons she had to be happy. She was pleased to be with her mother, she adored Olin, and she was glad that Stam was out of her life.

She did not know what had happened to Stam. Zad said the herders had nothing to do with it, but he would have said that anyway. Bez was saying nothing, but he had dropped a hint about the balance required by the gods. On the other hand, perhaps Stam really had, inexplicably, gone for a swim in the night and drowned.

Troon was enraged, but he did not know who to blame.

Yana was deeply thankful to be relieved of her unwanted boy-man. 'I'm just glad I'm too old to conceive,' she said. Fortunately, there were no more single men in Farmplace, Bort having already refused Yana, so Troon could not force her to couple with someone else.

In the heat of the day, when Pia felt she had to stop work or faint, Yana told her to go and look for crab apples in the wood. Pia exchanged her bag for a basket and gladly went into the relative cool of the trees. Olin made interested noises at the changed scenery. He was paying more attention to his surroundings.

Most of the early apples were so small that they were all skin and core, and Pia foraged through East Wood looking for larger ones until she emerged onto the plain. There she saw no herders and few cattle, which was odd. The herd had moved west. She walked in that direction, curious.

The cattle seemed to have been drawn to the Break, she saw, as she arrived there. Many of them were looking south, across the fields, where twenty or so farmers were working. When cattle were that close together the smell was overpowering.

The beasts seemed in a strange mood. They did not crop what little grass there was. They were abnormally still. To Pia they seemed menacing.

She had never been comfortable with cattle. By contrast, Han had moved among them as easily as among people. He had explained to Pia that it was important not to approach them from behind, as that could startle them, or directly in front, which they would see as a challenge. And he would talk to them so that they got used to his presence. He had been herding from the age of eight until he and Pia ran off together, so the lore had been instinctive with him. Pia remained nervous.

Now, she saw, the herders were in front of the beasts, trying to move them back, using long, slightly flexible herding sticks. She recognized Zad and Biddy. Their little girl, Dini, was watching from the edge of the wood with a group of herder children. What was going on?

She put down her basket next to the children and went to Zad. He was walking up and down in front of the herd, shouting and waving a leafy branch to scare them off. It was not working.

Pia said: 'What's the matter with the cattle?'

There was no sign of Zad's usual charming smile. He said curtly: 'They're thirsty, and they can smell the river.'

Pia was horrified. There were more cattle here than anyone could count. They were a threat of tremendous power, hardly contained. 'But if they cross the fields they will ruin the crops!'

Zad replied impatiently: 'That's why we're turning them back. We don't want a fight with your people.'

This was terrifying. The farmers could not afford to lose a single stalk of wheat. Yana's farm was farther downriver, so Pia and her family would not be directly affected, but if their neighbours were starving, it would be hard not to share – yet they had nothing to spare.

She looked at the farmers working in the Break. It seemed they were not aware of the danger. They could surely see the herd, but it was not obvious to them what the cattle might do. Pia had to warn them.

With Olin on her back she hurried across the field. The first person she came to was Deg, the son of Bort. 'Those cattle are trying to get to the river,' she said. 'You should be ready to get out of the way.'

He stood still, looking doubtful. 'The cattle have no right to come this way,' he said in a tone of protest. 'They'll destroy the crop.'

'Tell them that, then,' she said impatiently, and she moved on. She walked as fast as she could.

The next person she came to was Duff, carrying a bag of water to his field. He was a lot more sensible than Deg. She repeated her message.

Duff said: 'Right.' He emptied the water from his bag, making it lighter to carry. 'How about I warn everyone on the west side of the field and you take the east?'

She thanked the gods for a smart person. 'Good!' She hurried on.

She did as he had suggested, speaking to people on the east side of the Break. None of them was as stupid as Deg. They looked anxiously at the distant herd and thanked her for the warning.

By the time she had spoken to everyone she was within sight of the river. She stopped, panting. At that moment, Troon and Shen appeared. 'What on earth is going on?' Troon demanded angrily.

Olin immediately started to cry. Pia took him from her back and rocked him, and he calmed.

Troon said: 'Well?'

Pia pointed at the herd. 'The thirsty cattle can smell the river,' she said breathlessly. 'The herders are trying to turn them back, but they may cross the fields. I've warned the people working there.'

'This is outrageous!'

'No need to thank me for alerting everyone.'

He was impervious to sarcasm. 'They could ruin the crop of the entire Break!'

She lost patience. 'Well, do something about it, then, instead of standing there shouting at me.'

He turned to Shen. 'Round up people with weapons and send them to the north end of the Break, where the cattle are. I'll meet them there.'

Shen ran off.

Troon called after him: 'And bring fire!' He headed across the fields.

Pia was weary but she wanted to know what would happen next. She took a different route, hugging the edge of East Wood, where she could quickly take refuge in the trees.

She walked slowly, and she was overtaken by several young farmers with hammers and bows, presumably sent by Shen. Among them was Mo, now reluctantly Deg's woman, carrying a blazing torch.

Under Troon's direction, the farmers started to build fires. But the wood had to be collected, so the work went slowly. Also, the Break was a wide space: Pia thought the thirsty cattle would just run between the fires. They needed many more blazes, much closer together, to deter the herd – which was now edging south, she saw, forcing Zad and the herders to retreat.

Troon seemed to come to the same conclusion. He shouted orders, and the farmers started to pick up stones from the field and throw them at the cattle. The beasts hardly reacted to hits to their backs and sides, but when their heads or legs were struck they lowed angrily.

Pia retreated to the trees, covering the back of Olin's head with her hand to protect him.

She saw Zad turn around and walk towards the farmers, holding his hands out in front of him in a gesture of forbidding. 'Stop!' he shouted.

Some of the herders picked up stones and threw them back at the farmers.

This was turning nasty.

A farmer called Narod, who had been one of Stam's Young Dogs, grabbed a stone as Zad walked directly towards him. 'Don't anger them,' Zad said. 'You'll cause a stampede!'

Narod ignored him and threw the stone. It hit a bull on the face, near the eye. The beast roared.

Zad punched Narod in the face, and Narod fell down.

Pia yelled: 'Don't start fighting!'

No one was listening.

The farmers converged on Zad, yelling. He was attacked from all sides. He swung his herder stick widely, knocking one man down, driving them back. Then an arrow stuck in his upper arm. Beside Pia, Dini cried out: 'Dadda!'

But the herders had seen it too, and they raced to Zad's rescue. In no time a full-scale brawl developed, the farmers using hammers and arrows, the herders deploying herding sticks. Troon waded in, but instead of trying to stop the fighting he started attacking herders.

The sounds coming from the herd grew louder and more urgent. The farmers paid no attention, but the herders noticed. Suddenly all the herders ran from the fight, heading for the woods to the east or west of the Break. The farmers looked bewildered as their opponents turned from fighters into runaways.

The herd moved.

Pia cried: 'No, oh, no!'

The farmers at last saw the cattle moving and they, too, ran.

The cattle were slow at first. Zad and Biddy reached the wood where Pia stood with Olin and Dini. Then the pace picked up, and in moments the cattle were galloping, in a fog of dust, with a noise like the end of the world.

Pia was aghast to see Mo and Pilic disappear beneath the pounding hooves. The dust was so thick, and the scene so chaotic, that she could not see what happened after they fell, but she knew they could not possibly survive.

She backed into the trees, clutching Olin fearfully. The fugitive herders and farmers did the same, their fight forgotten. The cattle came frighteningly near, trampling the vegetation at the edge of the wood, crushing everything, but Pia got behind two big tree trunks, which the beasts avoided. All the same, she was terrified. The cattle seemed mad. Their lowing now sounded more like hooting. Pia stepped farther back so that Olin would not breathe the dust.

Then the herd passed. The thunder moved south, and the dust settled. The children around Pia were crying, but they were safe.

Zad spoke to a younger herder, who was strong-looking and long-legged. Pia guessed he was a quickrunner and she was right. Zad asked him to run to Riverhead and tell the elders what had happened. 'You could be there before dark today, couldn't you?' The boy agreed. 'Then the elders might be here by tomorrow evening.' The boy ran off, heading east.

Everyone else began to move south, following the cattle. Pia followed slowly, walking over the field. She looked with dismay at the destruction of the ripening stems of wheat, trampled and torn up by hooves. It was heartbreaking. She thought of the people who farmed these fields, and all the days they had spent carrying water from the river. Their efforts had gone to waste in a few short moments. What would they eat?

She was horrified to discover the corpse of Mo, badly trampled. Her body was completely crushed, barely recognizable as human, but strangely her face was untouched, and Pia could even see her freckles. Somehow this was worse than all the rest of the carnage, and Pia was suddenly too weak to stand. She sat down, feeling ill, staring helplessly at Mo's freckled face. Mo had seen only eighteen midsummers; she had been savagely mistreated by Troon; and now her life was over.

After a while Pia stood up again. She looked ahead and saw that the cattle had reached the river and were at last quenching their maddening thirst. The danger now, she felt, was angry humans, both farmers and herders.

When she caught up she saw that the cattle had spread out. Many were just standing in the shallows, drinking. Some had swum to the far side. Others had gone upstream or downstream to find places where they could bend their necks and suck up the water. They were calm now, their panic diminished, their mad rage spent. On the east side of the Break, in the fields that lay between the woods and the river, the crops were undamaged.

Unlike the animals, the humans had not calmed down. Men and women were weeping; others gave in to apoplectic fury. Troon was raging at Zad. 'People will starve because of what you've done!'

Zad was badly shaken, and bleeding from his shoulder wound, but he was not willing to take the blame. 'Who was the stupid fool who decided to plough up the Break?'

'That's ancient history. It's our land now.'

'Don't tell me, tell the cows.'

'None of that makes any difference. You've destroyed people's fields so now you have to save them from famine. You'll have to give this herd to us farmers, to compensate for the destruction you've caused.'

'You will not take a single one of these beasts,' Zad said angrily. 'If you do, it will be theft. And we know what to do with cattle thieves.'

'Be careful. Don't threaten me.'

'Then don't threaten to steal cattle.' Zad glanced to the edge of the herd. 'Look!' he said, pointing. 'That man is trying to lead a cow away!'

'Good for him,' said Troon.

Pia recognized the man. It was Bort.

Zad looked at Biddy and nodded. She put an arrow to her bow. Troon tried to stop her, but Zad stood in his way. Biddy released the arrow. It was a long up-and-down shot, and the arrow stuck into the ground next to Bort's foot. He was unhurt, but all the same he left the cow and ran away.

Troon said to Biddy: 'Lucky for you that you missed him, woman.'

Biddy replied: 'Lucky for him that he ran away before I could take a second shot.'

An arrow shot by a farmer curved through the air and landed next to Pia. She screamed, hugged Olin to her, and ran away, out of the herd and downstream. Then she looked back.

Another farmer tried to get away with a cow. Pia could not see his face and did not know who he was. A herder shot at him, and this time the arrow hit. The farmer fell.

After that no one else tried to steal a cow.

No more arrows were shot. The drama was over, except that it left a crowd of people facing starvation.

The afternoon darkened as the sun went down. The herders rounded up the cattle and drove them back through the Break. The farmers did not interfere.

Yana appeared at Pia's side. Pia said: 'Where have you been? The cattle stampeded. The crops in the Break are all gone, ruined.'

'I saw the whole thing,' Yana said. 'Come home with me. I've got something to show you.'

They walked along the bank of the river until they drew level with the house, then followed a narrow path up the slope. 'Look inside the house,' Yana said.

Pia looked inside and saw a cow.

She turned and grinned at her mother: 'You stole it!'

Yana nodded. 'Before the herders reached the riverside.'

'We can't keep it, though,' Pia said. 'Others need it more than we do.'

'I thought we'd give it to Mo,' said Yana. 'She and Bort have lost everything.'

'Mo's dead,' said Pia.

'Oh, no!'

'Trampled. I could see her face, though.'

'I'm sorry she's gone. She had courage.'

'Courage doesn't do a woman much good in Farmplace.'

Yana considered. 'We'll give the cow to Duff. His farm is in the Break. He'll have lost everything.'

'He'll probably share it with neighbours in the same position.'

'Good. I wonder what will happen tomorrow?'

Pia had the answer to that. 'The elders of the herders should be here before sundown. Zad sent a quickrunner.'

'I hope Han's mother is among them,' Yana said. 'She might knock some sense into people.'

On the following day Ani crossed the Great Plain with Keff, Seft and Scagga. She was ominously struck by how few cattle she saw. Joia had tried to count them and, as Ani did not understand the numbers, had simplified the result by saying: 'Where before we had four cows, now we have one.' Ani had been jolted.

Only the hardiest cows were calving, and the number of young did not match the number that had been slaughtered just to feed the herders. At some point there would be no cattle left.

The herd in the west had suffered from Troon's ploughing up the Break. They lost weight on the long roundabout route to the river. In good times, that could be tolerated, but now it had become crucial. The elders had to find a solution.

They went first to Old Oak. Zad had gone, Biddy told them, taking the herd out of the reach of the farmers, who wanted to seize cattle as compensation for their lost crops. 'Ridiculous idea!' said Keff. 'A thief steals your bow and, when it cracks, demands you give him a new one!'

Biddy walked with them to the Break. 'There was wheat here as high as your thigh,' she said. 'Now look.'

Nothing was left but trampled earth.

Pia and Yana met them crossing the Break. Pia was carrying Olin, now almost half a year old. Ani was thrilled to see her latest grandchild. She took him from Pia and he said: 'Ba ba ba ba,' and tried to grasp her nose.

'He looks just like Han when he was a baby,' Ani said.

They went to Troon's house. He was waiting outside with Shen, his minion, and half a dozen of the Young Dogs. Ani was not intimidated. Most of the farmer folk stood around, eager to see what would happen.

Troon did not offer a drink of water. He began by saying: 'You have destroyed crops, and you must suffer!'

Ani said calmly: 'We need to find a way to stop this happening again.'

Troon could not disagree with that.

She said: 'Seft has devised a scheme.' In fact she and Seft had worked it out together, but she knew Troon was more likely to accept something proposed by a man. She had high hopes for this compromise; Troon ought to welcome it.

Troon had been expecting an argument about who was at fault, and he was not prepared for this. He just nodded.

Ani looked at Seft. She remembered when he had first appeared at Riverbend, a handsome but downtrodden youth who had captured the heart of her daughter Neen. He was now a much-respected man, one of the leading figures among the herder folk.

Seft spoke with relaxed authority. 'You need to farm the Break, and we need to water our cattle. There might be a way for us both to have what we want.' He paused. The farmers looked interested. 'The cattle don't need the entire width of the Break to get to the river. All they need is a path about twenty paces wide.'

'Rubbish,' said Troon. 'They would leave the path to eat the crops.'

'Quite so,' Seft said calmly. 'That is why we would need to build a ditch-and-bank barrier between the path and the cultivated fields.'

Troon still looked sour, but Ani saw some of the farmer folk nodding.

Seft went on: 'The ditch would have to be deep enough, and the bank high enough, to make it impossible for cows to cross the barrier.'

Troon looked at the Break, seeming to imagine the path. 'It's a huge project,' he said.

Seft said: 'If the entire farmer community joined in the work, under my supervision, it could probably be done in about fifteen days.'

Troon was not thinking about the time it would take. 'Twenty paces wide, plus a ditch and a bank that would add another ten paces at least. It's a strip of fertile land thirty paces wide stretching from the plain to the river.' He shook his head. 'It's a huge area, as big as a farm that supports one family.'

Seft said: 'It's a tiny part of the entire farmer region.'

Troon shook his head. 'We need more land, not less. I can't lose that much precious fertile soil to make a road for cows.'

Ani was frustrated and depressed. She and Seft had felt this must appeal to Troon as a solution to a problem. But Troon was too greedy. No matter how much land they had, the farmers always needed more to feed their growing families.

Scagga was angry. 'You're crazy, Troon,' he said. 'You're the farmers' worst enemy. Here you have a fair offer that gives you nearly everything you want and you say no.'

'I rule this land. The herders have the entire Great Plain. This is mine and I decide.'

Scagga waved an arm, indicating the devastated Break. 'Don't you understand? The cattle decide, not you. If you go ahead and seed the land now, they'll probably trample it again this time next year.'

Some of the farmers murmured agreement, but Troon was obdurate. 'Next year we'll be prepared. We'll kill your cattle before they get near our fields. I'm warning you. We'll slaughter them, and any herder who tries to stop us.'

Ani despaired. This was the opposite of what she had hoped for. Instead of a cooperative way forward, they had an angry stand-off.

She could see that some farmers were dissatisfied. They would rather have the security of protected fields. But she could also see that they did not dare to defy their leader.

The conflict continued.

She would have to think of something else.

18

ANI AND SEFT were walking through Riverbend. Seft was explaining to Ani the concept of the sled, and how it would enable them to move giant stones much faster. Suddenly Ani put a hand on Seft's arm to interrupt him. 'Look at that,' she said.

She pointed at Cass, the brother of Vee, who was carrying a bundle of new green wood on his shoulder. The pieces were all about the same size, as long as Cass was tall. Some were entire trunks of young saplings, others the split trunks of slightly older trees. Seft said: 'That wood is yew.'

'So it is,' said Ani. 'Hello, Cass. Those look like staves for bows.'

'Yes,' he said. 'They're for the war.'

Ani suppressed the impulse to say, *What war?* The elders had discussed war against the farmers, and had decided against, at least for now. But something was going on behind her back, and she would find out more from Cass if she pretended she was in the know. 'How is that coming along?' she said.

'Very well. There are lots of young people working – more than I can count. I can hardly keep up with their need for wood.'

That was a surprise. Who was going to be killed by these weapons? Intrigued and anxious, she said: 'We'll walk with you and take a look.'

Cass led them to a clearing south of the village. Sure enough, there was a crowd of young men and women busy making weapons. Ani looked around, shocked and angry. Some were twisting together sinews from the legs of cattle to make bowstrings. Others were smoothing hazelwood arrow shafts or sharpening flints into triangular arrowheads. Someone was roasting the bark of a birch tree in an airless covered pit, turning the material into sticky birch tar. Older people were doing the most crucial job: fitting each arrowhead into a slit in the shaft and gluing the two together with tar. There were two piles of finished weapons, one of bows and the other of arrows.

The atmosphere was cheerful, a bunch of people engaged in a collective enterprise and enjoying it. You fools, Ani thought bitterly. War's not fun. It's smashed skulls and bloodshed and grieving families.

'Look who's in charge,' she said to Seft.

'Scagga.'

'Of course.'

'He's preparing for war.'

'And we have to stop him.' She picked up a finished arrow. Holding it in her hands, she approached Scagga. 'Are you expecting a war?' she said.

He looked guilty and defiant at the same time. 'Expecting? No, not expecting it. I'm going to make sure it happens.'

'And who will be your enemy?'

'Troon and the farmers, of course.'

'I recall that you were present at the meeting when the elders decided against war.'

Scagga sneered. 'Elders don't decide. They advise. If I want to gather a band of brave youngsters to go and teach the farmers a lesson, I may do so. And I shall.'

Unfortunately that was true, Ani thought with dismay. Elders had no power to enforce their decisions: they relied on the respect people had for their wisdom. Mostly that worked. But it was not difficult for a blowhard like Scagga to whip up an aggressive fever among young herders.

Ani said: 'You might have had the courtesy to tell your fellow elders that you planned to go against our decision, defy us, and undermine our authority.'

'Elders?' Scagga raised his voice so that those around could hear him. 'The elders yielded to the farmers eleven midsummers ago, when Troon ploughed up the Break.' Ani heard murmurs of agreement. That episode had not been forgotten. At the time, Ani and the other elders had acted for the best, avoiding war. But some people had felt that the herders had been humiliated. 'That's when we should have made war,' Scagga went on. 'The farmers have only got more arrogant since.'

'I agree that they've become more arrogant.' Ani touched the sharp flint arrowhead carefully. 'I don't think that's a good enough reason, though, to send our young people to have their flesh torn by arrows like this.'

'Troon said the farmers would slaughter any of our cattle that crossed the Break again.' Scagga raised his voice more, and Ani realized he was now speaking mainly for the benefit of the audience around him. 'But our beasts must have water, even if we have to fight for it.'

'If fighting would make it rain . . .'

One of the listeners laughed.

The laugh annoyed Scagga, and he became more belligerent. 'We outnumber the farmers. There are ten of us for every one of them. We can't lose!'

Some of the listeners cheered.

Ani asked her usual question, with the sourness she always felt. 'And when we have won, how many of these young folk' – she looked hard at them, meeting their eyes – 'how many will bleed to death on the battlefield, screaming in pain and crying for their mothers?' They were taken aback. They had not thought of war in that way.

Scagga saw that Ani had scored a point, and he said quickly: 'That's a coward's question.'

'It's a mother's question.'

'Mothers may be cowards.'

Insults of that kind had no effect on Ani. She said reasonably: 'We just think that violence should be the last resort, not the first.'

'And I just think we should kill the farmers!' Scagga shouted, and the youngsters cheered. 'Kill them all, burn their houses, and return their land to pasture for our herd!' They cheered more.

Ani wanted to howl with frustration. Scagga refused even to think about the consequences of what he proposed, and his supporters seemed not to notice his stupidity. But she was defeated. Dismally, she decided not to argue further. Anything she said now would be a cue for Scagga to rant more. She consoled herself with the thought that the issue would not be decided by Scagga and this group of young people. The majority of the herder folk would not be so eager for battle, and might decline to go to war.

She was getting ready to leave when Seft spoke. He had been listening to the argument with a thoughtful look, and now he said: 'The herd's way to the water is blocked by the woods. There is a gap in the woods, called the Break, but Troon now claims it as farmland, so we can't use it. But we don't need a war. We just need a new Break.'

Scagga thought he had won the argument, and so became emollient. He said: 'Look, I'd be in favour of a peaceful solution, but we tried that, and the farmers refused to cooperate.'

Seft shook his head. 'I'm talking about a different solution. The new Break could be in another location. We could clear a strip at the edge of the West Wood. Cut down the undergrowth, the bushes and saplings, but leave the big trees – the cattle can walk around them. That would allow for a path twenty paces wide plus a ditch-and-bank to keep the beasts off the crops. And Troon could hardly object. We would not be stealing his land.'

'No,' said Ani. 'But we'd be stealing the woodlanders' land.'

'It's a big wood. They'd hardly notice.'

'You're wrong. The wood is their livelihood. They'd notice if a strip was taken from them. They would be outraged.'

'I suppose so,' Seft conceded. He frowned. 'Could we give them something by way of compensation? You could negotiate with Bez.'

Ani nodded. 'The prospect of, say, some cows would be a big help to them in this drought.' Seft's idea had the makings of a solution, and her hopes rose. 'And perhaps the tribe could afford to lose a narrow strip of woodland.'

Scagga said: 'You two aren't thinking straight. You're talking about cutting down a mass of vegetation, from the plain all the way down to the riverside. Cutting it is hard enough, but to clear it all away is a huge job. Who do you think is going to do it?'

Ani looked around. 'There's a small army of strong young people right here.' She adopted a challenging tone. 'You said you'd support a peaceful solution, Scagga. Did you mean it? Could you take all these youngsters and put them to work clearing a new Break? Could you manage that?'

He hesitated, looked trapped, and said: 'Of course I could. We could do it in a few days.'

'That would be something to boast about. You could resolve the dispute without any of these young people getting killed.'

Scagga nodded reluctantly. 'Perhaps I could,' he said.

And so it was settled.

West Wood covered a large area, and Ani wondered whether she would be able to find the woodlander village. Struggling through the vegetation, she looked for signs of human settlement.

She hoped desperately that Seft's new scheme could work. The herd needed access to the river, especially now, in the crisis of drought. But the essential first step was the consent of the woodlanders. And that was her task today.

She passed a pond that still had water in it, and she guessed the woodlanders would have settled nearby. Sure enough, a little later she came to the village, just half a dozen houses around a central clearing. She paused at the edge, took a deep breath, and walked in.

Bez welcomed her warmly, as the mother of Han and Joia, but he was also wary. Gida was with him, and they all sat on the ground. Woodlanders gathered nearby, even though they could not understand the language. As always in warm weather, the women and children were naked, the men nearly so.

Ani's job was delicate. The woodlanders were friendly, but they did not think as herders did, and one could never be sure which way they would jump. She had to tread carefully.

She began by asking whether Bez had seen the stampede. Yes, he said, the whole tribe had watched it from the edge of the wood. 'Animals must drink,' he said. 'Just like people.'

Ani nodded. 'And that's why I'm here. We need to give our herd a new path to the river.'

'But how could you do that?' said Bez. 'Where would the new path lie?'

'It doesn't have to be as broad as the Break,' Ani said, avoiding the question for the moment. 'It would be only about thirty paces wide.' She remembered that the woodlanders could not count. 'From here to the pond,' she clarified. 'No more.'

Bez persisted with his question. 'But where would the path be?'

'Seft is deciding right now.'

'We saw him. He came soon after dawn.' The woodlanders always seemed to know what was happening in every part of the wood.

Ani decided to be candid. 'We need to use a strip on the eastern edge of your wood, next to the Break.'

Bez said something in the woodlander language, and the people sitting around made angry noises. Ani guessed he had translated. Reverting to herder language, he said: 'There are many hazelnut bushes there. We have pruned and shaped them for years.'

'I know. That's why I have come to offer you something in return for your sacrifice.'

'What could you possibly give us?'

'Cattle. We could give you cows, which you could slaughter for their meat. You would eat well now and smoke meat for the winter.'

Bez translated again. The woodlanders brightened. For them, beef was a treat.

Gida said something, and Bez said: 'How many cows would you give us?'

Ani was encouraged. The fact that they were asking about terms meant they were not going to refuse outright. She said: 'What do you think would be fair?'

Bez said: 'One cow for every hazelnut bush.'

'There's a lot more food on a cow than on a bush.'

'Yes, but a hazelnut bush feeds you every year for a lifetime. When you've eaten a cow it's gone for ever.'

He had a point, Ani thought. But she was pleased to be so close to agreement. This was about the survival of the herd. It was worth a few cows. She said: 'Let us go and look at the area, and count the hazelnut bushes that will be lost.'

'Yes,' said Bez, and he stood up. He could not count, but perhaps he could make sure none were missed as Ani did the counting.

Ani and Bez led the way. Looking back, she saw that the entire village was following. This would be a communal decision.

They found Seft and Tem marking the boundary of the area to be cleared. Seft was hammering stakes into the ground and Tem was digging a shallow trench between the stakes to make the line definite. They had worked fast, and had almost reached the river.

As they arrived, Troon appeared from the opposite direction, with Shen trailing in his wake. He shouted at Seft: 'What do you think you're doing?'

'None of your concern,' Seft said, and continued his work.

'I haven't given permission for this.'

'No need. Your permission isn't required.'

'Yes, it is. What you're doing might impinge on farmland.'

'It won't.'

'I don't believe you.'

'Wait and see.'

While Troon was trying to think of a reply, Bez spoke to him. 'It's my permission they need, not yours,' he said. 'You're in woodlander territory now. And by the way, watch out for snakes. There are vipers underfoot.'

Troon looked down anxiously, and Bez laughed. 'Better to keep out of the wood altogether,' he said.

Troon muttered a curse, turned around and left.

Bez spread the woodlanders out across the strip, at the river end, and told them to walk slowly north, staying inside the boundary Seft had marked, and looking for hazelnut bushes and trees. Each time they saw one they would call Bez and Ani.

When they came to the end of the wood Ani had counted twelve hazelnut bushes. She showed Bez the number with her fingers and toes. Bez said: 'We must have the cows before you start digging.'

'Very well,' said Ani. There were no cows nearby, but looking across the plain she saw a herd in the middle distance. 'Wait here, if you would,' she said.

The woodlanders sat on the ground and Ani headed off. When she reached the herd she was pleased to see Zad there. She explained her task. 'They are losing twelve hazelnut bushes, so we need to give them twelve cows.'

Zad was not happy about this. He said: 'That's very generous!'

'Not really.' Some herders did not share her sense of the rights of woodlanders. 'They practically live on hazelnuts, and they prune them and shape them to produce more. They're sacrificing something of great value.'

'I suppose so,' said Zad.

'Cut out twelve beasts from the herd. And don't bring me sick and dying cattle – the woodlanders are not stupid, they'll know, and they'll make a fuss.'

'All right.'

Zad separated twelve cows from the herd, with the help of a dog.

Ani said: 'You'd better come with me. We need to make sure the cows reach the village. After that it's up to the woodlanders to stop them wandering away.'

They drove the cows to where the woodlanders sat waiting,

then went on with the whole tribe. The woodlanders chattered loudly, excited to be going home with such a prize, perhaps looking forward to roasted beef.

They stopped at a point where Bez seemed to know they were close to the village.

Zad said to Bez: 'They don't need grass. They're browsers. They'll eat leaves, herbs, small plants, and even tree bark. They're fine in woodland. But if they hear the herd they may try to return, so you should tether them at night.'

Bez said: 'Thank you.'

The woodlanders drove the cattle into the wood. Zad and his dog returned to the big herd. Ani sighed with relief. She had succeeded.

She headed back towards the Break, to see how Seft and Tem were getting on.

The bank and ditch were now marked out. Troon had not reappeared. Perhaps he had realized that the new Break would do him no harm, and decided that he might as well leave the herders alone.

It was now late afternoon, and Scagga arrived with his young army.

Everyone sat down to eat the cold food they had brought with them. Tomorrow they would roast a cow.

Ani slept heavily and woke up when the camp stirred. The youngsters eagerly began work on the bank-and-ditch. Seft and Tem had done their job, and headed back for Riverbend. Ani went with them. She felt a profound sense of satisfaction. She and Seft had made a plan and seen it through, and a new Break would be made without quarrels, without violence. She was content.

The farmers had reaped their wheat and stored the grain. They had ploughed up the stubble. There was now no need to carry water from the river to the fields: they would not sow seeds until the spring. Pia's back no longer ached.

There was still plenty to do. They collected nuts and forest fruits and stored them for the winter. Yana made plenty of cheese, mixing the goat's milk with mallow leaves for a hard product that would last.

The younger farmers were curious about what the herders were doing on the edge of West Wood. One morning Pia, carrying Olin, strolled along to look, and found half a dozen others, including Duff, watching. There was a cold east wind, and Olin was wrapped in a lambskin.

The work was almost finished. They had built the bank-and-ditch and were now clearing a space on the west side of the strip, turning the earth, making a dark pathway a couple of paces wide.

Pia pointed at the dark pathway and said to Duff: 'What is that strip for?'

'I don't know,' he said. 'I asked one of the herders and he didn't know either. He said Scagga just wanted it that way.'

Between the bank-and-ditch and the dark pathway was a pile of vegetable detritus half as high as Pia and about twenty paces wide. It would have to be cleared before the path could be used by cattle. That job would take many days, she guessed.

Scagga was lining up his workers along the strip, facing into the new gap and with their backs to the wood. Pia noticed that each of them carried some kind of implement: a flat shovel, a wide piece of wood, an old worn leather mat.

Then several more people came along with blazing torches, setting fire to the pile of cut greenery in the middle. 'Oh!' said Pia. 'I didn't know they were going to do this!' It would be a lot quicker than carrying the debris, she realized.

Duff said: 'The dark path is a fire break, to prevent the flames spreading to the rest of the wood.'

Pia frowned. 'I wish it was wider,' she said.

Duff said: 'The people standing there with shovels and so on are there to beat the fire if it threatens to spread.'

Pia was somewhat reassured.

The debris caught quickly and blazed up. Everything in the wood was dry after three summers of drought. It was surprisingly fierce, and Pia and the other farmer spectators moved away and stood behind the line of beaters, for safety.

The fire made a roaring sound. Smoke rose in the air, and Pia could feel the heat. The flames reached higher, and sparks flew over the heads of the beaters into the virgin wood. The beaters moved quickly to put out small fires. Pia and the other farmers moved farther back.

Pia noticed that some woodlanders had appeared and were watching with scared faces from behind the bushes.

She wished she had not brought Olin. She decided to get away from the fire and just go home. She turned towards the river.

There was a gust of wind. Suddenly dozens of small fires broke out around Pia. The beaters could not put them all out, and those they failed to reach spread quickly. Pia's way to the river was blocked by flames, and she turned west, breaking into a run, heading deeper into the wood. Olin instantly felt her stress, and began to cry.

The fire grew with terrifying speed. Trees were aflame, their branches and leaves blazing; bushes and saplings crackled and smoked; the dry brown grass was consumed. The beaters gave up and ran with the farmers, and a feeling of panic spread. Pia suffered the appalling fear that she and Olin would be caught in the flames and would burn to death. Terror gave her a choking feeling.

It was hard to run in the dense woodland. In her rush she

stumbled and fell to her knees, but no one stopped to help her up. She struggled to her feet and staggered on.

Forest animals came out of hiding and ran past her: a pair of roe deer, a fox family with cubs, a dozen hares. Countless smaller creatures scurried between her feet: voles, dormice, squirrels and hedgehogs.

The other farmers were getting ahead of her, because she was encumbered with Olin and could not run so fast. Then one came back to help her. It was Duff. He took Olin from her so that she could move faster. She saw that he held the baby securely, pressing the little body to his chest, with one hand under Olin's bottom and the other behind his head. Together they stumbled and dodged through the vegetation. The heat on Pia's back eased and she knew she was getting farther away from the advancing flames. Duff might have saved her life.

He angled south-west, heading for the river, and she followed. They ran just ahead of the flames. Suddenly Pia felt an agonizing pain on the top of her head and realized that her hair had caught fire. She screamed. At that moment they burst out of the wood onto the riverbank. Duff put an arm around her and the three of them fell into the water. Pia's head went under and the agony on her head changed to soreness. She surfaced and looked for Olin.

Duff was swimming on his back, holding Olin in front of him so the child could breathe, heading across the river. Pia could have wept with relief, except that she did not have the energy to cry. She was not much of a swimmer but she could doggy-paddle a short distance, and they both made it to the other side.

The vegetation was low scrub. No sparks flew here from the fire: the wind was in the wrong direction for that. All the same, Pia and Duff moved away from the river as far as the start of the hill before they sat down, exhausted.

Pia took Olin from Duff. She removed his lambskin, now

sodden, and rubbed him dry with leaves from a bush. It was only when he fell silent that she realized he had been crying ever since she started running.

She slipped her shoulders out of her tunic, held Olin to her bare chest, and let him suckle. The heat of her body and the warm milk soothed him.

She looked across the river. West Wood was ablaze. She could feel the heat even from here. The fire was rapidly moving west, driven by the east wind. Surely, she thought, it wasn't possible that the entire wood should be consumed? Then where would Bez and his tribe live?

She looked at Duff. 'You came back for me,' she said to him. 'No one else helped me, but you ran back into the fire.'

'I saw that you couldn't run fast enough, carrying the little one,' he said. 'The fire was going to catch up with you.'

'You risked your own life.'

'I didn't think about that.'

She looked hard at him. Why did he care enough to run into fire for her? It was almost as if . . .

She would ask her mother.

The wind dropped suddenly, and the effect on the fire was immediate. It became less intense, and the roaring diminished. Duff noticed it too. 'Perhaps part of West Wood may be spared,' he said.

Pia hoped so.

They sat staring at the obliteration of West Wood. The rushing sound of flames was the dying gasp of the wood. Pia looked upstream and saw a small group of woodlanders standing on the riverbank, hugging each other and weeping.

She felt like crying herself. Something precious had been destroyed. And how would those woodlanders feed their children now?

The wind came around to the west, a stiff breeze. Perhaps that would halt the eastward advance of the fire.

Olin stopped suckling. Pia put one shoulder back into her tunic and stood up, still holding him close. She said: 'Let's get back to Farmplace.'

They walked along the riverbank. On the other side, a few blackened trees grew in a field of ash. When they reached the village they had to swim back across the river. Duff carried Olin again while Pia doggie-paddled.

Where they got back on to dry land Troon was talking intently to some farmers. Pia was curious, and joined the group. Duff did the same. Troon ignored Pia but spoke to Duff. 'We must plough the ashes into the ground before the wind blows them away. Ash is good for the soil.'

Duff was surprised. 'We're going to farm the burned woodland?'

'Yes. It's not woodland any more. But it's fertile soil, perfect for farming.'

Pia was shocked. 'We can't do that!'

Troon looked at her with irritation, then decided he needed to respond. He said: 'Why not?'

'Because it belongs to the woodlanders.'

'They have no concept of property. Anyway, it's no good to them now. Everything's gone – the deer, the birds, the nut trees.'

'All that will come back, eventually.'

'Eventually!' Troon rolled his eyes. 'Eventually means a lifetime. Meanwhile, farmers are hungry. We'll have a crop next year if we act fast.'

Pia glanced past Troon and was surprised to see Bez approaching. Troon followed her gaze and saw him. All the farmers looked the same way, and silence fell.

Bez stood still and quiet for a moment, then said: 'Our home has gone. Only a small area of the wood is left, far too little to feed the tribe. We will starve.'

Troon was quick to say: 'The herders lit the fire, not us. Farmers had nothing to do with it.'

Pia said: 'But now Troon is going to plough up the burned wood and sow seeds in the springtime.'

Troon gave her a look of such fury that she knew he would have killed her there and then if he could.

Bez turned his gaze back to Troon. 'Then the woodland will never come back. It will be farmland for ever.'

'If we wait for the woodland to come back we'll all be dead before it happens.'

'My tribe must eat,' Bez said. 'The herders who lit the fire will have to feed us. And you, if you farm our land, you must feed us too.'

Troon said: 'We can't feed your tribe. We don't have enough for our own.'

'You must, and the herders must. You are taking everything from us. The gods require a balance.'

'I don't care what you think, I'm telling you it's impossible.'

'Very well.' Bez turned and walked a few steps away. Then he turned back.

'The gods will have a balance,' he said.

He turned again and walked into the ashes of the wood.

19

BEZ WALKED FROM Farmplace through the length of what
had been West Wood, kicking up the powdery ash, skirting the
still-burning logs and the glowing embers, trudging through the
sad remains of his home. The scattered tribe joined him in small
groups on his pilgrimage. They passed the pond but could see no
trace of their village.

They saw the burned corpses of the cows Ani had traded them.
That morning, when they had first smelt the smoke of a big fire,
the cows had become restive and the woodlanders, fearing they
might run away, had tethered them, never imagining that the
distant fire would eventually consume their village and the poor
tethered cows with it.

Eventually they reached the last remnant of the wood, a small
area like a toenail on a foot. It had been spared from the blaze by
the change in the wind. Although still green it was devoid of
animal life: no birds in the trees, no little creatures in the

undergrowth, and probably no deer, which would have found it difficult to hide in such a small area.

The tribe were subdued, grieving, but also fearful for the future. Everything that had made them safe was gone, and they had no idea how they would find their next meal.

They sat down in a clearing, and Bez told them about his conversation with Troon. He also repeated what Pia had said about the farmers taking over the burned area so that the woodland would never come back. The tribespeople were indignant but not surprised.

While they were discussing their plight, some other woodlanders appeared. Bez recognized them as members of the nearest neighbouring tribe, from Round Wood. They had seen the smoke and come out of curiosity, to look at the devastation. A woman Bez knew, called Ga, asked how it had happened, speaking the pidgin that woodlanders used on their summer trek.

'The herders lit the fire and the farmers are going to plough the burned land,' Bez said. 'They don't deny what they've done but they won't give us food.'

'That's wrong,' said Ga. 'They should replace what they've destroyed.'

'They say they simply don't have the food,' said Bez.

He was waiting for Ga to ask if there was anything her tribe could do to help, but she did not. In the end he said: 'Would you allow some of our women and children to join your tribe?' He knew better than to ask her to accept men. No woodlander tribe would do so willingly: it led to trouble. Women were less quarrelsome.

Ga said: 'If any of your women are close relatives of ours – for example, if the woman's mother is in our tribe – then we will welcome them, in accordance with the custom. Otherwise, no. We haven't enough food for the tribe as it is.'

It was the answer Bez had expected, and he was sure he would get the same response from any tribe on the Great Plain. And as woodlanders did not often couple with those from other tribes he would not be able to settle many, if any, of his people by appealing to that tradition.

Ga and the Round Wood folk soon left, and Bez resumed speaking to the tribe. 'We're desperate,' he began.

Several people nodded. They had followed the same train of thought. They knew that the tribe might soon be extinct.

He went on: 'Here in this little patch, which is all that is left us, there is not enough for more than one family.'

They could all see that.

'Other tribes cannot help us, and why should they? They did not light the fire.'

They all knew that too, and they waited to hear what he would say next.

'So that leaves us with just one possibility.' He paused, looking around, seeing the faint signs of hope in their faces, and he finished: 'What they refuse to give us, we must steal.'

'There was a great deal of vegetation to be disposed of,' Scagga told the elders. 'We burned it, as the quickest and most efficient way of dealing with it. And we made a fire break two paces wide to prevent the flames spreading. Unfortunately, there was a strong east wind that morning, and the fire break was not sufficiently wide.'

Ani exploded. 'You set fire to West Wood?' she said, in furious incredulity.

'It was an accident,' Scagga said, in a tone of injured innocence.

'What did you mean by starting a fire at all?'

'I told you, it was the only way to deal with all that vegetation – a huge pile.'

'Nobody told you to burn it. And you never told anyone that was your plan.'

'What else could we do?'

'Carry the debris to the plain, of course!'

'That would have taken days.'

'Did anyone tell you there was a rush?'

Scagga did not answer.

She said: 'How far did the fire spread?'

'Fortunately it did not go the whole length of the wood.'

'Not the whole length? How much was burned? Half of it? Three-quarters?'

Scagga looked down. 'More than that. A small area is left at the west end.'

Ani said: 'Bez and his tribe will starve! They'll just die!' Then she burst into tears. 'You fool,' she said, with bitter grief. 'You've killed a whole tribe.' She turned and walked away from the elders, head bowed, sobbing. 'A whole tribe,' she said quietly. 'You fool.'

Bez knew nothing about cattle. He had never had anything to do with tame animals apart from dogs. Cows made him nervous because he never knew what they were going to do. But he had come up with the idea of stealing them, and naturally he had to be the first of the tribe to try to do it.

The herders minding the cattle were the real danger, because they had bows and arrows. Bez was armed with a heavy club and a flint knife.

He thought about this as he and Gida headed for the herd. There were few cloudy nights in the drought, so they had picked the next best thing, a moonless night, for their first attempt at theft. They were not invisible, but they would be hard to see when moving among a herd of cattle.

The nearest herd was usually just north of East Wood, but Zad had taken it farther away when the farmers started talking about getting cows as compensation for the stampede. Bez guessed Zad had moved the beasts north-west, but not too far, because he needed frequently to take them to water.

Bez smelt the herd before he saw it – which was a good sign: it meant that he and Gida were downwind and the herders' dogs might not pick up their scent.

Bez's biggest worry was noise. Both he and Gida were barefoot – woodlanders hated shoes – and they had the woodlander skill of moving quietly, but dogs had extraordinarily good hearing and could instantly tell the difference between the footsteps of a human and the hooves of a cow.

They stopped at a lone oak tree and stood either side of it, positioning themselves half behind its massive trunk, to study what was in front of them. Bez could not see any herders. Certainly one or more of them would be there, so they must be on the far side of the herd. Most of the cows were standing, but a few were lying down. Bez did not know whether they could sleep standing up. He did not really know whether they slept at all.

He and Gida waited patiently. If the herders were walking around they would come into view sooner or later. But they did not, so probably they were sitting down somewhere. After a while Gida said: 'Let's move.'

This was a dangerous moment. They had to walk upright across empty grassland, in plain view, with nowhere to hide. Bez stared hard as he walked, looking for herders, but it was Gida who spotted them first. Without speaking she dropped to the ground and lay flat, and Bez did the same a heartbeat later.

There were two people. At this distance Bez could not tell whether they were male or female. They were walking slowly. Fortunately they were looking at the cattle, and seemed not to have seen Bez and Gida.

There was a long wait while the herders continued their circuit. As soon as they disappeared, Bez and Gida stood up and walked briskly across the remaining ground.

When they reached the herd they knelt down with their heads on the same level as those of the beasts. On their knees they mingled with the herd, so that their scent would be masked somewhat by that of the cattle.

The animals were used to humans. A bull grunted at Bez, then decided not to worry. Cows glanced at the newcomers and looked away, uninterested.

Bez and Gida stopped and listened hard, trying to hear where the herders were now. People were rarely completely silent. They would talk, cough, sniff, whistle a tune or sing. If asleep they would mutter or snore. After some moments Gida pointed north-west. Bez nodded. He had heard nothing, but he knew she had better ears.

He looked at the cattle around him. None of them was fat or even meaty. They had all suffered in the drought. Bez wanted a healthy young beast, a heifer or a bullock – young female or castrated male – either of which was likely to be obedient, and might be gently led away without noise. He pointed at a heifer and mimed a query to Gida.

She had a leather bag slung over her shoulder. She took from it a handful of fragrant fresh meadowsweet, found in a little clearing in what was left of West Wood. Neither Bez nor Gida knew whether cows would eat out of your hand, as dogs would.

Gida stood up, risking that the herders would notice her.

The cow sniffed the meadowsweet, then turned away. That was disappointing.

Gida tried another cow. Its long tongue came out, wrapped around the herb, and transferred it rapidly to its mouth, then it chewed with a satisfied look.

As it was eating, Gida slipped a rope over its head.

She stepped away, pulling on the rope, and it followed her.

They had captured a cow.

Gida stopped to give it some more meadowsweet, then walked on, pulling gently. The cow went along, making no noise.

Bez stood up and walked behind Gida. They had done all this without alerting the herders. Clearly silence was the key. They had got away with it – so far.

Suddenly Bez felt the brush of a wing against his cheek. He gave an involuntary shout of shock and fear. He heard a small animal squeal loudly and desperately. Gida screamed.

At his feet Bez saw a pigeon hawk struggling with a long-necked weasel. The hawk was big, its wing span as long as a man's arm, and the weasel no bigger than a man's hand, but the little creature was fighting back, wriggling and biting. Nevertheless, the hawk rose into the air with the weasel in its talons, and a moment later was lost in the darkness of night. The weasel's screams faded to nothing.

And the herders' dog was barking maniacally.

'Go that way,' Bez said to Gida, pointing towards the oak tree. 'As fast as you can, but don't scare the cow. I'll go in the opposite direction and create a distraction. Meet me in Round Wood.'

Gida calmly set off at a jog-trot with the cow.

Bez ran, bent over, around the outside of the herd towards a point east of where the barking was coming from. When he had covered a significant distance he stopped and drew his flint knife from his shoulder bag. He stuck the point into the rump of a bull and quickly stepped behind another beast, putting the knife away and taking into both hands the heavy club.

The bull bellowed loud and deep, a noise that could be heard throughout the herd. Bez knelt down and listened carefully to the barking of the dog. He was able to tell that, as he hoped, the dog was moving towards him and away from Gida. He lifted the club and held it over his right shoulder, ready to strike.

He remained still. The dog came on, barking, and Bez could hear the running steps of the two herders. However, the dog moved faster among the cows, and in moments Bez saw it.

The dog saw him and bared its fangs. Bez knew he had to silence the dog with just one blow. The dog leaped at him. Bez swung the club and hit the dog in mid-air, striking it on the head just behind its ear. The dog fell to the ground and lay still.

Bez turned and ran.

He got out of the herd. Far to his right he could just about see Gida running with the cow behind her. She was well past the oak tree and would soon cross a rise and drop out of sight. To keep the attention of the herders away from her Bez angled left. There was a patch of woodland ahead of him, too small to be home to a tribe: if he could reach that they would never find him.

He was confident he could outrun herders. They were not hunters and rarely had reason to run, except for their quickrunner messengers. Woodlanders hunted deer, so had to run fast.

The herders might have come to the same conclusion, for the running footsteps behind him ceased. He glanced over his shoulder and saw that they had not given up, but had stopped to aim their bows. He immediately began to run in a zigzag, to make it difficult for them to sight on him. Two arrows went wide and landed ahead of him, but he knew their aim would improve. He quickened his pace with a huge effort, and doubled his zigzags. The arrows came closer, but none hit, and soon they began to fall short. He was out of range. The herders started running again, but it was no good: he was too far away. They stopped, doubtless reasoning that they could not catch him now.

He made it to the copse and slipped into the bushes. Looking back through the leaves, he saw the two herders walking disconsolately back to the herd, carrying their bows.

We did it, he thought. We are now cattle thieves.

He began to think about how to do it better next time.

The elders met at Riverbend to discuss a message brought from the west by a quickrunner, a young woman called Fali. She had said: 'Zad asks me to tell you that we are losing one cow every night to thieves. We assume they are woodlanders of Bez's tribe. They come at night and quietly lead a cow away without making any noise.'

Scagga immediately said: 'This cannot go on. We herder folk will be wiped out if we carry on losing cattle at this rate.'

Ani was outraged. 'It's your fault!' she burst out. 'They wouldn't need to steal if you hadn't destroyed their habitat!'

'I couldn't help it!' Scagga said.

He would have said more but Keff interrupted. 'Ani and Scagga, there's no point in arguing about whose fault this is. We have to look to the future. What are we going to do to stop the thieving?'

Jara spoke. She was a new elder, the sister of Scagga, but more reasonable. 'We can't stop it,' she said. 'They will carry on stealing cows because their alternative is to starve to death.'

She was probably right, Ani thought despairingly.

Scagga backed his sister. 'We have to wipe out the entire tribe of Bez,' he said. 'Otherwise we will starve instead of them.'

Ani decided to oppose Scagga's belligerence by raising a practical issue. 'Do you know where Bez's tribe is living?'

'West Wood.'

'What little is left of it?' Ani shook her head. 'They're not stupid; they'll be hiding out somewhere.'

'Not necessarily. Perhaps they are stupid.'

Ani said: 'Let me go and investigate.' Her heart sank at the thought of another long walk across the Great Plain, but at least it would force Scagga to postpone violence for a few days. 'I'll see if I can learn where the tribe is hiding.'

Scagga looked ready to argue, but his sister said reasonably: 'That makes sense. Before we send an army, we should find out where the enemy is.'

Ani found the sight of the burned wood horrific. Nothing green remained. The ground was covered with a layer of grey ash as far as the eye could see. A few trees stood still, bare of leaves, their trunks and branches blackened and lifeless, ghostly plants growing out of a dead landscape.

But farmers were at work, digging the ground, turning the earth over to bury the ash. Their furrows ran east to west, parallel with South River, so that the rain – if it ever rained again – would be retained in the field instead of running down the slope and into the river. Little clouds of ash lifted and sank as the shovels worked. The land would be green again next summer, but with regular shoots of growing wheat instead of the fecund jungle of wild woodland.

Troon had enlarged his territory, Ani thought. At a stroke he had added a huge area to his domain. She wondered if he would do the same to East Wood one day.

Yana and Pia were not there. Presumably Troon had not favoured them with an allocation of the new lands. Ani found them in one of their old fields, Pia carrying baby Olin strapped to her back. Both women were thin but not unhealthy.

They sat on the ground to talk. Ani said: 'I'm here because someone is stealing our cattle.'

'We know,' said Pia. 'Zad thought it might be the farmers. He came here, and Troon let him look everywhere for beef, cow hides and cow bones. He didn't find any.'

Ani nodded. She was not surprised that the farmers were innocent. 'So who do you think it is?'

'Oh, Bez, obviously,' said Yana. 'There's really no other possibility.'

'And where is Bez? In the remnant of West Wood?'

'No. It's too small for a whole tribe.'

'Then where?'

'We don't know,' said Yana. 'No one knows.'

Ani walked west along the bank of the river until she came to the small surviving area of woodland. She walked all around it and satisfied herself that it was not big enough to hide a tribe, no matter how clever they might be at concealing themselves.

She then went into the wood and found a small settlement, just two houses. A handful of woodlanders were sitting around while a spitted joint of meat roasted over a fire.

It smelt like beef.

An old woman was sitting by the fire, turning the spit occasionally with a veined brown hand. Ani sat beside her. Some of the children came closer to stare at the stranger with frank curiosity. Ani noticed that they were wearing new-looking leather tunics.

She said to the old woman: 'I am Ani.'

'I know you,' said the woman.

She spoke the herder language. That was helpful.

'You had a son called Han,' the woman added.

'He's dead now.'

'I know. Stam killed him. Stam killed Fell, too.'

'And now Stam is dead.'

'The balance was restored.' The woman nodded in a satisfied way.

Everyone suspected that the woodlanders had killed Stam for murdering Fell, but no one could be sure. And even this woman's statement was enigmatic: a balance had been restored, but by whom? She was not saying.

Instead she said: 'I am Naro.'

Ani said: 'You're cooking beef.'

'Venison,' said Naro, firmly.

Ani looked around. She saw mainly old people and children. There were two young women, one heavily pregnant and the other breastfeeding a newborn baby. Ani was glad the children had food, but the tribe could not go on living by theft.

She said to Naro: 'Where are the others?'

'Hunting,' said Naro.

'When will they be back?'

'Soon.'

Ani reached out and touched the garment of a child standing near her. She said: 'This is cow hide.'

Naro shook her head. 'Deerskin.'

Ani said: 'I'm a leather tanner. I know the difference between one skin and another. This is not deer, it's cow.'

'Hard to tell them apart.'

'Not for me.'

Naro became cross. 'What are you doing here?'

'Looking for Bez.'

'He's not here.'

'But he comes here, and he gives you cow hides and beef.'

Naro said nothing.

'When Bez leaves here, where does he go?'

'You should leave now,' said Naro. 'We don't want you here.'

Zad told Ani that he was sick at heart because he could not fulfil his duty of protecting the herd. She believed him.

The herd he supervised took up one-third of the Great Plain, but for as long as anyone could remember, it had needed only half a dozen families to take care of it.

Those days were over.

Ani sat with Zad, Biddy and their daughter Dini on the ground outside their house. Biddy said plaintively: 'They come creeping so silently! If something goes wrong, they run and we can't catch them. Otherwise we never see them at all, but next day someone says: "Where's the bullock with the white patch over one eye?" and we realize we've been robbed again.'

Ani said: 'I went to the remnant of the West Wood. Only old people and children were there. A woman called Naro told me the rest of the tribe were away hunting.'

'She always says that,' Zad said. 'But we never see them.'

'Where could Bez be living?'

'No one knows.'

If they could not be found, they could not be massacred, which was a relief to Ani. But they could not hide for ever. At some point their secret would be revealed, and then there would be a bloodbath. 'Let me ask you something,' she said. 'Is there a way to stop the thefts without killing everyone in the tribe?'

'I think there is,' said Zad.

Ani said eagerly: 'How?'

Biddy answered: 'Double the guard.'

They had obviously worked this out between them, and Ani was encouraged.

Zad said: 'Where there are two herders now, there should be four. And they must patrol all night, walking around the herd continuously, without sleeping.'

Biddy added: 'And every woman and man should carry a bow and arrows.'

Zad said: 'And if four is not enough, we must have six, or eight.'

That could work, Ani thought. It obviously involved killing woodlanders, but not all of them. It was a grimly cold calculation. But it was what she was looking for, a way to restrain Scagga and prevent a massacre.

She said: 'How many people would you need altogether?'

'There are six families in this village. That makes twelve herders. And there are two more villages here in the west of the plain. I can't count that high.'

'Nor can I,' said Ani. 'But you need three new villages each with twelve herders.'

'And soon,' said Zad. 'We're losing a cow almost every night, remember.'

'Soon,' Ani repeated.

'This is how it works,' Ani said to the elders when she got back to Riverbend. 'Bez and most of the tribe have gone into hiding, no one knows where. They might have persuaded another tribe to share their territory.'

'Unlikely, in a famine,' said Keff.

'I agree. But in that case they must have left the Great Plain altogether. They may have crossed the South River and found a hideout somewhere between the river and the Great Sea; they could have climbed the Scarp and disappeared into unknown regions north of here; but most likely they're in the North-West Hills, a region they're familiar with.'

'So that's where we look for them,' said Scagga.

'Wait a minute, Scagga,' said his sister. 'Listen.'

Ani resumed: 'They come back to the plain at night. They approach a herd silently. They rope a cow and lead it away. Often the herders don't know it has happened until daylight, when they notice that a cow is missing. I assume the woodlanders lead the cow to their hideout and butcher it there. Later, probably travelling at night, they take some meat and hides to the remnant of West Wood to give to the old people and children living there. Then they disappear again before dawn.'

'We'll find them,' said Scagga. 'It may take a while, but we'll find them, and then . . .'

Ani said: 'The herders in the west have come up with another proposal, a way to stop the thefts without sending an army to search unknown territory outside the Great Plain.'

Keff said: 'That would be very good indeed.'

'Zad believes he could protect the cows if he had double the number of herders. Where now two people watch over a herd, he wants four. We would need to create three new villages in the western plain, each with twelve people. And all armed with bows and arrows.'

'We have plenty of bows and arrows,' said Scagga. He had created a stockpile and was impatient to put the weapons to use.

Ani ignored that. 'If we're agreed on this, we need to do it as soon as possible, before we lose many more cattle.'

Keff said: 'We can send the new people tomorrow.'

Ani said: 'That would be good.'

For some days Bez had been surreptitiously preventing Lali from going on a cattle raid. In fact he had wanted her to stay in West Wood, where she would have been safer, but she was a woman now, and having a romance with a nice boy called Forn, and Bez could not pretend she was a child. However, he kept suggesting other couples to go cow-stealing, and had pretended not to hear her when she volunteered; but she saw through him and demanded to be sent. At last he had to give in. Lali went with Forn to steal a cow.

That night he lay awake beside Gida, worrying.

Lali returned in the dawn light. She had no cow and no partner, and she was bleeding.

The wound was an arrow cut on her shoulder. A little more to the centre and it might have been her throat.

Gida pressed healing leaves on the wound and Bez bound the leaves with vines. Then they and others questioned Lali about what had happened.

'There were two herders, and another one, and another one,' she said, using the woodlander words for numbers. 'And every one had a bow. They walked around the herd constantly, with their dogs, hardly stopping to rest, and never sleeping!'

Bez said: 'So you couldn't reach the cattle?'

'Well, we felt we had to. So in the end we slithered on our stomachs across the ground, and we reached the herd without being seen. I got a rope around a cow's neck, that wasn't difficult.'

Gida said: 'But then you had to escape across open ground – with the cow.'

'We tried to. I made the cow gallop, and Forn ran alongside, but the beast didn't want to run, and it slowed down. So the herders got close enough to shoot. And they hit Forn, and he fell.' She began to cry. 'He must have turned around to look, because the arrow was in the front of his thigh, and he was bleeding so much. And I knew he was going to die, and I would too if I stayed, so I ran, leaving him behind. And one arrow hit me but it wasn't bad and I could run faster than the herders.'

Bez kissed her. 'You're a brave girl,' he said. He was close to tears himself.

Gida said: 'I wonder if they have done this, doubled the watch, for all parts of the herd.'

Bez said: 'If they haven't yet, they will soon. It's their new strategy to stop us stealing.'

Gida nodded. 'It's clever. We have to find a way around it.'

'Yes,' said Bez. 'Or rob someone else.'

20

'IGNORE THE HOUSES,' Bez whispered to the others. 'The food is in the little stores.'

They were a small group of woodlanders, and they were at Farmplace in the dead of night. There was no moon. Bez had split them into three groups of three. The plan was that each group would rob one farm and they would rendezvous in the remnant of West Wood.

Bez was sounding more confident than he felt. This was their first attempt to rob farmers, and he did not know what difficulties they might encounter. He knew it was dangerous, but they had to do it or starve. If they got into trouble, he would try to save Lali and Gida.

'Let me show you how to deal with the dogs,' he whispered. 'And from now on, silence.'

He had a plan, but he did not know if it would work.

He led them across a field of stubble, then approached a house with a dog tethered outside. The dog saw them and barked. Bez lay flat, and the others followed suit.

They watched as a man came out of the house and looked around. Seeing nothing, he muttered a curse at the dog and went back inside.

Bez stood up and walked closer. The dog barked again, and the woodlanders again lay flat.

The man reappeared, this time carrying a bow. He would not be expecting to see thieves, which were little known in Farmplace, but he was ready to shoot foxes or possibly a wolf.

He walked all around the house, then went to the nearby store, walked in a circle around it, and looked inside. Bez hoped he would not come where the woodlanders were lying. He seemed to look straight at them, and Bez held his breath, but a moment later the man turned away. As Bez had hoped, in the dark they were indistinguishable from the ground around them.

Seeing nothing unusual, the man spoke angrily to the dog and returned to his house.

The woodlanders crept forward on their bellies. The dog probably could not see them, but could surely smell them. Confused now, it growled, barked briefly and uncertainly, and fell silent.

When they got close, Bez stood up. The dog barked loudly. Bez stepped forward, knife in hand, and cut its throat. It died quickly and silently.

He stared at the doorway to the house. The knife in his hand dripped dog's blood. But the man did not come out.

Without speaking, Bez directed two teams to neighbouring farms, then led his own team – himself, Gida and Lali – to this farm's store.

It was pitch dark, so they had to leave the door open for the sake of the little light it let in. They stood still while their eyes adapted. Eventually Bez dimly saw three large pottery jars. On top of one was a cup with a long handle. Bez picked up the cup, removed the lid of the jar, and dipped the cup into some kind of liquid in the jar. He tasted the liquid: it was milk. He spat it out. Milk gave people stomach ache.

The second jar contained curds and whey, milk that had soured and separated into lumps and a watery liquid. It was not part of the woodlander diet and Bez guessed it would have the same unpleasant effect as milk.

But the third jar contained wheat grains, the staple food of the farmers. Woodlanders did not grow wheat but ate the grains of wild grasses. Cultivated grains were similar but fatter.

Meanwhile Gida and Lali explored the store, mainly by touch. Gida found a big leather bag full of apples, and Lali a wooden box containing cheese. They took all three prizes.

They left the store, Bez closing the door quietly.

They crossed the fields, staying away from the buildings. Bez kept looking around, fearful that some sleepless nightwalker might see them and raise the alarm. However, it was not a human but an animal that saw them.

They passed a farmhouse at a distance and then, from behind the house, came the biggest bull Bez had ever seen. Its shoulder was higher than his head, and its huge curved horns spread as wide as Bez's legs were long. It bellowed, and Lali gave a little scream.

Bez realized it was an aurochs, a type of wild cattle that was rarely seen. He guessed it was on its way to the river to drink. He hefted his club, but knew that such a weapon would not save him from those mighty horns.

The beast looked at the three of them as if trying to decide whether they were food. They were paralysed in its stare. Then, seeming to lose interest, it turned and trotted away, heading down to the waterside.

Weak with relief, the three woodlanders hurried on. Bez

thought the people in the house must have heard the bellow, and possibly Lali's scream too, but they seemed to have decided it was safer to stay inside than to investigate.

Lali whispered: 'What was it?'

'A wild bull,' Bez said quietly. 'A type called an aurochs. You don't see them often.'

'I'm glad about that,' she said.

After that they reached the edge of the cultivated land without incident, and headed across the ashy former woods. As they got farther away from Farmplace, Bez began to feel safe. He hoped the other two teams had had the same luck.

They reached the little village at the far end of what had been West Wood. Bez woke Naro. 'Get the children up,' he said. 'We have food for them.'

The children came rubbing their eyes. They seized on the apples and Naro gave them cheese too. The old folks tucked in too, as did the pregnant woman and the nursing mother. Soon the children went back to bed with full stomachs.

The other two teams arrived safely, bringing smoked pork, nuts, and the carcass of a wild boar. They gave some of the loot to Naro, who wrapped it in leaves and dug a shallow pit in which to hide it, in case Troon came looking tomorrow morning.

Bez and his thieves left carrying the rest of the food. They crossed the plain in starlight and headed for their hideout.

The news spread across the fields on the following morning. Pia heard that three families had lost precious stores, food laid away for the winter. In each case a dog had been killed. The robbed people were especially anguished about the wheat they had lost.

They had toiled all summer, carrying the water from the river to the fields, then reaping the wheat – stoop, slash, gather, bind and stoop again, all in the heat of the sun – and now the reward for all that labour had been snatched away by people who came creeping in the night to steal.

She was grateful that she and her mother had lost nothing. They had stores of wheat and cheese and root vegetables, for all of which they had worked until they ached, and they were relying on those stores to keep them and baby Olin alive through the winter. It would have broken her heart to lose them.

Troon was angry – not blustering, as was his usual way, but coldly furious and determined. What he was determined to do was not clear to Pia, nor to Duff or anyone else she spoke to. But he gathered together the usual group of Young Dogs. Even they did not know his intentions, though he had told them to arm themselves.

Perhaps they would go looking for Bez and his tribe. But how could Troon know where to find them? He could spend weeks searching and not come across any trace of them.

Some of the farmers gathered around Troon's house as the Young Dogs prepared to leave. It was Duff who had the nerve to stand in front of Troon and say: 'Who are you going to kill, Troon?'

Troon gave him an evil look and said: 'You – if you don't shut your mouth and get out of the way.'

Pia feared that he meant it, but Duff was not scared. He said: 'The woodlanders are robbing people because they have to. Did you not think of that possibility when you decided to plough up their land?'

'I'm not answerable to you, you young fool.'

'The Big Man ought to explain himself to the farmer folk, don't you think?'

Pia was full of admiration. Duff was not giving in.

Troon put the point of his knife to Duff's chest, exactly over the heart, and Pia felt it would take only the slightest provocation for him to push it in. 'You don't tell me what to do,' he said. 'I tell you what to do. Now get out of my way.'

There was a pause. Pia wanted to say, *Give in now, Duff. You've made your point, you don't need to die for it.*

Duff seemed to have a similar thought. 'As you wish,' he said, and to Pia's relief he stepped aside.

Troon grinned, as if he had made a fool of Duff, but Pia saw it the other way around. She said quietly to Duff: 'Troon couldn't defend his actions, and you made everyone see it.'

'Good.'

'Weren't you scared when he drew his knife?'

'Terrified. But someone's got to tell him. His foolishness makes trouble for all of us.'

'You're very brave,' she said.

'I'm glad you think so.'

Troon marched down to the riverbank, followed by the Young Dogs. They turned west and headed upstream. They might have been going to the remnant of West Wood, but they would not find Bez there, not in broad daylight, Pia felt sure. So what was Troon up to?

As she walked back to the farm, she noticed that the sun on her back had lost some of its heat, and she looked up to see clouds in the sky. Her heart leaped. Could it be that rain was on the way?

She half expected Troon to be away for days, but he and the Young Dogs came back that afternoon. Everyone went to Troon's house to see whether he had found the tribe. But Troon did not speak, and no one had the nerve to ask him questions.

After he disappeared inside, the Young Dogs went to their homes in silence. People who shouted questions at them were ignored. None of them spoke.

Once again they all returned to their homes.

It would come out one day, Pia thought.

Few things remained secret for ever.

Bez and his tribe raided the far eastern end of the farming country, almost halfway to the Monument, where the strip between river and woodland was narrow, and the houses were far apart. The trick with the dogs worked a second time, and they came away with lavish prizes of meat, grain and cheese. They made their escape through East Wood and met up on the edge of the Great Plain. From there they set off west, following the border line between wood and plain. They had a long walk ahead of them, but Bez thought they could make it before daybreak.

Everything was going well. Bez congratulated himself on a second triumph. They would go to the remnant of West Wood and give some of this food to the young and old there, then carry the rest to their hideout. His tribe would survive, despite all efforts to wipe it out.

They had almost reached the Break when they came upon a herd, and quickly knelt down to be less visible. They had no interest in stealing cattle – they already had too much to carry – but the herders would assume the opposite. However, they could not see any herders, and they moved on cautiously.

A strong wind sprang up, and it began to rain.

It came down so hard that Bez could not even see the length of a cow. In no time he was drenched. It was difficult to maintain his grip on the slippery pottery jar he was carrying.

It was exactly like the rainstorm that had occurred at this time last year, and Bez wondered whether it represented a new pattern.

He heard dogs barking in the distance. They must belong to herders, Bez thought. Fortunately they sounded far away – though it was difficult to be sure in the wind and rain.

They stumbled on, slipping on the muddy ground, wiping the water from their blinded eyes. The rain would revive the dried-up hazelnut bushes, Bez thought, then remembered that nearly all his bushes had gone up in flames.

The barking was suddenly loud and close and, before Bez could react, a pause in the rain revealed a line of herders, no doubt alerted by their two dogs. Every herder had an arrow to his bow ready to shoot.

In a moment that lasted as long as the blink of an eye, Bez considered saying, *We're not robbing you, we're robbing the farmers!* then realized the herders would kill them anyway; and he decided to flee.

The woodlanders dropped their burdens and ran, but Bez saw two fall to arrows beside him, and another stumble, then run on. While the herders were putting fresh arrows to their bowstrings the woodlanders made it to the edge of the wood and burst into the vegetation with two dogs at their heels.

They split up then, all finding different routes away from the herders, who were crashing through the bushes behind them. Now, Bez thought, his people were in their element, and could move a lot faster than the herders. If they had remained together, they might have turned and fought back, but it was too late to wish for that now.

However, they could not outrun the dogs. One was behind Bez. He turned and struck it with his club. The dog whimpered and ran away.

He came to a tall tree and considered taking refuge in its invisible heights, but decided it was wiser to put more distance between his pursuers and himself.

The herders quickly became discouraged. They must have realized they were losing ground. Anyway, they were probably tripping over tree roots and falling in puddles, being unused to the terrain. Soon Bez could no longer hear them, and he stopped to rest. They would not be able to sneak up on him because, unlike the woodlanders, herders could not move silently.

He hooted like an owl, and immediately heard an answering hoot. He repeated the sound, and a few moments later Omun appeared. They both hooted, and a second woodlander, Arav, arrived. Then three more.

Two had fallen to arrows, and another had been hit and probably had not escaped the herders. This was all that was left of the raiding party.

'Our bounty is lost,' Bez said to the others. 'The herders will have taken everything. We should head west, through the wood as far as it goes, to make sure we don't encounter them again.'

They were a dismal party, trekking through the rain in the dark. Three companions had died and they were empty-handed. Bez's idea that they could live by stealing was not working out. Still, he did not know what else they could have done.

They reached the Break. There was no risk that they might be seen at a distance by farmers, for the rain was still blinding. The sky was black with rain clouds, but Bez sensed that a hidden dawn was near. They hurried across the fields in the dark. When the ground underfoot changed they knew they had reached what had been West Wood.

As they continued to walk west, the rain eased from downpour to drizzle, and Bez saw a faint light in the east.

There was no sunrise, for the clouds were still thick, but the light strengthened, and as they approached the remnant of woodland they were able to see clearly.

Before they reached the houses, Bez was shocked to see a

woman lying on the ground in the rain-wet mud. She was on her front, but her head was turned to one side, and he could see her face. It was Naro.

She was not breathing.

He knelt beside her and touched her. She was cold.

Poor old Naro. The children would weep.

She must have got up in the night, he supposed, with nobody noticing, and then wandered, perhaps confused. And for some reason she had fallen down and died. That was the only explanation he could think of for her body being out there, untended.

The villagers would still be asleep. He would take her body to them and rouse them. He bent down and picked her up. She was a thin old woman and she weighed little.

Ahead of him he heard Omun say: 'Bez, look at this.'

He walked on. Omun was staring at something on the ground. Bez followed his gaze. It seemed like a child, but it could not be. He looked harder. It *was* a child, a boy, six or seven midsummers old, lying on his back, eyes open and staring lifelessly at the branches above.

His throat had been cut.

'No,' said Bez. 'No, no.'

Omun picked up the child and they walked together into the clearing in front of the houses, and there they saw a scene so vile, so horrifying, so unbearably tragic that Bez could not take it in.

They were all dead.

All the children, all the old folk, the pregnant woman and the nursing mother and her baby. Some had been clubbed to death; some had had their throats cut. Some had run and been caught, and their bodies lay on the ground in poses of flight.

Bez put the body of Naro gently on the ground. As he did so he saw something he had not noticed before: a bloodstained hole in her tunic, just over her heart.

The faces of his companions all wore the same look: mouths open in shock, eyes staring in disbelief.

He walked around, looking at each corpse. He wanted to weep, but he could not: he was too stunned.

At last he began to think sensibly. The bodies must be treated with respect. He tried to speak, but his throat constricted and he could not utter words. He breathed in and out slowly, and tried again. 'We should lay them all down, side by side, here in the clearing,' he said. 'With their legs straight and their arms folded. Come, let's do right by the dead.'

They did as he said.

The mother and baby were left until last, perhaps because their deaths were hardest to contemplate. In the end it was Bez who bent over her. Mother and baby were both naked. He lifted the baby from her chest. It was a boy.

The baby cried.

Bez was so shocked he almost dropped it. 'Alive!' he said.

He wondered whether the child had been overlooked. Or perhaps the murderers, despite the evil they were doing, had simply found themselves unable to cross that final line of depravity.

He stood up with the child in his arms. Its eyes were open and its legs kicked. Its skin was cold, but probably it had been kept alive by the warmth of its dead mother. Bez fell automatically into the eternal position, holding the baby to his chest, one hand under its bottom, the other hand protecting the head. He felt its lips moving on the skin of his shoulder and realized it was seeking a nipple.

Omun said: 'What are we going to do with him, Bez?'

'Take him to Round Wood. There will probably be a nursing mother in the tribe. They will take him, when we tell them the story of . . . this.'

The child cried again, and Omun said: 'He's hungry now.'

Bez looked at the baby, then at the dead mother, then back at the baby. Why not? he thought. It's life or death.

He knelt down. With his left hand he lifted the dead mother's shoulders until she was in a sitting position. Then he held the baby to her chest. It turned its head, lips making a sucking shape, until its mouth found what it was searching for; and at last its eyes closed in contentment as it began to feed.

21

THE MEN AND women of Bez's tribe sat in the clearing in the remnant of West Wood. It was cold, but they had lit a big fire and huddled around it.

There were no children or old people: they were all dead. They had been killed here in this clearing, and farmers were the murderers. Pia had confirmed that to Gida. The Young Dogs had been silent at first, but they had not been able to keep their foul secret very long, and the truth had come out in whispered confessions to mothers and wives, until everyone in Farmplace knew it.

The faces around Bez were pale and tense with grief. They had all lost parents or children or both. So many bodies had been cremated here that there was still ash in the bushes and trees.

'I have never known anything like this,' Bez said.

None of them had.

'The balance is not just upset, it has been destroyed.'

Omun said: 'Where there is murder, there must be killing.'

366

Gida said: 'But who should die? The hammer of the gods must fall upon the guilty.'

Several people in the crowd repeated the familiar phrase: 'The hammer of the gods must fall upon the guilty.'

Bez said: 'The herders are guilty, because they burned our wood.'

Many people nodded. Bez waited for someone to disagree, but no one did.

'The farmers are guilty, because they murdered our children and old people.'

The crowd agreed.

'To restore the balance, we must kill herders and farmers.'

Several people shouted: 'Yes!'

Bez said: 'And they will all be at the Monument for the Midwinter Rite.'

The high priestess, Ello, was ill, too ill to get up. Joia had been doing Ello's job for some weeks. It was Joia who had proposed painting all the crossbars with red ochre. The priestesses had enjoyed the work and the colour enhanced the Monument.

Today she rehearsed the priestesses for the Midwinter Rite. This was an evening ceremony, so the practice took place in the morning. Outside the circular bank, trading was in noisy progress.

Joia tried not to think about Ello dying. It would be wicked to hope for such a thing. But she knew she would be the next high priestess, and then she would be free to pursue the tremendous project of a stone Monument. Still, she must leave everything in the hands of the gods.

That autumn it had rained as it used to, before the terrible years of the drought. The cattle were healthier, though not fatter:

the grass would not grow again until spring. Supplies of fodder were low, and many beasts would be slaughtered at midwinter and turned into smoked beef, because they could not be kept alive until spring. The famine was not over, but perhaps its end was in sight.

Optimism was in the air as people gathered for the Midwinter Rite at the Monument. Many farmers were there, though men only.

Herders from distant regions to the north, which had escaped the worst of the drought, brought fat sheep and cattle to trade for flints and pottery.

The gossip was about a rumour that had spread all over the plain and even farther. Terrible evil had been done, people said. No one had seen it, but everyone spoke of it. Children and old people of Bez's tribe had been slaughtered. Farmers said they knew nothing about it, but rumour said the Young Dogs had done it on Troon's instructions.

The thefts had stopped abruptly. Cattle no longer vanished from the herd at night, and there were no more raids on farmers' stores. Some woodlanders left Bez's tribe and wandered on the plain. Joia saw a couple grubbing for roots in the grass, and Seft said he saw one trying to catch fish in a stream that had been refreshed by the storm. It was unusual to see woodlanders outside their territories, but the reason was obvious to Joia: Bez's tribe had lost their territory.

Today was the shortest day of the year, and people began to gather inside the circular bank as soon as the sky darkened. The ceremony celebrated the setting of the sun on Midwinter Day, but more often than not the sun was behind clouds in winter, so its setting had to be assumed. Today, however, the cloud cover broke in the west, and the crowd looking south-west watched, mesmerized, as a huge red sun, seen against blood-red and flint-grey clouds, slowly sank beyond the Monument and disappeared over the edge of the world.

Going from the Monument to Riverbend for the feast, Joia found herself walking next to a farmer called Duff, an amiable young man she had met before. She asked him about the rumoured massacre. 'It was a tragedy,' he said.

'But who did it?'

'I don't know,' he said, his amiability diminishing.

'But you must have your suspicions,' she persisted.

'It's best not to discuss suspicions.'

'Of course,' she said, backing off. 'I hope I haven't embarrassed you.'

With a sudden access of candour, he said: 'Thank you for not forcing me to lie.'

That was a complex remark, and she moved away from him to think about it. He was intelligent and honest, she thought, and he knew who had committed the massacre, but if he said it he would be putting himself in some kind of danger. And what danger could a young farmer fear? It could only be some threat from Troon.

A few moments later Troon's minion, Shen, came alongside her and said: 'So, you've been talking to Duff.'

Troon's people did not miss much, she thought. 'I've been trying to talk to him,' she said. For his sake she would make it clear that he had told her nothing. 'He's a very ignorant young man, isn't he?'

Shen seemed surprised. 'What makes you say that?'

'Well, every time I asked him a question he answered: "I don't know." Is he always like that?'

'I don't know,' said Shen.

'Oh, go away.'

Shen went away.

At the feast Joia joined with her family: her mother, Ani, plus

Neen and Seft, with their three children. As always they sat cross-legged on leather mats, with bowls and spoons. Joia remembered the ones who were not there: her brother, Han, and her father, Olin. But she kept her sad thoughts to herself.

After the meal a poet told of a time when people were giants, and could fight bulls and bears and wolves, and kill them with their hands. *But the people became arrogant, the poet said, and they started to say: 'We are bigger and stronger than any other living thing, and we fear nothing, so we should be called gods.'*

The listeners murmured their disapproval. They knew that arrogance was a mistake that would be punished, at least in a story.

There was a man called Ban Highspeaker who could talk to the gods, and he said to the Earth God: 'We are gods.' This offended the Earth God, who made people small to teach them a lesson.

The result was dreadful: a bear could kill someone with one blow of its huge paw; a bull could gore a person with its horns; a wolf could tear anyone's throat out with its teeth.

The people said: 'We have learned our lesson, and we will never again call ourselves gods.' Then Ban Highspeaker reported this to the Earth God, and said: 'We want to be giants again.' However, the Earth God refused, because he knew that if he made them big, they would just become arrogant all over again.

Many listeners nodded agreement.

Then he thought: 'I wonder what would happen if I made them the smartest of all living things.'

'Yes!' said one of the listeners, and others repeated it.

When they were clever they made arrows to kill bears, and sharp flints to cut off the bulls' testicles, and they stole puppies from the wolves and fed them and made them friends, and called them dogs, so that when a wolf came to the village the dogs would chase it away. And the people said: 'We don't want to be giants and we know we are not gods but we want to stay clever.'

And Ban Highspeaker spoke again to the Earth God and said: 'We are happy now.'

The Earth God said: 'Why are you happy?'

And Ban Highspeaker said: 'It is better to be clever than big.'

By the time the story ended, a half-moon shone irregularly through gaps in the clouds.

Seft and Neen took the children home. Anina had fallen asleep during the poem, and Seft picked her up without waking her. A secret that not even Neen knew was that Anina was his favourite child, and he hugged her close as he carried her.

He often recalled how badly he had longed for this, a family who loved one another and were kind. Now when he thought of his childhood it seemed like something that had happened in a bad dream. This was real life, Anina in his arms and Neen walking beside him holding the hands of Ilian and Denno.

When they reached the house, Ilian and Denno lay down immediately. Seft put Anina down beside them. He said to Ilian, the eldest: 'Did you like the story?'

'Oh, yes! I can remember all of it.'

Denno said: 'Can you tell it? I want to hear it again.'

Seft said: 'Tell it again, Ilian.' It would send Denno to sleep. 'All right.'

Seft kissed each of them, and Neen did the same, then they got ready for the revel. They took off their tunics and put their shearling coats back on for warmth. Neen picked up a hefty stone that she carried in a pouch; it was for men who forgot, in their excitement, that a woman could say no, even at a revel. They headed for the outskirts of the village, where the action would be getting under way.

When they were first together Seft had not wanted to take part in the revel, feeling that sex with Neen was all he would ever desire. But after a couple of years he had begun to feel differently. He had kept this to himself for a while in case Neen would be hurt but, when eventually he told her, she confessed that she, too, wanted to go, and they had been enthusiastic participants ever since.

They always told each other what they had done. Neen often lay with a stranger from the north, someone she would probably never see again; she enjoyed the feeling that what she was doing would have no consequences. Seft hoped to find a group of women and men all having sex with each other at the same time. There was no love in it: that was part of the attraction.

They came to the edge of the village. Fires had been lit at intervals, taking the bite from the winter air. Most people were still looking around, some alone, some in pairs, a few in small groups, searching for whatever it was they liked. A few had begun, and several shearling coats were humping up and down already.

Seft and Neen kissed affectionately. Neen said: 'Have a good time.'

Seft said: 'You too.'

Then they went in different directions.

Sometimes Joia envied those who liked sex with people they did not love, or did not even know. It might be fun to enjoy the pleasure then forget the person. But she could not do it. She had tried, with a priestess at a revel, but it had left her unmoved and reluctant to try again. So, when the poet ended his story, she headed back to the Monument.

There would be a few traders outside now, she expected, guarding the goods left there overnight. Some would be walking around, chatting to each other, while others would be asleep.

However, as she got closer she realized that it was not so. She could hear strange noises and she smelt smoke. She broke into a run.

The possessions of the traders littered the ground outside the earth bank, but there seemed to be no one guarding them. Looking closer, she saw a boy peeping out from under a leather blanket. She recognized him as Janno, grandson of El the flint-knapper. She knelt down beside him. 'What's happening, Janno?' she said.

He was terrified and barely coherent. 'They killed my sister!' he said hysterically. He pointed, and Joia saw the body of a young woman on the ground.

'I'm very sorry, Janno,' Joia said. 'That's very sad. But you must tell me something else. What did they steal?'

'Nothing!' he said.

Joia was baffled. What did they want? And who were they?

She looked towards the Monument. The moonlight showed her five or six figures on the circular bank, presumably traders who had been guarding their pitches. At first she thought they must be dead, but then she saw that they were moving. They seemed to be peeping over the edge – as she had done so many midsummers ago – but what were they watching? There could be no ceremony going on: none was scheduled, and the priestesses were still at Riverbend.

Fear seized her.

She ran to the bank and up the slope to the top, then looked into the circle. She was horrified by what she saw.

The Monument was burning.

Some thirty men and women were there, and by their bare feet she knew they were woodlanders. She could see the remains of the dry twigs they had used as tinder, and she could smell the

373

birch tar they had applied to make sure the timbers blazed up quickly. Now all the posts were on fire and some of the crossbars were already smouldering.

Two figures lay still on the ground, and Joia knew by their long tunics that they were priestesses. They must have decided to skip the revel and come straight home, as Joia had. But they had been ahead of her and had tried to stop the woodlanders burning the Monument. The positions of their bodies, and their splayed limbs, told her they were dead.

One of the woodlanders was Bez.

Joia stood upright at the very top of the ridge and yelled: 'Bez! Bez! This is me – I am Joia!'

All the woodlanders looked at her. She could tell by their faces that their blood was up and they wanted to kill her. She had acted without thinking – again – and she had done something stupid and dangerous.

But she could not stop now.

She walked slowly down the slope into the circle, making herself appear calm while inside she was terrified. Speaking loudly, but not shouting, she said: 'Stop, please, Bez.' She hoped they could not hear the tremor in her voice.

Bez said: 'The gods demand a balance.'

One of the woodlanders ran at her and hit her with a club. She dodged, and the weapon missed her head but hit her shoulder, and she fell to her knees. I'm going to die now, she thought. And I have so much yet to do!

She looked at the man as he raised his club again. Then she heard Bez shout: 'Omun!' then something peremptory in the woodlander tongue.

The man called Omun lowered his club and backed away.

Joia's shoulder hurt like fire but she struggled up. She looked at Bez, his face lit red by the flames. He spoke again in the

374

woodlander tongue, and pointed at the break in the bank that served as the entrance and exit. Some of them spoke back angrily to him, and she guessed they wanted to kill her. But Bez prevailed, and reluctantly they turned away from Joia and began to run.

She shouted: 'Why are you doing this, Bez?'

'The gods demand a balance,' he said. 'For a fire, there must be flame; and for a death, there will be killing.' Then he ran after the others.

She watched them leave the circle and charge along the path that led to Riverbend. What were they planning to do in the village? Whatever it was, they would meet more resistance there than they had at the Monument.

She had no way to warn the people in Riverbend. She could not run faster than woodlanders, so she could not overtake them and warn her family, and there was no means of giving the alarm at a distance.

Instead she knelt by the two priestesses on the ground. But her first instinct had been right: neither was breathing. Their heads had been smashed with clubs.

Struggling not to cry, she looked at the burning Monument. She took off her tunic and tried to fight the fire with it. She wrapped the leather around a burning post and succeeded in dousing the flames, then moved to the next post; but a moment later both posts collapsed, and the crossbar – also burning – fell to the ground.

There were seventy-five pieces of timber in the Monument – she was one of the few people who could count that high – and she realized that on her own she could do nothing to prevent the whole thing burning down.

She sat on the ground and cried.

A woman Seft had met for the first time that afternoon was on top of him, kissing him, while his hands explored two other people, a man and a woman, one on each side of him. Then he began to hear shouts and screams that were not sounds of delight. He fell still. The woman on top of him said: 'What's the matter?' Then she heard it too, and said: 'It sounds like a fight.'

It was a fight. Seft scrambled out from under her and got to his feet. He saw a barefoot woodlander coming towards him at top speed, club raised. He moved without thinking: he dodged the man then tripped him, causing him to fall flat, then grabbed the club out of his hands. The man got to his knees but, before he could stand, Seft brought the club down hard on his head. The man fell on his face and lay still. For two or three moments Seft had acted mechanically, without emotion, but now he was filled with rage, and he hit the man again, three times, until his head was a pulp and he was undoubtedly dead.

He looked around, suddenly alert and fearful. In the light of the fires he saw that the man who had run at him had not been alone. A small army of woodlanders was attacking, using clubs and flint knives. He thought of his three children, fast asleep at home, and knew that he should go to them even before he searched for Neen.

He broke into a run, swerving around pairs and groups of fighting people, desperate to reach his children; but someone came at him from behind, catching him by surprise. He was hit on his head and fell on his front.

As soon as he landed he rolled, in fear of his life, knowing the man would strike him again, as mercilessly as Seft himself had struck moments ago, and he looked up to see a woodlander raising a stone hammer.

Then the woodlander was in turn hit from behind. A hand holding a stone came down on the back of the man's head, and he staggered.

Seft jumped to his feet, still determinedly holding the club. He saw that the person who had saved him was Neen, and he felt a jolt of elation, seeing that she was unharmed. But the fight was not over yet. The woodlander spun round and raised his hammer to hit Neen. Seft swung his club to hit him in the side exposed by the raised arm, and the overwhelming impulse to protect Neen gave him supernatural strength. He connected with the woodlander's right shoulder, and the man dropped the hammer and staggered sideways. Neen hit the woodlander's head with her stone, and Seft hit him with his club, and the man fell.

Seft was filled with savage fury and would have beaten the fallen man to death, but Neen said: 'The children,' and they ran together, not waiting to find out whether their attacker was dead or alive.

They raced through the village to their house. They went inside and found all three children sleeping. Tears of relief ran down Seft's face into his beard.

He bent over the children, staring hard at each in turn, looking at their peaceful faces. It seemed strange that they could sleep through a battle, but perhaps a few shouts in the night were not so unusual. In any case, the noise was dying down.

Seft looked outside. There were bodies of woodlanders and herders on the ground, but the only living people he saw were herders. Those woodlanders who were not dead must have retreated, he deduced. Wounded herders were being helped by those who had escaped injury.

It seemed the woodlanders had not stolen anything. Clearly robbery was not the purpose of the raid. So it must have been revenge. After what had been done to them, it was hardly surprising.

Cruelty begets cruelty, Seft thought, and violence begets violence.

The elders met in the morning, as the smoke of cremation formed a dark cloud over Riverbend. Everyone was still shocked. Nothing like this had ever happened to them. Even Scagga, always spoiling for a fight, seemed shaken. However, he took his usual belligerent attitude, albeit with a tremor in his voice. 'We have to make sure these savages can never do anything like this again.'

Ani said: 'Best way to do that would be not to burn woods again.'

Scagga shook his head. 'We can't allow these people to live.'

She said angrily: 'Do you really not know that what happened last night was your fault?'

'Don't you dare say that, you stupid bitch.'

Keff intervened. 'No more of that talk, please, both of you. Concentrate on what we need to do now.'

Scagga said: 'All of Bez's tribe must be killed. It's the only way for us to be safe.'

Ani said: 'There may not be many left to kill. The farmers murdered all the children and the old. We know that a certain number have simply left the tribe. And a lot were killed last night.'

'I don't care!' said Scagga. 'If there are two left, we must kill them. Or one!'

Ani stopped arguing. From conversations earlier that morning, she knew that most herders felt the same as Scagga. For once she had no alternative to propose. Scagga could at last have the war he had been advocating for years.

He would be happy.

Bez sat with his back to a tree in the remnant of West Wood, with Gida by his side. He had been wounded in the raid. A herder had stabbed his backside with a knife. He had struggled to walk from

Riverbend to West Wood. Next day the wound became swollen and painful, and soon the whole of his leg turned a nasty shade of brown. He felt hot.

When the wound began to stink, he knew his life was coming to its end.

The tribe no longer existed. Half had been killed by farmers in the massacre. Half of those who remained, the adult men and women, had died in their attack on Riverbend. The rest were drifting away in ones and twos. They talked loosely of leaving the Great Plain. Some headed for the North-West Hills, where they knew the landscape. Others favoured crossing South River. It was unknown territory, but that was its appeal. They would try to exist on squirrels and hedgehogs and wild vegetables, and hope that some day another woodlander tribe might welcome them.

Bez covered his leg with earth to suppress the smell. He had stopped eating, but he had a jug of water beside him. Gida sat with him during the day, and lay beside him at night, under their shearling coats.

She would not talk about where she might go after he died.

They recalled their life together, with its joys and sadnesses. 'How lucky we are to have Lali,' said Bez. 'So smart, and almost as beautiful as you.'

'Much more so,' Gida said, with a laugh. 'But how sad that Fell died.'

Bez touched the necklace of bear's teeth at his throat. 'Worst time of my life,' he said. 'Until they burned our wood.'

Gida brought up a more cheerful memory. 'Remember the time we tried to make love in a tree?'

Bez laughed. 'We were young, we thought we could do anything.'

'I don't believe we really considered how dangerous it was.'

'You held me so tightly!'

'I was afraid you'd fall.'

They ran out of memories and began to sing. There were songs about hunting deer, and finding birds' nests, and falling in love. Sometimes they sang the songs that sent children to sleep.

As the afternoon darkened, Bez said: 'The woodlander life is happy. We eat hazelnuts when we're hungry, we make love with anyone who's willing, and we accept death when it comes, as animals do. But our way of life cannot go on. Soon all the people will be herders or farmers, jealously guarding their cattle and their fields, working hard and living unhappily.'

'It's a shame,' said Gida. 'But we had a good life.'

'Yes, we did,' said Bez. Then he closed his eyes, as if to sleep.

Joia watched the young men and women getting ready to march. They had been told that the survivors in Bez's tribe had returned to the remnant of West Wood, and they were going there to kill them.

Some looked angrily determined, no doubt aiming to avenge the deaths of family members. Others were laughing and joking, happy to be part of Scagga's army. Herders loved to go somewhere in a huge crowd on some mission. As they put arrows into quivers and measured bowstrings, they must have known that the object of the exercise was to kill and be killed; but that did not seem to spoil their mood.

No one in Joia's family was involved. Neen and Seft were the right age, in their twenties, but neither wanted to kill woodlanders, despite what had happened on Midwinter Night. Ani was too old but she would not have gone anyway. Neen's children were too young, happily. Joia wondered whether Ilian would be eager to fight in a few years' time. So many adolescents were.

Scagga appeared and shouted: 'Time to go – now! Everybody! It's a short day and we don't want to be walking half the night.'

They began to move through the village. People came to their doorways to wish them well. The marchers relished the attention, the cheers and smiles, the blown kisses and a few real ones.

On impulse Joia joined them. She did not know what was going to happen, but she wanted to be there and see it. And with Ello ill, there was no one to reprimand her. Without telling anyone, she walked with them out of the village.

They were about fifty, she counted. They sang rhythmic songs that helped them keep a steady pace, and they had funny chants that made no sense but rhymed. The effort of an all-day walk with nothing to eat was part of the fun.

The festive mood struck Joia as grotesquely inappropriate.

Water was scarce, and they followed a predetermined route that took in some of the few streams and ponds left by the drought.

It was dusk when they smelt roast beef and knew they were near the village of Old Oak. Joia guessed that Scagga had sent a quickrunner forward to tell Zad to slaughter a cow.

They all had to sleep in the open, but it did not rain, and as Joia drifted off to sleep she had the impression of some romantic activity around her. That would be another attraction of a long march.

In the morning there was hot soup and cold beef. Then they set off on the final leg of the journey. Now the mood was sombre: today they had to kill an entire woodlander tribe, or what was left of it, and there was no doubt that the woodlanders would fight back.

They passed Farmplace and saw the women and men in their fields. There were fewer farmers since the massacre.

Going west, they passed the shocking sight of the burned wood. The few trees left standing were black and leafless, stark monuments to the dead forest. In the distance, a green blur was the remnant of the wood. As they got closer they strung their bows and readied their arrows. Joia, who had no intention of killing anyone, stayed at the back of the march.

She expected that at any moment the woodlanders would burst forth from the greenery brandishing their clubs and axes, but the place was oddly quiet. Could it be an ambush? The herder army entered the wood cautiously and immediately came to a clearing with a couple of houses but no people.

Joia noticed flakes of black in the bushes and in the trees. Then she saw a flash of white on the ground. She thought about what these things might mean.

Scagga ordered his army to spread out and search the remainder of the woodland. Joia remained at the clearing, waiting for them to come back. She knew how it would be and, sure enough, they returned to report that there were no woodlanders anywhere.

The young men and women of Scagga's army now looked bewildered.

Joia remembered that she was a priestess, and thought that perhaps the gods had led her here for a reason. She decided to speak.

She raised her voice so that everyone could hear. 'This is a cursed place,' she said, and she had their attention immediately. 'Here the little children and the old folk of Bez's tribe were murdered by the farmers.' She spread her arm to indicate what was all around. 'Open your eyes. In the bushes, on the leaves, even in the trees, you see flakes of ash.' They all looked and saw what she meant. 'So many people were cremated here that their ashes have not all blown away yet.'

Everyone knew about the massacre, but standing here where

the helpless children and old folk were slaughtered brought it vividly to their imagination, and they looked appalled.

Scagga clearly did not know what to say.

Joia picked up the white object she had seen on the ground. 'You may have seen this necklace before,' she said. 'It's made of bear's teeth. A woodlander called Fell had it, and when Fell died it went to his brother, Bez, the leader of the West Wood folk. Somehow it survived the cremation.' She looked directly at Scagga. 'You came here to kill Bez, but you're too late. He's already dead, and all that is left of him is his necklace.'

She paused to let that sink in, then added: 'The rest of his tribe are either dead or gone away. There is no one left to kill.'

They were silent for a long moment.

Then Joia began to sing the song for the dead. Some of the marchers looked at her as if she was mad. But she kept on singing, for she could see people weeping. Another woman put down her bow and joined in the song, then a third and a fourth did likewise. Scagga was angry but bemused, not knowing what to do; and soon most of his army were singing, many crying at the same time. The birds fell silent in the trees, and the leaves quivered as the voices shook the air. The sad remnant of West Wood trembled with a lament for the people who now lay, silent for ever, beneath the soil of their ruined homeland.

22

THE SIGHT OF the burned Monument was heartbreaking to Joia: the timbers were scorched, tumbled, broken and scattered. It would have been worse if she had not intervened and berated Bez, but that was small consolation. The Monument was all-important. It brought everyone together on special days and reminded them that they were part of a community. And it preserved their knowledge of the movements of the sun and moon, ensuring that precious learning was never lost.

Three things had to be done immediately: repair the damage, resume the ceremonies, and confirm that the Monument was the heart of the herder society of the Great Plain.

But long term there was another vital task: to rebuild the Monument in stone, so it could never burn again.

'We must start repairing the timbers today,' Joia said to Ello.

'I don't see the urgency,' said Ello, languidly. 'Everyone knows it's not our fault.'

The high priestess lay on the floor of her house, close to the fire, her head on a leather pillow stuffed with straw. Joia stood to talk to her: she had not been invited to sit down.

Joia said: 'We can't restart the ceremonies until we have at least a temporary Monument.'

'Well, then, the ceremonies may have to lapse for a while.'

Joia was appalled. Let the ceremonies lapse? How could a high priestess even think that? But her response was mild. 'The trouble is that people might begin to imagine that the ceremonies don't matter. Then they'll ask why they have to feed priestesses who do no work.'

Ello could not help seeing the force of that. 'Oh, very well. But it will take you more than a day to repair. Several weeks, more likely.'

'I know. So we have to do a makeshift job first.' Joia had thought about this. 'Most of the timbers are not burned through. Some will be re-usable, and we'll begin with those. We may have to use untrimmed branches to finish, but we can have a temporary Monument in a few days. Then, as soon as we can, we'll replace the damaged timbers with new ones.' Or stone ones, she thought.

'Well, all right.'

Joia had won her case. Ello was never going to enthuse about her plans, or even approve them, but as long as she did not actually forbid something Joia considered herself authorized. 'Thank you,' she said lightly, concealing her feeling of triumph. 'I hope you feel better soon.' And she went out.

The priestesses were still in the dining hall. Some were missing: they had left, too frightened to remain. Breakfast was over but they were waiting for instructions. The normal routine had collapsed after the raid.

When Joia walked in, all conversation stopped and all heads turned to her. She made them wait a few moments, then said: 'Exciting news!'

They smiled and looked eager.

'We're going to rebuild the Monument!'

They cheered.

'Not all the timbers are re-usable, but today we'll begin with what we've got.'

They liked the idea of starting right away.

'Our first job is to pick up the timbers – they're all quite cold now, don't worry – and lay them down where they need to go, one upright to each hole, and the crossbars in place too. If you're not sure what I mean, I'll show you now. Follow me!'

They all left the dining hall, chattering enthusiastically. They entered the circle and went quiet as they confronted the dismal state of their Monument. Only a handful of the seventy-five timbers remained in place.

'Come on!' Joia cried. 'Let's see how much we can get done today.'

They set to, picking up timbers and putting them in place. Each piece of wood took at least four priestesses to move. They chose the least damaged ones first, then those that might serve at a pinch. They made a pile of those that were clearly too bad to be used at all. The priestesses put their hearts into the communal effort, and in a surprisingly short time, they turned a mess into something ordered.

Now Joia noticed a feature she had not been able to see before the Monument was wrecked: the flat tops of the posts each had two dome-shaped bumps. They had been carefully carved, so must have a purpose, but she could not figure out what that might be. She found a crossbar and examined it, and saw that it had two dome-shaped hollows. Clearly the domes must fit into the hollows. That would keep the crossbar securely in place.

I had no idea, she thought.

Following the original design, the crossbar reached from the top of one upright to the top of the next. But when the priestesses tried fitting a crossbar to the tops of two uprights lying in place on the ground, they found that the pegs and holes did not meet. Of course, Joia realized: Seft, or one of his cleverhands, had measured each individually, and a crossbar would fit only the pair of uprights for which it had been made. It would be the work of the world to match them all up. They could spend weeks moving huge uprights around trying to recreate the original sets. And not all the timbers were re-usable.

She stood staring at the posts and crossbars, thinking hard, but she was stymied. And the priestesses could tell. They became restless.

She had to maintain their enthusiasm. 'There's a difficulty,' she said, 'but I know who can help us – Seft.' They perked up right away. Everyone knew that Seft was the one to see if you had any kind of practical problem. 'Sary and Bet, go and find him, please. Tell him that Joia badly needs his advice.'

She knew he would come. He was fond of her in a brotherly way. At that Midsummer Rite so many years ago, when he was trying to escape from his brutal family, she had been kind to him. She had not done much, in her own eyes, but he had never forgotten it. In those days few people had been kind to Seft.

The two priestesses ran off. Joia continued to study the salvaged wood. When originally installed, the posts must have been all the same length, so that the circle of crossbars would be level; but now the partly burned timbers were of different lengths. How would their tops be made level? Something else to ask Seft about.

Sary and Bet returned with Seft and his son, Ilian, a precocious boy who was learning his father's craft. Joia explained the problem, and Seft immediately came up with a solution. 'Turn the crossbars upside down and make new sockets to fit whichever posts you choose. The old sockets, on top of the crossbars, will be too high to be seen.'

It was obvious, Joia thought, once it had been said.

The new sockets would have to be made by a carpenter. Seft had already thought about that. 'Ilian and I will make the sockets,' he said.

'That's absolutely wonderful,' said Joia.

Riverbend needed a fillip. People were down in the mouth, apathetic, pessimistic. Ani could tell by the way they walked around, moving sluggishly, heads down, faces glum. They needed to be inspired.

'After the horror of the Midwinter Rite, we have to prove that we are back to normal,' she said to the elders. 'We want people to forget the woodlander attack. We need a success. The Spring Rite must be the best ever.'

Scagga's sister, Jara, said: 'How would we achieve that?'

'Put the word out, attract lots of people. Tell them there will be a big feast, with the best poets.'

'Don't be ridiculous,' said Scagga. 'We're in the middle of a famine. No one expects a great plateful of beef.'

Scagga drove Ani mad. 'This attitude will ruin us,' she said forcefully. 'Don't be so pessimistic about everything. We're not in the middle of a famine. We're probably at the end of it.'

'We hope.'

The elders decided to give people just enough meat, and nothing else came out of the meeting.

On the day before the Spring Rite, Ani realized they would not need much beef anyway. Normally people started arriving two or three days ahead of time. They came early to be sure they did not miss it. But this time, worryingly, there were only a handful of visitors on the morning before. A few traders arrived during the day, but nowhere near the norm. This was very disappointing.

The opening ceremony, next morning, celebrated the Halfway, one of the two moments in the year when day was as long as night. It had never been among the most exciting rituals.

In reconstructing the Monument the priestesses had made the best of a bad job: much of the timber was damaged and scorched. Ani began to feel that the place might truly be cursed. It was beginning to look that way.

Some of the traders packed up their goods and left at midday.

One way and another, the Spring Rite was a disaster.

Ani talked to the flint-knapper El, whose granddaughter had been killed by the woodlanders. El needed to buy unimproved flints – called 'blanks' or 'cores' – so that he could turn them into useful tools by shaping them and sharpening the edges. As usual she marvelled at how the knapper knew exactly where to hit the surface of the flint to make a flake fall away. It took a long time to acquire the skill, and most learned by watching a parent for years.

Sitting cross-legged outside the earth circle, with his grandson Janno beside him, El had a fresh flint in his left hand and a round stone in his right. His face bore the grey defeated look of grief. 'There's only one man here selling cores,' he said. 'And his flints aren't the best – not floorstone.'

The hard black floorstone came only from underground mines. She said: 'Where are the miners?'

'Some of them were talking about going to Upriver to trade.'

That would be it, Ani thought despondently. The village of Upriver was nearer to the mines, which were along the north side of the Great Plain. 'But they've always come here in the past,' she said.

'They're afraid of more attacks by woodlanders.'

That was ridiculous. 'The tribe that attacked us no longer exists! Those who are still alive have scattered. West Wood, or the remnant of it, is deserted.'

'I know that.' El shrugged. 'But people think this place is cursed.'

She had had the same thought herself, but was horrified to hear it from someone else. And there was no way to prove that a person or thing was *not* cursed, so the accusation usually stuck.

El added: 'I'm only telling you what others are saying.'

'I'm not blaming you, El,' said Ani. 'Thank you for letting me know.' She thought for a few moments. 'Did they use that word?'

'What word?'

'Cursed.'

'Yes,' he said. 'They say the Monument is cursed.'

One morning Pia took Olin into East Wood, to a place where strawberries grew early. After a rainy winter the Great Plain was enjoying a sunny spring. Sure enough, she found the small, dark-red berries growing low on the ground, half hidden by their leaves. She showed them to Olin, saying: 'Look! Strawberries!'

Olin repeated, 'Look!' but he could not manage to say 'strawberries'. He had seen only one midsummer, and could say just a few words.

Pia picked a strawberry and ate it. Olin immediately held out his hand for one. She picked another and put it into his hand. In grasping it he squashed it, but he got the remains to his mouth and held out his hand for another.

They ate some more, then Pia began to put them in her basket. 'For Grandmamma,' she said.

Olin said: 'Gamma.'

Pia picked half the strawberries and left the rest for the woodlanders who lived here. She had noticed that they never picked a bush clean, and she followed their custom.

She lifted Olin and walked out of the wood. Their dog barked a greeting, and Olin pointed at the animal and said: 'Dog.'

'Very good!' Pia said. 'Clever boy!'

Her mother, Yana, had been weeding, and was now resting outside the house, drinking water and talking to Duff. Pia put Olin down to crawl around, then sat with them and offered strawberries to the visitor.

Duff said: 'I've been in the wood too.' He picked up a basket from the ground beside him and passed it to Pia. It contained wild leaves and spring onions. 'Those leaves are bitter, but something in them gives you a happy feeling,' he said.

Pia smiled. 'Happy leaves,' she said.

'I brought you a message as well as some vegetables,' Duff said. 'Troon wants to speak to everyone at midday outside his house.'

Pia glanced up at the sky. It was mid-morning.

Duff read her mind and said: 'You've got plenty of time.'

She asked him: 'Do you know what it's about?'

'No, but I can tell you that the herders' Spring Rite was poorly attended, and Troon is gloating over that.'

Pia shrugged. 'We'll soon find out.'

Duff got to his feet. 'I'll see you at noon.'

When he was out of earshot, Yana said: 'What a nice young man.'

'Yes.'

'Did you know that he puts his aunt Uda's shoes on for her every morning, and ties the laces, because she can't bend?'

Pia laughed. 'I didn't know that. He's always kind to me.'

'I think he's more than kind.'

391

Pia knew what her mother was getting at, but she asked the question anyway. 'What do you mean?'

'You told me he saved your life in the great fire.'

'That's true. I couldn't run very fast because I was carrying Olin. Then I fell over, and no one helped me up. I was really desperate. Duff was ahead of me, but he came back. He carried Olin and we ran together.'

'He came back,' Yana repeated. 'Towards the fire instead of away from it. To help you.'

'You think he's in love with me.'

'I'm sure of it.'

'But I love Han. It's only a year since he died. I haven't forgotten him. I never will.' This was true, but not the whole truth. She really liked Duff, and thought about him at night, wondering what it would be like to kiss him. But that seemed disloyal to Han, and she felt terribly guilty about it.

'Of course you won't forget him. But while you remember him, you could open your heart to the possibility of loving someone else, one day.'

Pia looked at Duff walking away across the field. He was so different from Han: small and neat, with curly dark hair that he kept short – she guessed Aunt Uda cut it for him. Do I love him? Not in the way I loved Han, she thought. That was an overwhelming passion, something out of my control. I never examined my feelings, never even thought about them, I was just crazy for him. It will never be like that with Duff. But perhaps I could love him in a different way, and be happy.

She did not know.

She and Yana returned to the field and weeded the rows for the rest of the morning. Then it was time to go and hear what Troon had to say.

Optimism was in the air as the farmer folk gathered in front of Troon's house. The drought seemed to be over – and they were all survivors – so they hoped for a good harvest, full bellies, happy children and well-stocked stores.

Duff and Uda came and stood with Yana, Pia and Olin.

Troon came out of his house and stepped up onto a tree stump so that everyone could see him. The crowd went quiet.

He said: 'The herders' Spring Rite this year was a washout. Our people who attended did hardly any trading. There were too few people there. Everyone is scared to go there. They think the Monument is cursed. They're probably right.'

He's enjoying this, Pia thought, but where is it going?

She soon found out. 'This year, on Midsummer Day, we farmers will hold our own feast!'

There was a burst of surprised comment in the crowd. Pia said to Duff: 'I wasn't expecting that.'

'Nor was I.'

'I think he's worried about inbreeding.'

'Because the farmer women are no longer going to the revel?'

'Exactly.'

Troon said: 'And we will have a poet!'

Troon let them talk excitedly for a few moments then held up a hand for quiet. 'We will hold the feast here in the village centre, beside the river. And naturally people will be encouraged to trade.'

Pia wondered how the herders would react to this. It was a direct challenge to their Midsummer Rite, which was important to them. They would not take it lightly. But what could they do?

'First we need to spread the word,' Troon said. 'I'm appointing six people to travel, in pairs, west, north and east, to tell everybody. When I call your name, please come forward.'

Pia thought he might send the Young Dogs, but he was smarter than that. He began to recite the names, and they were all women.

That was unexpected, when Troon still would not allow women to go to the Monument for the Rites.

The chosen ones moved to the front, as instructed. To Pia's surprise she was among those picked. She wondered why Troon was willing to risk her leaving the farmland. How did he know she would come back?

She was paired with Rua, a woman of her own age who had a son of ten or eleven midsummers called Eron. She made her way to the front, still carrying Olin. When she looked at the other women she said: 'Oh, no.'

They all had babies or children.

Pia understood now why Troon was so sure they would return. She knew what he would say next.

'I'm confident that all of you will gladly return to Farmplace. But just in case there might be a traitor hiding among you, you will have to leave your children here.'

Reflexively, Pia held Olin tightly to her chest. She did not want to leave him. He would be perfectly well cared for by Yana, his grandmother, but Pia's feeling was instinctive.

She and Rua were assigned to the north, where the flint pits were. They had to tell the miners they could trade their flints for wheat and barley and cheese, with no danger of being killed by woodlanders.

Troon finished by saying: 'You leave tomorrow.'

Ani decided that she should have an ally in the elder group, now that Scagga had brought in his sister. She invited Kae, the kind-hearted mother of Vee and Cass. Now there were two wolves and two does, with Keff to keep order.

They met to discuss the shocking news that the farmers were going to hold a feast on Midsummer Day.

Keff said: 'They have sent messengers all over the Great Plain. And if people go to the farmers' feast, they can't come to ours.'

Ani said: 'This is terrible news. Our Spring Rite was so lacklustre. The Monument is unimpressive now that it's damaged and rickety. The farmer festival could even overtake ours in popularity.'

'The Monument has nothing to do with it,' said Scagga. 'The people stayed away from our Spring Rite for fear of another woodlander attack.'

Jara nodded. 'I think that's right.'

Ani thought it was neither one thing nor the other, but both. She said: 'In any case, what are we going to do? The herder community is in crisis, and we are their elders. What do we say to them?'

Scagga said: 'We must resist the temptation to act as if better times are already with us. We've had some rain, that's all. It might be a short interlude in a long drought. Until we know, we must continue with rationing and serve less meat at the feast.'

'So our Midsummer Rite will be even less attractive.'

'It will use up less of our shrinking herd.'

'May I suggest an alternative approach?'

'Waste of time.'

Keff directed an annoyed look at Scagga and said to Ani: 'Of course you may. Please go ahead.'

'Thank you.' She took a breath. 'Our Midsummer Rite has always been the event of the year for the Great Plain and beyond. The ceremony, the feast, the poets, and the revel – people often say it has been the most exciting time of their lives.'

Scagga said: 'So what?'

'The beautiful grassland of the Great Plain represents only half of our prosperity. The other half is what we gain from having traders come to us, instead of us going to them. Flints and all the other things we need to trade for come here, and they're traded for what – in normal times – we have in abundance: livestock. We *must* attract people back.'

Kae put in: 'Otherwise we'll just see a slow decline into nothing.'

There was a short silence. Scagga opened his mouth to speak but Keff forestalled him. 'I don't think we need to hear from you again, Scagga. I think you're right. This isn't the time to spend a great deal of effort organizing a spectacular event. I fear no one would come to it.'

Ani had lost. Timidity had won. She took her leave politely.

She had one more hope.

She walked through the village and across the plain to the Monument.

Joia was with the priestesses, practising singing. Ani heard her say: 'We must begin each word together, and end each word together. You have to listen as well as sing.'

My daughter, the perfectionist, Ani thought fondly.

She listened as the priestesses sang again, and she was struck by the difference when they began and ended words precisely together. It was almost magical.

Joia had seen Ani, and when the song was over she said: 'That's enough for today. Well done, everyone.'

The priestesses drifted away, and Ani and Joia sat on the ground to talk. Ani told her about the elders' meeting that had just finished. Joia agreed with Ani, not surprisingly. 'We really need to rebuild the Monument from scratch,' she said. 'That's the only way it will look decent. And we could do it. But Ello keeps saying no.'

'Let's go together and ask her again,' said Ani.

They went to Ello's tent. She was lying down, but perfectly alert. 'In these trying times we must expect less,' she said, when

Ani and Joia had made their pitch. 'We can't have everything we want. Priestesses must reduce their ceremonies and spend more time gathering wild vegetables.'

It made Joia cross. 'Priestesses don't exist to gather food!' she said. 'We're here to count the days of the year and pass on the knowledge acquired by generations of our forebears.'

'Yes, and we'll do that again, but not now.'

'The drought is coming to an end—'

'Leave me now. I'm tired.'

Ani and Joia stared at Ello in exasperation, but there was nothing they could do.

They left.

At the end of the day, just when it was getting too dark to weed the furrows, Duff would come strolling along the riverbank to Yana's farm, and would chat to Pia in the dusk. One evening he said to her: 'Can I ask you a question?'

'If you like.'

'A rather personal question.'

'I don't know. Try me.'

'How long do you think it will take you to get over Han?'

That was very direct. She did not answer immediately.

He said: 'Have I embarrassed you?'

'No,' she said. 'It's a good question – one I should ask myself.'

He waited in silence.

After a while she said: 'I will never forget Han and I will always love him. The real question is whether I might be able to love someone else.' She paused again. Then she said: 'Someone like you.'

He was surprised. 'Do you mean that?'

She said: 'Someone who is kind and strong and loves me enough to risk his life to save me and my child from a fire.'

He looked pleased.

She said: 'Someone who ties his old aunt's shoelaces in the morning.'

He laughed. 'Who told you about that?'

'My mother. She also told me to open my heart to the possibility of loving again.'

'Do you think you can?'

'I don't know, but I want to try. But if I find I can't, I'm afraid you'll be sad.'

'Not as sad as I'll be if you never give me a chance.'

'All right, then.'

'All right?'

'Yes, all right.'

He looked as if he was not sure what to do next. After a moment he said: 'Can I kiss you now?'

'Yes.'

It was a gentle kiss, but long. His lips were soft and his skin smelt good. He stroked her hair and she touched his beard. She felt a glow of excitement, a sensation she had almost forgotten.

When at last they broke the kiss, she said: 'Oh, how lovely.'

He smiled. 'Yes,' he said. 'Lovely.'

Joia found her mother looking depressed on the day before the herders' Midsummer Rite. 'It's going to be as bad as the Spring Rite, if not worse,' said Ani. 'Look around. How many traders are here?'

'Twelve,' said Joia. 'But they're still arriving.'

One of the traders overheard and said: 'They've all gone to the farmers' feast.' The speaker was the flint-knapper, El.

'But not you,' said Ani.

'I can't walk that far. But lots of people can.'

Joia said: 'Someone told me the farmers haven't got much food for the feast.'

El shrugged. 'Maybe not, but people are curious to find out for themselves.'

'Well, we're here, and the ceremony tomorrow is going to be beautiful.'

It was. The singing practice had taught the priestesses to sing together, not just at more or less the same time. It made the music a different experience, and the small audience listened with open-mouthed astonishment and fascination. The appearance of the sun, and its slow rise above the edge of the earth, was as moving as ever. It was a pity there were so few people there to experience it.

Joia went to Ello's house to tell her how good it had been – but Ello was dead, her head on the pillow beside her fire, her eyes half closed as if she had been dozing. Joia felt for a heartbeat but there was none.

She could not feel very sad. Ello had always been against her. A burden had been lifted.

This meant a great change for the priestesses. There would be a new high priestess, and it would probably be Joia, although such things could not be taken for granted.

Next day the priestesses cremated Ello inside the earth circle, and sang the funeral songs as her smoke rose into the air over the Monument.

Afterwards they had a late breakfast in the dining hall. Sary, still small and thin but no longer timid, came up to Joia and said: 'We all want you to be high priestess. No one disagrees. It's you.'

'Let me speak to them,' said Joia.

Sary looked worried. 'Don't you want to be high priestess?'

'It depends.'

Joia stood up and they all went quiet. 'I love you all,' she said. 'It's wonderful to sing and dance with you. I'm fascinated by the study of the sun and the moon, and the way they move in the sky. And I really want to be your high priestess.'

They began to cheer, but she held up her hand for silence. 'However, I will not be your high priestess with a ramshackle Monument and a nearly empty circle. Our Monument must be a great sight to see, and our public ceremonies should be viewed by great crowds of awestruck people crammed inside the earth circle. We are the spiritual heart of the Great Plain. But right now the community is drowning in a river of pessimism and timidity.'

She studied their faces. No one scowled, looked indignant or shook their head. They knew she was right. Her words were true.

'If I become high priestess, you must be prepared for a challenge. We must have a spectacular Monument and crowds of followers. It is our holy duty.' She saw their faces lighten. This was what they wanted to hear. 'If you want a quiet life, say so now, and I'll withdraw, and let someone else be high priestess.' Several women shook their heads. 'But if you've got the courage . . .' a murmur of agreement began and got louder '. . . the courage to make the Monument truly amazing . . .' the murmur became a shout '. . . say so, and . . .'

Her words were drowned out in a chorus of acclaim. She stopped speaking. She had said enough.

She was high priestess.

23

SEFT SOMETIMES FELT guilty because he did not produce any food. He knew that this feeling was irrational. He did essential work, as did leather tanners such as Ani and flint-knappers such as El. When he confided this feeling to Neen, she said: 'You're probably the most valued person in the community – they always come to you for help.' Still, sometimes he felt he had no right to eat food others had put into his bowl.

However, he did not let this depress him. He was happy, especially when he remembered how his life had been before he came to Riverbend. Now he felt so lucky that he sometimes found himself hoping this was not a dream.

After Neen and his children, the person he liked most was Joia. The feeling was not romantic. He liked her because she was smart and kind and courageous. So when, soon after she had become high priestess, she asked him to meet her at the Monument, he went along right away.

As they stood looking at the makeshift restoration, she said: 'We're losing respect, and this is part of it.'

He was glad she was high priestess. Ello had been content to leave everything just as it was. Joia was different. She was always looking for improvements. Even before she became leader she had changed the way the priestesses sang and danced, making the whole performance more dramatic.

Now she said: 'It's time for the stones.'

He was thrilled. They had been talking about building a stone Monument for years. Now that she was high priestess they could do it – or at least try.

He began to walk around, looking at the timbers, and Joia went with him. He said: 'You want it exactly like this?'

'It must be. This is how we count the days. Nothing can be changed, except the material.'

'So the stones will go in the holes that the posts are in now?'

'Yes.'

'We'll have to dig the holes wider and deeper, but that's easy. What about the volunteers? We need crowds and crowds of people to drag the stones here from Stony Valley.'

'I'm going to make a speech at the next Midsummer Rite, asking for volunteers. I'll appeal to their sense of adventure. I'll tell them that this is a holy mission, but also an extension of the festival. I think we'll get the two hundred people we need. And we'll start for Stony Valley the next day.'

It was the first time Joia had revealed this plan to Seft, and he took a few moments to absorb it. He wondered how people would respond to her appeal. She was exceptionally charming and persuasive, and he just had to have faith in her.

But he thought of another snag. 'If this works, we'll be taking many strong young men and women away from their regular work.'

'I hope so!'

'I'm afraid I think we'll need the elders' consent.'

Joia made a stubborn face, and he thought she was going to disagree, but she said nothing.

'Think about it,' Seft said. 'If the elders forbid this, some young people might defy them, but others would hesitate to get into a dispute. And then you might not have enough people to pull a stone.'

Joia nodded reluctantly. 'You're right,' she said. 'A project this big, this important, can't begin with a clash between us and the elders. We must have them on our side from the start.'

'That's what I think.'

'All right. I'll talk to my mother.'

Walking back to Riverbend, Seft had a fateful sense that this might be the day his life changed. The more he thought about it, the more he longed to rebuild the Monument in stone.

There were many stone circles. One of the biggest was on the far side of the North River, in a village called Pits, where there were many flint mines. But the circle at Pits, like most stone circles, consisted of untrimmed boulders in a rough ring. It was nothing like what the Monument would be if Joia got her way.

She had said firmly that the rebuilding must follow the pattern of the existing timbers. The stones would stand in a perfect circle, equidistant from one another, with an exactly fitting crossbar joining each pair. In the middle would be an oval of detached pairs, each with a crossbar. It would be astonishing and unique.

Building it would probably take the rest of his life, Seft realized, with a doomy feeling. But then his stone Monument would last for ever.

He nodded to himself as he reached his home, thinking: That would really be something.

Keff opened the meeting. 'The grass is green, the streams are running again, and the cows are calving. Let's pray to the Earth God to continue this weather, and never again afflict us with drought.'

Everyone agreed with that.

'But the demise of our Midsummer Rite is very bad for us. I was hoping to trade for some young bulls from the north, to bring new blood into the herd. But no bulls were brought. And we're hearing that the farmers' feast was well attended.'

Ani said: 'That's what I hear. And I agree with Keff that this is a disaster for us. Our four Rites every year have always been of great benefit to us. We've been able to trade things we have plenty of, like beef and leather, for what we lack, such as flints and pottery. We've constantly improved our herd by mating our cows with bulls from elsewhere. And in the same way, at the revel, we've strengthened the blood of our own folk.' She looked around. 'It would be very bad for us if we let these events diminish.'

Jara said: 'Let's be realistic. We may simply have to endure a period of hardship. Eventually people will realize that the woodlander attack is not going to be repeated, and they will forget it and come back to us.'

Ani said: 'Or they may continue to go to the farmers' feast because by then they will be used to it. People like whatever is familiar.'

Scagga said: 'Perhaps we could get some woodlanders to attack the farmers' feast.'

It was a stupid idea and no one responded.

Keff said: 'Well, Jara's idea, simply to wait and hope, seems to be the only option.'

Ani said: 'I have a better solution.'

'Good!' said Kae.

Scagga rolled up his eyes.

Keff said: 'Let's hear it.'

Here goes, Ani thought. 'We need to make a spectacular gesture to attract people back and show them that we are still the leaders of the Great Plain.'

'A gesture,' Scagga said scornfully.

Keff said: 'What gesture do you have in mind, Ani?'

'We must rebuild the Monument – in stone.'

They were all silent, surprised. Then Keff said: 'That would take years.'

'I suppose so. But right from the start it will be something new and surprising that people will want to look at.'

Scagga said: 'There aren't enough stones on the Great Plain!'

'Have you counted them?' Ani said sarcastically.

Jara said: 'Wherever the stones may be found, they will have to be dragged to the Monument. That will take people away from their normal work.'

Ani said: 'We all know that the regular work of a herder is not very demanding. We could manage our herd with half the people, especially now when so many cattle have died in the drought.'

'But this could go on for years!' said Jara.

'You don't know how long it will take.'

'There's a lot we don't know about this idea.'

Ani did not have an answer to that.

Keff said: 'How many people would be required to drag a stone from wherever it's found to the Monument?'

Ani hesitated.

Keff said: 'You don't know, do you?'

'A crowd,' Ani said. 'More than any of us can count.'

'I'm sorry, Ani,' Keff said, 'but there's too much we don't know about this proposal. We don't know where the stones can be found, we don't know how many people it would take to move one, and we don't know how long it would take.'

Ani now saw that she had failed to prepare this proposal sufficiently. She said desperately: 'I just feel it's our only chance.'

Keff plainly felt forced to refuse. He said: 'I'm afraid we have to turn you down.'

Seft and Tem were making a bed for Neen, and Joia was watching them. Neen got so cold sleeping on the floor, and Seft had said that before next winter he would make a bed that would raise her by the span of a hand. She would be warmer like that, he had promised. They had brought two large logs, the same width, to support the platform, and they had smoothed three broad planks for the surface she would lie on.

They all knew that the elders were meeting, and Seft felt tense. He had allowed himself to imagine the grandeur of the finished stone circle, and he had made the mistake of enjoying in advance the sense of achievement he would feel. The work he was doing now soothed his anxiety while they all waited for the verdict.

Seft and Tem were drilling holes through the planks and into the logs, and Seft's son, Ilian, was whittling pegs to fit the holes, when Ani returned from the meeting. Seft could tell by her face that she had bad news. 'They turned us down,' she said.

Joia said: 'Oh, no!'

Seft's dream evaporated. He felt bereft. He said: 'Why?'

'Too many uncertainties,' Ani answered. 'How many people, how many days, how far.'

'I suppose they're right,' Seft said dolefully. He felt the disappointment like a blow. It depressed him.

Tem, who had not shared Seft's eagerness, said: 'The whole

notion was quite shaky. Perhaps we've been saved from a catastrophe by the elders' caution.'

'Perhaps,' said Seft, sadly. 'But it would have been the adventure of a lifetime.'

Ani said: 'I didn't have the answers to their questions. I should have foreseen their arguments and planned my responses.'

'Oh, well,' Seft said, 'I suppose it's back to real life.'

Joia had tears in her eyes, but her jaw was set in a familiar look of determination. She was not ready to surrender. 'Don't give up so fast,' she said. 'I have another idea.'

Seft smiled. That was Joia, never daunted. He wondered how she thought she could rescue this. 'Go on,' he said hopefully.

'We'll move just one stone.'

Seft did not see how that would help. 'All right, but . . .'

'That will prove it can be done.'

He nodded. It made sense. Joia usually made sense.

Ani said: 'That may not be enough to change the minds of the elders.'

'Wait,' said Joia. 'You haven't heard it all. It will also tell how many people we need to move a giant stone, and how many days it will take to bring a stone to the Monument.'

'Answering the elders' questions.' Seft's hopes lifted. 'They might consent to that.'

Ani said: 'I sensed that Keff would have liked to consent, but felt the arguments against were too powerful. He might back this more modest proposal.'

Joia said: 'It has to be worth a try.'

And this time the elders consented.

Joia, Seft and Ani were euphoric for a while, then they started to make plans. They would move the stone after next year's Midsummer Rite. They had a lot to do in advance.

Joia started the priestesses making ropes. She got an elderly couple of rope-makers, Ev and Fee, to come and show them how it was done. They were grumpy but expert.

First the priestesses had to collect honeysuckle vines. Honeysuckle grew everywhere, on trees and sometimes on houses too. It could flourish in all kinds of soil provided it got some sunshine. Its sweet scent and bright yellow flowers made it easy to find. The priestesses went first to Three Streams Wood, where the plant was abundant. They enjoyed the outing: it was a change from their usual routine.

Fee showed the priestesses how to cut the vine just above the lowest set of leaves, to ensure that it would regrow quickly. She told them to strip the vine of leaves and branches, leaving the debris on the forest floor to return to the soil, coming home with only the tough, flexible main stems.

To braid the vines together into a rope was a job for two people. Ev and Fee demonstrated: Ev took three vines by their ends and held them tight, and Fee twisted them. Both had to pull to keep the vines taut, and this was where tempers frayed. Fee said Ev was pulling too hard, making it difficult for her to braid the vines, and Ev said that if he didn't pull hard the rope would be loose and weak. They must have been quarrelling about this for years, Joia thought, hiding her amusement.

Next they would take another three vines, overlap them generously with the first three, and twist again, splicing the two lengths together.

Joia had a long discussion with Seft about how long the ropes should be. The largest stones were about as long as four men lying head to toe. The rope would have to be twice that length and a bit more to go all the way around the stone. Then each grab line had to be long enough for forty people to be able to pull it at the same time without treading on the feet of the person in front and the one behind. That requirement would quadruple the length of rope needed.

Inside the Monument they made thirty priestesses lie on the ground head to toe – which made the women giggle. As men were slightly taller they added two more. Then they dug lines in the turf to mark the beginning and end of the rope.

When Ev and Fee had two strands that length, each of three vines, they then twisted the two together, this time twisting in the opposite direction. Fee explained that the opposite twist locked the two yarns together.

After that, the process could be repeated any number of times until the rope was of the needed length and thickness.

Once the rope-making was under way, with Ev and Fee dropping by daily to make sure the priestesses were maintaining high standards, Seft and Joia decided to go to Stony Valley.

While Joia was getting ready, Ani told her that Scagga was desperate to know more about what was going on at Stony Valley. 'He's looking for something to complain about,' Ani said.

Joia frowned. 'I don't know why he's so against us,' she said. 'Is it just a habit?'

'He's frightened,' Ani said immediately. 'People who bluster like that, and constantly propose aggressive action, do so because they're scared. They want everybody to be disciplined, and work to store up resources for the future, and they're nervous of anything new. They always see disaster coming.'

'That's very wise,' Joia said thoughtfully.

'You'll be wise, if ever you calm down,' Ani said, and they both laughed.

Joia noticed that her mother had a bracelet made of sea shells. 'That's new,' she said, pointing.

'A traveller was here yesterday,' Ani said. 'I gave him a small piece of leather, enough for a pair of shoes. Do you like it?'

'It's pretty.'

'The traveller was curious, like Scagga. He asked me why herders had set up camp in the North Hills.'

'How did he know about that?'

'He said everyone was talking about it.'

I might have guessed, Joia thought. Gossip travelled fast on the Great Plain. 'What did he say?'

'I asked him what he had heard. He said no one knew what the herders were up to.'

'Did you enlighten him?'

'No. I told him to come to the Midsummer Rite, when all will be revealed.'

'Well done! That's what we want. Lots of curious people at the Rite.'

Next day, Seft and Joia set out along the riverside path. 'The great advantage of following a riverbank is that there are no hills,' Seft said.

The path was well-trodden, but rough in places. 'The ideal would be a trackway of poles laid flat and hammered into the earth, but that would take too long and use more timber than we could get. Anyway, we don't really need it here on level ground. Perhaps we'll do it farther along, when we have to divert away from the river, and there are some uphill stretches. Here we'll put down rough branches, which will get trodden in and be better than nothing. '

'The stones are awfully wide,' Joia said. 'Parts of this path are too narrow for them to pass.'

'We'll have to widen it by cutting back the vegetation,' Seft said. 'We can spread the debris on the path to level the surface.'

'But in a few places the path is narrowed by rising ground on the side away from the water.'

Seft nodded. 'We can dig out the ground. And the earth we remove can be spread on the path to smooth it. It will be a lot of work, but we've got a year.'

Joia was pleased that he had gone so far in working out the details. But there was more to come.

Seft halted at a point where the river widened into a small lake. 'We'll need stopping places, especially on the way back, when we're dragging a stone and the volunteers will need rests. And it makes sense to pick them out in advance, so there will be no need for time-wasting discussions on the journey. This place is about a quarter of the way to Stony Valley. And we must get Chack and Melly to start thinking about how to feed our volunteers. They can't haul giant stones if their bellies are empty.'

'Chack and Melly will like this,' Joia said. 'It will be a change from just catering the feasts. And they love a challenge.'

They walked on to the village of Upriver, which Seft said was roughly halfway. They rested in a large meadow alongside the river. 'Our crowd of volunteers can pause here,' he said.

'Two hundred of them,' Joia said. 'Yes, I think there's room.'

A little north of the village Seft turned away from the river, heading north-west across a corner of the Great Plain. 'Last time I was here there was a large herd,' Seft said. 'I talked to two of the herders. They told me they often moved the cattle here for new growth, but it's a little early in the year for that.' He smiled, remembering the encounter. 'The woman, Revo, was pregnant. I suppose she has a baby by now.'

After a while the landscape changed to hills, and Seft stopped again at a place where a stream emerged from a valley. 'Here, where the plain ends, is about three-quarters of the way. After this it gets more difficult. We'll be travelling in the other direction when we move the stones, so the hard part will come first.'

'That's good,' Joia said. 'The volunteers will be fresh.'

They reached Stony Valley at the end of the day. The village had grown. Under Tem's direction the cleverhands had stockpiled timber. They had particularly cut lengths of stout oak, about as long as a person is tall, to use as levers when raising the half-buried stones from the ground. Soon they would collect the antlers that the red deer shed, and store them for digging.

'I've got something to show you,' Seft said to Joia, 'but it had better wait until tomorrow.'

'Good,' she said. 'I'm looking forward to sleep, after today's long walk.'

They all ate together. When they had finished, but were still sitting in a circle, Seft said: 'The first big task is to clear the riverside pathway. We're going to be using it a lot even before we start moving stones. We need to bring the ropes the priestesses are making, and later Chack and Melly will bring supplies of food plus cooking utensils. The more we use the path, the smoother it will become.'

Seft was putting his heart and soul into this project, Joia realized, as she lay down to sleep. Yet he could not succeed without her. She had to summon the volunteers and motivate them. If she failed, the whole enterprise would collapse.

From where she lay she could look up the slope to where the shepherd lived. She wondered if she would see a gleam as the setting sun was reflected off a head of bushy fair hair. But it did not happen, and she went to sleep.

Next morning Seft showed Joia the sled.

It stood behind the houses, a huge object as big as several houses put together. It was hidden by a cover made of the skins of a small herd of cows. Seft and Tem together pulled the leather off.

The sled was enormous, longer and wider than the biggest stone in the valley. Joia recalled the single runner Seft had shown her. Now there were two, and the entire edifice rested on them. The parallel runners were polished and greased. They were joined by lateral planks. Rising from the planks were short, very thick sections of tree trunks. They in turn supported a platform which, Seft explained, would hold the stone.

Joia thought it was a beautiful object. It seemed to her perfectly designed for its purpose and lovingly assembled, but it also spoke of great strength. Like the trees from which it was made, it seemed impossible to improve.

'If this works the way I think it will,' Seft said, in a tone that made Joia feel he was saying something of great importance, 'I think a crowd of strong young men and women could drag the stone from here to the Monument in two days.'

Joia was astonished. Could that possibly be true? Two days? With her arithmetical brain she saw immediately that the stone would be travelling at half the speed of an ordinary person walking. It did not seem impossible. 'That would be fantastic!' she said.

'If I'm right,' Seft said sombrely, 'it would indeed be fantastic.'

After breakfast Seft announced that they needed to lift a stone upright – not one of the largest, for he wanted only to examine the underside.

The one he picked lay flat, half buried in the earth, and they started by digging all around it to loosen it. When they had revealed the underneath edge they all got down and excavated earth from the underside as far as they could go.

Next Seft picked the strongest ten people, told them to take stout oak levers from the stockpile, and stood them in a line on one long side of the stone. Following his instructions they pushed the ends of their levers into the gap under the stone. Then, acting together, they lifted the edge of the stone. As soon as it had risen the width of a hand Seft shoved a branch underneath so that it could not sink down again, and those with the levers relaxed.

After a short break they stuck their levers in again and lifted once more, and Seft was able to insert another branch. Now the two supporting branches were hammered into the gap so that they would not slip out.

They repeated the process again and again. As the stone rose and the gap widened, Seft stuck short lengths of wood upright underneath it to act as props.

While they worked, a mouth-watering smell of beef and onions encouraged their efforts.

When at last they got the stone upright on edge and secured it, they ate their midday meal with relish.

After the meal, Seft said he wanted to find out how difficult, or easy, it was to flatten the underside of the stone – a process Joia considered essential because, when the stone was upright in the Monument, what had been the top and bottom surfaces would become the highly visible inner and outer faces.

First he carefully brushed the underside, removing earth and insects and some kind of oily growth, then wiped it thoroughly with a scrap of leather. 'I need a clean, dry surface,' he explained to Joia.

The only tool for shaping a stone was another stone. Seft picked up from the ground a roundish stone that fitted neatly into his hand, and began to attack the underside of the giant sarsen. Joia expected to see a lot of dust, but there was very little. She wondered whether that was because the stone was so hard.

When the aged dark surface cracked and fell away, the stone underneath was revealed to be a vivid mid-grey, very distinctive. Joia said: 'What a beautiful colour! Our new Monument will be that shade all over. Won't that be wonderful?'

Seft attacked the lumps and bumps on the underside. The rock was hard, and he had no experience of stone masonry. Joia realized that dressing these stones might be a long job. Perhaps people who were too old to pull the sled could do the work during halts.

She frowned, suddenly feeling that she was being watched. Looking around, she saw a woodlander gazing at her. There was a large wood on the other side of the hill, she had noticed, so it was not surprising that there were woodlanders. As she thought this, several more appeared, stepping from behind trees.

One of them she recognized. It was Lali, the daughter of Gida – and, perhaps, of Bez. She was still beautiful, though she looked older. In just one year she had lost her home and most of her tribe, and the bereavement showed on her face. She had left the Great Plain, Joia presumed, and had found a welcome here.

Lali said: 'I am ashamed to speak to you.' Bez had taught her the herder language.

Joia thought there was no point in blaming a girl for what had been done by her tribe. She said: 'My people and your people have done each other great harm.'

'I have found a new tribe.'

'I'm glad. What happened to your mother?'

'I don't know.' Lali looked sad. 'She insisted that we split up. She said a young woman on her own would have a much greater chance of finding a home.'

Gida had probably been right about that, Joia thought, but what a wrench it must have been.

Lali said: 'These people, my new tribe, didn't believe I could speak the herder tongue, so they made me talk to you to prove it.'

'Well, now you've proved it.'

Some of the other woodlanders spoke to Lali. She listened, then said to Joia: 'They would like to know what you are doing in this valley. You take branches from trees and lay them on the ground. Now you are chipping a stone. They find these acts mysterious.'

'We're going to take this big stone to the Monument.'

Lali stared at her incredulously. 'They will not believe that.'

Joia shrugged. 'I don't blame them. It will be very difficult.'

Lali turned to the others, now crowded around her, and spoke in the woodlander language. They gave cries of astonishment.

There was some discussion, then Lali turned back to Joia. 'They say it is too big to move.'

'It is very big, but we will move it.'

Lali translated. After more chatter, she said: 'Why do you want to do this?'

'Our timber Monument was burned and we want to rebuild it in stone, which does not burn.'

Lali looked embarrassed. It had been her tribe who had done the damage. She translated, then asked: 'Why do you want such a big stone?'

Joia thought for a minute, then said: 'To please the gods, and to make the people gasp with wonder.'

The tribespeople made noises of assent. They understood.

They drifted away, all talking animatedly about what they had learned.

Seft started flattening the other side of the stone. Both he and Joia wanted the stones to look smooth, for a greater contrast with other, inferior, stone circles. Some of that work might be done while the stone was in transit.

She looked up to see two people approaching from the south. As they came closer she recognized Scagga and his sister, Jara. She cursed quietly. They were here only to cause trouble. That was certain.

Although there was a resemblance, she noticed that the big eyes looked good on her, but not on him.

His greeting was characteristically oafish. 'What do you fools think you're doing?'

Seft remained cool. 'Hello, Jara, hello, Scagga. Glad to see you both. You can help the people trimming tree trunks. We need a lot of branches. Pick up a couple of flint-headed axes and get to work.'

Scagga did not reply, but walked slowly around the giant stone and the people standing beside it. As he did so he said: 'You probably thought you were hidden away up here. In fact practically everyone on the Great Plain knows where you are.'

Joia said: 'We've no reason to hide. What are you doing here, if you haven't come to help?'

Scagga completed his circuit, looked at Joia, and said: 'Surely you don't imagine you can transport this enormous stone to the Monument?'

'Wait and see,' said Joia.

'It's impossible!' Scagga's eyes bulged.

Seft said: 'If you're right, then you'll look clever, and I'll look foolish. You'll enjoy that.'

'No, no, no,' said Scagga. 'This must stop. Look at all these herder folk wasting their time here. And many of them living here, to judge by the houses! None of them doing anything to benefit their fellow herders.'

Jara said: 'Just as we feared. This is growing out of control. Countless more people will be needed to move that stone. You'll have crowds up here helping you try to do the impossible. And meanwhile back at home their useful work will be neglected. The elders never anticipated this.'

So that would be the line of attack, Joia deduced. They would say she had gone beyond what the elders had authorized. She said: 'They won't be away from their work for long.'

'Well, then, how long?' Jara demanded.

Joia went out on a limb. 'Four days,' she said. 'A day to get here. A day to load the stone onto the sled. Two days to drag the sled to the Monument.'

Scagga said: 'Impossible! If you can move it at all, it will get stuck twenty times a day. Half your people will get fed up and go home. You'll keep at it, though, obstinately, day after day. This is going to be a disaster.'

Seft put down his stone hammer and turned to face Scagga. 'Don't you think I've thought of all that?' he said. 'You've been here a few moments and imagined some snags. I've been thinking about this for more than a year, and I'm an expert, so I've foreseen many more problems than the few you've dreamed up. And I'm finding solutions for them, one by one, instead of just squealing about things being impossible.'

Joia was impressed. Seft did not often take part in arguments. In fact he went to some trouble to avoid conflict, perhaps because of his brutal childhood. It was interesting to see how formidable he could be when he chose.

Neither Scagga nor Jara had an answer for him. After a pause Scagga said: 'We'll see about that!' very emphatically, then turned and walked back the way he had come. Jara hesitated – perhaps wondering where else they were going to spend the night – then followed him.

When they were out of earshot, Joia said: 'Thanks for backing me up.'

Seft shrugged. 'Of course.'

'Can we really do it in four days? What do you think?'

'Well,' Seft said, 'now that you've said it, we'll just have to.'

Joia returned to Riverbend, hard on the heels of Scagga and Jara, suspecting he would call a meeting of the elders as soon as he got home, and knowing she had to be there to defend herself.

Keff was irritated, and he let it show as he opened the meeting.

'We have already approved of Joia and Seft erecting a stone within the Monument as part of the rebuilding,' he said. 'I believe they've already done a good deal of the preliminary work. But now, Scagga, you ask us to reconsider our decision urgently. It seems very unfair when they're halfway through. But you must give us your reasons.'

He might as well have said, This had better be good, Joia thought.

It was Jara who replied. 'You haven't seen the stone, Keff,' she said. 'We have. Dragging it to the Monument is probably impossible, but they will spend weeks trying, and that means the herder community will lose its youngest and strongest workers for much of the summer.'

Kae spoke next. 'If I may point something out . . .'

'Go ahead, please,' said Keff.

'Joia will call for volunteers at the Midsummer Rite.'

Keff said: 'Yes, that's what I understand.'

'They won't all be herders. There will be farmers, flint miners, and plenty of people from beyond the borders of the Great Plain. Probably no more than half the volunteers will be herders.'

Jara said: 'That's just a guess.'

'I say it's likely, that's all.'

Scagga got tired of letting his sister lead the argument, and burst out: 'We can't take the risk! We haven't yet recovered from the drought!'

Joia said: 'You're assuming the volunteers will be needed for a long time. That's not so.'

Scagga butted in: 'Here we go, another fantasy.'

Keff said: 'How do you know this, Joia?'

'Seft has built a sled that will carry the stone and make the journey much quicker. I've seen it. Scagga hasn't, because he didn't stay at Stony Valley long enough to get the full facts. I discussed the timing with Seft and he is confident in our estimate of four days.'

Scagga looked flustered. He could not pour scorn on the sled because he had not seen it. There was nothing he could say.

Keff said: 'I think we're agreed, then, that Joia may continue.'

'Thank you,' said Joia.

24

NEXT YEAR, IN the days preceding the Midsummer Rite, Joia anxiously watched the early arrivals. She and Seft had agreed that the least number of volunteers needed to move the stone was two hundred. She had taken time to teach Seft the priestesses' way of counting, and he had grasped it quickly. 'No less,' he had said. 'I wouldn't mind a few more.' The old and the very young were not included, of course, only fit and strong adults. As the visitors arrived, in ones and twos and families, Seft and Joia worried whether attendance would be high enough.

Seft had built the track, a remarkable achievement. Most of it consisted of branches and earth, but the steepest climbs had a surface of embedded logs that would make the work of the volunteers less difficult and faster.

Chack and Melly had organized the feeding of two hundred people for four days. The drought was over, and in addition the herders had called on their reserves. At Stony Valley, and at scheduled stops between there and the Monument, there were sheep and cattle to be slaughtered and roasted and baskets of vegetables and early wild fruit. Members of the Chack-and-Melly clan would head off at the end of the Rite, to get ahead of the volunteers.

Joia planned to speak to the crowd immediately after the sunrise ceremony, but she and the volunteers would depart the following morning. Seft had worried about this. 'I wonder whether you should set off right after the ceremony, when you've got them all worked up. During the rest of the day and overnight they could go off the boil.'

Joia shook her head. 'I don't want to ask them to give anything up. They'll want to trade. Then they'll be looking forward to the feast and the poets and the revel. The next day will be different. Then they'll welcome an excuse to extend the festivities. That's what I'm hoping, anyhow.'

Seft nodded. 'We're not sure of anything at this point, are we?'

That was the truth.

She sent the priestesses out to mingle with the visitors and tell them there would be a big announcement tomorrow after the ceremony. 'Don't say what it is. Say you don't know, but be excited.' She wanted everyone to be curious and expectant.

On the day before the ceremony, people began to arrive in big numbers, and Joia was somewhat reassured. The effect of the rival farmers' feast had worn off, and everyone wanted to know what was going on at the Monument. They had come, and now it was up to her to win their support.

Her mother was thrilled by the high attendance. 'They're inquisitive,' she said. 'They know something big is about to happen and they can't wait to find out what it is.'

Joia agreed. People on the Great Plain travelled more than they needed to because they wanted to know what others were saying and doing.

Towards sundown Joia ran into the farmer Duff. He looked well, she thought. His curly hair was longer, which suited him. Farmer women still could not attend Rites, so Joia asked Duff about Pia and their baby. 'They're wonderful,' he said.

Joia was glad that Duff was enthusiastic about his stepson.

'Let me ask you something,' Duff said. 'Why is Troon telling us farmers not to let you lead us on a wild-goose chase?'

Joia was immediately concerned. 'What has he been saying?'

'Something about a giant stone. He's been talking to Scagga.'

So Scagga was trying to discourage volunteers even before they had been asked. Shrewd of him. 'I'm going to make an announcement tomorrow morning,' Joia said. 'You'll know everything then.'

Duff grinned. 'I can hardly wait.'

Joia wondered how much effect Scagga's insinuations would have. Not much, she began to think. Troon was a famous killjoy. Young farmers such as Duff might even be attracted to something because the tyrant banned it.

She left Duff and returned to the priestesses' quarters. Previous high priestesses had occupied a house, sometimes with a lover. Joia had never had a lover and she preferred to bed down in a communal building with her sister priestesses around her. She found it reassuring to hear them breathing and shifting as she drifted off. 'I didn't become a priestess to be alone,' she sometimes said.

The night was warm and most of them slept naked. Joia lay down next to Sary, the second high priestess, and they discussed the number of visitors. There were fewer than in the glory days, but many more than at the last Spring Rite. Everything would depend on how they reacted to Joia's rallying cry. 'There's nothing more I can do until tomorrow,' she said, and soon after that she was asleep.

She woke before dawn, as always. She put on her ankle-length leather tunic, then made sure everyone else was awake. She went to the dining hall, drank some water, and ate a slice of cold mutton.

Looking into the Monument circle, she saw visitors gathering for the ceremony in the moonlight. There were many people standing on the earth bank for a better view. The circle was not packed full, as it had been in the past, but she estimated there were six hundred people. If one in three volunteered she would have enough.

She knew what she was going to say to them, but not the exact words. She had practised the speech often, but it came out slightly different every time. If she tried to say it exactly the same, she found herself hesitating and speaking mechanically. She had to be natural, even though it felt risky.

Joia picked up a heavy pottery disc that was part of the ritual. It had a lightning zigzag marked on its face. Then she lined up the priestesses in pairs, ready to begin. She and Sary were side by side at the front. Sary was smart and well liked, and might well end up as high priestess one day.

The singing and dancing needed to be perfect today. Joia wanted to impress people before asking them to do something unprecedented. We've rehearsed enough, she thought; it should be stunning.

A narrow smear of grey appeared at the eastern end of the black sky. The crowd in the Monument went quiet. Joia began the chant and moved forward. Glancing behind, she saw the priestesses all moving together and in time. A good start.

They entered the circle and Joia carefully placed the pottery disc in front of the first of the upright posts to her left, indicating that today was the first day of the first week of the new year. Tomorrow another disc would be put on top of the first. The priestesses had twelve altogether, each with a different symbol carved into its face, and when they were all used up it was time to move to the next upright and a new week.

At the end of the final week, in almost a year's time, the Rite would move to the central oval, and five different discs would be placed, one per day, in front of the paired uprights. There were three hundred and sixty-five days in a year, and this number was the core of the priestesses' knowledge. Joia had known that for so long that she found it difficult to imagine how ordinary people could not even count that high. She also knew that every fourth year had an extra day, and there was a special ceremony for that.

Having placed the disc, Joia led the group in a dance around the entire timber circle, singing a song that counted the posts, as the dawn light spread across the sky.

Finally the priestesses knelt on the ground, still in pairs, facing east. They sang as they watched the eastern sky turn slowly from grey to pale yellow to red. Then a bright gold orb inched up over the edge of the world. For those spectators in exactly the right position, it was seen to appear exactly between two uprights, as if in a doorway. The priestesses sang louder, coming to a climax and stopping precisely when the low edge of the orb broke free of the earth.

After a moment of dramatic silence, the crowd roared their delight that the Sun God had once more kept the promise.

Now Joia had to move quickly. She ran across the middle of the timber circle, followed by Sary. When they reached the posts at the halfway mark, at the point furthest from the entrance, Sary cupped her hands, Joia stepped on them, and Sary heaved her up far enough to scramble onto the wooden crossbar, where she stood up.

This had never happened before, and people stared in surprise. Some of the crowd had started to leave, but they turned back to see what was going on. And Joia began to speak.

'Herders – farmers – miners – visitors – I have news for you.'
She had learned to speak in a carrying voice, louder and deeper
than her normal tone, and they all seemed to hear her. 'I have
found . . .' she paused for effect '. . . the biggest stone in the world.'

Their expressions said, Is this true? It's interesting, true or false.

'And tomorrow I am going on a walk. And I want you to come
with me.'

To her dismay, a few people looked away and moved on. She
was in danger of losing them, she saw. That last part had been
uninspiring.

She tried again. 'We will all go together on a holy journey – to
see the giant stone!'

That was better. A murmur of interest arose.

'It is one day's walk from here, in the North Hills, and I will
leave tomorrow. And if you are fit and strong you must come with
me. Because we are not going merely to look at the stone. Do you
know what we're going to do? With the biggest stone in the world?
We're going to bring it here!'

There was a buzz of conversation. Now they were really
interested. She felt a thrill at her power to hold their attention.

'We are going on a sacred mission to please the Sun God. We
will tie ropes around the biggest stone in the world. And we will
bring it home to the Monument!'

She felt they were getting excited.

She said: 'It will be hard work. Only healthy and strong people
should volunteer. No one lazy. No one who would prefer to doze
in the sun. No one who gives up easily. Only people with
enthusiasm and a love of adventure!'

Now some of them were putting their hands up.

'Are you with me?'

A cheer went up.

'Spend today trading. Feast with us this evening, and hear the poets. Do whatever you like tonight. And if you are brave and strong, come here to the Monument tomorrow at dawn. Will you come?'

There was a shout of assent.

'Don't be late!' she cried. 'We leave at sunrise!'

She clambered down from the lintel. 'What do you think?' she said to Sary.

Sary was flushed and breathless. 'They love you!' she said.

'But will they still love me tomorrow?'

'Oh, yes,' Sary said, in the tone of one who makes a vow.

'I hope you're right,' said Joia.

Outside the Monument, as Ani was watching the trading begin, she was accosted by Scagga. His face was red and his eyes were bulging. He was so indignant that he spat saliva as he spoke. In an angry, challenging tone he said: 'How many volunteers do you expect Joia to take to the North Hills?'

Several people nearby looked up to see what the fuss was.

Ani said quietly: 'Really, Scagga, you can't speak to me like that. I won't be bullied and interrogated by you or anyone else. Where are your manners? Speak to me politely, or don't speak to me at all.'

'Look here—'

'What do you normally say when you meet someone?'

He looked impatient and irritated, but he said: 'May the Sun God smile on you.'

'And on you, Scagga. Now tell me, calmly, what's on your mind.'

'The number of people Joia is going to take on this mad mission of hers.'

'If this is business for the elders, there should be more than two of us.' Ani was not going to let Scagga pick people off one by one. 'Let's bring Keff in, at least.' Keff was not far away, talking to an arrow-maker. His belly was growing again, Ani thought; a sign of the improved weather this summer. She caught his eye and waved him over.

Keff said: 'What is it?'

Scagga said to him: 'When we elders discussed Joia's scheme, how many volunteers did you imagine she would take to the North Hills?'

'I'm not sure I had a definite idea,' Keff said. 'Why do you ask?'

'Come on, you must have had a notion.' Scagga showed both hands, pointed to both feet, and showed both hands again. 'That many?'

'More,' said Keff.

'Twice that many?'

'Perhaps.'

'Three times?'

'At most.'

'And having seen the reaction to her speech this morning, how many of those cheering youngsters will she take away from their work?'

'I don't know,' said Keff. 'Nor do you.'

'Precisely,' Scagga said triumphantly. 'We don't know. And that's why I think we should set a limit. Otherwise it's out of control.'

Keff said: 'That's sensible, I suppose.'

Ani's heart sank. Joia would be furious. And who could tell how many people would be needed to move a giant stone?

She said: 'What limit do you suggest?'

Scagga again indicated both hands, both feet, and both hands again, and said: 'Keff envisaged three times that number, so that should be our limit.'

'Very well,' Ani said reluctantly.

'I'll leave you to tell Joia,' Scagga said to Ani.

'No, you won't,' Ani said firmly. 'It's your idea – you tell her.'

Scagga pretended not to care. 'All right, then,' he said. 'I'll tell her.'

Some days earlier, Joia had acquired an entire pig, slaughtered and salted, ostensibly for the priestesses. Salt was a luxury, produced in small quantities by seaside dwellers who boiled sea water in giant pans until the water disappeared leaving only the salt. Salt pork was a treat. Joia had used all her charm to get this boon.

Chack and Melly and their family were frantically busy preparing the feast – thin Chack humping great carcasses, fat Melly boiling nettles and dandelion leaves with wild garlic – and Joia, wanting their goodwill because she needed them to feed her volunteers on the mission, did not wish to trouble them on their busiest day of the year, so she had built a roasting frame at the back of the houses. At the end of the day, she and Sary spitted the pig. Cooking slowly inside its skin, it would roast all night, turned by a couple of novices. The fire would deter owls and other creatures from stealing the pork.

Joia had just lit the fire when Scagga appeared.

She expected him to demand to know how come she had a whole salted pig, but he was too focused on what he had to say to notice what she was cooking. He had a gratified look, as if he had been proved right about something. He said: 'You've been limited.'

With weary patience she said: 'What now, Scagga?'

'The elders never gave you permission to take an unrestricted number of volunteers away from their work.'

'As far as I know, the elders never specified numbers.' Anyway, they struggled to count above thirty, she thought, but she did not say it.

'Well, they have specified numbers now.' He made the sign for thirty, then said: 'That many, three times.'

Ninety, she thought. Nowhere near enough.

She was about to protest when she had second thoughts. Perhaps the time for opposition would be tomorrow morning, when – all being well – the eager volunteers would have gathered. Scagga would have to try to stop people doing what they wanted to do, and that would be extremely difficult. How would he decide which hundred people had to stay at home, and – more importantly – how would he enforce his decision?

There was nothing to be gained by protesting now. However, she did not want to look too compliant – that would make him suspicious. So she said: 'That may not be enough.'

'You should have thought of that before.'

'You say the elders agreed to this?'

'Yes.'

'Including my mother?'

'Yes.'

Under protest, I expect, Joia thought. 'I'll speak to her,' she said.

'She won't change her mind. Keff backed me against her.'

'We'll see.' She turned away and went into the dining hall.

She hoped she had misdirected him. He was now expecting a new row among the elders. He would not be prepared for mass resistance tomorrow morning.

After deploying two novices to mind the pig, she went in search of Seft to tell him what was going on. She found him just outside Riverbend, on the riverside path. The track he had built had been disarranged. Seft was picking up scattered branches and putting them back in place. 'This isn't wanton damage,' he said to Joia. 'It's just the effect of many people walking on the track.'

Joia said: 'What can we do?'

Seft scratched his dark beard. 'We'll have to maintain it constantly. It will be less of a problem farther north, where there are fewer people. When the stone is on the move, we'll have a team going ahead to do last-minute repairs.'

'That sounds manageable. I'm not so sure about Scagga's latest dodge.'

'What's he done?'

'Persuaded the elders to limit the number of volunteers we take.' She had taught Seft the priestess way of counting, so she could discuss high numbers with him. 'They have ordered us not to take more than ninety. You and I decided we needed twice that number.'

'Can we change their minds?'

'I think we should just ignore them.'

Seft frowned. 'What do you mean?'

'Say nothing, and let them try to enforce their rule tomorrow, when there are a couple of hundred eager volunteers raring to go.'

Seft grinned, nodding, and said: 'That's just brilliant.'

25

JOIA WOKE EARLY, as always. Her first thought was that this was Day One of the four days she had to bring the giant stone to the Monument. That was the reckless promise she had made.

She went to the roasting frame and put out the fire under the pig. She had been told by Melly that it was best to stop the cooking a good while before carving the meat.

Then she woke the priestesses. They chattered excitedly as they dressed. Today would be a big day.

Several of them picked up sharp flints and began cutting slices off the pig and putting them into baskets.

Dawn broke, and volunteers began to arrive as the silver light touched the Monument. All Joia's friends came, which pleased her. She saw daredevil Vee, her cousin and childhood friend; Vee's amiable brother Cass, who had kissed her once, to no great effect; Boli, a quickrunner; and homely-looking Moke. Zad of the confident grin came with his dark-eyed woman, Biddy, and their daughter, Dini. There were several farmers, including Duff.

Two priestesses with baskets of sliced pork appeared and volunteers crowded around them, jostling. Joia heard Sary say: 'One slice each! Only one, please. Leave some for others.'

More volunteers arrived, and Joia began to think they might have the two hundred they needed. The mood was festive, the boys and girls flirting. Ani came to wish Joia well. Scagga was lurking outside the earth circle, wearing his habitual scowl. What would he do?

When the sky on the horizon turned yellow, Joia started the priestesses singing the song of sunrise. Looking around, she was sure she had at least two hundred volunteers. They all watched the sun come up, and cheered when it was fully risen; then Joia cried: 'This is the moment! Now we go!'

This was also the moment when Scagga would try to stop them.

Joia and Seft led the party out.

Scagga was outside. 'This is too many!' he yelled at her.

Joia spoke without stopping. 'No, we're exactly the number you said was the limit,' she lied.

He walked backwards in front of her, his face twisted in angry frustration. She knew he could not possibly have counted. It was too difficult to count crowds, and like most herders he did not know high numbers.

Joia marched on determinedly.

Scagga started yelling at the volunteers, telling them they could not go, the elders had forbidden it. They ignored him, talking to one another, laughing and joking. He stood in front of one young man and got pushed away. Joia had a moment of severe anxiety, fearing a fight might break out.

Then there was an intervention by a woman volunteer. 'How dare you tell me what to do?' she said to Scagga. Joia recognized the fair curly hair and wide mouth of Dee, the Stony Valley shepherd's beautiful daughter. In her surprise Joia stumbled and almost fell.

When she recovered her balance she heard Dee say: 'Get out of the way, before someone picks you up and throws you.' The people around her laughed. Mocked and threatened, Scagga reddened, turned around, and stamped off.

Joia found herself panting for no reason. She tried to calm her breathing, then spoke to Dee. 'Well done,' she managed.

'He needed to be shut up.'

'Yes, and, um, you did it very effectively. Thank you.'

Dee gave the wide-mouthed smile that was like the sun coming out.

Joia ended the conversation before she could embarrass herself but, as she walked, she was continually conscious of Dee behind her. She would have liked to talk to her some more. She wondered how she might get to know her better. Then she asked herself why she was thinking this way. It had never happened before.

They marched along the path to Riverbend. Joia looked back and saw that Sary and Tem were bringing up the rear, as she had instructed them, encouraging stragglers.

As they passed through the village everyone came out of their houses to cheer, egging them on.

They came to the river and turned north on the path. Seft's track was now in better shape, but no doubt it would be disarranged again by two hundred marchers. It could not be helped.

A group of young men started singing. It was a marching song with a left-right left-right beat. People sang it on long walks to help them keep up the pace. Soon everyone joined in. They sang it again and again until they tired of it.

The sun rose higher in the sky and the marchers got warm. People stopped often to drink from the river.

After a while the volunteers started a risqué song that everyone knew.

A boy loved a girl
But she didn't care for him
So he said, Mother, what shall I do?

She said, Give her a ring,
And then show her your thing,
And she's certain to fall for you.

So he gave her a ring
And then showed her his thing,
And she said, I don't know what to do.

There were many verses, in every one of which the courtship ran into a comical snag, each one greeted with hilarity. They were treating the march as an extension of the festivities, just as Joia had hoped. It was another excuse to fool around and have fun.

Duff came up to her and said: 'A word in your ear.'

'Any time,' said Joia. She liked Duff.

'I just want to let you know that some of Troon's Young Dogs have joined us. His son Stam is dead now, you probably heard, but Stam's best friend, Narod, is here, with a handful of others.'

Joia frowned. 'Thank you for letting me know. I wonder what they want.'

'Troon might have sent them just to keep an eye on what we're doing.'

'Perhaps. More likely they want to undermine us.'

'I don't see how.'

'Troon may have thought of something.'

She mulled it over until they came to the large village of Upriver. It was almost noon, and Seft had picked this as a place to rest because there was a wide meadow beside the river. Many of the marchers threw off their tunics and jumped into the river to cool off.

The villagers were interested and amused by this invasion of cheerful people, and some residents offered them snacks and honeyed drinks.

Dee sat down by Joia. This time Joia was not startled and she managed to keep calm. Dee said: 'I came to the Rite with some hoggets to trade.'

Joia knew that hoggets were year-old sheep. She said: 'What did you get for them?'

'Some flints. My brother is carrying them home for me.'

'Do shepherds use special tools?'

'We need very sharp knives to cut a sheep's fleece close to the skin.'

'What do you use the fleece for?'

'To stuff leather pillows. Much softer than straw.'

Joia looked at the crowd. 'I was afraid a lot of people would drop out on the way, tired or bored, and perhaps a few did, but I can't see any significant fall in our numbers. They might stay the distance. I'm relieved.'

Dee said: 'The sunrise ceremony was wonderful yesterday. This is the first time for some years that I've seen it, and it seemed more coordinated.'

Joia smiled. 'I've been working on that.'

'I've been told that when you dance like that you count the posts, and somehow that enables you to know what day of the year it is. Is that true?'

'Yes, that's right.'

'I can't imagine how it works. Could you tell me?'

'Yes, although it will take a while. I'll gladly explain it when we've got time. Right now I need to get these people marching again.'

'Oh, of course.'

Joia went around telling the volunteers to get out of the water and put on their tunics. They were slow but they obeyed, and soon they were on the way. Once again Sary and Tem were left to round up the slow ones.

So Dee was curious about the days of the year. Joia felt lucky. The woman who made her heart beat faster wanted to learn. That would make it easy to get to know her better. Why do I want to know her better? I'm not sure, she seems like she would be a good friend.

After Upriver they came to the Great Plain, then turned away from the river. There were no cattle. Joia remembered Seft saying the herders sometimes moved the beasts there in summer, but they had not done so yet.

Halfway through the afternoon they began to climb into the North Hills, and the walking got harder. The ground was uneven and the landscape went up and down. They followed Seft's track – undamaged here – and found that it cleverly avoided steep slopes.

From this point on, Joia felt, people were unlikely to drop out. They were more than halfway to their destination.

She allowed herself to feel a thrill of triumph. She had won over her volunteers and she had brought them this far. Until this moment she had hardly dared to believe she would manage it. But here they were.

They passed only one village, half a dozen houses standing on a hilltop. No doubt the position enabled the residents to see their sheep, which were grazing the hillside. Two hundred marchers made a noise even when they were not singing, and the villagers came out of their houses to stare. Some volunteers waved at them, and the shepherds waved back. Joia asked Seft the name of the place, and he said he did not think it had one.

The afternoon dimmed. The walkers were tired when they reached the valleys. The hillsides were green and the tall trees were in leaf. Bold squirrels scampered from one tree to the next. Bees sipped the nectar of the wild flowers that dotted the grass. It was a pretty sight.

When at last they arrived at Stony Valley they found it covered with oxeye daisies, tall flowers with long white petals and a golden yellow centre.

Seft's track led straight to the stone they had chosen – not the one they had lifted last year, which had been only medium-sized, but one of the largest. There were many other stones about the same size, and uniformity was important in the Monument.

The volunteers were thunderstruck. They had never seen such big stones. There was a buzz of surprised conversation. Cass walked all around it, wide-eyed, and said: 'This is a Monument all on its own.'

Joia raised her voice to speak to the crowd. 'You're probably wondering how we're going to move it.'

There were nods of assent and sounds of agreement.

'I'll show you.' Along the track, ten paces from the stone, stood a large object shrouded in hides. Joia nodded to Seft, and he and some of his cleverhands began to remove the covers to reveal the sled. The volunteers broke out into a buzz of astonished conversation. They were impressed because they had never seen such a large work of carpentry, and they were intrigued because they could not see, at first glance, what its purpose was. The greased wood gleamed in the evening light. Joia thought again how beautiful it was.

She turned to practicalities. 'You can probably smell your dinner.' There was a strong aroma coming from several roasting pits. 'Just one rule. You see the stream running north–south along this valley? To the east of the stream we eat and sleep. To the west, we shit and piss. No exceptions! Even if it's only a midnight piddle, you have to cross the stream. Now rest. Tomorrow we work hard.'

Seft came to stand beside her and they looked at the sled together. 'It's so graceful,' Joia said.

'And strong!' Seft said. 'It has to take a great strain.'

'It looks stronger than a house.'

Seft laughed. 'It's a lot stronger than a house.'

'I think it should be guarded, especially at night.'

'Really? Who would damage it?'

'A farmer boy called Narod is among the volunteers, with some of his cronies. He was close to the late Stam, the thuggish son of Troon. They might be here just to enjoy the mission, but let's not take any chances.'

'I agree. I'll have half a dozen men sleep next to the sled.'

'Good.'

She left Seft and went to see the cooks, a small group led by Chack's daughter, Verila. Dee was helping them. She said to Joia: 'I suggested they lay the cow hides on the ground for somewhere to put the meat when it's carved. I hope you don't mind.'

'Great idea,' said Joia. 'Thank you.' She liked people who used their initiative.

She took some meat for herself and found a quiet place to sit on the grass and eat. After a while Dee joined her, taking off her shoes and rubbing her toes. She had shapely feet, Joia noticed.

The evening was darkening and some of the marchers were slipping away in pairs. There was going to be a revel, clearly.

Dee said: 'Something I don't understand. How can you count the days of the year when the highest number is . . .' She touched the top of her head, for twenty-seven.

'We have a different way of counting. First, every number has a name.' She ran through the first ten numbers on her fingers, saying the names of the numbers up to ten. Then she touched

Dee's little toe. 'Imagine that your toe represents the same number as all my fingers together. Then if I touch your toe and hold up one finger, we get the next number after ten. Is that clear so far?'

'How can you remember all the names of the numbers?'

'It's not that hard. You don't have to remember the higher numbers. You can make up the names according to a formula. Just as someone who didn't know your name could call you Hol's granddaughter.'

Dee picked it up quickly. She said: 'If a toe is worth all the fingers, is there something else that's worth all the toes?'

'Yes! You've worked it out without me telling you.'

'But that means you could go on counting, up and up . . . for ever.'

'That's exactly what I said when they taught me.'

'I have to think about this.'

'I said that, too!'

They sat quiet for a few moments. Night had fallen. Dee lay down, and Joia did the same.

As Joia closed her eyes, she thought how much she liked Dee. She could be a really good friend, long term, she thought.

Like Seft.

26

JOIA WOKE UP feeling that so far she had not really achieved anything. The stone still lay where it had been since the world was young. True, she had created an army of volunteers and marched them from the Monument to Stony Valley, and that had not been easy. But the really difficult part lay ahead.

Today they had to raise the massive stone upright. Such a thing had never been done before. There were stone circles on the Great Plain and elsewhere, but none featured a stone half as big. The task might turn out to be impossible.

Equally new and difficult was the challenge of mounting the stone on the sled. And, regardless of what Seft might say, there was no way of knowing how much weight the sled could withstand. The stone might simply crush it, turning it into firewood.

An added worry was Narod and the Young Dogs. Joia suspected they were biding their time, waiting for an opportunity to sabotage the mission, but she could not stop them in advance. In the farmer society troublemakers were dealt with harshly, but the herder folk were different, and Joia did not have the authority to send Narod away.

As she got up and pulled on her tunic it occurred to her that her future held many days when she would wake up anxious and struggle, with others, to do something that had never been done before. She felt both excited and dismayed.

Dee woke up too, although it was still dark. Joia went to supervise the breakfast and Dee followed along to help her. With Verila they cut up the remainder of the beef and laid it on the hides. By then a pale light was seeping into the dewy valley.

Seeing Dini, the daughter of Zad and Biddy, Joia asked her to wake up the other children and gather berries.

Joia ate some beef, then went to the stone. Seft was already there, with Tem and other cleverhands, frowning at the stone, contemplating the task in front of them. They did not look unhappy. A challenge such as this energized them.

Joia did not relish the challenge. All she could do was fret about whether they would succeed. Seft had a plan for today, she knew. She also knew that he was not sure it would work.

The volunteers gathered quickly, some of them munching beef, eager to hear Seft tell them how to achieve the impossible. Seft gave an impression of confidence, which, she knew, he did not feel, as he said: 'Here's how we do it.'

Pointing, he went on: 'That end of the stone is thicker than the other, and the thicker end will become the base. The thin end is the top. The first thing we're going to do is dig a hole under the base.' Using an antler pick, he scratched a rectangle in the earth showing where the hole should be. 'The depth of the hole will be half the height of a person.'

Simple enough so far, Joia thought.

Seft stood facing the long side of the stone and stretched out both arms wide. 'So, when we lift the thin end of the stone . . .'

he tilted his body so that his right arm went up and his left arm down '. . . the thick end will tip gently into the hole.'

The volunteers were nodding. Everyone could understand that, especially with the vivid gesture.

Joia was encouraged by Seft's plan and, even more, by his air of command.

'So, let's get working.'

Here we go, Joia thought.

Tem had a stock of antler picks and wooden shovels. He pointed to two volunteers, who happened to be Zad and Biddy. He gave the pick to Zad and the shovel to Biddy. Men were usually better at breaking up the soil, women at shovelling it, no one knew why. They accepted willingly, Zad giving his typical grin, and began to dig the hole under the thick end.

Seft moved to the thin end. 'The stone is partly buried in the soil, so we need to loosen it,' he said. 'We can have a dozen or more people working on this at the same time.'

Tem gave out more picks.

'Dig all around until you can see the bottom edge of the stone. Then scrape away the earth under the stone, especially at the thin end, where we need enough space to insert levers.'

They all went to work energetically. Their enthusiasm heartened Joia. With all these eager helpers, she thought, we can do anything.

Anything humanly possible, at least.

At this point the biggest job was the hole under the thick end. They had to dig directly under the stone so that its end jutted out over the hole. Tem saw that Zad and Biddy were tiring, and replaced them with another couple. They finished the job, so that there was a hole into which the thick end of the stone could slide.

Next, Tem picked out five strong men and one woman, a flint miner called Bax. He gave each of them a stout oak lever about as long as they were tall, then stood them in a line at the thin end, and told them to shove one end of the lever under the stone as far as it would go.

Joia realized that this would be the first time they tried actually to shift the stone from its place. If we can't do this, she thought, we can't do anything.

Tem told them to push forward and upward on their levers until the thin end of the stone lifted clear of the ground.

They braced themselves, heaved, and nothing happened.

Joia said: 'Harder, harder!'

They tried again, grunting with effort. Bax became frustrated and red in the face. The stone did not move.

We're going to fail right at the start, Joia thought.

Someone in the crowd said: 'This will never work.'

That was Narod's voice, Joia thought in disgust.

Seft was not daunted. 'We just need more people lifting.'

Tem chose more big people and gave them levers. It turned out that the most that could stand side by side without jostling was eleven. Seft decided it might also help to have levers at the sides of the stone. They would be less efficient but all the same it might be somewhat helpful. Tem placed four people crosswise.

Joia took over the job of encouraging those wielding levers. She was better at that sort of thing than Seft or Tem. Now she said: 'Ready . . . take the strain . . . heave!'

The stone seemed to move.

'More, more!' Joia cried. 'You can do it, I know you can!'

The stone came up a finger's breadth, and the watching crowd cheered.

'Keep going, keep going!'

The stone came up the span of a hand. Seft quickly shoved a log into the gap so that the stone could not sink down. Joia held her breath, fearful that the log would be crushed, but it held, and

Seft put in two more. Under the weight of the stone they sank a little into the earth. That would make them stable, Joia realized.

'Well done!' she cried jubilantly. 'Now relax.'

They dropped their levers. Some sat down, drained. Bax said: 'Gods help us, that was hard.'

Wasting no time, Tem chose another fifteen of the strongest and told them to pick up levers. When they were ready, Seft stood by with another log.

Joia said: 'Ready . . . take the strain . . . heave!'

The stone moved a fraction.

'Just a bit more, just a bit more!'

They grunted and cursed and became red-faced, and the stone lifted enough for Seft to put in another log on top of the first three, then add more.

The volunteers dropped their levers, and one man said: 'I'm done in.'

This is very hard, Joia thought, but we're doing it.

Another fifteen were deployed.

Soon the top of the stone was above the ground by the length of a forearm from elbow to fingertip. 'Look how well you're doing!' Joia said. 'You're lifting the biggest stone in the world! You're heroes!'

The exhausted volunteers looked pleased.

The process went on with a change of team each time. Soon Seft was placing short upright lengths of tree trunk in the gap. Joia noticed that at the other end the base of the stone was tilting into the hole. She felt a warm glow of triumph, but told herself it was not finished yet.

Dini appeared with a basket full of strawberries. 'Look how many we got!' she said to Joia. 'And we ate lots too.'

'Well done!' said Joia. 'Take the basket around and offer them to everyone.'

The volunteers ate with relish and congratulated Dini, which made her happy.

Then they ran into a snag.

When the stone was about a quarter of the way to upright, and its thin end was level with the heads of the volunteers, the levers no longer worked as levers. The volunteers found themselves merely pushing at the stone.

To Joia's surprise, Seft admitted that he had not foreseen this.

Tem said: 'We could rope the top of the stone and pull.'

'That might do it,' said Seft. 'Especially if we could weight the thick end so that it would slide into the hole sooner.'

Joia was unnerved by their uncertainty. She said briskly: 'Well, are we going to try that, or what?'

Seft said: 'I'm not sure how we would weight the base.'

Joia said impatiently: 'Get ten people to stand on it.'

Seft and Tem laughed, but Seft said: 'That could work. They'll have to jump off before it lands.'

Tem tied a rope around the top of the stone, made it very tight, and knotted it. The priestesses had made the ropes very long so that there would be generous grab lines. Volunteers lined up, holding the rope.

The first to stand on the thick end were two priestesses, Duna and Bet. Another eight people joined them, holding on to one another to steady themselves. Joia frowned. When she had so quickly suggested this, she had not taken into account that the surface of the stone was uneven.

She heard Narod laughing, saying: 'This is stupid!'

Joia said: 'Ready . . . take the strain . . . heave!'

The stone moved, but not as expected. The thin end did not rise and the thick end did not drop into the hole. Instead, the stone slid laterally.

The volunteers jumped off, but one of them slipped. It was

Duna. She landed in the hole with the stone still inching across the gap above her. Joia saw that the stone was going to crush her. She screamed at those pulling the rope: 'Stop, stop, stop!'

Bet fell to her knees and reached into the hole for Duna. The stone had momentum, and did not stop moving even when the volunteers dropped the ropes. Bet got hold of Duna's arms and Duna grabbed Bet's neck. Bet hauled Duna out just in time.

The base of the stone ran into the far side of the hole, lodged in the earth there, and stopped.

Joia felt terrible. It had been her idea to stand people on the thick end and she had almost killed Duna. If Narod says, *I told you so*, I will kill him, she thought. She put on a brave face and said: 'I think we're almost there.'

Seft said thoughtfully: 'The people pulling are now lower than the top of the stone, so they're pulling *down*. We need to be higher than the highest part of the stone, so that we're pulling *up*. Then it may come upright.'

Tem said gloomily: 'If there was a tree nearby with a branch conveniently at the right height, we could loop a rope over it. Then when we pulled on the rope it would lift the stone. But I don't see such a tree.'

Joia looked around carefully. Tem was right.

She did not like this indecision in front of the volunteers. It could undermine their morale, which at the moment was high. She glanced at the sky: it was midday. 'Everybody, let's have lunch!' she shouted, and they cheered. Speaking quietly to Seft, she said: 'We need a new plan by the time they've eaten.'

'I'll do my best,' said Seft.

Verila and her team were handing around slices of smoked pork. Joia took some and looked around for Dee, hoping to sit with her. But Dee was deep in conversation with Bax. Feeling mildly annoyed, Joia went back to sit with Seft and Tem.

447

They were working on something, she saw with relief. The ground around them was scattered with flints and hammers and ropes. Also on the ground were two poles, very long, longer than the stone. Joia guessed that each pole was the entire trunk of a tall, slender tree.

Seft and Tem were tying the two poles together with rope. The knot was nearer to one end of the poles than the other. The thing they were making was like a giant with two long legs and two short arms. While she watched, they took one pole each and raised the structure upright. Both men nodded, as if finding it satisfactory.

They put it down again and did some more work on it. They added a crossbar so that the legs could not move closer together or farther apart.

Then Tem said: 'We don't want it to fall flat at the wrong moment.'

Seft grunted agreement, and as Joia watched they fixed two shorter legs to the crossbar, front and back, so that if the giant leaned forwards or backwards the short legs would stop him falling to the ground.

Joia wondered how this strange four-legged thing would help, but she suppressed her impatience and kept quiet. All would become clear in time.

Finally they sharpened the feet of the giant into two long points.

The volunteers were finishing their lunch and gathering for the afternoon's work, and they stared at the giant with the same baffled curiosity that Joia felt.

Seft and Tem now positioned the giant flat on the ground with his arms towards the thick end of the stone. Then they took the rope that was tied around the thin end and laid it so that it passed between the giant's arms, across the knot, and between the legs.

He told ten volunteers to grab the end of the rope.

Then he and Tem lifted the giant. It came up, lifting the rope, which was draped across the knot. The pointed feet sank into the ground. Seft stopped them when the giant was still leaning slightly towards the stone.

Now the rope ran from the stone over the knot of the giant, then down the other side into the hands of the volunteers.

Joia began to see the purpose of the giant. It would do the same as the convenient tree branch that Tem had wished for. Although the volunteers were on the ground, the height of the giant meant that the stone would be pulled upwards, and would therefore come upright instead of sliding along the ground.

Seft and Tem were still holding the giant's legs. Seft said to the volunteers: 'Take the strain.'

They pulled the rope taut.

As they pulled harder, they drove the pointed feet of the giant deeper into the ground, making the whole set-up more stable. The harder they pulled, the deeper the legs would sink. Joia was struck by how clever that was. Seft was brainy in a special way. She should have known to trust him. But there was so much at stake.

Still holding a leg of the giant, Seft nodded to Joia. She said: 'Ready . . . take the strain . . . heave!'

The stone did not move.

Seft said: 'Ten more volunteers, please.'

More women and men took hold of the rope.

Joia said: 'Ready . . . take the strain . . . heave!'

The thin end of the stone lifted off the ground.

'Keep going, keep going!' Joia yelled.

It moved higher.

Seft said: 'Some of you get ready to shovel earth into the hole around the fat end. But wait for my word.'

Several volunteers grabbed shovels.

The stone continued to rise. The sight filled Joia with pride.

When it was approaching the upright position, Seft said: 'Try to hold it still now.' He turned to those with shovels. 'Fill the hole and tamp the earth down.'

When that had been done he turned to those holding the rope and said: 'Very slowly, very slightly, release the tension.'

Joia bit her lip.

The stone rested back a little.

'A bit more.'

The stone seemed to settle.

'And again.'

The stone did not move.

Everyone stared hard. It remained still.

'Drop the rope,' Seft said quietly. 'We've done it.'

Not many people heard him and, anyway, his tone was too matter-of-fact for such a joyous announcement. Joia raised her voice. 'We've done it!' she yelled. 'We've done it!'

The valley rang with shouts of triumph and delight.

And Seft dreamed that up while we were having lunch, Joia thought in amazement.

Whenever Joia was feeling triumphant she would ask herself what she needed to do next. Now she looked at the sky and said to Seft: 'If we're to keep to our timetable, we must get the stone onto the sled today, so that we can leave first thing in the morning.'

'You're a hard taskmaster,' he said, but he smiled.

'And you love it,' she rejoined.

He laughed. 'All right.' He turned to a group of volunteers. 'Pick up the giant and move him to the thin end of the stone, please,' he said. 'Handle him carefully, we'll need him again.'

He recognized Vee and addressed her. 'Can you see three big logs over there, a few yards away?'

The logs were thick. Seft's cleverhands had felled an oak tree and divided its trunk into three parts. Joia had noticed the logs but had not been able to guess what they were for. She was about to find out.

'I see them,' Vee said. 'You need them?'

'Yes. You and your friends bring them here. They're heavy, but if you roll them it won't be too difficult. Put them right next to the stone, two on the ground and the third on top of the other two.

'Next we need to move the sled until it's touching the logs. Ten or twelve of you, push it along the track, carefully.'

When the sled was in place, Joia saw that the pile of logs was slightly higher than the load-bearing platform of the sled, and now she understood what the logs were for. Seft had long been worried about lowering the stone onto the sled. At first contact the entire weight of the stone would be on one end of the sled and might crush it. But this way the stone would first rest on the logs, and they would take the weight until the stone was almost flat with its thin end on the front of the sled. Then the logs could slowly be removed, allowing the thick end to come down gently onto the sled.

The giant was raised, and volunteers grabbed the rope. Now they would not be raising the stone but letting it down. More volunteers were ordered to dig the earth out of the hole, to free the thick end, while those holding the rope took the strain as the stone began to tilt over the sled.

The huge stone sank with majestic slowness. It made Joia think of a hunted aurochs finally giving in to many arrow wounds and lying down to die.

The thin end touched the sled. The logs were slowly removed and the thick end sank the last few finger-widths. Joia's heart seemed to stop as the total weight of the giant stone rested on Seft's wooden sled. But the wood was stout and the carpentry was sound, and the sled took the weight.

Seft supervised the roping of the stone to the sled, making sure the knots were as tight as they could be.

Joia smelt roasting mutton. Dinner was being prepared. She was surprised to see that the sun was going down. The afternoon had passed swiftly. But they were on schedule. She thought of the obstacles they had overcome. At midday she had feared the task might be impossible, but Seft had brilliantly solved an unforeseen problem.

Now she was exhausted. But what a victory the day had been. Perhaps tomorrow would be easier.

27

ON THE THIRD day Joia woke before dawn, but she could see the valley clearly in the light of a full moon. Glancing to her side, she was surprised to see Dee leaning on one elbow, looking at her with an expression of friendly curiosity. Joia was vaguely pleased. She decided not to get up just yet.

She said to Dee: 'I saw you talking to Bax.' Then she bit her tongue. It had come out like an accusation, which she had not intended.

Dee seemed not to notice. 'I was interested in her. She's got the shoulders of a man.'

'What did you say to her?'

'I asked her if she liked being so strong. She said yes, she did, but her mother told her that men don't like strong women.'

'Did Bax mind that?'

'She said it doesn't matter because she doesn't like men.'

Joia laughed, then said: 'Do you like men?' As soon as she had asked the question she felt embarrassed. It was so personal.

Two blurts in four sentences, she thought; I'm getting worse.

Once again Dee did not mind. 'I don't dislike men, but I never fall in love with them, if that's what you mean.'

Joia decided to stop asking questions and share something of her own. 'I really love Seft,' she said. 'But I'm not in love with him – which is a good thing, because he's partnered with my sister.'

'Seft is terribly handsome.'

'He's kind, too. He endured so much cruelty as a child that he wants never to make other people suffer that way. He told me that.'

'Have you known him long?'

'Thirteen midsummers. When I met him I was a naughty girl.'

Dee smiled her ear-to-ear smile that showed gleaming teeth. 'Naughty how?' she said, and there was a tone in her voice that made Joia breathe a little faster.

'I peeped at the priestesses doing a naked dance,' Joia said. 'They caught me.' She remembered the fright she had felt. Her offence seemed trivial now, so many years later, but the memory of guilt and fear was still unpleasant. 'I was taken to the high priestess, who was called Soo. I expected her to punish me, but instead she taught me to count.'

'I want you to teach me to count. You told me the theory but I need to know the names of all the numbers. Then I'll be able to count my sheep.'

Joia decided to risk another question. She was very curious to know whether Dee had a partner, but she paused to think of a tactful way to ask. 'Are you alone up there in the hills?'

'In fact my place is not far from here, to the east. But, no, I'm not alone. I live with my brother and his woman.'

No partner, then. 'And you don't know how many sheep you've got, because you can't count them.'

'But I really want to learn.'

'I can teach you some of it in the next two days. We've got a lot of walking to do. Speaking of which, we should get up.'

Verila was carving cold mutton. Vee was helping her, and Joia introduced her to Dee. 'Vee's my oldest friend,' Joia said. 'She was with me when we spied on the priestesses.'

Dee smiled and said to Vee: 'Was Joia really such a bad girl?'

'Yes,' Vee said. 'She persuaded others to join in with her adventures, and we all got into trouble.'

Dee turned to Joia. 'And now you have a whole army of people joining in with your adventure.'

That was perceptive. 'I suppose you're right.'

They helped serve the mutton, then ate some themselves. Joia found it very chewy.

As the sun came up, everyone gathered around the stone.

The stone and the sled stood on the track, already looking like a monument. The cleverhands were busy encasing the ensemble in a kind of rope bag, which sheathed the stone and the sled, spreading the tension and ensuring that the stone could not fall to the side. Every rope had a long grab line, and these were neatly laid out in front of the stone, ten of them, straight like dead snakes, ready for the volunteers to pick up.

All was ready, and Joia was biting her lip. What if it wouldn't move?

Seft had a last-minute thought. With Tem's help he lifted the giant and tied him to the stone. 'We'll need this when we erect the stone at the Monument,' he said.

The volunteers took hold of the ropes, more than twenty people to each rope. There was some shuffling as they found places. Seft, Tem and Joia had to encourage people to stand as close together as possible. 'Make room – you'll be glad of the extra help,' Joia told them.

She and Seft had agreed that they needed two hundred

volunteers, making that calculation on the basis of Seft's experience with the farmer's stone, which had been much smaller. They could not be certain but they had no other way of estimating. Today they were going to learn the truth. Perhaps they would discover that they needed five hundred volunteers, in which case they would all go home with their tails between their legs.

She noticed that they had an audience. Yesterday she had seen a handful of woodlanders watching. Today there were more, fifty or sixty men, women and children, all staring at the mad people trying to move a giant stone. A handful of shepherds were observing too, with folded arms and sceptical expressions. Clearly this was the most interesting event to happen in the North Hills for many years.

The sled was at the end of a long track formed of logs embedded in the earth, made by Seft and the cleverhands over the winter. The track curved gently then headed south in a straight line up a long rise to the top. It had taken some months and many felled trees, but both Seft and Joia had felt strongly that the beginning of the journey should not be discouragingly hard.

The volunteers splayed out in front of the sled in a flare shape, the leaders of each rope looking eagerly at Joia, waiting for the word. When she was sure they were all settled, she said: 'Ready . . . take the strain . . . heave!'

They leaned in, bending their knees, straining at the ropes. Most chose to get a shoulder under the rope, then hold it with both hands in front of the chest. A few preferred to face the stone and pull backwards. Joia watched their faces as they began to realize the enormous weight they were up against. They bent lower and pulled harder.

The stone did not move.

The ropes creaked. Would they snap? Would the timbers of the sled break?

She heard Narod's voice again: 'It's not going to move. This is a waste of time.'

He was not popular among the volunteers, and someone shouted: 'Oh, shut your mouth, Misery-guts.'

It was Joia's worst nightmare.

Seft said to her: 'I want to try something else.'

Joia's hopes rose. She shouted: 'Relax, everyone. We're going to do something different.' They let their ropes go slack with relief.

Seft said to her: 'Tell them to pull and relax, pull and relax. We want to rock the sled forwards and backwards. When I think it's ready to move on, I'll nod, and you can tell them to give it all they've got.'

Joia repeated the explanation to the volunteers. They seemed to understand, many nodding.

Joia felt it might help, though she was not sure why. Perhaps there was a kind of stickiness between the blades of the sled and the ground, a stickiness that was reduced by the rocking. Anyway it was worth a try.

She called: 'Ready ... take the strain ... heave! ... Relax ... heave!' She continued, watching for signs of movement. Suddenly the woodlanders joined in, not using the ropes but pushing the sled. Joia was not sure how much help they were, but they certainly did no harm.

At last she thought she saw the sled rock slightly, forward and back. 'It's working!' she yelled. 'Heave! Relax ... heave! Relax ... pull harder! Harder!' The sled was rocking now, and Seft gave her the nod. 'Relax ... pull! Big effort next time ... Relax ... heave!'

Two hundred people strained at the ropes, panting with the effort, their feet digging into the earth, and at last the sled shifted, jerking forward a mere finger-width. 'Keep it moving!' Joia yelled. 'Keep it moving!' To her delight the sled continued to move forward, with painful slowness, and the volunteers, jubilant now, kept pulling.

She walked backwards in front of them. Once the sled was moving, its momentum made the pulling a little easier. As the track curved to the side, Joia moved in that direction, shouting: 'Follow me, follow me.'

After the curve, the route sloped up, and the task became heavier again. Halfway up she saw them tiring, and shouted: 'We've passed the halfway mark! Not far now to the top!'

They breasted the rise. The log track gave way to a flimsier version of branches and earth, which was less smooth, but the downhill incline more than compensated, and Joia could see the young volunteers recovering from the strain. As the stone began to move a little faster, it occurred to Joia that if a volunteer should fall they could be crushed. She needed to speak to them about what to do if there were such an accident.

In any route from the hills to the plain, the movement would be mostly downhill, Joia figured; something she had never before thought about. However, hills were hills, and they went up and down; and soon there was another rise.

The volunteers were tired now, she saw. It would be wise to give them a rest at the top of this rise.

But the notion occurred to her too late. Halfway up the volunteers began to falter, a few dropped out altogether, and the sled came to a halt.

Joia was dismayed. If they collapsed this early, how could they hope to pull the stone all the way to the Monument?

Making a virtue of necessity, Joia called: 'Rest time, everybody.' She looked around. They were in a scrubby dale with little grazing. Behind them was a stream they had crossed almost without noticing it. 'Drink some water,' she said. Many of them headed for the stream, others just lay flat, exhausted. Verila and two of her cousins had been following with baskets, and they now produced smoked pork and handed it round. Perhaps rest, water and a little food would restore the volunteers.

Seft placed logs behind the blades of the sled so that it could not move backwards. 'I'm being cautious,' he said. 'I don't think this could move of its own weight even on a slope a lot steeper than this one.'

'Which is a good thing,' said Joia, 'otherwise it might run on ahead of us and crash. We have no way of stopping it.'

'A design fault,' Seft said. 'I'm to blame.'

'Don't fret,' Joia said. 'What you've done already is astonishing. No one else could have achieved this.'

Seft smiled and nodded. What Joia said was true, and he knew it.

She gave the volunteers plenty of time. When everyone had drunk and eaten and rested, they began to mill around socially, and Joia reckoned they were ready to start pulling again. She called them to the ropes.

They began to pull, but the stone did not move. Joia realized with alarm that restarting would be especially difficult on an upward slope. Neither she nor Seft had thought of that. They had made a bad mistake.

In future she would make sure that any stop took place on a downward slope. But they had to deal with this now, or there would be no future.

'Relax,' she said to the volunteers.

Tem said: 'We could run the sled back down the hill and a little way up the opposite slope. Then we'd have a downward start.'

'I hate to go backwards,' Joia said. She also thought it would be demoralizing. 'We'll do that as a last resort.'

Tem nodded.

Joia called to the volunteers: 'We'll try rocking again.'

She called all the cleverhands and Verila and Verila's cousins to the ropes. She and Seft and Tem took hold of ropes. No one was left watching.

She shouted: 'Ready . . . take the strain . . . pull! . . . Relax . . . take the strain . . . pull!' They got into the rhythm. When the sled was rocking she said: 'Relax . . . huge effort this time . . . pull! And keep pulling!' And the sled inched up the rise. 'Keep it up!' she yelled. 'Don't falter!' The sled kept moving. Joia stayed on the rope, heaving with the rest, her elation giving her strength, until the sled perched at the crest of the rise.

There she called a short rest. 'Well done, everybody,' she said. 'With luck we won't have to pull that hard again.'

Soon afterwards they passed the nameless hilltop village they had noticed on their way to Stony Valley. The people were ready for them this time – Joia wondered how news travelled so fast in apparently empty country – and they came running down the hill. At first Joia feared they might be hostile, then thought they would hardly dare to confront a couple of hundred people.

In fact they brought water in jars and small gifts of mutton, which the volunteers consumed without stopping. They asked excited questions. A couple of adolescent girls kissed several boys each.

The younger villagers joined in, pulling the ropes. Joia wondered how far they planned to come along.

Joia heard Dee say: 'These people have never seen anything like this before.'

Joia was worried that all this might somehow delay their progress, but everyone managed to keep going, and eventually they left the village and its people behind.

At noon they emerged from the hills onto the plain. It had been deserted when they passed through on their way to Stony Valley, but now there were several hundred cattle. This was a pre-selected resting place, and more of Chack and Melly's children and grandchildren were there with cold meat. The sun was high, and many of the volunteers cooled themselves in a nearby stream.

Seft climbed on top of the giant stone and began to work on the surface, smoothing it by knocking flakes off it with a round stone he held in his hand.

Joia sat in the shade of a low, wide hornbeam tree, her back against its distinctive fluted trunk, to eat cold pork. Dee sat beside her, her hair wet from the stream, her curls plastered to her head. They had not spoken since before dawn, when they had chatted in the moonlight about all sorts of things.

Dee said: 'This is the hardest thing I've ever done. As a shepherd you don't often go long distances. I've walked to the Monument, of course, but not pulling a great big stone.'

'I'm finding it hard too,' said Joia.

'How old are you?'

'Twenty-seven midsummers.'

'Same as me,'

'We're young, but most of the volunteers are younger.'

'A few are older.'

'Very strong older people,' Joia said thoughtfully. 'What made you join this ambitious mission?'

'Oh, I don't know,' said Dee, without meeting Joia's eye. 'To do something different, perhaps.'

Joia thought she was avoiding the question. However, if there was something Dee wanted to keep to herself, Joia was not going to press her.

Seft approached with two strangers. He said to Joia: 'These are the herders I met before, Dab and Revo.'

The woman, Revo, said: 'And this is Lim.' She was carrying a toddler.

Joia and Dee stood up and made a fuss of the child.

Dab said: 'I can hardly believe you're moving that enormous stone!'

Seft said: 'Yes, and now we must move it on.'

The sled was stopped on a slight downward slope, so getting started was less difficult. It was still hot, but the day would cool soon. The volunteers talked a little as they pulled, and Joia even heard snatches of songs.

They came to the East River and followed its bank south until they came to Upriver, where they planned to spend the night in the broad riverside meadow. The cattle were already roasting on spits.

The volunteers dropped the ropes with enormous relief. Some people just lay flat where they were. Others threw off their tunics and cooled themselves in the river.

Joia happened to see Dee's bare body, and it had a strange effect on her. She stared, fascinated. She had seen many naked people, and had never taken much interest, but now she could not tear her eyes away. Dee was slim but muscular, no doubt from pulling stupid sheep out of swamps and other places where they got stuck. She had lovely round breasts, and Joia could not help thinking about kissing them. The hair at Dee's groin was much darker than the fair bush on her head. This, she realized, was not how one thought about someone who was going to be no more than a good friend.

In the river Dee talked to Bax, the two of them naked in the clear water. Joia felt with annoyance that Bax was not good enough to be Dee's girlfriend. It was an unkind thought but Joia could not get rid of it. The idea of a romance between Dee and Bax just bothered her.

When night fell there was not much romantic activity. The volunteers ravenously ate roast beef then lay down and slept. It had been a hard day.

And they had to do it all again tomorrow.

28

THIS IS THE last day, Joia thought as soon as she woke up. Today we will deliver the giant stone to the Monument – and I will have done it in four days, as I promised the elders.

People who said it was impossible will admit that they were wrong. Visitors will come from far away just to look at it. More people will come to the Rites; more trading will be done; more girls will want to become novice priestesses. This will be a rebirth for the people of the Great Plain.

And if we can move one stone, we can move more. We can rebuild the entire Monument. But not right away. The volunteers will want to go back to their everyday lives. The only way we can get enough people will be by doing this every midsummer. But if we can do that . . .

Nothing must go wrong today.

Beside her, Dee woke up with a moan. 'I ache all over,' she said.

Joia was not sure why Dee always slept beside her. Dee had made friends with several people on the mission, and chatted amiably to everyone, but last thing at night she always lay down by Joia, who tried to hide how much this pleased her.

Now she thought of offering to rub Dee's shoulders, but she hesitated; and Dee got up, so it was too late.

A lot of the volunteers were stretching their legs and backs, trying to relieve aching muscles. Joia realized that if she had rubbed Dee's shoulders, Dee might have done the same for her. How nice that would have been.

Her hands were sore, and the fatty meat on offer for breakfast gave her an idea. She took a particularly greasy piece and rubbed it all over her hands. Then she took Dee's strong, broad hands and shared the fat with her. They smiled at each other while they rubbed hands, and it made Joia feel happy.

At sunrise they moved to the sled and took up the ropes. The ground alongside the river was mostly flat, but they had stopped the sled on a slight downward slope, which was now standard practice, so rocking was not needed, and they got the stone moving quickly, albeit with a lot of grunting and groaning. The terrain was easier today, and Seft's track of branches ran straight, and levelled out the bumps and dips in the ground. And the task was now familiar.

They stopped briefly at mid-morning and then for a longer break at noon. While they were eating, Joia spotted Narod and his friends quietly slipping away.

She frowned. What did that mean?

She got up and sought out Duff. 'The Young Dogs seem to have left us,' she said.

Duff was surprised. 'Which way did they go?'

'South, towards the Monument.'

'I can't think why. I don't really know why they came in the first place.'

'Nor do I, which worries me.'

'They didn't achieve much with their negative comments, except to make the volunteers dislike them.'

'Troon may have told them just to keep an eye on the mission.'

'Well, I'm glad to see the back of them.'

Joia nodded. All the same, she had an uneasy feeling as the volunteers set off again, pulling the great stone along the bank of the river.

Before the mid-afternoon break their progress stopped dead.

Someone had destroyed the track.

The branches had been scattered all around, some thrown into the river. The damage continued along the riverside path as far as they could see. Joia stared in dismay. She could hardly believe her eyes. They were less than half a day's journey from the Monument, yet the mission had been wrecked. The volunteers dropped their ropes. Joia sat on the ground and cried.

Seft approached her. She wailed: 'What are we going to do?'

Seft was calm. 'Repair the track,' he said.

She was almost angry with him for not being more upset. 'We won't get to the Monument by the end of today, so we won't have done the job in four days.'

'We should still repair the track and continue on. Or do you want to leave the giant stone here?'

She realized she was being silly. 'I just can't bear to hear that fool Scagga say: "I told you so."'

'I feel the same. But let's put that behind us.'

Joia sighed. 'You're right, of course.' She wiped her eyes and got to her feet.

'We've a workforce of two hundred,' Seft said. 'It won't take us long to repair the track.'

Joia nodded. 'I'll tell them what to do.'

'We can re-use all the branches we can find, and I'll send some cleverhands forward to cut extra ones. There are plenty of trees along the river.'

Joia stood on a tree stump and shouted: 'Listen, everybody. We have to repair the track.'

There was a collective groan.

'Consider it a rest period. It's easier than pulling the stone.'

They laughed at that.

'Collect up the scattered branches and lay them back where they were. Don't separate them, but push them together so that they interlock, then stamp on them. Throw earth on top to make it more stable. Tread everything down. Come on, let's get started. We're nearly home.'

She got down on her knees and began work on the nearest damaged section, showing people how to do it; and volunteers watched her for a while, then moved farther along to do the same.

Dee knelt beside Joia. 'How do you think this happened?'

'I know how it happened,' Joia said. 'Narod and his friends did it. I saw them leaving at midday. Obviously they went ahead to do their dirty work. Troon will be pleased with them.'

Dee did not understand. 'But why would farmers want to stop us doing this?'

Joia thought for a moment before replying. It was a serious question and Dee deserved a considered answer. She said: 'After the woodlanders burned the Monument, people stopped coming to our Rites, and the farmers started their own midsummer feast. Troon saw a chance to increase his power and influence. I feel sure he dreams of being Big Man of the entire Great Plain, not just of Farmplace. So he doesn't want the Monument to be rebuilt in stone. He doesn't want it to regain its status as the focal centre of the people of the plain. Our mission threatens his dream.'

Dee was shocked. 'I had no idea.'

In silence they continued repairing the track until they caught up with the people in front, then they stood up. Joia said: 'I need to know how far this damage continues. Come with me and we'll walk to the end.'

Trees shaded them as they went along the riverbank. Dee observed: 'Wrecking this track was a quicker job than rebuilding it.'

Joia nodded. Somehow that made the destruction more reprehensible.

To get to the end of the damage took as long as it takes to boil a pot of water. Suddenly the track ahead was pristine. 'They gave up here,' Joia said. 'They got bored, and told themselves they had done enough.'

Dee said: 'Why did you want me to come with you?'

'So that I can teach you to count on the way back.'

'Oh, good!'

'And at the same time we'll find out how many paces it is.'

She counted each step, Dee repeating the number. They stopped when they reached the point where the track was already repaired. Joia said: 'One thousand, two hundred and eighty-four paces.'

Dee was dazzled. 'How can you keep such numbers in your head?'

'It's not so difficult when you get used to it.'

Seft came up and said to Joia: 'How much more to do?'

She repeated the number.

Seft looked at the sky, and Joia did the same. The sun was sinking in the west. Seft said: 'I don't know . . .'

'Nor do I,' said Joia.

Ani was at the Monument, looking out for the volunteers and the giant stone.

Seft's track skirted the village of Riverbend and approached the Monument from the north across the plain. It ran through the entrance to the Monument all the way to the large hole in the ground where the giant stone would be erected. Ani could hardly wait for the sight of the sled appearing in the distance, pulled by a crowd of excited volunteers with Joia at their head, and storming over the plain like a cloud across the sky. Even more thrilling would be the knowledge that her daughter had achieved the ambition that so many people had thought unattainable.

Ani was not the only one eagerly waiting. Her daughter Neen was there to greet her man, Seft, and their three children were looking out for their dadda. A crowd had gathered at the Monument in the late afternoon. They were sitting or standing on the earth bank, all looking north. This was easily the biggest event of the year, if not the biggest ever. Just about everyone in Riverbend was there, and some from more distant villages.

There was a smell of roasting meat, but it was not for the crowd. Chack and Melly were preparing a meal for the exhausted volunteers when they finally arrived. Expecting a wait, some families had brought their supper with them. Neighbours chatted, youngsters flirted, and children climbed the bank and rolled down again.

And there were some hoping that Joia would fail. Scagga was present, wearing the scowl that seemed now to be permanent. He had his family around him: they always supported him, though sometimes with a lack of enthusiasm they could not quite hide.

She wondered what was behind Scagga's hostility. It was likely he resented Ani, who was the longest-serving elder after Keff and was generally expected to be Keff's successor as Keeper of the Flints. He probably thought he should be Keeper of the Flints, and felt unjustly overlooked. Ani's influence was all the greater for having a high priestess as her daughter. And Scagga's belligerent attitude did not win him many friends.

Keff appeared and sat beside Ani. 'Well,' he said, 'will she do it?'

'Or die trying,' Ani replied. She looked west, and saw that the sun was setting. 'Although she doesn't have much daylight left.'

'We need people like her,' Keff said. 'Sometimes she upsets folk, but she tries new things, and such people are essential. They keep us from becoming complacent and lazy.'

'I'm very glad you think so,' Ani said sincerely. She was pleased when people appreciated Joia's strengths.

The spectators began to drift away, taking children home to bed. Scagga came over, looking as if he had been vindicated, and said: 'She's not here, is she? Nor is there a giant stone.'

Ani said coldly: 'She'll be here.'

'I said it was impossible.'

'Indeed you did.'

'Well, perhaps you'll listen to me next time.'

'I always listen to you, Scagga.'

'Huh.' He walked away and, a few moments later, left with his family.

Chack and Melly, looking frustrated, put out the fires under the spits. Chack said: 'The meat will still be warm in the morning,' and Melly added: 'But it won't be as tasty.'

Keff got up, but he stood silent for a few moments. At last he said: 'When do you think Joia might get here?'

Ani stood up too. 'Right now,' she said, 'I have absolutely no idea.'

The volunteers were tired, and the stone moved slowly now. They knew they could not reach the Monument today, and that disheartened them. When darkness fell they dropped the ropes. They lay down where they stopped, too tired even to look for a comfortable place to sleep.

Joia half expected some of them to give up now and disappear back to their homes. But it was dark and they needed rest.

The frustrating thing was how close they were. The track was just about to divert from the river and head across the plain. Their destination was not far away. They had almost made it.

She spoke to Boli, who was a quickrunner, a tall, slim woman with muscular calves. 'I know it's dangerous to run in the dark, but could you find your way to Riverbend, just walking fast?'

'Sure,' said Boli. 'There's starlight, and no cloud.'

'I need you to speak to my mother.'

'That's easy. I know where Ani's house is.'

'Just tell her that everyone is well, we've been delayed, but we'll reach the Monument early tomorrow morning.'

'Early tomorrow morning.'

'But go carefully, don't hurry, be safe.'

'I will.'

'Ani won't mind being woken up.'

'Good.' Boli went off.

Joia lay down next to Dee. 'Such a shame it's ended this way,' she said dolefully.

'Don't feel discouraged. You've done something remarkable. No one else could even have begun.'

'But I needed this to be a triumph. I've even planned my victory speech. Instead our lateness is going to be portrayed as a failure. You know how people talk.'

Dee reached out and took her hand. 'I'm sorry I can't cheer you up.'

'Thank you for trying.' Joia's eyes closed and she fell asleep holding Dee's hand.

Ani awakened in the middle of the night. Looking at her doorway she saw, outlined against the starry sky, the slim silhouette of the quickrunner Boli. 'Oh, hello,' she said. Joia had failed to arrive yesterday and she realized with a chill of fear that this could be bad news. 'What's wrong?'

'Joia says that everyone is well.'

'Thank the gods.'

'They've been delayed, but she wanted you to know that they will be here early in the morning.'

'Oh, good,' said Ani. 'Early this morning. I'll spread the word.'

Then she went back to sleep.

Joia awoke at first light. Worried that the volunteers might be slow to get up today, she went around waking them. They got to their feet and rubbed sore muscles.

There was no breakfast. All they had was water from the river. In consequence everyone was grumpy. 'There's beef waiting for us at the Monument!' Joia shouted. 'We're not far!' Some of them perked up. She kept her eyes peeled for deserters, but she saw none.

At sunrise they reluctantly picked up the ropes. 'This is our day of triumph!' Joia shouted, but they did not respond. They just wanted to get this over, she guessed. 'All right!' she yelled. 'Ready . . . take the strain . . . heave!'

A slight downward slope enabled them to get the sled moving on the first try, and Joia was heartened.

Seft's track followed a wide curve to the west, onto the Great Plain, then turned south to climb a gentle rise.

Joia heard a soft, distant noise that sounded vaguely like a crowd.

The volunteers leaned into the ropes as they hauled the stone up the rise. Joia was terrified that they would falter now, so close, but they kept on.

They breasted the rise, and ahead they saw the Monument. The volunteers made noises of relief and happiness, and Joia had to shout: 'Keep going! Keep going! We're nearly there!'

There seemed to be a lot of people gathered around the Monument and on the earth bank. As the stone moved closer, some of them began to run towards the volunteers. There was a sound of cheering. Joia's spirits lifted. There was a welcome party, even though they were a day late.

In fact, she saw as she got closer, there were hundreds of people waiting to meet them, the entire population of Riverbend and more. It was almost too good to be true.

The advance guard of the welcome party reached the volunteers and wanted to kiss and hug them. 'Don't stop!' Joia yelled. 'We're not there yet!'

Some of the welcomers grabbed the ropes, trying to be helpful – or perhaps just wanting to tell the tale, one day, of how they had helped bring the stone to the Monument. Some volunteers gratefully stepped aside and let them take the strain. Joia had an anxious moment: the newcomers might not have the strength or stamina – or the sheer grit – to do the job. But the stone did not stop.

She walked ahead along Seft's track for the last hundred or so paces, holding her head high. She had made this happen, and she was proud. She led them through the entrance to wild cheers from the crowd.

She followed the track to the hole Seft had prepared. She turned to halt the sled at just the right moment, then shouted at the top of her voice: 'You are heroes!'

The crowd erupted.

Chack, Melly and most of their large extended family appeared with baskets of roast beef, still warm, and the hungry volunteers fell on the food. People crowded around Joia, congratulating her, then moved to the volunteers, hugging and kissing. The volunteers revelled in the adulation, forgetting their aching muscles and their crabby mood of this morning. Joia heard snippets of conversation: 'I thought it would never move . . .'

'I was so hot I just threw myself into the river . . .'

'That night Janno had sex with three girls and in the morning he couldn't walk . . .'

They were already telling the stories, true or exaggerated, that would turn the journey into a legend.

When the excitement began to die down, and everyone had had enough to eat, Joia said to Seft: 'We must erect the stone now, while everyone is watching.'

'It hasn't been properly dressed,' he said. 'I've done a bit, but it needs more. Can't we postpone it?'

'No,' Joia said decisively. 'It won't have the same impact then.'

'True. All right. We'll have to work on it later.'

He and the cleverhands untied the ropes that attached the stone to the sled, but not those around the stone itself. Seft said: 'If we've positioned it right, the stone should slide off the sled straight into the pit.'

Joia persuaded the volunteers to pull one more time on the grab lines. The crowd went quiet as the stone slipped, with majestic slowness, along the top of the sled. As it came to the end of the sled it began to tilt. They continued to pull, and the thick end of the stone tipped gently until a quarter of its length was in the hole.

Now the stone had to be pulled upright, and – as with many of the challenges they had met in the last three days – they knew how to do it. Seft freed the long-legged giant that had ridden all the way on top of the stone. He and Tem laid him in place and positioned the rope, then the volunteers took the strain. Seft and Tem lifted the giant, the volunteers pulled, and the great stone slowly came upright.

The crowd gasped with admiration when the full height of the stone was made evident. They had never seen anything like it.

More volunteers quickly filled the pit with earth and tamped it down hard. Everyone stood back, and the crowd applauded.

Joia looked with awe at what she had done. Here, surrounded by spectators, the stone seemed even bigger, and the people were dwarfs, or perhaps acolytes. It looked like something divine.

This was the moment to make a speech.

She climbed up on the sled, so that more people could see her. As the crowd realized she was going to address them they became quiet, people shushing noisy neighbours. Looking around she spotted Shen, the sidekick of Troon. He would report everything said and done here today to his master. Let him, she thought; Troon will be as sick as a dog.

The crowd became silent.

Making her voice deep and loud, she said: 'This was hard.'

There was a murmur of agreement from the volunteers.

'We toiled in the sun. We got discouraged. We feared we would fail.'

They shouted: 'Yes!'

'But we did it.' She paused.

'Talk about people who are strong.

474

'Talk about people who are brave.

'Talk about people who never give up!'

She felt tears run down her face. She pointed at the volunteers, and her voice shook with emotion she had not expected. 'Here they are!' she cried. 'These are the great people of the Great Plain!'

The crowd roared their approval.

She let her voice go a little quieter. 'The gods are pleased with us today.'

They were hushed.

'We have honoured the Sun God. And I believe the god wants to see more stones in the Monument. Today the central oval has one stone and nine wooden uprights. Next year . . .' she paused for effect '. . . next year, friends and neighbours, the god wants to see ten upright stones!'

There was a murmur of amazement.

'That means that, after next year's Midsummer Rite, we will bring nine more giant stones to the Monument!'

She heard a rising noise of people reacting to this and commenting to those around them. She caught Seft's eye: he was open-mouthed in astonishment. She had not forewarned anyone of this.

'Spread the news!' she cried. 'Next year we want to see a huge attendance at the Midsummer Rite! Every person in the Great Plain who has a sense of adventure, and many more from farther afield, will come to the Rite. They will attend the ceremony of the sunrise, they will trade, they will feast with us, and the next morning we will all march again to Stony Valley.'

She needed them to commit. 'Shall we do this?'

There was a shout of 'Yes!'

Joia felt inspiration seize her. 'Shall we please the Sun God?'

They shouted louder. 'Yes!'

'Shall we go again to Stony Valley?'

Now the volunteers joined in. 'Yes, yes, yes!'

'Shall we bring back nine stones? *Nine stones?*'

Loudest of all: 'Yes!'

They continued to cheer as Joia got down from her platform, shaking with emotion. The applause went on. She had won them over. She felt woozy with success. She saw Dee in front of her and felt faint. Her vision blurred and she fell forward. She knew that she was caught in Dee's strong arms, and then she passed out.

Joia recovered quickly, and life began to return to normal with a speed that felt a bit disappointing. As noon approached, Dee asked if she could share the midday meal with the priestesses. 'I'd like to know more about them,' she said.

'You're welcome, of course,' Joia said.

They sat on the ground in the dining hall and ate cold meat left over from the volunteers' breakfast with some of the vegetable leaves that were plentiful in summer. Dee sat next to Bet, a small, round-faced girl who always had a happy smile. Dee said: 'What made you become a priestess, Bet?'

'When I was a little girl I always loved the way they sang and danced at the Rites,' Bet said. 'And then when I was older my father died, and my mother got a new partner who didn't really like me.'

'And now you dance and sing with the priestesses.'

'To be honest, I'm not naturally very graceful.'

The other priestesses protested. 'You're fine,' said one.

'Well, I've improved.'

Dee said: 'Don't you get bored, doing the same thing every day?'

'No! It's hard to remember the songs. We have hundreds of them. Joia knows them all, and so does Sary, but I'm still learning them – and I've been here five midsummers.'

Dee turned to Sary. 'Do you really know hundreds of songs?'

'Yes, of course,' said Sary, being uncharacteristically curt. 'That's what being a priestess is all about.'

Joia was surprised at her abrupt tone. She wondered whether Dee had done something to offend Sary. She could not think what it might have been.

Dee showed no sign of having noticed. 'And you all must feel favoured by the Sun God.'

'We hope so,' said Bet.

The flint miner Bax came into the room and said: 'Forgive me for interrupting. I came to say goodbye to Dee. I'm heading home.'

Dee stood up. 'I'll walk a little way with you.' She looked at the priestesses. 'Thank you all for sharing your meal with me.' She turned to Joia. 'I'll see you this evening.'

They left, and the others broke up to do their afternoon chores.

Outside the hall, Sary confronted Joia. 'May I have a few words?'

'Of course.' Now, Joia thought, I'll find out why she was unfriendly to Dee.

Sary said: 'If Dee becomes a priestess, are you going to make her second high priestess instead of me?'

Joia was surprised by the question. 'Why do you think Dee will become a priestess?'

'Why do you think she came to eat with us?'

Joia was taken aback. 'Well, she's never said anything about becoming a priestess.'

'It's obvious to everyone else. She's been sleeping next to you every night.'

'I don't know what that's got to do with anything.'

'Don't you? Why did she say she would see you this evening?'

'Because she's coming to supper with my mother.'

'Really?'

Joia got fed up with this. 'Look, Sary. You're second high priestess and that's not going to change, no matter who may join us. You're good at what you do and you're a very good friend. I'm sorry if I've done something to make you think that's going to change, because it's not.'

'All right.'

'You do believe me, don't you?'

'I suppose so.'

'Will you give me a hug, then?'

Sary stepped forward and they hugged.

Joia went to Ani's house. She had not yet had a chance to talk properly to her mother. She found Ani cleaning the inside of a sheepskin, using a wood scraper so as not to tear the hide. Joia sat beside her, enjoying resting in the summer sun.

While Ani worked, Joia told her the whole story of the mission. Remembering everything that had happened, she was quite shocked at all they had done. They had dealt with one problem at a time, but now that she related them one after another they made a formidable list.

'You were clever,' Ani commented.

'Seft was the clever one, really, thinking up ways to do things that have never been thought of before. I just tried to keep the volunteers' spirits up.'

'Which might have been the most important thing of all.'

Joia lay on her back. It was a pleasure to be still and not have to go anywhere or heave on a rope. She closed her eyes. 'I don't think it was the most important thing of all,' she said. 'But it was important.'

Ani said something that Joia did not hear well, but it did not matter. She was luxuriously weary and the sun was a warm blanket. In a few moments she was asleep.

Ani woke her, shaking her shoulder. 'You slept all afternoon!' she said.

'Did I?' Joia was momentarily confused. She looked at the sky and saw that it was evening. 'Why did I sleep so long?'

'Because you're tired. Dee is here.'

Joia turned her head and saw Dee smiling down at her. 'You were sleeping like a baby,' Dee said.

Joia sat up, afraid that there was something she had failed to do; then she remembered that the mission was over, and she had no obligations, not today anyway. She could relax.

Ani had put away the sheepskin and was stirring a pot at the edge of a fire. Joia smelt sorrel and mutton. She felt happy. The three of them would eat and talk as long as they wanted to. She could not think of anything nicer.

Ani got bowls and spoons and served the stew, meat and small white carrots. When they had eaten their fill, she said to Dee: 'I guess you became a shepherd because your parents were shepherds.'

Dee nodded. 'Both my mother and father died when I was quite young. I'd seen only twelve midsummers when I was left to look after my little brother.'

Joia had not known this. 'That must have been hard!' she said.

'Well, I knew how to look after sheep, which was the important thing.'

Ani said: 'Did neighbours help you?'

'A little, but shepherds aren't very neighbourly. They live far apart and, anyway, they tend to be independent types. But my grandfather helped me. He's a shepherd. Joia has met him.'

'And now?'

'I live with my brother and his woman, and we take care of the sheep together.'

'What's his woman like?'

Ani often questioned people in this way, but they never seemed to mind. She had a way of doing it that disarmed them. She never judged them. And they were flattered that she was so interested in them.

Dee said: 'I get on all right with her, though I sometimes feel the two of them could manage the flock without me. All those years it was my responsibility to keep my brother alive – but now he doesn't need me.'

'Do they have children?'

'A baby girl.'

Something else Joia had not known.

There was more that she wanted to know, but Dee asked Ani about her life, and Ani told her of the deaths of Olin and Han, and talked about what it was like to be an elder. The evening passed quickly and darkness fell. The three women lay down to sleep in the house.

Joia thought over the conversation and concluded that Dee was restless. She was feeling superfluous in her own home. Perhaps she was looking for a new life.

Or was that just wishful thinking?

Dee was returning home in the morning. Joia had the feeling that in the last five triumphant days she had somehow missed an important opportunity.

For breakfast they ate the cold leftover stew, then Joia said: 'I'll walk with you to the river.'

They passed through the village, which was waking up to the morning light. Joia had a hundred things to say but did not know how to say any of them. They walked to the start of the long path that led to Upriver and beyond. There they stopped to say goodbye.

Feeling desperate, Joia said: 'You don't always come to our Rites.'

'My brother used to bring the hoggets to trade on Midsummer Day, but now he wants to stay at home with the baby.'

'So will you come again next midsummer?'

Dee said: 'Do you want me to?'

'Oh, yes, I want you to,' Joia said fervently.

Dee smiled. 'Then I'll come back.'

'Promise?'

'I promise.'

Dee kissed Joia's lips gently and tenderly, and the kiss lasted longer than Joia expected. She could have held it for ever, but Dee broke the embrace. 'Goodbye, dear Joia,' she said.

'Until next year.' It sounded like for ever.

Dee turned and walked away, and Joia watched her until she turned around a bend and was out of sight.

29

THE PEOPLE AT Farmplace were agog to know how Joia's mission had ended. Several young farmer men had joined the volunteers, and their parents, their wives and their children were waiting to hear news.

The first to return were the Young Dogs, but their report was indecisive. They said they had so damaged the track that the sled could not possibly have reached the Monument. No one was sure whether to believe this.

Then Shen arrived. As he walked through the settlement to Troon's house, people followed him until there was a small crowd. Pia was among them, with Yana and Olin. Troon and Katch came out of the house to meet Shen.

'She did it,' Shen said. 'She got the stone to the Monument, and it's standing there for all to see. And, my gods, it really is the biggest stone in the world.'

Troon cursed. 'Where is that fool Narod?' he said, looking around.

Narod was in the crowd, and could not hide himself because of his height.

Troon said: 'You told me you had stopped them!'

Narod protested: 'We destroyed the track!'

Troon looked at Shen, who said: 'They destroyed part of the track. The volunteers repaired it. That made them a day late, but no one cared.'

Narod said indignantly: 'We wanted to smash up their sled. That would have ruined everything. But the sled was guarded all the time. We waited until halfway through the last day, then realized we were never going to get the chance, so we messed up the track.'

'Stam would never have been satisfied with a bit of petty vandalism,' Troon said. 'You're pathetic. Get out of my sight.'

Narod disappeared.

Shen said: 'She wants to do it again next midsummer. She says she'll bring nine stones then.'

Pia felt a glow of satisfaction. What a woman Joia was!

'This is intolerable,' Troon said. 'One giant stone will be a huge attraction, but nine will be the wonder of the world. People will come to see it from . . .' he waved a hand vaguely in the air '. . . from over the water. The herders will be dominant again. We farmers will be regarded like the woodlanders, people of no account. Hardly anyone came to our midsummer feast this year – no one will come next year!' He paused for breath. 'That woman . . . she wants to be the ruler – the Big Man of the Great Plain.'

Pia murmured to Duff: 'The Big Woman.'

'Well, we're going to stop her,' Troon went on. He was breathing hard, as if he had been running. 'We have a year to prepare,' he said. 'Next time I won't send a handful of boy thugs.' He looked as if he was going to announce a plan, but stopped himself. 'We'll have to think of something else.'

Ani had a little pile of leather offcuts and decided to make them into a bag. Using a flint knife she sliced the offcuts into thin strips, each the width of a baby's finger. Then she stood a wide log on end and draped some of the strips over it. Next she had to weave the remaining strips into those on the log. She had just begun the process when she felt someone watching her. She looked up to see the frog-like eyes of Scagga glaring at her. He had a dead swan slung over his shoulder and was holding it by the neck.

Irritated, she said: 'Go and gawk at someone else, why don't you?'

He ignored that. He said: 'I doubt we'll be hearing any more about nine stones.'

She wanted him to go away, but on second thought she decided she had better find out what he was getting at, so she played along. 'Why do you think that, Scagga?'

'You'll find out, soon enough.'

He was probably saving his argument for the elders, but he looked as if he was bursting to reveal it. Ani said: 'Oh, you're just making this up.'

'No, I'm not. And you could work it out if you had enough sense.'

'I'm sure I could.'

He could hold it no longer. 'She took five days to bring one stone to the Monument.'

'Everyone knows that, Scagga, and no one cares that she was a day late. What she did was heroic.'

'But it took five days,' he insisted. 'And now she wants to bring nine stones. That will take nine lots of five days. All those people will be away from their work half the summer!'

Ani had not looked at it that way. She could not figure out nine times five – she would have to ask Joia – but it sounded like an awfully long time for the fittest of the herders to be away from their beasts. She felt quite sure the elders would baulk at that – which was worrying.

She said: 'Perhaps Joia has a different plan.'

He laughed scornfully. 'But you don't know what it is, do you? I can tell.'

'No, I don't. But I'll find out before you do.'

'Hmm.' He went away, the limp wings of the dead swan flapping against his back as he walked.

Ani thought about what he had said, and decided it was so serious that Joia needed to know about it at once. She picked up her unfinished bag, and the log it was draped over, and put both inside her house with the knife; then she headed to the Monument.

She could see the new stone from the outskirts of Riverbend. It stood up, grey and massive, above the ridge of the earth bank, and was probably visible from even farther away.

It occurred to Ani that Joia might spend her life rebuilding the Monument in stone. That might be a good thing. Joia would always need some endeavour upon which to expend her inexhaustible energy.

Ani wondered how Dee was going to fit into that future. It was no surprise that Joia had fallen for Dee, who was strikingly attractive. Not many people were as clever as Joia, but Dee was one of the few. Plus she was likeable and kind and she laughed a lot. Ani had no doubt that Joia was deeply in love with her, though whether Joia knew it was another question. And Ani thought Dee probably loved Joia, too.

Ani would be glad if they became a couple. Joia deserved to be loved long and well by someone who knew how special she was. And it would be nice, Ani thought, to know that there's someone to care for her when I'm gone.

She found Joia in the dining hall, supervising the cooking of the priestesses' midday meal. She looked happy. It was a great thing, Ani thought, to see your child happy.

Joia left Sary in charge and took Ani outside. They entered the Monument and walked to the new giant stone. Ani stroked its cold surface, feeling its ridges and hollows. She wondered why the Earth God had put it in Stony Valley. Perhaps so that it could be found by Joia. You could never fathom the motives of the gods.

She told Joia what Scagga had said.

Joia looked anxious. 'To tell you the truth, I haven't even thought about this,' she said. 'The crowd was so strongly supportive when we arrived that I imagined they would go along with anything.'

'And they would have, on that day,' Ani said. 'But such hysterical enthusiasm wears off.'

'I suppose so. And we can't sustain our mission if the elders oppose us.'

There was silence as the two of them digested that. Joia's project to rebuild the Monument in stone could fail, despite the triumphant first stone that towered over them now.

Ani said: 'I suppose you can count nine times five days.'

'Forty-five. But I don't accept his assumptions. We won't have the same two hundred people move one stone after another – it would take too long: Scagga is right about that.'

'So what's the answer?'

Joia was thoughtful. 'We'll need several teams. But that's possible. We'll get many more volunteers next year, I'm sure of that. What we did is going to be talked about farther afield than the Great Plain. There will be at least a thousand volunteers.'

Ani did not know what a thousand was.

Joia was still figuring. 'If we had six teams, and the first three came back for a second run, we could move nine stones in nine days. Say ten days, in case of unforeseen snags – though there shouldn't be many of those, as we've now made the trip once and learned a lot.'

'Ten days is one working week. That might just be acceptable to the elders.'

'Good.'

'But are you sure so many people will volunteer? I can't do numbers the way you can, but it seems to me you'll need something like half the able-bodied population of the Great Plain.'

'That's about right. But we'll also have people from beyond the plain.'

'It's a lot to hope for,' said Ani.

'I know,' said Joia.

After the midday meal Joia gathered the newer priestesses in the Monument to teach them a chant. This one was about the number twelve. There were twelve days in a full week – ten working days and two rest days. The chant was about how many days there were in two weeks, and three, all the way up to thirty.

The lesson was interrupted by Seft. Uncharacteristically, he was in a rage. He came striding into the circle, red-faced and furious. 'What's this nonsense about nine stones in ten days?' he demanded.

Joia was not intimidated by Seft. She had known him since he was sixteen midsummers old and lovesick for her sister, Neen. 'My goodness, that got around quickly,' she said. 'Who told you?'

'Not you, obviously, though you should have spoken to me before anyone else.' He was really bitter about this.

Joia told the priestesses to leave, saying she would finish the lesson later.

'I'm sorry,' she said to Seft. 'I talked to my mother, because she brought me the news of what Scagga was saying. I haven't discussed it with anyone else.'

He was not mollified. 'You've given people the impression that you had my agreement. I'll look a fool when we have to confess that it can't be done.'

'Why are you so sure it can't? We learned so much, the first time – like that two-legged giant you made for getting a stone upright – that everything will go faster the second time.'

'True, but we still can't move nine stones in ten days.'

That word *true* was a concession, a sign that he was softening. She knew that the way to get around Seft was to start him thinking about the practical problem. She said: 'We should at least talk some more about it. Suppose we had six teams.'

'What? Six teams each the same size as the one we had this year? Are there that many people in the Great Plain?'

'There are twice that many people in the Great Plain. And they'll come from elsewhere too.'

'But what if we don't get so many?'

'If we don't, Seft, we'll do our best with what we get, and at least bring some giant stones to the Monument, and hope to do better the following year.'

'All right, as long as we don't start making ridiculous promises.'

'Let's work it out. On Day One all the teams walk to Stony Valley. On Day Two, three stones are lifted and put on sleds – you'll have to make more sleds – and sent on their way. They arrive at the Monument at different times, the last by the end of Day Four. Day five is a rest day for them.'

'All right, that seems possible.'

'They walk back to Stony Valley on Day Six. On Day Seven another three stones are dispatched, and arrive by the evening of Day Nine.'

'That's six stones.'

'The other three teams are just a day behind, and their stones reach the Monument by the end of Day Five. They don't need to return to Stony Valley for a second run, but I wouldn't be surprised if they were glad to go back and help the others.'

'You have to allow for unexpected snags.'

'I've added an extra day. My timetable has all the stones at the Monument on Day Nine, but I've told people we need ten days.'

Seft clearly did not think that was enough, but by now he was losing the argumentative spirit. 'I'm not sure the elders will approve this,' he said weakly.

'There are only five people who matter at an elders' meeting,' Joia said. 'Scagga and Jara will oppose us, my mother and Kae will support us, and Keff will make the decision. Any other elders who may show up will go along with Keff.'

'I agree, but how does that help us?'

'It means we need to convince Keff *before* the meeting.'

Seft nodded.

He was extraordinarily clever about physical stuff, Joia knew, but surprisingly unimaginative when it came to dealing with people. Fortunately I can do that part for him, she thought.

She said: 'We should go and see Keff now.'

Seft was taken aback, but he had got used to Joia's perpetual wish to do things immediately. 'All right,' he said.

They left the Monument and found Keff outside his house in Riverbend. When they arrived he was sharpening a flint. This was a skill most adults had, because everyone used flints and flints often needed sharpening. However, the operation demanded concentration. Keff placed the point of an antler carefully near the edge of the stone and pressed hard, leaning over the antler. A perfect little flake came off the flint, leaving the edge sharper. This was a technique called pressure flaking.

Keff looked up at Joia and smiled.

'We've come to ask your opinion about something,' Joia said tactfully. What she really wanted was to convince him of her own opinion, but it would help to give him the illusion that he was dispensing wisdom.

'Sit down,' he said. 'You won't mind if I carry on with my work.'

They sat, and Joia said: 'We're trying to think how to continue the building of the Monument with the least possible disruption of normal herding.'

Keff pressed another flake off his blade and said: 'That's a good start.'

'We'd like to complete the next stage in a single working week – ten days.'

'I've heard rumours. Nine stones in ten days sounds ambitious.'

That meant Scagga had already talked to Keff. Never mind. Joia leaned forward. 'This whole enterprise – rebuilding the Monument in stone – depends on one thing,' she said, and Keff looked up. 'Enthusiasm,' she said emphatically. 'The volunteers must feel a sense of achievement. They must want to do it, like doing it, feel proud after doing it, and hope to do it again.'

'So I imagine,' Keff said coolly, but she knew she had his interest.

'If we move one stone a year, everyone will know that, long before the Monument is finished, we will all be dead and our children will be dead too. Moving the stones will become a tedious annual chore. That won't do.'

'What did you want my opinion on?'

'The risk,' Joia said. 'We have a timetable for moving nine stones in ten days, and we hope to do it, but we know we may not succeed. Do we take that risk? Or do we follow a less ambitious course, and accept that none of us will ever see the completed stone Monument?'

She looked at Keff. So did Seft. There was a long wait. Keff was looking down at the flint he was sharpening, but he had paused, and he sat motionless.

At last he answered her. 'Let me think about that,' he said.

The elders' meeting was stormy. When Ani presented Joia's plan, Scagga ridiculed it. He was even more insulting and contemptuous than before. Jara, his sister, looked embarrassed. Twice Keff ordered him to be polite.

The discussion took its expected course. Kae backed Ani, Jara unenthusiastically backed Scagga, and everyone looked to Keff.

Keff said the elders should approve Joia's plan.

Scagga erupted. 'You people never listen to me!' he raged. 'Everything I say here is contradicted or ignored. I'm sick of it.'

None of this was true. Ani's wishes had often been frustrated by Scagga in these meetings. But he was not rational now.

Jara, his sister, said: 'Scagga, please!'

Scagga was not listening. He pointed an accusing finger at Keff. 'You want Ani to be the next Keeper of the Flints. I know, people have told me. You do everything she wants. You must be her lover.'

Kae, sitting next to Ani, gasped.

Keff stood up. 'I will not permit such talk,' he said.

'Don't worry! No need to forbid it. You won't see me at any

more meetings. I'm off, and I'm not coming back. Get yourself another pet dog.'

He stood up and walked away.

We won, Ani thought.

Joia said to her mother: 'I miss Dee so much.'

'I can tell,' said Ani. She did not like to see her children sad, but this was a different sadness. It was the kind that could easily turn into joy.

Joia had been caught in a summer shower and had taken shelter in her mother's house. Through the doorway they could see the rain. Joia said: 'I wonder if she'll come to the Autumn Rite.'

Ani shook her head. 'She won't have anything to trade in the autumn. No one wants lambs – they're too liable to die in their first year. Everyone with any sense trades for hoggets. At one year old they've survived a winter and proved they're sturdy. We won't see Dee or any other shepherds until the next Midsummer Rite.'

Joia nodded. 'Dee said she'd be here for that.'

'Then that's what she'll do. She seems like a person who does what she promises.'

'I'm afraid she might change her mind.'

'It's possible, but I'd be very surprised.'

'I love her.'

'I guessed.'

'Do you think she loves me?'

'I can't see inside her heart but, yes, I think she adores you.'

'Adores?'

'That's what I think.'

'Why me? She must have so many people in love with her.

When she's laughing, with her mouth wide and her hair shaking like a tree in leaf, anyone would fall in love with her.'

'She's very alluring.'

'I haven't felt like this before, Mamma. I thought there was something peculiar about me because I couldn't understand why girls talked all the time about kissing and sex. I've never loved anyone like this. Now I know why people are obsessed with it.'

Ani smiled. 'You've taken an awfully long time to get to this place.'

'Was it like this for you with Dadda?'

'Exactly like this.'

'Do you think she's the one for me?'

'Yes. I'm not in any doubt. She's the one.'

The rain stopped. Joia looked out through the door, as if Dee might be there. 'I hope she comes back,' she said. 'I do hope so.'

30

ON THE DAY of the Spring Rite, Joia was happy. The drought was over. Last summer the farmers had had their first decent harvest for four years. The winter had been mild and wet. On the Great Plain, the cows were pregnant and the herd was growing again. The sun was shining.

The gods must be pleased about the giant stone, she thought.

The number of priestesses had doubled. The thrill of rebuilding the Monument was one of the reasons, but people also said that recruits wanted to join because of Joia. She would not have said that herself, but in her heart she knew it was true.

The priestesses spent every afternoon making rope. Each of Joia's six teams would need its own supply. To relieve the boredom Joia got them practising songs while they worked.

The Autumn and Midwinter Rites had attracted larger crowds. Everyone wanted to see the stone. Attendance today was greater again, with hundreds more people. Joia was thrilled. Her project was bringing people back.

And the people were different. No one was scrawny or sick. They no longer walked slowly and looked scared. They did not scan the ground for something edible: a bone, a dead bird, a puppy. There was a spring in the step, a tune on the lips, a look of optimism.

It was easy to identify the different communities. The farmers were always muddy. The miners had abrasions on their hands and arms, from working with sharp stones. And those from beyond the Great Plain looked subtly different: they had longer or shorter tunics, shoes of a different pattern, odd-looking hairstyles.

Life would have been perfect for Joia if Dee had been with her. But the Midsummer Rite was soon – and it would arrive more quickly if only Joia could stop thinking about her all the time.

Meanwhile, the priestesses performed the Spring Rite at sunrise, with the more disciplined singing and dancing that Joia had introduced. Today for the first time she encouraged them to wear feathers in their hair. And she had introduced a rattle – a wooden box with pebbles inside – that Sary shook rhythmically to keep them all in time.

There was one change to the Monument, introduced overnight, probably not even noticed by most spectators: leaning up against the giant stone was a ladder, a slender tree trunk with notches cut into its sides. Seft had made it.

When the ceremony ended, Joia and two novices did not exit the Monument but instead ran to the giant stone. While the novices held the tree trunk steady, Joia climbed it, using the notches as hand- and footholds. She had practised five days ago, as soon as Seft had finished it, but she was still unsteady. It wobbled, despite the efforts of the novices, and she had one or two anxious moments. But she pressed on as fast as she could go, and with great relief reached the top.

She stood up and raised her arms, and the astonished crowd

roared their appreciation. She was famous now, and those who did not recognize her guessed who she was. She revolved slowly, arms still raised, until she had turned full circle. Then she made calming-down gestures with both hands, and they quickly went quiet.

It amazed her to have such control over so many people.

She repeated what she had said at the Autumn and Midwinter Rites: that the next Midsummer Rite would launch another holy mission. Again she would be calling for volunteers, fit and strong and ready for adventure. And this time they would bring nine giant stones to the Monument. 'Tell your friends and neighbours,' she shouted. 'We need many more people than before. And remember: at the end we will be exhausted, but we will be so very proud!'

They cheered and she climbed down the pole. The novices looked at her with shining eyes, thrilled that their leader had been cheered rapturously by the crowd. She hurried out through the entrance, eager to avoid getting waylaid by admirers, and took refuge in the priestesses' dining hall.

She rested for a while. She was surprised at how tiring it was to be idolized. She let the hysteria die down, and when she judged that people would be concentrating on trading, she went out again.

Many people shook hands with her in the herder style, holding their hands up and clasping. Right-to-right was formal; right-to-left was casual; right-to-left and left-to-right together was affectionate. Most people offered her the four-handed clasp, even if she had never met them.

She found her mother trying to resolve a dispute – her frequent duty after Rites. A basket-maker wanted a flint, but the flint-knapper said the basket was not worth a good sharp flint. The basket-maker was outraged, and wanted to insist on the deal. Ani was trying to explain to him that the flint-knapper was free to refuse if he wished, but the man did not want to hear that.

Joia left her to it and moved on. She ran into Seft. He had spent the winter at Stony Valley, making sleds, and Neen had moved there with the children. They were back for a short visit. Joia would have to go there soon, to make sure everything necessary was being done.

Seft said: 'The climbing pole worked all right, then?'

'As you saw,' Joia said. 'Thank you for making it.'

'They loved it when you stood on top of the stone. To those who couldn't see the pole, it seemed as if you had flown up.'

'People love to think they have seen a miracle.'

'You should do the same thing after the Midsummer Rite.'

'Absolutely.'

She spotted Scagga's sister, Jara, who caught her eye and came over. 'My brother will attend the next meeting of the elders,' she said.

Joia tried to say something neutral. 'He's changed his mind, then?'

Jara went on: 'I agree with his cautious approach, but I hope you and I may be polite to one another.'

This was disarming. 'I hope so too,' Joia said.

'Thank you.'

Jara moved off. Joia would have liked a little time to think about what Jara had said. It had seemed like a peace offering. But people were crowding around Joia to clasp hands, so all her conversations were short.

The flint miner Bax shoved through the crowd and said: 'Is Dee here?'

Bax had made Joia foolishly jealous by talking to Dee naked in the river. Now Joia suppressed her resentment and said: 'No, but she's coming at midsummer.'

'She's a fabulous woman. I'd like to see her again.'

'Me, too.'

'Oh, don't be coy. She fell for you just as hard as you fell for her.'

Ani had said something similar. Joia was embarrassed to think that her private feelings were so obvious to everyone.

Bax went on: 'Lucky you. And lucky her.'

That was such a nice thing to say that Joia hugged Bax.

Then someone else wanted to clasp hands with her and she had to turn aside.

She noticed Shen, Troon's sidekick. He was there to snoop, of course. He would go back to Farmplace and tell Troon everything he had seen and heard. Troon would be angry about Joia's popularity and her big plans. Joia gave a mental shrug. So be it.

A few days later, Joia walked to Stony Valley.

The track looked good, to her surprise. It had bedded in, probably because of winter rain and snow, and the branches had sunk into the ground. It would need fresh branches to be added, but a useful base had formed.

She took a group of priestesses with her, including some of the new novices. They all carried coils of rope they had made. They were young, and a day's walk was no challenge to them, even carrying rope.

As they began the climb into the North Hills, Joia became vividly conscious that she was now near Dee. 'My place is not far from here, to the east,' Dee had said, when she and Joia were camped in Stony Valley. It had not occurred to Joia then to ask for more precise details. If it was close, Joia might have been able to walk there and back in a day. Or Dee might come to Stony Valley to check on her grandfather. It was painfully tantalizing to know she was close but not know where.

The sun was sinking as they arrived at the ridge and looked down into Stony Valley. Half the trees in the valley had disappeared. She had noticed en route that some of the flimsy branches-and-earth track had been replaced by embedded logs. Also, Seft's team had built decent houses for themselves and their families, replacing the makeshift shelters of last year. She saw four new sleds in a row and one still being made. Ropes were coiled and stacked.

Her sister, Neen, came out of one of the houses and welcomed her. 'Have supper with us tonight and we can chat,' Neen said.

'With pleasure.'

'The food's almost ready.'

'Let me make sure my priestesses are all right.'

She told the priestesses to build a fire and gave them some beef and a large cooking pot. Chack and Melly were not required to cater for the relatively small number here: their speciality was cooking for large crowds.

Joia returned to Neen's house. The children were there too, and she was pleased to see her nephew and two nieces. They ate together, then put the children to bed and sat talking until dark.

Joia remembered the night she had fallen asleep holding Dee's hand. She imagined she was doing the same now, and again fell into a contented slumber.

That spring in the farmer country green shoots appeared in the ploughed furrows, and Pia and Duff weeded regularly. They liked to be together in the fields. Pia loved Duff as much as she had loved Han, but in a different way. She had adored Han, but she saw Duff as an equal partner.

Yana was getting creaky and could no longer manage the

bending, but she kept busy with the goats: three were pregnant. Little Olin was going to be tall like Han. His hair was fair, so perhaps one day he would have a blond beard like his father. He had seen only three midsummers, but all the same, Duff, his stepfather, was teaching him which green shoots were wheat and which were weeds.

Troon announced that the farmer community was not well prepared to defend itself. One or two people wondered aloud who on earth might want to attack them, but Troon brushed aside such questions and ordered every man in Farmplace to equip himself with a bow and at least six arrows.

A few farmers already had such weapons, but most did not: farmers did not hunt. Troon got a hunter called Wel, who lived alone on the south side of the river, to show the farmers how to make bows and arrows. Duff had to find a flexible yew branch a little longer than he was tall, and some shorter branches of hazel to be made into arrows, and he had to get sinews from carcasses to twist into a bowstring.

When the bows were made they all had to practise shooting at targets in East Wood. At first they were hopeless. Duff joked that the safest place to stand was in front of the target. But they got better.

Pia said to Duff: 'He says all this is for defence, but it looks more like we're getting ready to attack someone.'

Duff said: 'Well, there's no point in attacking the herders. There are too many of them.'

'Troon thinks they're too cowardly to fight.'

Duff said: 'He might be planning to burn more woodland – East Wood, perhaps, or Round Wood.'

Pia shuddered. 'I hope not. The woodlanders take revenge – dear gods, we should have learned that lesson.'

Troon also announced that no one, man or woman, would be

allowed to go to the herders' Midsummer Rite. They would all be expected to stay and support the farmers' feast. So few people came to the feast that this measure was obviously unnecessary, and Pia was sure Troon had some secret scheme.

Duff told Pia he would go to the Midsummer Rite at the Monument anyway. He had taken part in Joia's mission last year and wanted to do it again. Several other young farmer men felt the same: the event had been the best festival ever. Troon did not have the same hold on men as he did on women, and Pia thought the young men might go in defiance of Troon's edict.

A few days later Troon's woman, Katch – who was Pia's aunt – appeared while Pia was weeding. Katch was carrying a piglet, black with a pink snout and big ears. She showed the baby pig to Olin, who giggled.

She said to Pia: 'I'm sorry to interrupt you in your work.'

'It's all right. I need a break. That's a healthy-looking piglet.'

'Would you swap a goat kid for a piglet?'

Pia had never had pigs, but they were not difficult to raise: they fed themselves by scavenging much of the time. 'I'll have to ask Duff and Yana,' she said, 'but it seems like a good idea. We've only got one kid so far this spring. Do you want to see?'

The goats were not tethered during the day, and kids never wandered far from the mother. They were at the edge of the wood, eating the leaves of low bushes. Pia picked up the baby, and it bleated for its mother. She had to hold it tight. 'It's strong,' she said.

'If Yana and Duff agree, bring the kid to my house tomorrow and I'll give you this little wriggler.'

'All right. Thank you.'

Katch lowered her voice, though there was no one else around, and she spoke nervously: 'Something I want to mention to you.'

Pia thought this was probably the main reason for the visit.

Katch went on: 'I heard that Duff and some of the young men are planning to go to the herders' Midsummer Rite, despite Troon's ban.' She held up a hand to silence any denial. 'Don't tell me whether it's true – I'm not asking.'

'Then I won't.'

'And I'm not telling Troon anything.'

Pia believed her. Katch, who had no daughters, was fond of her niece Pia.

Katch said: 'Don't let Duff go on the mission.'

'What?'

'Please, I beg you.'

'But why?'

'Because you've already had one man killed.'

She was talking about Han. And Pia was chilled by the dreadful thought that Duff might be killed as Han had been. 'Are you saying Duff could die on the mission?'

'Not just Duff.'

'A massacre?'

'I'm not saying any more than I've already said. I'm just begging you to prevent him going.'

'But I don't understand.'

'If Troon finds out I've spoken to you in this way, he will beat me half to death.'

That made Pia reluctant to ask more questions. She said: 'Well . . . thank you for the warning . . . I suppose.'

'But never say who told you.'

'All right.'

Katch nodded, acknowledging a promise made; then she turned and walked away, still carrying the piglet.

She might look like a mouse, Pia thought, but she's a brave woman.

Katch could not confront Troon directly, and she had not been able to help when Troon forced Yana to marry Stam, but she could act covertly, as she just had. All the same, she was risking a beating.

Pia mulled over this warning while she carried on weeding. At midday Duff and Yana returned from different fields – Yana walking with one hand on her back, just above the hip, where it ached – and they sat down with Olin in the shade of a tree to eat porridge with soft goat's cheese. Olin could feed himself now, though Pia kept an eye on him and stopped him making too much mess.

Pia said: 'I had a visitor this morning. I've promised not to say who.'

'Intriguing,' said Duff, light-heartedly.

Yana, more sensitive to the seriousness in Pia's tone, looked worried.

Pia said to Duff: 'I have been warned that you could be killed if you go on Joia's mission after this year's Midsummer Rite.'

Duff said incredulously: 'Who would want to kill me?'

'The only other thing I know is that you might not be the only victim.'

Yana said: 'Oh, no!'

Duff said: 'A massacre? *Another* massacre?'

'I'm not sure.'

There was silence while they tried to digest this news.

Finally Yana said: 'Who could be behind it? That's the next question.'

Duff said: 'The woodlanders, I assume. They were responsible for the last one.'

'But that tribe has been wiped out,' Yana pointed out.

'Another tribe, then?'

'As far as I know, no tribe has a quarrel with the herder folk, or with anyone else. And, even if they did, would they ignore the grim lesson of what happened to Bez's tribe?'

That seemed unlikely to Pia. Woodlanders were not stupid.

Duff looked serious and said quietly: 'Perhaps Troon intends that we farmers will be the aggressors. If we create a violent incident at the Monument, it will discourage people from attending the Rites, and then they would come to our feast.'

Pia said: 'My visitor said the mission was the target.'

Yana said: 'This makes more sense than any other explanation.'

Duff said: 'But it would be madness for us to attack the herders. I've always said that. They outnumber us.'

'And Troon has always said the herders are too cowardly to fight,' Pia said. 'Remember when he took over the Break? He said they would do nothing about it, and he was right.'

'That's true.'

'In any event, Duff, you have to stay at home.'

Yana said: 'But what about the others? Duff, you said that some of your friends are planning to defy the ban.'

'Five or six.'

'They might be killed by their own people!'

'I'll have to warn them.'

'Wait,' said Yana. 'That many people can't keep a secret. Troon is going to find out that you warned them. You'll be in deep trouble, and your visitor could be found out too.'

'You're right.' Duff looked bewildered. 'I don't know what to do.'

There was silence for several moments, then Yana said: 'We have to warn Joia.'

Duff shook his head. 'That means going to the Monument. If one of us disappeared for two or three days, Troon would guess we were up to something. And Shen would find out where the person had been, and probably even whom they'd spoken to.'

Yana said: 'I agree. So let's one of us go to Old Oak and tell Zad and Biddy.'

Pia said enthusiastically: 'That's a better plan! We could be there and back in half a night.'

'And they'll find a way to get the warning to Joia.'

Pia felt good. If the herders were prepared for the attack, it could be fought off. At least it would not be a massacre. At any rate she would have done her best. 'I'll go to Old Oak,' she said. 'I'll slip away unnoticed. I know East Wood well and I can find my way through by night.'

Duff looked as if he wanted to argue, but in the end he said: 'When will you go?'

'Tonight. No point in postponing these things.'

They returned to their fields and worked until sundown. By the time they finished supper it was dark. Pia kissed Olin goodnight and left.

The sky was partly cloudy. Stars showed now and again. Pia went slowly through the wood, not finding it as easy as she had thought, stumbling sometimes over tree roots and fallen branches. It would be better on the other side where she would have nothing more than a grassy plain to negotiate.

She emerged from the wood and paused to get her bearings. There was no herd in sight, though she could smell it not far away. No herders were in view. But there was someone, and before she could slip back into the wood he said: 'Hello, who's that?'

It was a farmer, she could tell by the accent. He had been sitting on a log, and now he stood up. He was tall and wide, and she recognized him as Hob, a crony of Troon's.

She tried to appear relaxed. 'Hello, Hob,' she said. 'What are you doing? Spying on people who flit about in the dark?'

He walked towards her. 'It's Pia, by the voice – and the attitude.' She realized that she had had a chance to run away unrecognized, and had missed it. 'Spying?' he went on. 'I suppose I am. Troon likes to know who's going in and out of the farmer territory. You're going out, I see. He'll be interested in that. Women are supposed to stay at home.'

'Don't give away my secret, Hob. I'm in love with a herder boy.'

'Well, if that's the case you'd better go home. You know Troon has banned fraternization with herders.'

A question occurred to her. 'If I'd gone another way you wouldn't have seen me, would you?'

'I'm not the only sentry, lass. There are six of us at different points on the perimeter. You'd be very lucky not to be seen by one of us.'

This was bad news. 'I didn't know Troon had set guards on us,' she said, not hiding her disapproval. 'It makes Farmplace seem like a pen to stop animals wandering. Is that what we've come to, Hob? Are we to be treated like animals now?'

'Don't ask me, I just do as I'm told. And you'd better do the same. Start by going back to your house.'

'Very well. Goodnight, Hob.'

'Goodnight.'

Defeated and depressed, Pia headed back through the wood to her home.

Troon came visiting in the morning.

Pia and her family were depressed as they ate the usual cold leftover porridge for breakfast, sitting outside the house in weak sunshine. They had failed and they did not know what to do next. Only Olin was carefree.

Pia had been caught the moment she left farmer territory, but she was determined to try again. She would need to evade Troon's guards. Was there a chance she could slip between two of them, perhaps on a particularly dark night? Could Duff distract one long enough for her to get away unseen? She would have to think of something. Troon could not be allowed to commit mass murder.

He appeared while she was trying to think of a way to outwit him.

He came with Shen and Hob. Hob was carrying a stick of oak, shaped and smoothed, clearly a club meant to hurt people. They sat down uninvited.

'So, Pia,' Troon said with pretended amiability, 'you were on your way to see your herder lover last night, when Hob here met you.'

She said defiantly: 'I didn't know that we farmers are penned in, like animals that must not stray.'

Troon ignored that. 'Your man Duff here doesn't seem very upset about your lover.'

Pia said impatiently: 'What are you doing here, Troon? What do you want?'

'You're a cocksure bitch,' he snarled. 'But you'll suffer for it.'

Yana said: 'People never used to talk like this in Farmplace. Whatever happened to good manners?'

Troon did not reply to her. He said to Pia: 'You weren't going to Riverbend – you had no food with you for the journey. So you must have been going to Old Oak. But which herder is your lover?'

'Zad,' she said.

'If that was true you wouldn't have said it so fast.'

Pia realized that he had outwitted her. Because he was brutal she was inclined to underestimate his brain. Brutal men could be cunning too. She needed to remember that.

Troon went on: 'No, you didn't go there for romance. So what was your purpose? I wonder if you were planning to send a message – to Ani, perhaps, the mother of your man Han, the one who died.'

'Murdered by your son Stam.'

507

'Oh, let's not rake up the past. But what might you have to tell Ani that was so important?'

'A lot,' said Pia. 'I haven't seen her for years, because you forbid women to go to the Rites. So she doesn't even know that her grandson has all his teeth now.'

Troon's face twisted in a smug grimace, and Pia knew he was about to say something he thought would shake her. He said: 'Katch paid you a visit yesterday.'

Pia was horrified. How did he know that?

Troon answered her unspoken question. 'Shen happened to see her.'

Shen nodded and smiled, pleased to be noticed.

Shen seemed to see everything.

Pia quickly collected her thoughts. 'Yes, your woman wanted to trade a piglet for a goat kid.'

He stared at her with his little dark eyes. 'So it's just a coincidence, is it, that you tried to leave Farmplace just half a day after Katch visited you?'

'It's not much of a coincidence.'

'I don't think it's a coincidence at all. It looks to me more as if a message was to be passed: Katch to Pia, and Pia to Zad, then Zad to that quickrunner, Fali, and finally Fali to Ani at Riverbend. Very neat, and all in a couple of days.'

'And all in your imagination.'

But that was bravado. He knew the truth; he had worked it out. What would he do now? She began to feel scared. She decided to stop challenging him. He would always win.

Troon said: 'So what shall I do with you? Left alone, you'll try again. Even now you're dreaming up ways to get past my guards.'

She almost shuddered. He knew what she was thinking.

He went on: 'Given long enough you'll probably succeed. You may be foolish, but you're sly.'

That was not unlike the way she thought of him.

'So how do I make sure you don't have a chance to betray me to my enemies?'

Pia had a nightmarish premonition of what Troon was about to say.

'I have to tether you, like wandering goats.' He stood up. 'From now until after Midsummer Day you will all be kept in your house, with the door permanently in place, and an armed guard outside.'

Duff said: 'You can't do that!'

'Shut your mouth, you young fool, or Hob will shut it for you with his stick.'

Hob hefted his club.

Duff still looked outraged, but he said nothing.

Troon went on: 'You'll be let out, one at a time, to go to the river and wash each morning, supervised by a guard. Yana can also milk the goats.'

Yana said: 'But what about the wheat growing in our fields?'

'It will still be there after midsummer. You'll just have a lot of weeding to do.' He bent and swiftly picked up Olin. Pia screamed and Olin cried. 'Now get inside, all of you,' Troon shouted, 'or I'll smash this little brat's skull.'

Yana, Duff and Pia went into the house. Pia stood in the doorway and reached out for Olin. Troon handed the boy to her.

Pia said: 'But it's still many days to midsummer. What are we supposed to do, stuck in this house all that time?'

'You can reflect on how foolish it is to go against me,' Troon said, and he walked away.

31

ANI WAS STANDING in the shallows of the river, washing a
cow hide prior to scraping it, when she saw Biddy, dusty and
perspiring, evidently having walked there from Old Oak. 'Hello,'
Ani said. 'What are you doing here? Where's Zad?'

'Zad's minding the herd, and Dini's with him,' she said. 'She
loves working with her father.'

'And you're here.'

'I came to see you.'

'Then I'd better get out of the water.' Ani climbed the low bank,
dragging the hide behind her. It was as clean as water could make
it, she decided. But before she started scraping it she had better
find out what was on Biddy's mind.

'I'm worried about Pia,' said Biddy.

Ani suddenly felt cold. Something was wrong with her
daughter and perhaps her grandchild. 'Tell me why, quickly,' she
said.

'I wanted to get some goat's cheese from her.'

Ani wanted to tell her to spare her the narrative, but suppressed the wish and tried to summon patience.

Biddy went on: 'There are guards all around the farmer country now, stopping people going in and out.'

Ani was startled, and wondered what the reason was for such a bizarre happening, but she said nothing.

'I said I was going into East Wood for hazelnuts and they let me pass. So I got as far as Pia's house, but there was another guard there.'

Ani was now mystified. 'Why?'

'He wouldn't say. But he did tell me that they were all in the house – Pia, Yana, Duff and the little brat for that matter, he said – but I couldn't see or speak to them.'

'Did he offer any explanation?'

'No, he just said they would be released after midsummer. Then he told me to go back through the wood.'

'So this is something to do with the Midsummer Rite?'

'I suppose so.'

'Come with me. We've got to tell Joia.' She glanced up at the sky. 'It's almost suppertime, anyway.'

They walked to the Monument and found Joia in the priestesses' dining hall. Someone was cooking sheep's livers with onions in a big pot. Ani asked Biddy to repeat her story. Joia asked the same questions and got the same unsatisfactory answers.

They discussed the mystery while eating a rich liver stew. Joia said: 'Troon is planning some mischief at the Midsummer Rite.'

Ani nodded. 'And Troon is afraid that Pia will find out about it and tell people. That's why she and her family are being kept inside until then.'

Joia said: 'Our Rites are more popular than his feast, especially since we brought the giant stone. Troon might want to blight our celebration so that more people will go to his.'

Ani felt frustrated. 'I can't just sit here wondering! I must at least try to see Pia. I've got to go to Farmplace.'

Biddy said: 'I'm going home tomorrow. We could travel together.'

'Perfect,' said Ani.

Two days later Ani did what Biddy had done, and approached Farmplace through East Wood so that she would be hidden until she emerged a few steps from Pia's house. But when she was halfway there she heard the voices of a group of men and she stopped, listening.

She could not make out the words, but she could tell that they were farmers, not woodlanders. The voices seemed casual and amiable. The men were involved in some more or less harmless activity, she guessed.

She crept closer, staying in thick vegetation, until she glimpsed them. She saw one carrying a bow, then another shooting. There was quiet while he aimed, then muted comment afterwards, presumably on how accurate he had been.

They were doing archery practice.

She diverted around them, well out of their sight, and continued on her journey. She asked herself why farmers needed shooting practice. It seemed unnecessary. Arrows could bring down the largest deer, but farmers rarely hunted: they were too busy tending their crops.

She reached the southern edge of the wood and stood in the shade, taking in what was in front of her.

A burly guard stood outside Pia's house. The doorway was firmly blocked by a full-size wicker gate, which was unusual at this time of year: in warm weather everyone used a half-gate, which let the air in. Pia's goats were roaming free, and eating the wheat shoots in the ploughed field.

Ani could not see a way to get into the house, so she decided to shout through the walls.

The guard was sitting down and concentrating on something he was doing with his hands. Ani watched for a moment and figured out that he was making string. He was rolling tough, flexible animal sinews on his thigh to twist them together, and he had a basket beside him that probably contained more cleaned and dried sinews. A long, thin branch leaning against the side of the house was the right length and heft for a bow. It lacked a bowstring, and clearly that was what the guard was making.

It seemed the farmers were arming. But what for?

She walked across the field towards the house, stepping softly. The guard continued to focus on his string.

She was almost there when he saw her out of the corner of his eye. He looked up, stared for a moment, then shouted: 'Hey, you! Go away!'

She spoke without stopping. 'I just want to talk to Pia. You wouldn't stop me, would you?'

He stood up and strode towards her.

Ani yelled at the top of her voice: 'Pia! Are you there? It's Ani!'

Pia's voice answered her, muffled by the walls of the house but just audible. 'Ani! I'm in here!'

'Are you all right?'

'We're prisoners.'

The guard came close to Ani but she dodged him and shouted: 'Is Olin all right?'

'Yes, but I have to tell you something.'

The guard struck Ani with his club from behind, a hard blow

on the head that was agony. She fell to the ground, hurt and dazed. She could hear Pia shouting but could not make out the words. She wanted to get up but she could not summon the energy. She got on her hands and knees and tried to focus her eyes. Pia was shouting something about Joia's mission, but Ani could not make it out, and the guard started yelling at her.

She felt herself picked up off the ground and carried away, across the field. Every step of the guard's stride hurt her head. 'You've got to leave Farmplace and never come back,' he said to her. 'But I'm not leaving you at the wood. I'm taking you all the way to the Break.'

He stopped and let her down, holding her arm so tightly it hurt, then he marched her across the fields, past farmhouses and stores. The people at work stared at her. Many of them would recognize her. Probably they all knew what had been done to Pia and her family.

Ani took everything in and would reflect on it all when her head stopped hurting.

The guard did not let her go until they were at the northern edge of the Break, where grassland took over from cultivation. He pushed her on and said: 'If I ever see you again, I'll kill you.'

She staggered on until she was out of sight of the farmland, then lay down on the turf and rested. Slowly the pain in her head receded and she began to think straight.

Pia and her family were all right, though living very uncomfortably. But something dangerous was developing in Farmplace. Target practice, bowstrings, guards: the farmers were getting ready for war. And it was going to start on Midsummer Day.

'I told you so!' Scagga roared. 'I said we'd have a war with the farmers one day, and now I've been proved right!'

Keff said: 'Yes, Scagga, you were right. Now, how do we prepare for it?'

Scagga was enjoying himself. 'Luckily for you,' he said, 'I've got a store full of bows and arrows that I had made after the stampede three midsummers ago. We can arm practically our whole adult population.'

'Weapons still in good condition?'

'The bows might need new strings, but that's all.'

Ani said: 'I saw the farmers doing target practice. We should do the same.'

'I'll gather together the fittest young men and women, as I did last time, and train them.'

Ani really did not want Scagga in charge. He would be impulsive and reckless. But she had taken discreet soundings before the meeting and, of the few people who knew what was going on, most thought Scagga should lead. He had the right attitude. Ani would have to find ways to restrain him.

Ani said: 'Pia has been shut away until Midsummer Day, which must mean the attack will come then. We will have crowds of visitors for the Rite on that day. How shall we manage our defence?'

Scagga said: 'I'd like to see our people striding around with their weapons, looking so fierce that no one would dare touch them.'

That was obviously a terrible idea, and Keff stamped on it right away. 'That doesn't give us what we need, Scagga. We don't want to wait until they've reached us before we fight them. We'll be able to see them from some distance away, across the plain, and we should meet them long before they get to the Monument.'

Jara agreed, surprising Ani by going against her brother. 'We should have lookouts north, south and west, and they should be briefed to light a big, smoky fire as soon as they see the enemy. Scagga, you should be watching for those fires and ready to lead our force into battle.'

Scagga liked that idea.

Ani said: 'I think it's important to keep our weapons out of sight of the visitors. They could be stashed in the priestesses' dining hall. We can't be sure the farmer army will come – something may go wrong, Troon could change his mind. And don't forget that the Monument may not be the target. Pia seemed to think the farmers would attack the volunteers on the mission. Let's not scare our visitors before it becomes absolutely necessary.'

Scagga disagreed, of course. 'We should show people that we're strong and ready to fight, and that anyone who attacks us is in for a beating.'

'I agree with Ani,' Keff said firmly. 'We should be strong and ready to fight, but we shouldn't boast about it because that will frighten people away – as well as offending the gods, who feel that they alone have the right to decide who wins and who loses. Between now and midsummer, tell no one that we're expecting an attack.'

Jara said: 'People will see the archery practice. It's too difficult to hide.'

Ani said: 'We could say we've heard that farmers are planning to steal cattle in the far west of the plain, and just in case the rumours are true we're preparing to go and get them back by force.'

'Good idea,' said Keff.

Jara said: 'It's not many days now until midsummer. I suggest that every day I report to Keff and Ani on how the preparations are progressing. That way, Scagga, you'll be able to concentrate on what you're doing without the distraction of a meeting.'

And the elders could monitor the preparations without having rancorous conversations with Scagga, Ani thought. Clever Jara.

'Very good idea,' Scagga said.

The day before midsummer, Seft and his team came back from Stony Valley. All preparations had been made. The sleds were finished, the ropes stacked, the track ready. There was food at the stopping places, and people to cook and serve.

When he arrived, Joia told him about the threat from the farmers. He was shocked and alarmed. This changed everything. If war broke out on Midsummer Day, no one would be dragging stones from Stony Valley to the Monument. The whole project was in danger.

He reckoned the farmer community must amount to about four hundred people. Leaving out children and old people, they could probably muster an army of two hundred. That many could do a lot of damage.

The danger had been kept secret. Even Joia could not count the number of people who had arrived in the days leading up to midsummer. The visitors' houses were crammed. Many slept in the open air as the weather was fine. There was a good chance Joia would have the volunteers she needed. But they would not volunteer for a war.

Seft went home and took a nap before supper, tired by the long walk and happy to be in his own home. He fell into a light doze and dreamed he was fighting Troon. He knocked Troon to the ground and was about to kill him when he noticed that Troon had the face of Seft's father, Cog. Terrified, Seft hesitated.

Then he woke up.

Joia was hoping that Dee and her year-old sheep would arrive early. She had been missing Dee for a whole year and now the time had arrived when they would be reunited. But by midday on the eve of the Rite she had not come.

Joia told herself this was not surprising. A separation of a year could be fatal to a romance. Dee might have met someone else. Or her memory of Joia might have faded.

Even if it was like that for Dee, it could never be that way for Joia. Dee might have other loves in her future; Joia never would. For her it was Dee or no one. Her feelings had not changed at all in the past year. She felt now the way she had when Dee had tenderly kissed her goodbye. She might spend her life remembering that kiss, and never kiss anyone else.

The sun set. Joia was due in the dining hall for supper. Tonight, on the eve of the most important day in the priestesses' year, she could not possibly be absent. She made her way there in the gloom of twilight.

She tried to hide her feelings during the meal, and she thought she had succeeded. When the meal was over they all lay down to sleep.

Joia remained awake. Tomorrow morning she had to lead the sunrise service and then make a speech that would inspire hundreds of people. She was so dispirited that she felt she could not do either. She had no energy and no enthusiasm. She would probably fall off the climbing pole before she reached the top.

She stayed awake a long time, drowning in misery, but eventually she did sleep.

She was not the first to wake, which was unusual. Most of the priestesses around her were making bracelets of wild flowers and putting feathers in their hair. They had taken to heart her suggestion that they decorate themselves for public ceremonies.

Sary reported that she and Duna had put the climbing pole in place, up against the giant stone. They had also surveyed the Great Plain all around by starlight, and had seen no sign of a farmer army.

Joia joined in as best she could, faking enthusiasm and laughing when they laughed. She was not sure how well she was masking her feelings, but at least no one asked her what was the matter.

Dawn broke and the sky turned swan white. The priestesses lined up in pairs. Joia went to the front and summoned the energy to lead them. They entered the Monument singing. A huge crowd was there, more like two thousand than one thousand, Joia thought. It should have thrilled her but left her cold. There was only one person she wanted to see.

This will be a disaster if I don't pull myself together, she thought; but she could not pull herself together.

Scagga was standing on the ridge of the earth circle, looking west. Jara was beside him. They were watching out for the pillar of smoke that would serve as the alarm. Evidently they had so far seen nothing to worry them.

Joia scanned the crowd – and there, near the front, was a mass of fair curls like a tree in autumn, and under the curls a wide mouth and two rows of even teeth. Dee had come after all. Joia almost left the procession and ran to embrace her, but managed to control herself. Then, amazingly, Dee caught her eye.

And smiled.

Joia smiled back. Melancholy left her, like a black crow taking flight, and she was herself again. She sang louder, stepped more lightly, and smiled at the world. She was able to concentrate on the dance and song, and effortlessly led the priestesses through the ceremony. When it ended, and most of the priestesses headed out of the circle, she ran with Sary and Duna to the climbing pole.

She gained an extra burst of energy knowing that Dee was watching. She ran up the pole a little too hastily, and slipped halfway up. Sary and Duna held the pole steady. Joia banged her shin but regained her footing. She went more carefully up the rest of the way and stepped onto the top of the great stone.

As before, she raised her hands in a victory gesture, and as before, the crowd went wild. She turned through a full circle, and saw Dee again, smiling. Joia quieted the crowd, then took a deep breath and spoke with the carrying voice she had learned.

'Tomorrow,' she began, and they cheered again, so that she had to pause and wait. 'Tomorrow,' she said again, 'will be the greatest day of my life – and the greatest day of your life, if you join me.'

She turned slowly as she spoke, so that everyone could get a look at her face. She also checked that there was no smoke signal.

'At a holy place in the North Hills there are nine stones, which were put there by the gods when the world was young. They are for us, so that we can build a stone Monument. They are waiting for you and me to come. This is their destiny – and ours!'

The cheering told her that she did not need to say much more. They were already converted devotees. She did not need to whip up their enthusiasm, arouse their passion, ignite their spirits. They were with her already.

'Tomorrow morning we meet here at dawn. We will set off when the sun rises. We are going to build a Monument that people will marvel at for ever. People unborn today, and their unborn children, will look at our stone Monument and ask: "Who were the people who conceived this? What brave men and women overcame all obstacles to create this? Who were the giants who made it?" And the answer will be – us!'

The cheering was so loud she could hardly continue.

'If you want to be one of those giants, join me here tomorrow at dawn. Will you come?'

They shouted: 'Yes!'

She repeated: 'Will you come?'

They yelled louder.

'Will you come?'

They roared their answer, and Joia waved, then climbed down the pole and ran back to the priestesses' quarters.

She lay down, limp with exhaustion. She wanted to see Dee but if she went back out there she would be mobbed. Besides, she had no energy left, and in moments she was asleep.

Pia and her family were waiting for the guard to remove the wicker gate to their house and take them, one by one, to the river. After a while Pia shouted: 'Guard! Guard! We're all awake now.'

There was no reply.

She peered through the gaps in the lattice and saw no one.

'I think he's gone,' she said.

Duff looked out. 'No one there,' he said. 'I'll break us out.'

It did not take long. The gate was made of interwoven branches and secured with light withies. After a few kicks it fell over.

They all stepped outside: Pia, Duff, and Yana carrying Olin. The sun was shining. Pia half expected to see the guard on the ground, dead of some sudden seizure, but there was no sprawled corpse. 'It must be Midsummer Day,' she said. 'I think we're free.'

She looked at the fields. They were overgrown with weeds. The sooner the family went back to work, the better.

First they went to the river to wash. It was a delight to be all together outside. Duff played a game with Olin, disappearing under the water then surfacing in a different place, which made Olin squeal with laughter.

When they got out, Pia looked up and down the river and across the fields, and said: 'I don't see many people.' There was an old woman washing laundry in one direction, and a man watering cows in the other.

Pia recalled Katch's warning: *Don't let Duff go on the mission*. The farmers were on the warpath, she felt sure.

They walked along the bank to the man, who turned out to be Bort. Pia said: 'Where is everyone, Bort?'

'They left yesterday,' he said. 'All except the children and people like me who are too old to walk long distances.'

'Where did they go?' Pia asked, although she thought she knew the answer.

'They didn't tell me. All I know is that all the men had bows.'

Duff said: 'They've gone to Riverbend.'

Pia indicated that they should move away, back towards their farm. When they were out of earshot of Bort, she said: 'I did my best to warn Ani, shouting through the wall of the house, but I don't know whether she heard.'

'Too late now,' said Duff. 'If they left yesterday they will be at the Monument, or near it, by now.'

'Then it's in the hands of the gods,' said Pia.

When Joia woke up, the sun was high. She heard birdsong and the noise of a thousand people bargaining. She had slept for half the morning. Clearly there had been no farmer attack. Yet.

She felt refreshed and triumphant. But she knew she needed to fix people's commitment, to move around, greet people and remind them of their early-morning promise. She had won the hearts of more than a thousand, and now she had to make sure their enthusiasm did not fade.

And most of all she wanted to see Dee.

Sary and Duna were waiting to escort her. She ate a slice of cold pork and went outside with them. She walked around, stopping every few paces to clasp hands, listen to what people wanted to say to her, and answer their questions. She enjoyed it, and knew she would meet Dee today, sooner or later.

She noticed Scagga and Jara walking around the ridge of the earth bank, surveying the distant horizon.

However, she still had not come across Dee when the sun began to go down and people started packing up and getting ready for the feast. Would this be the moment when the farmers struck?

There were hundreds of cattle, sheep and goats tethered outside the Monument, but Joia went all around without spotting that head of light-brown hair and that wide smile. Now she was mystified and troubled. What could have happened? Was Dee ill, perhaps, or – gods forbid it – dead?

She sat through the feast and the poet's recitation, then left the village as the revel was beginning. She walked around the Monument and saw the folk who had stayed behind guarding the goods. She ran into Scagga and Jara, still on the lookout. Shortly they were going to get four younger members of their family to patrol all night. But they did not think the farmers would come in the dark when they could end up killing one another. Shooting arrows accurately was difficult enough in daylight.

If the farmers were coming, Scagga and Jara now expected that they would attack at dawn, before volunteers left on their march and the rest of the visitors drifted away. If it was an atrocity that Troon planned, he needed to do it when the maximum number of people were there to suffer it.

Joia examined her feelings as she walked towards the communal house where she always slept. Her speech had gone well and the farmers had not attacked. But Dee was missing and the farmers could strike at the volunteers later. She wondered if she would be able to sleep.

Then she saw Dee, waiting by the house, moonlight silvering her wonderful hair. Joia trembled with pleasure, ran to her and kissed her.

Dee broke the kiss sooner than Joia wanted to.

Joia said: 'Where were you? I've been looking for you all day!'

'I got here late last night and had to tie up my flock in the dark. I must have made a bad job of it, because this morning, after the Rite, I found that they had loosed their tethers and wandered everywhere. It's taken me the whole day to find them all.'

'I'm so sorry! I've missed you every day since we said goodbye.'

'And I've missed you,' said Dee, but she said it coolly, reporting the fact rather than agonizing over the separation.

Something was wrong. 'What is it?' Joia said. 'I'm so happy to see you – aren't you happy to see me?'

Dee did not answer the question. 'I have just spent the most miserable year of my entire life.'

This was bewildering. 'Is that my fault?'

'Yes.'

'Why? What have I done?'

'Nothing – and that's the problem. In all the time we spent together last summer, you never gave me the least indication that you loved me. You hardly touched me. We lay side by side every night and did nothing but talk. I held your hand once, and all you did was fall asleep. I waited day after day for you to say something. I still hoped, right up until the moment that was our first kiss – a goodbye kiss! Even then I thought you must say something. But you maintained your calm, and I went home heartbroken.'

It was all true, but Joia had not known she was doing wrong. 'I'm so sorry,' she said. 'I didn't know what I was supposed to do.'

'Surely you know that people in love touch each other?'

'I didn't know it was love! I only realized when you'd gone; and I missed you so badly, and it hurt so much, that it had to be love.'

'How could you get to the age you are without knowing the simplest things about love?'

'I don't know,' Joia said miserably. 'I always knew I was peculiar.'

Dee had tears in her eyes now, but her voice was still firm. 'I find this very hard to understand. I'll think about it.' She half turned to leave.

Joia said: 'But you'll come on the mission tomorrow?'

'I'll think about it,' Dee repeated, and she turned her back and walked away.

32

JOIA SPENT MOST of the night lying awake, listening for the sound of an approaching army. She was scared for herself, but much more for her family and Dee and everyone else. She remembered with horror the woodlander attack, the flames and the violence and the dead bodies.

Eventually she slept, then woke up suddenly, frightened, but there was still no sound. She got up in the dark and made her way to the Monument by starlight. There was no farmer army.

Troon might have changed his mind, but Joia thought it more than likely he had decided to attack the volunteers on their mission. They would have to be ready for anything.

She smelt cooking. Verila, who had become caterer to the volunteers, was now boiling salt pork to send them on their way.

Joia was still reeling from last night's conversation with Dee. She felt mortified that she had caused such unhappiness to the one she loved. She had done it out of ignorance, but knowing that made it even worse. And she did not know whether the damage could be repaired, or even if Dee wanted to repair it.

At dawn the volunteers started arriving, and each was given a fragrant slice of pork. Scagga was not there but Jara, his sister, turned up. 'He doesn't like to rise early in the morning,' she explained.

Joia said: 'There's no sign of the farmer army, happily.'

'Good. However, they may attack the volunteers on the mission.'

'That was always a possibility.'

'So we need to arm the volunteers.'

Joia hesitated for only a moment. She hated weapons but she could not let her volunteers go defenceless. 'Yes,' she said. 'They should each have a bow, six arrows, and a leather protective wristband.'

A moment's thought told her they could not possibly have enough bows for the number of people she was hoping to take on the mission, and she went on: 'When we run out of bows we should tell people to bring axes or hammers, or even just clubs. I don't want anyone to be vulnerable.'

'I'm coming on the mission myself,' Jara said, surprising Joia. 'I'll keep an eye on the volunteers' preparedness.'

Jara would probably be a better military leader than me, Joia thought.

As volunteers streamed into the Monument, she did her best to estimate numbers and figure out whether she would hit her target. The dawn light grew stronger, more people arrived, and she began to think she would succeed.

Then she saw Dee in the crowd. That bucked her up. With Dee on the mission there would be many opportunities to talk. Joia would have a chance to put matters right. She would apologize abjectly and beg to be allowed to start again. She would not hesitate to humiliate herself. The rest of her life hung on this.

Volunteers were still arriving when the sun rose. Joia, feeling cheerier now, decided to set off right away. It would take time to get so many people moving. Latecomers could join the tail end.

She led. They would not follow anyone else.

Last summer Joia had walked beside Dee. Today Dee was somewhere in the crowd behind, and Joia was walking with Jara.

All morning they followed the East River under a hot summer sun, and they reached the village of Upriver at midday. Joia and Jara and many others crowded into the river to cool off. As they rested in the clear water, Jara looked back at the route they had travelled and said: 'The farmers won't attack here, beside the river. It would be a bad choice for a battlefield.'

'Why's that?' Joia asked.

'The land rises on the other side of the path. The only flat area is the path itself. There's no space to fight.'

Joia found that convincing. Jara probably spent a lot of time talking with her family about battles, especially the two occasions when the Monument had been attacked.

When they moved off again, they turned away from the river into a wide stretch of grassland being grazed by the herd. Joia said: 'It's like this until we reach the North Hills.'

'Gently sloping and unobstructed,' Jara said. 'This will be our danger zone.'

At suppertime in Stony Valley Joia saw Dee sitting alone, in a bed of oxeye daisies, under one of the few trees that Seft had not felled. Joia took her beef and sat next to Dee without asking.

Unluckily, a young woman chose to sit near them, looking as if she wanted to chat. 'That's a long walk!' she said.

'Indeed,' said Joia.

Dee said nothing.

The woman looked at them, realizing she was not welcome. 'Oh,' she said, 'you're Joia.' She looked at Dee. 'And you're the one who fascinated Joia on the last trip.' She got up. 'I will leave you two alone.'

Joia said: 'I'm sorry if we've been unfriendly.'

The woman did not seem to mind.

As she walked away, Joia said to Dee: 'Thank you for joining in the mission. Last night you said you'd think about it. I'm glad you decided to come.'

Dee did not reply, but looked at her expectantly.

Joia said: 'I'm bitterly sorry for what I did to you. I didn't intend it, but it seems that makes no difference.'

Dee seemed to agree with that, though she did not say anything.

'I do love you,' Joia said, 'even though I failed to show it. But now at least I've said it.'

Dee spoke at last. 'Yes,' she said, 'at least you've said it.' And with that she got up and walked away.

Joia wanted to scream. She could not figure out what Dee wanted, and Dee would not tell her.

She was determined not to cry. She was the leader and had to be strong. She took a deep breath and stood up, dry-eyed. She began to walk around the valley, talking to the volunteers. 'How do you feel? A bit tired? Me, too. Get some sleep! Be ready for tomorrow.' She could see that many of them were forming couples, and she guessed they might not get a full night's sleep, no matter what she said.

Jara set up a night watch in case of a sneak raid by the farmers. She stationed volunteers on the outskirts of the camp, in pairs to stop one another falling asleep.

The sun set, and in the dusk Joia looked for a place to sleep. Her eye fell again on Dee, already lying down.

Joia lay facing her.

Dee opened her eyes but said nothing.

Joia said: 'I am not going to let this happen.'

'What?'

'I am not going to lose you. I'm determined.'

'Is that so?'

Joia said: 'I've had sex twice, once with a boy and once with a girl, both times at the revel. I did it because I wanted to find out what it was like.'

Dee raised up on her elbow and said: 'What was it like?'

Joia was encouraged. She's talking to me, she thought. She said: 'I knew the boy, though not well. He kissed me and put his tongue in my mouth, then he felt my body all over. He asked me to rub his cock, so I did, but he said I was doing it wrong and he showed me how he liked it. Then he sploshed. It smelt funny.'

'And that was all?'

'I don't think he enjoyed it much, and I didn't enjoy it at all.'

'What about the girl?'

'I didn't know her. She kissed me all over then lay on top of me, rubbing her pussy against mine. After a while she made a little noise then rolled off me. I asked her if it had been nice, and she said: "Not very. Was it nice for you?" I said: "Not really." And that was that.'

'So that's your whole sexual history?'

'I'm not sure.'

'What do you mean?'

Joia raised herself on her elbow, mirroring Dee. 'A year ago you kissed me, and it was so lovely that I've been thinking about it ever since. If sex was like that I'd do it every day.'

'Really?'

'Would you kiss me like that again? Please?'

Dee shuffled closer to her, leaned forward, and kissed her lips. The kiss was soft and loving, just like before. This time it lasted longer. When at last Dee moved away and took a deep breath, Joia said: 'That's right, exactly like that. Would you do it again?'

Dee gently pushed her down until she was lying on her back, then leaned over her. 'What you did before, with the boy and the girl at the revel, that wasn't really sex,' she said. 'It was going through the motions.'

'What makes the difference?'

'We love each other,' Dee said. Then she kissed Joia again.

After a while Dee sat up and pulled her tunic over her head. Joia did the same. They lay down again, and Joia said: 'What should I do?'

'Do you ever stroke yourself?'

'Yes.'

'Where do you touch yourself?'

'My nipples, and my pussy.'

'Anything you do to yourself, you can do to me.'

Dee's breasts seemed to shine in the moonlight. Joia felt an eager impulse to fondle them. And she suspected that this was what Dee wanted, although she could not be sure with Dee in this mood. She reached out with both hands and touched them. Dee's skin was warm. Her breasts were bigger than Joia's. Joia touched the nipples experimentally, stroking them lightly. Dee breathed a little harder, and Joia felt a thrill to realize that she had caused that.

Then Dee pushed Joia's hands away, seeming almost impatient, and bent her head to Joia's breasts. She kissed them all around, then took a nipple into her mouth. Suddenly Joia felt a deliciously pleasurable sensation, and she said: 'Oh!'

Dee moved her mouth to the other side, then back again, in a way that Joia found frustrating and thrilling at the same time. And there was another thrill: that of doing such intimate, such private things, not with just anybody, but with Dee.

Dee moved again, took Joia's hand and placed it on her pussy.

Joia had never touched anyone's other than her own, and she found the experience strange. She moved her hand a little, experimentally, and Dee said: 'Yes.'

Joia wanted to do anything and everything to please Dee. Her fingertip found a small damp place, something that happened sometimes when she touched herself. She wanted to push her finger inside. It would be shockingly intimate, and that was what excited her. She had never even done it to herself. But she sensed that Dee wanted her to do it. So she did, and Dee gave a quiet moan of pleasure.

She had the strangest feeling that she was no longer in the familiar real world. She and Dee were doing the oddest things. Yet Dee liked what they were doing, and as for Joia, she had never felt this good before, ever. She hoped this was not a dream.

Dee put a hand over Joia's and pressed, then began to move her hips rhythmically. The motion was the same as that of the girl who had lain on top of her at the revel. But that girl had closed her eyes, whereas Dee looked lovingly at Joia as she moved. She seemed to be in a trance, concentrating. On impulse, Joia kissed her, and the kiss had an immediate effect, as if Dee had been waiting for just that. Dee gave a low cry, one that might have been pain or delight, and froze for a long moment; then she slumped, saying: 'Thank you, thank you, thank you.'

As Dee caught her breath, Joia said: 'That was so lovely.'

'It's not over yet,' Dee said. 'Lie on your back.'

She knelt between Joia's legs and began to kiss her body. Surely, Joia thought, she won't kiss me down there; but she did. Joia was glad she had bathed in the river that day; then she had the thought that Dee would not have cared anyway.

Dee seemed to know Joia's body better than Joia did. Everything Dee did was just firm enough, in just the right place, for just the right length of time. She was shocked to feel Dee's tongue inside her, and she thought: Do people really do this? She stopped asking questions and, reaching down, buried her fingers in Dee's hair, feeling her head move from side to side and up and down. Losing herself in sheer delight, she heard herself cry out, and then, slowly, the sensation faded, and she felt as if she was waking from a dream.

Slowly she returned to normal, and after a while she said: 'So that's what all the fuss is about.'

Joia woke up full of optimism. Another day and a night had passed without an assault by the farmers.

That morning, raising the first stone and roping it to a sled seemed less challenging than it had last year. Then they had been working out how to do it as they went along. Today they knew what to do at each step. To Joia's delight the stone was ready to go by mid-morning. 'I was right,' she said triumphantly. 'It can be done.'

Joia and Jara led the first team off. Seft's embedded-log track eased the first climb, and they soon passed out of Stony Valley.

Boli was in the first team. Seft had suggested having a quickrunner with each team, so that the teams could communicate.

Dee was also in the team, just because Joia wanted her. She was her old self again, loving and talkative. As they walked, Joia said: 'What happened last night . . . that was what you wanted?'

'Oh, you noticed?'

Joia giggled, but she had a serious question. 'Why didn't you just tell me that?'

'Because then you would have faked it.'

Joia was taken aback, but had to admit that Dee was right. She would have done anything Dee asked, regardless of her own feelings. And subservience was not what Dee wanted. She had doubted whether Joia loved her sexually.

And now she knew, Joia thought, with a private smile.

They pulled the sled between two hills – like Dee's breasts, Joia thought, her mind now moving along new paths – and came to the plain at midday. As they followed the straight line of the track through the grazing herd, Joia was astonished to see a girl of about three midsummers, alone, wearing nothing but a pair of tiny shoes, crying.

She ran to her and picked her up. 'Are you Lim?' she said, remembering the baby that Revo had carried.

She stopped crying long enough to scream: 'I want Mamma!'

She had probably wandered away from her mother and got lost in the herd. Revo was somewhere out there, frantically searching for her. Joia scanned the herd, but she could see no one.

The sled was still moving, and she walked alongside it, carrying Lim. She hoped Revo would see or hear the volunteers. Two hundred people and a giant sled made a lot of noise. She kept scanning in all directions.

Then she suffered a shock. The track had been vandalized in the night. The volunteers dropped their grab lines and the sled stopped.

Joia looked at the branches scattered widely over the grassland and felt despair. The damage had not been done by the cattle: it was too thorough, too complete. Troon had done it. He had not changed his mind, after all. He was still on the attack. Now, with all the regular challenges of moving giant stones, Joia had also to deal with sabotage by enemies.

Then she saw the bodies.

There were two dead people, a woman and a man, and Joia had a dreadful feeling that she knew who they were. She turned Lim away so that she could not see.

Seft turned the bodies over. It was clear how they had died:

both had multiple wounds – piercings from arrows, cuts from sharp flints, and crushing injuries from clubs. They must have tried to stop the farmers destroying the track.

This had been their punishment.

They were Dab and Revo. Tears came to Joia's eyes and overflowed. They had undoubtedly led peaceful lives, minding cattle, but their time had been brutally cut short, and now they were gone, and their bodies were lifeless.

And Lim had no mother, no father.

Dee appeared and took Lim from her. 'You have to decide what to do about the track,' she said.

Joia pulled herself together.

She considered moving the stone without a track, dragging it over the bare ground. The hardest part of the journey was over, and from now on the way was mostly flat. All the same, progress would be slow, and she would certainly fail to keep her promise of nine stones in ten days. No, she decided, it was better to spend time mending the track. That should be quicker in the long run.

There were two hundred people in this team. With luck they could get the stone moving again before sundown.

She set them to work. She told them to pick up all the strewn branches and replace them in the track. She sent half a dozen people to search for logs for the pyre. There were a few bushes on the plain, dry now after the warm spring, and they too would serve for firewood.

Once that process was under way she talked to Jara about where the farmer army might be now. It had been here, where they stood, but had gone. 'Perhaps they're heading home,' she said optimistically. 'Troon might feel he has made his point.'

'I doubt it,' Jara said. 'They've killed two herders, and they've inflicted some damage that looks as if it can be repaired by the end of today. That's not going to satisfy a man like Troon.' She looked around the rolling landscape. 'They'll be west of here, so that they can retreat home if things go wrong for them; but they're not far away, so they can attack again quickly. They'll be hiding in a shallow valley behind a ridge, watching for a favourable opportunity.'

Joia was chilled by that thought.

She said: 'The second team should have left Stony Valley by now. They could be here by sundown, barring accidents. That will give us another two hundred people, making four hundred in all.'

'I don't understand your numbers.'

'It's more than double the number the farmers are expecting, and probably double the size of their force. We have a huge advantage.'

Jara nodded. 'But the herder society is unused to violence. We hardly ever fight, even when we should.' She was thinking of the time when Troon seized the Break, and the herders had done nothing about it, Joia guessed. 'Farmers are violent people. Think what they did to the woodlanders.'

Joia said: 'So what can we do to protect our people?'

Jara had clearly been thinking about this, for she had her answer ready. 'This part of the route, between the twin hills and Upriver, needs to be patrolled day and night.'

Joia was calculating. 'If, say, twenty people were spread evenly across that distance, each could shout to the one ahead or the one behind, and so an alarm could be sounded along the whole stretch.'

'That sounds right,' said Jara. 'But we'll double the number and send them in pairs, so that they can stop one another falling asleep.'

Joia did not want the guards to get hurt. 'Tell them that if they see the farmers they should give the alarm, then run away. They mustn't try to fight the farmer army alone. They'll be slaughtered.'

'I'll tell them that, and I'll send them out right away, in case the farmers are already on the move.'

'Good.'

Jara went off and Joia looked around for Dee. She found her kneeling down, mending the track, with the dubious help of Lim, who had stopped crying and was bringing small pieces of vegetation to her.

Joia said: 'I want to talk to you.'

Dee got to her feet. 'That sounds ominous.'

Joia said seriously: 'For some people, there is only one love. I'm like that. My mother told me I just have to wait for the right one. Now I've found you.'

Dee smiled. 'That's the nicest thing anyone has ever said to me.'

'And now that I've found you, I'm not going to lose you.'

'I'm glad.'

'So I want you to go home.'

Dee was taken aback. 'Why?'

Joia pointed across the plain. 'Because the farmer army that killed Lim's mother is on the plain, somewhere west of here, not very far away. There will be fighting. You told me that your home is a short distance from here. Go there, please, and be safe with your brother and his woman. And we'll meet again when the danger is past.'

Dee shook her head. 'I love you for saying that, but you haven't thought enough about what it means to be a couple. From now on we do everything together: wonderful things, like last night, and dangerous things, such as we're doing now.' She looked solemn. 'If I'm going to die, I need you to be with me when it happens; and if you're going to die, I want to hold you as you take your last breath.'

Joia had a choked feeling. It was a few moments before she could speak. She wanted to argue but she could not. Dee was right. Living together should include dying. She had not thought of it in that way. She took Dee's hand. 'I used to think I was wise,' she said ruefully.

They stood like that for a moment; then Dee went back to mending the track.

A long stretch had been destroyed, and it took until late afternoon to repair. Joia decided to resume moving the stone for what was left of the day. At the same time she sent Boli, the quickrunner, to Upriver to tell the cooks there to bring food as the volunteers would not reach there today.

Before leaving they cremated Dab and Revo. Dee took Lim behind the stone so that she could not see. Joia and the others stood around the pyre and sang the song for the dead. They had to leave before the bodies were consumed: they could not spare the time.

The sled made good progress in the cooling afternoon, and they stopped when the sun went down. Joia looked back across the plain and was pleased to see the second stone catching up with them.

The food arrived from Upriver. The patrolling lookouts were called in, and fresh people took over. Dusk turned to night.

Joia and Dee lay wrapped in each other's arms, with Lim alongside them. 'I don't think I can sleep,' Joia said. 'I'm too nervous, wondering where the farmers are.'

'Me, too,' said Dee. 'I think I'm too nervous for sex.'

'That's how I feel.'

They held each other close. They could hear the volunteers all around them, shuffling and murmuring, and the cattle grunting and lowing. Joia touched Dee's hair. A full moon rose. They kissed a little, and eventually they did have sex, after all. It was different this time. Joia no longer felt embarrassed about her ignorance, and did just whatever occurred to her. Dee responded to her relaxed mood by being more spontaneous.

In the end they did sleep.

Joia woke up with a frightened start, again, then realized the farmers were not there, and tried to stop her heart thumping.

They had breakfast; then two teams of volunteers heaved on the ropes and pulled two sleds, each bearing a giant stone, away across the plain. Forty people stayed behind, twenty from each team, to maintain the day and night patrol. Their strength was missed, but the hardest terrain was behind them, and the depleted teams managed.

Joia, Dee and Jara did not leave with the stones. Dee passed Lim to Sary, who was thrilled to take charge of her and carry her to safety at the Monument. 'Do you think we might keep her?' Sary said, with bright eyes.

'Perhaps,' said Joia. 'We'll talk to the other priestesses.'

'Just think,' said Sary. 'We could raise her, all of us. She would have many mothers.'

Joia could not give thought to this right now. 'I don't know,' she said. 'We'll discuss it later.'

Joia and Dee walked with Jara back along the track as far as the two hills. There they met the third team, which had started from Stony Valley that morning. They returned with that team across the plain and, to Joia's surprise and relief, they saw no sign of the farmers. They left the third team not far from Upriver, and returned again for the fourth.

With the fourth they stopped halfway across the plain and waited for Seft, Tem and the fifth team. This meant they had two teams, four hundred people, in case the farmers attacked.

However, Joia felt hopeful. There had been no trouble in the past day and night. Perhaps there would be no more.

Joia and Dee had supper, lay down, made love, and fell asleep.

33

SEFT CLIMBED THE fifth stone, grabbing the ropes to pull himself up, carrying his bow slung across his shoulder and a quiver of arrows at his belt. Tem followed him. At the top they stood upright and looked around. There was a full moon that intermittently disappeared behind clouds.

All around the fourth and fifth stones hundreds of volunteers lay on the ground, most of them sleeping, all with weapons beside them. Jara had picked out the strongest and most aggressive young men and placed them at the western edge of the camp, forming a front line. Beyond the camp, the herd stretched west across the plain as far as Seft could see. The cattle were quiet and calm, undisturbed, which meant the farmers were not yet on the move.

Seft was deeply unhappy. When he had left his father and formed a couple with Neen he thought he had left violence behind for ever. That was how he had lived, never even smacking his children when they were naughty. Now he was preparing for a battle.

When he thought of all the problems he had solved, and the obstacles he had overcome, to bring the stones to the Monument, it seemed outrageous that all his efforts might be brought to nothing by jealous farmers with bows.

Neen and the three children were not here, but in Riverbend, which was a comfort.

He stared across the plain. Was there movement in the distant herd? Darkness could play tricks with eyesight. He thought he saw a black mass within the dappled herd. The moon came out from behind a cloud, and he saw that he was right. A dark wave was moving slowly through the cattle, and he thought he heard the distant hooting of protesting cows.

He said to Tem: 'Do you see what I see?'

'Yes,' said Tem. 'The farmers are coming.'

Joia dreamed that she was lying on a grassy bank of a stream, with Dee next to her, enjoying the sunshine. They were watching Dee's flock. Dee thought she should walk around the sheep to make sure they were all still there, but Joia counted them every now and again and told Dee she need not worry. Then the sheep began to make noises of shock and distress, first one then another and soon all of them. Dee seemed not to know what to do, and Joia was close to panic. Then she realized that the noise came not from sheep but from people who were shouting: 'Alarm! Alarm! Alarm!' She opened her eyes and saw that it was the moon, not the sun, that was shining on her, and in the same moment she jumped to her feet. 'It's the farmers!' she said, and Dee stood up too.

She could see the great black shapes of the two stones and their sleds, one behind the other on the mended track. All around the stones, four hundred men and women were jumping to their feet, finding their weapons, shouting questions and advice at one another. In the distance, startled cattle hooted in distress and dodged out of the way of an approaching crowd. The attackers were making noises, whoops and roars and animal sounds, to help them feel brave, she imagined, and to scare their enemies.

Someone thrust a flint knife into her hand. It was Jara, moving through the crowd, arming those who had not armed themselves. Joia saw Dee take a bow and arrows, and tie a leather band around her wrist to protect it from the impact of the bowstring.

She wondered despairingly how it had come to this. She had had a vision of a stone Monument, and now a little girl called Lim had lost her parents because of it. She wished she had never had the vision. She realized that Dee was going to be a target for the farmers' weapons, and she wanted to weep.

A dozen or so archers climbed up on the two stones with Seft and Tem.

Seft had had very little practice with the bow. Just to pull the string and bend the bow took a surprising amount of effort. When aiming at a tree trunk six paces away he sometimes missed. But he was good at estimating the trajectory of an arrow fired into the air.

As the archers put arrows to their bowstrings, he said: 'Not yet! They're too far away.'

The youngsters were impatient but they did what he said. They all watched the army approach.

'Get ready now,' Seft said, and he put an arrow to his bow. 'Aim upwards, like this.' He showed them. 'Copy my angle.'

They did so.

He waited another moment, then said: 'Shoot!'

The arrows showered down on the close-packed farmer army, and Seft heard shouts and screams as some of them found targets. The youngsters cheered with delight and took out more arrows.

Seft did not cheer. When the farmers were in range, the reverse must also be true: the herders were now in range of the farmers' arrows.

Joia heard a hissing sound, and suddenly there was a rain of arrows. In front of her a woman fell to the ground with an arrow in her shoulder. Someone screamed behind Joia. Joia screamed too, not in pain but in fear. She felt they would all be savagely killed. She looked at Dee and saw she was unhurt. She wanted to grab Dee and run away.

Then she noticed Seft and a group of young people with bows standing on top of the stones, shooting arrows as fast as they could. The oncoming farmers were closely massed and there were shouts and screams of pain as several of them fell. Their advance faltered, and Joia felt a surge of hope: perhaps the farmers would retreat, recognizing a larger force in front of them.

But the top of the stone was a vulnerable place for archers, for they had to stand up to shoot, which made them highly visible targets; and now several of those were hit, and fell, some tumbling off the stone all the way to the ground. She yelled: 'Seft! Get down!' but he did not hear.

More archers climbed the stone, and fresh fusillades hit the farmers. Joia was shocked at how courageous the archers were, which made her realize that she was behaving like a coward. If I must fight, I should fight bravely, she said to herself.

As the farmers approached, Seft saw, they drove some of the cattle before them. Seeing the massed volunteers, most of the cows turned aside, but some came on, charging into the camp, panicking, shouldering people aside, creating confusion.

Seft and Tem clambered down from the stone. When the two armies met and fought at close quarters bows would be useless. Seft dropped his and took an axe from his belt, and Tem changed his bow for a hammer. They ran forward through the crowd, dodging the cattle. They reached the edge of the camp just as the farmers got there. A few volunteers were running away, but others fought back fiercely with axes and hammers. A wave of angry herders fell on the farmers' front line, driving them back.

But the farmers regrouped and attacked again, and this time it was the herders who fell back.

Joia moved forward with the knife in her hand, scared but determined, and many other volunteers did the same.

Then she was in the thick of the battle. She knew many of the fighters by sight, but the only way to tell whether someone she did not know was a farmer or a herder was the direction in which they were moving.

Next to her a farmer swung a hammer at Cass, the brother of Vee, and Joia foolishly yelled: 'Leave him alone!' and not so foolishly stabbed the farmer with her knife. Its point went into the man's forearm and he dropped his hammer. Cass, who seemed to have arrows but no bow, stuck an arrowhead into the man's throat, and he fell.

It was the first time Joia had ever drawn another person's blood, but instead of thinking about that she looked around wildly for Dee. She saw a man running towards Dee, but Dee had already drawn her bow and she shot an arrow into his belly, and he bent double and hit the ground.

When Joia turned to face the enemy again a farmer was in front of her with an axe held high. His mouth was open, his teeth were bared, and an animal noise came from his throat. All Joia could do was scream. Then the man collapsed, and Joia saw behind him a herder called Yaran, wielding a hammer. Yaran looked pleased with himself, but only for a moment, because in the next breath an arrow hit him from behind, piercing his neck and then, horribly, coming out through his throat.

Joia realized she had dropped her knife. She could not see it anywhere so she picked up an intact arrow from the ground.

She could not tell who was winning the battle, if anyone was.

She saw Narod, who had pretended to be a volunteer last year, and had wrecked a section of track. He spotted her and grinned widely, coming at her with a flint axe. She jumped backwards, and he stumbled, tipping forward. Without thinking she thrust the arrow at him. She aimed at his belly, but he fell so far forward that his face was level with the arrow, and it went into his eye. Joia instinctively pushed harder, and the arrow sank deep into Narod's head. He fell to the ground. Joia jerked at her arrow but the shaft came out without the arrowhead. Narod lay still.

The hand-to-hand fighting was vicious, and people on both sides fell, but Seft could see that the onward rush of the farmers had stalled. They had been stopped by the more numerous herders with their two-to-one advantage. Now the herders pressed forward.

Then Seft found himself in front of Troon.

The farmer leader had a club in one hand and a flint knife in the other. He swung the club at Seft's head and readied the knife for a stab. But Seft was quick and stepped back. Troon's club swept through the air without hitting anything, and Troon staggered. Seft raised his axe – but his dream came back, and suddenly Troon had the face of Seft's father. Seft hesitated. In that moment another farmer stepped in and swung at Seft with a stone hammer. Seft brought the axe down on his assailant a moment before the hammer struck his left ribs. The assailant fell, spurting blood from his neck.

Seft spun around, looking for Troon, but he had vanished.

Suddenly the moon was obscured by a cloud, and the scene went dim. Now it became even more difficult to know whether the dark figure in front of you was an enemy or a friend. There was a lull. Tem reappeared at Seft's side. 'The farmers are walking backwards,' he said. 'Are we winning?'

Walking turned to running, and Seft heard a voice that sounded like Troon's shouting: 'Retreat! Retreat!'

Seft's heart lifted. The herders had won.

Some chased after the fleeing farmers, felling every one they could catch; but Seft did not have the heart for that. He put his arm around Tem's shoulders. 'Let me lean on you,' he said. 'My ribs hurt.'

After a while the herders gave up the chase and came back, shouting and laughing, thrilled with their victory and glad still to be alive.

Joia was stunned, terrified and exhausted. She stared at the corpses on the ground, knowing she had to do something about them: she had to take charge again. The volunteers gathered around the stones, rejoicing.

Joia came to her senses and her instinct for order returned. She set the volunteers to dealing with the dead. 'There's no time to burn them all,' she said. 'We must dispatch them in the way of the ancients – sky burial.'

Some of them knew about sky burial; others did not. 'We must build a platform, higher than a man, wide enough for all the bodies,' she said. 'Seft will show us how. Then we will sing the song of the dead and leave them to the birds.' Dealing with a practical problem restored her.

Some of the older volunteers had a little knowledge of healing, and they attended to the injured herders, washing wounds, bandaging them with leaves, and tying the bandages with shoots.

Seft came to her. He was walking slowly and had one hand on his chest, as if it hurt. However, he spoke with his usual confidence. 'Tem is building the platform,' he said. 'But there's another problem. We have twenty dead and about the same number wounded too badly to continue to drag the stone. We've also sacrificed people to guarding the route. We've got the fourth and fifth stone here, but we haven't enough people to move them both.'

Joia said: 'Shall we take people from the fifth stone to make up the team on the fourth?'

'Yes.'

'But what do we do about the fifth stone?'

'The team pulling the first stone should have arrived at the Monument yesterday – a day behind schedule because of the vandalized track. If they leave again this morning they will be here by early afternoon. Some of them can make up the depleted team on the fifth stone.'

'Good,' said Joia.

'The track has been damaged by the battle, but not as much as I feared,' Seft said. 'Most of the fighting took place to the west of the stones. I'll set Tem and a few men to checking and repairing it.'

The work took until daybreak. Then everyone gathered around the funeral platform.

Joia and Dee stood side by side and looked at the bodies. Joia said quietly: 'I did this.'

Dee protested: 'The farmers did this!'

Joia took no notice of that. 'I brought all the volunteers together,' she said. 'I led them on the march, made sure they were fed, and persuaded them to haul giant stones. If it were not for me, they would be at home now, with their families, having breakfast. But they're dead, and they're dead because they did what I asked them to do.'

She recited the service for the dead with tears streaming down her face; then she led the singing. She had never before heard the song for the dead sung by so many voices, more than three hundred. The singing changed everyone's mood. The music rang out over the Great Plain, and Joia's spirits rose with the sound. She shook off her melancholy, and her determination revived. When the song came to an end, she raised her voice and said: 'Now, everyone – let's take these stones to the Monument!'

Early in the evening of the fifth day, Joia arrived at the Monument with the fourth stone. She was greeted by a wildly enthusiastic crowd. They rejoiced in her triumph. She was closely followed by the teams pulling the fifth and sixth stones. All the stones were parked outside the Monument. They would be trimmed there, then dragged to their assigned places later.

Looking at the six huge stones, Joia shared the astonished delight of the crowd. Six of the nine stones had been brought here in five days, despite everything that had happened.

She was less euphoric when she thought about tomorrow. She needed three teams to walk back to Stony Valley and do the same thing all over again for the last three stones. They were tired and they had suffered a violent attack. Would they be willing to carry on?

She had talked to some of them on the last leg of the journey, as they pulled the stone alongside East River, and she had been pleasantly surprised by how many of them said they were more determined than ever to finish the job, if only to defy the farmers, whom they now hated. A tribal spirit had set in. Others, however, did not say much about what they would do next, and she concluded that they would not be in the party returning to Stony Valley.

Now, looking at the volunteers, she realized that some had already vanished. She was dismayed, but she could hardly blame them. Offered a fun challenge, they had found themselves fighting for their lives. It was understandable that some had quit. But she needed only six hundred, half the original number, to move the last three stones. It could still be done.

Dee said: 'You should speak to them.'

'Of course. But what do I say about the risk that the farmer army is not yet defeated and may attack again?'

'Tell the truth. You never do anything else.'

'They may walk away.'

'In that case, so be it.'

That was wise, Joia reflected grimly.

Dee added: 'But the sun is setting. You need to do it now, while they're all here.'

'You're right,' said Joia. 'Let's fetch the climbing pole.'

They placed the pole against the stone they had brought last summer. The sun was now a low, dark-red circle in the west, turning the grey rock to a soft pale pink. When she reached the top and stood up, its rays made her glow.

She did not make her usual triumphant gesture, but they cheered her all the same. She was still a hero.

She began: 'I'm tired.'

They laughed and clapped and shouted that they were tired too.

Then she said: 'But I'm going back.'

They cheered.

'I'm going back tomorrow. We haven't finished the job, but I have to give you a warning.'

The noise died down. This was not how Joia usually spoke.

'Yesterday some of our friends were killed. And when we bring the last three stones to the Monument, we may be attacked again, and more of us may be killed. So I must say to you: there will be no disgrace, no shame, for those who decide not to return with me to Stony Valley tomorrow morning. No one will reproach you. Your life is your own, and no one has the right to give it away.'

They remained quiet, subdued.

'Speaking for myself, I want to finish the job. I want to defeat the farmers.'

There was a cheer for that.

'I'm going back – whatever the danger.'

The cheers became louder.

'If you want to finish the job – if you're willing to risk your life – then come with me.'

They roared their approval, and she raised her voice to a shout. 'We leave at sunrise!'

She climbed down. Dee was waiting. 'You did it!' she said, amazed. 'You told them their lives would be at risk, and they cheered!'

'Good,' said Joia. 'But let's see how many show up in the morning.'

Joia watched them in the dawn light, streaming into the Monument in hundreds, but there were fewer than before. They chewed their salt pork and chatted excitedly, and more and more came in.

When the sun rose she calculated that she had just over six hundred, more than she needed. She breathed a sigh of relief and led them out of the Monument and across the plain towards the East River. Jara marched by her side.

Seft had roped the now-empty sleds ready for the volunteers to drag them back to Stony Valley. Though very solid and heavy, they were light by comparison with the stones, and people bent to the task cheerfully.

Their mood was good but Joia felt she was pushing them as far as they would go. In future years she would avoid this level of intensity. Never again would she promise to move nine stones in ten days.

They all had weapons. Joia carried a bradawl, a flint tool with a very narrow point, used by carpenters to make holes in wood. However, they walked to Stony Valley without encountering the enemy. The track was in good repair all the way. Once again Joia entertained the hope that the farmers had given up and gone home. Once again she suspected that was wishful thinking.

She slept in Dee's arms that night in Stony Valley. Dawn brought the seventh day, and Joia was still on target to deliver nine stones in ten days.

Seft, supervising what was now a practised routine, got stones seven and eight onto the sleds and away by early afternoon. The ninth and last stone was loaded by sundown, and would leave first thing tomorrow.

Next day Joia led the last march out of the valley and over the ridge.

At mid-morning they passed between the two hills. From there the route rose and fell gently, with cattle on both sides of the track. They climbed a slope, and Joia called a rest stop on the other side of the ridge, providing a long downhill slope for the restart.

She heard Dee say: 'Oh, no!'

She looked ahead.

She could see in the distance that the route was blocked. A crowd of about a hundred and fifty men stared angrily at the volunteers and the giant stone. It was undoubtedly the farmer army, and clearly they wanted a fight.

They had timed this carefully. This was the last stone: there was no one following, no reinforcements that could catch up.

Joia felt sick with disappointment and fear.

Jara was brisk. 'I think we have the advantage,' she said. 'They lost a lot of men in the moonlight battle.'

'This isn't a game!' Joia protested. 'If we fight, some of our people will die, even if we win!'

'Of course,' said Jara. 'It's a war. The only alternative is surrender.'

'I can't accept that,' said Joia. 'I will not be responsible for more deaths.'

Jara said sceptically: 'So what is your plan?'

Joia did not have one, but she was not prepared to give in. 'Let me think,' she said, and she walked away, leaving the track behind.

A cow with a calf looked at her warily, and another grunted. What could she do? She could tell everyone to run away, leaving the stones; but that would be so dispiriting that she might never again be able to motivate volunteers. This project was far-fetched: only her leadership had made people believe in it. If once it was labelled a failure, it would never be resuscitated.

On the other hand, even that downfall would be better than getting people killed.

She looked around the Great Plain, now occupied by a giant stone, two armies, and hundreds of cattle, and she realized she had another potential army: the herd.

A plan began to form in her mind.

She had heard about the stampede of the herd at the Break, when the beasts had been mad to get to the river and drink. She had not witnessed it herself, but someone who had was standing near her: Zad. He had managed the herd in the west of the plain for more than ten years, so he probably knew everything there was to know about cattle.

She said to him: 'You and the other herders can make the beasts go where you want to, can't you?'

'Of course,' he said, with his usual charming grin. 'Otherwise we wouldn't be able to move them to fresh pasture when necessary.'

'And you were present at the Break when they stampeded for the river.'

He looked embarrassed. 'We tried to stop them, but we couldn't.'

'Could you make this herd stampede?'

'*Make* them stampede?' For a moment he looked nonplussed. 'It's never been done . . .' he was thinking, imagining it '. . . but I don't see why not.'

'Could you make them stampede the farmer army?'

He thought some more, and Joia kept quiet. Then he said: 'We'd have to circle around the back of the herd from here, then down both sides so they don't divert. It will take . . . I don't know how many people . . . the more the better. And then . . . But, yes, we can do that.'

She looked him in the eye. 'Then do it, please,' she said.

He stared hard at her for a moment, as if making sure she was not mad; then he said: 'Right.'

She watched him move through the crowd, speaking quietly to herder men and women, who nodded and followed him. She began to wonder whether she had done the right thing. A stampede was uncontrollable, wasn't it? Otherwise it would not be a stampede. Had she started something that could turn bad? But Zad, though surprised, seemed confident.

Joia looked south across the plain at the farmers. Something about the way they moved made her think they might be getting ready to advance. If so, she hoped they would not get here before Zad could start the stampede. She wished he would hurry.

He gathered thirty or forty people around him at the north end of the herd, then deployed them so that they formed a rough half-circle around the cattle, leaving the southern end open. Some of them had picked up sticks or cut branches to use as whips or prods. The other volunteers could see that something was happening and they watched with puzzled looks, no doubt wondering what was the point of this exercise.

Joia looked again at the farmers and saw that they were coming, brandishing their weapons.

Then she noticed that the cattle around her were drifting south.

It was beginning.

The smell of the herd became stronger, perhaps a sign that the beasts were anxious.

The cattle continued to move south and began to walk faster. The herders were prodding and smacking them with their sticks, heading them towards the farmers, and at the same time keeping them closely massed, preventing them from spreading out east or west.

Joia said to Dee: 'Oh, gods, I hope this works.'

She looked ahead, over the cattle, to the farmers. They had halted their advance and were staring at the herd, apparently puzzled. Any moment now they would realize their peril. But where would they go? They could not escape to east or west because the herd was too big. If they went backwards, the herd would catch them. Some of them might climb a tree but there were not many trees.

The herders began to beat the cattle with their sticks while whooping and yelling, and the beasts panicked and started to run. Their hooves thundered and kicked up dust from the dry summer ground. The farmers ran in all directions. Joia imagined the carnage that was about to happen, and felt sick.

The volunteers around her were not so sensitive. They cheered and yelled and ran after the herd with their weapons. Joia grasped her pointed bradawl hard and ran with them.

Ahead, the herd met the terrified farmers and ran over them like a wave. Some tried to dodge through the animals; some climbed trees; several stood in a pond and watched the herd divide around them. The cattle pounded on, leaving a bloody litter of dead and mangled bodies on the ground. The volunteers fell on the few survivors, and there was a fierce though one-sided battle.

Joia saw with dismay that many of the smashed bodies lying on the ground were not lifeless. Some struggled to move, bleeding into the grass; others moaned in pain and cried out for water. A calf lay on its side, bleating, crippled and abandoned.

Joia heard someone say: 'Bitch.'

She knew that voice, and her heart missed a beat. She looked around and saw the small dark eyes and familiar scowl of Troon. For a moment she was scared, then she saw that he was too badly injured to be a danger to her or anyone. One arm and one leg lay unmoving in positions that showed they were broken, and there was blood on his face.

Joia had no sympathy. He was a cruel and violent man, and everyone on the Great Plain – farmers, herders and woodlanders – would breathe easier when he was gone.

The farmer army was no more. The farmer community would be hard hit. Their able-bodied men now lay on the Great Plain. How would they manage? The women would have to run the place.

There was an irony. Joia almost smiled.

Troon moaned and said: 'Water. Give me water.'

Joia knelt over him, her knee pinning his one good arm.

He said: 'Have mercy.'

That plea maddened her. 'Mercy?' she cried. 'Han was my brother!' And she thrust her bradawl into his throat, leaning on it so that it penetrated skin and flesh and went deep into his neck.

When she pulled it out, blood fountained from his throat and splashed on her arms. Then it abruptly slowed to a trickle, and Troon stared at the sky with lifeless eyes.

Joia stood up and looked around. The fighting was over. The volunteers stood around waiting for her to tell them what to do next.

The herd had come to a halt not far away, and had resumed cropping the grass.

34

WHEN THE CELEBRATIONS were over, and the crowd had at last gone home to their beds, Joia and Dee sat on one of the nine stones, looking in the starlight at what they had done. It was the end of the tenth day, and Joia had achieved her target.

She had ordered the stones to be unloaded outside the Monument, at a spot a few paces north of the earth bank, where the cleverhands could work on them before setting them upright inside the Monument.

'You're a hero,' Dee said to Joia.

It was a warm summer evening, and they were holding hands. Joia said: 'People think I'm a hero – and that's good, because it makes them willing to follow me – but I think you know I'm really just an ordinary person.'

'Not quite ordinary,' Dee said, with a smile.

Joia knew that was true, but she also knew that she *felt* like an ordinary person. Even when she was standing on a giant stone whipping the crowd into a frenzy, a small voice in the back of her head said: This isn't really me.

Then Dee said, in a casual tone: 'I must go home tomorrow.'

Joia was shocked. 'But why?' she said woefully.

'I have sheep to mind, and a baby niece I'm missing.'

'You're going just for a few days?'

'No . . .'

'But . . . I thought we were going to be together from now on.'

Dee let go of Joia's hand, and Joia felt it like a blow. Then Dee said: 'And what do you imagine I would do, if I didn't go home?'

'I don't know, but . . .'

'You didn't think about it.'

'I just thought our love was strong enough to deal with any difficulties.'

'I can't spend my life following you around and watching people worship you.'

Joia knew she was adored. Dee was not the first person to tell her so. But she did not feel that she deserved their veneration, and because of that she never thought of herself as adored. She said: 'But that's the last thing I want.'

Dee took hold of both Joia's hands and looked into her eyes. 'My love—'

'Am I your love?' Joia interrupted. 'Truly?'

'Yes, you are.'

Joia whispered: 'Thank you.'

'But if we're to be together, one of us must give up the life she's been living.'

'But I assumed . . .'

'You assumed I'd give up mine.'

Joia felt ashamed. 'I suppose I did.'

'You've just announced to the people that next year you'll

bring five crossbar stones from Stony Valley, each to be placed across the tops of two uprights, on the pattern of the timber Monument.'

'Yes.'

'You committed yourself to another year as a priestess without talking to me about it.'

Joia bowed her head in shame. 'That's true.'

'Would you give up your life as a priestess, here at the Monument, to be with me?'

Joia wanted to say yes, but could not. 'I've promised to rebuild the Monument in stone . . . Thousands of people are expecting me to do it and want to support me. How could I walk away?'

'You believe your life is more important than mine.'

'I didn't mean to say that.'

'But you thought it.'

'I did, and I'm sorry, because I know that your life is just as important as mine. But what are we going to do?'

'We both need to think very hard.'

'Couldn't you stay with me while we do that?'

'No. That would mean we had already made the decision.'

Of course it would, Joia saw that. Still she protested: 'I can't bear for us to part again.'

'I'll come back.'

'When?'

'Midsummer.'

'A whole year? Can't you come earlier?'

'Perhaps. I'll see.'

There was a long silence, then Joia said thoughtfully: 'It's the second time you've done this.'

Dee frowned, not understanding. 'Done what?'

'Knocked me flat.'

'I don't know what you mean.'

'The first time it was because you were afraid I didn't love you in a sexual way. You thought I might just want to be friends.'

'I was wrong about that.'

'Now you're afraid I don't respect you as I should. You think your wishes will always be secondary to mine.'

Suddenly Dee was upset. Tears ran down her face and she said: 'I'm sorry I hurt you. I'm sorry I've hurt you again. You're the one I love.'

'Then you will come back.'

'I promise.'

'I'm not going to lose you. I will not let it happen.'

'I'm glad,' said Dee.

Pia, Duff and Yana worked hard on their farm, trying to make up for the days they had lost as prisoners. They weeded and hoed from dawn to nightfall, and continued on the eleventh and twelfth days of the week, which were supposed to be rest days.

At the beginning of the following week Zad and Biddy came looking for them, and found them in a field. 'There was a battle,' Zad said. 'I was there. All the farmers were killed.'

Duff said: 'All of them? No survivors at all?'

'Joia told me to stampede the herd, and the farmers were trampled.'

Yana gasped. 'That's terrible,' she said. Beginning to understand the consequences, she went on: 'It means that most of the women in Farmplace have lost their men.' After a moment's thought she added: 'We'll have to go round and tell them.'

Pia said: 'We'll have to do more than tell them. The young widows will struggle to manage their farms, and the older ones will be unable to get their harvest in – unless we can organize to help them.'

Duff said: 'I don't see what we can do – every family will be stretched thin.'

'Some are better off than others,' Pia said. 'A young mother with a fourteen-year-old and a twelve-year-old will do better than an old woman with no one. The young mother could let her children help the old woman a couple of days a week.'

'But who's going to organize all that?' said Duff.

'We are.'

They divided up the mothers and each took a third. But that did not work well. Pia's first call was on Rua, whom she found forking leafy fodder into a manger for her cows. 'I bring bad news, Rua, I'm sorry.'

Rua put down her wooden pitchfork. 'He's dead, isn't he?' she said immediately. Tears came to her eyes but she did not sob.

'Yes,' said Pia. 'Our men lost the battle and they're all dead.'

Anger overcame Rua's grief. 'Thanks to that pig-headed fool Troon.'

'At least you've got Eron to help you.'

Rua nodded. 'He'll have to be the man now.'

'Your neighbour Liss hasn't got anyone, now that Jax is dead.'

'Poor soul.'

'Would you let Eron work for her a couple of days a week? It would make a big difference to her.'

'I don't know . . .'

'We're asking all the women with half-grown children to help in this way.'

'Was it your idea?'

'Yes, why?'

'What does Duff say about it?'

'He's in favour.'

'Hmm. Let me think about it.'

Pia hesitated. 'I was hoping you'd agree right away. Surely you want to help your neighbour?'

Rua was miffed. 'I've said I'll think about it.'

Pia gave in. 'Well, thank you for that.' She took her leave.

She met up with Duff and Yana at midday. They sat in the sunshine eating goat's cheese. 'How did you get on?' Pia said to Duff.

'Fine,' he said. 'They all agreed right away.'

'And you, Mother?'

Yana said: 'Not so well. Most of them said maybe.'

Pia said: 'And did they ask you whether Duff had agreed to the scheme?'

'Yes.'

'Mine did the same: prevaricated, and asked about Duff. I was afraid of this. They won't follow the lead of a woman.'

Yana nodded. 'I'm sure that's what it is.'

Duff said: 'But that's crazy! They've been complaining for years about stupid men telling them what to do. Now Troon's gone and they've got a chance to run their own lives, they insist on male authority.'

'Crazy it is,' said Pia, 'but we've got to deal with it.'

'How?'

'From now on, we pretend that you're the boss, Duff, and I'm just doing what you tell me. But you have to go and see the women who haven't yet agreed. As soon as you personally ask them, they'll join up.'

'All right,' said Duff. 'I'll visit the waverers this afternoon. I'll be the male boss.'

'Don't let it go to your head,' said Pia.

A week later Shen returned.

The area immediately outside the Monument, where the nine stones had been put, was turned into a workshop by Seft. All the stones had to be trimmed to the same size and shape, with their tops flattened so that the crossbars could sit securely. The cleverhands were hard at work.

It was difficult, Seft knew. The only tool for the task was a stone hammer. The mason had to study the block carefully and guess where the weaknesses lay, then place his blow with great care and use just the right amount of force. It was like making a flint blade, but trickier, because sarsen did not flake as readily as flint.

However, Seft was worrying about the crossbars, still lying on the ground in Stony Valley but due to come to the Monument next midsummer. The uprights were a lesser problem. He knew how to get uprights in place and secure. It was not easy, but he had established the method and his team understood what they had to do. By contrast, when the crossbars arrived they would present a whole new set of problems.

A crossbar was less than half the size of an upright. However, each one had to be lifted to the top of a pair of uprights and set in position. To follow the pattern of the inner oval of the timber Monument, the crossbar had to fit exactly on top of a pair of uprights, edges and corners strictly in line. Trimming the crossbar to the right size and shape was not impossible, with careful measurement and skilled trimming. The two new challenges were: first, lifting the crossbar to that height; and second, adjusting its position precisely.

He discussed the problem with Joia when she came to the workshop to check on progress. His son, Ilian, listened attentively.

Joia said: 'Once you've got the crossbar on top of the uprights, surely you can adjust its position?'

'No,' said Seft. 'It's far too heavy to be nudged this way and that.'

'Couldn't you rope it?'

'We might have to try that, but it's impossible for a hundred men pulling ropes to make tiny adjustments, perhaps move a giant stone no more than the width of a thumb.'

At that point Ilian broke in. He had now seen thirteen midsummers, and his voice had changed from a childish treble to a shaky bass. He had learned a lot and was already a competent carpenter, and Seft was proud of him, but perhaps he was not yet ready to interrupt an adult discussion of a problem. However, Seft let him speak.

Ilian said: 'Remember the peg-and-hole joints we made for the timber crossbars in the old Monument?'

'Yes, but that was different,' Seft said. 'We needed to secure the wooden crossbars so that they wouldn't slip off, for example in a high wind. The stone crossbars are far too heavy to be shifted by wind or anything else. Once we get them up, they'll be there for ever.'

Ilian persisted. 'I'm thinking about getting the crossbar in exactly the right position, square on top of the upright. If there were pegs on the uprights and sockets in the crossbars, both carefully positioned, then each crossbar would just naturally slide onto the upright in the correct spot; in fact it could hardly rest on the top without slipping into place.'

'Oh,' said Seft. He thought about it. 'That might work.' He looked at Ilian. 'Good thinking.'

Ilian said: 'And we could carve the pegs on the uprights while they're here, lying down, more easily than later, when they'll be standing up.'

Seft nodded. 'Go and tell the men.'

Ilian went off.

Joia said: 'That was amazing, for one who is hardly more than a child. You must be proud of him.'

'Very proud.' Seft smiled and nodded. 'Though what I'm most proud of is the way he's been raised. He's never been beaten. Never been told he's a fool. No one played mean tricks on him. He was a happy child, and now he's turning into a happy adult.'

'Not the way you were raised.'

'That's right,' said Seft. 'Not the way I was raised.'

Pia was surprised and dismayed at the return of Shen. I shouldn't be surprised that he survived the war, she thought; it would be like him to slither away when things got tough.

He had moved into Troon's old house, sharing it with Katch: Pia wondered how Katch felt about that.

The wheat stood high in the fields, almost ready to be reaped, and Pia was making a scythe, fixing sharp flint flakes into a curved stick, ready for the harvest, with Olin watching her. She discussed Shen with Duff and Yana when they came back to the house for the midday meal.

Duff was angry. 'How dare he show his face here? He was the closest ally of the Big Man who was responsible for the deaths of more than half the men in Farmplace!'

Yana said: 'I suppose this is his only home. It's about four weeks since the stampede: he may have tried to find somewhere else to live, and failed.'

'No one would have him,' Duff said, speculating. 'And we won't either. He must be thrown out.'

Pia said firmly: 'Let's not start acting like Troon.'

Duff saw sense immediately. He calmed down and said: 'You're right. Those days are over. All the same, we've got to do something. He's sly and mean, and we don't know what he may have planned.'

Pia said: 'Surely we can't allow a return to the old ways?' The prospect was chilling.

Yana said: 'I don't know . . .'

'We need to know more,' Pia said. 'I'll talk to Katch. I'm her niece, she likes me. She'll tell me what Shen is up to. I'll go after we eat.'

Katch and Shen were in Troon's big rectangular house. Shen was sitting cross-legged, eating what looked like a roast swan, dark oily meat on a bony carcass. He was wearing a long-sleeved tunic that must have belonged to Troon, the only person in Farmplace who owned more than one tunic.

When Katch saw Pia she looked nervous, perhaps fearing a quarrel between Pia and Shen. Shen continued eating, taking no notice of Pia, but she could see by the way he sat that he, too, had tensed.

Pia spoke to Katch. 'How are you?'

'I'm all right,' Katch said.

'Your wheat is ripening nicely.'

'Yes.'

Everyone's wheat was ripening nicely. Pia was making small talk in the hope of getting Katch to relax.

Without looking up from his food, Shen said: 'Get me some water, woman.'

Pia watched as Katch filled a bowl from a jar and gave it to Shen. He took it without thanking her.

This is awful, Pia thought. He's just walked right in and started to behave as if nothing has changed. We can't let this happen.

She concealed her worry and said: 'Katch, you must be glad to have Shen to help you bring in the harvest. Life will be easier for you now.'

Katch made a noncommittal noise, and Shen looked cross.

Pia decided to push. 'Shen, as well as helping Katch you must work with Liss, my neighbour, one or two days a week.'

He gave her a look that said: You cannot be serious.

She persisted. 'We're all doing this now, to support the women who have been widowed by Troon's stupid war. If we all do our part, then perhaps no one will starve this winter.'

Shen looked disdainful. 'I see you've been giving orders, as if you were the Big Man,' he sneered. 'Well, that's over. Women can't give orders.'

'Is that so?'

'You know it is.'

'So, Shen, who do you imagine will be giving the orders now?'

'If you don't know that, you're even more stupid than most women.'

Pia caught Katch's eye and smiled, but Katch looked away anxiously. Well, Pia thought, after living with Troon as long as she did it's going to take her a while to realize she doesn't have to be a slave to the next man who walks in the door.

She said: 'Katch, just let me know if you need anything, won't you?'

Katch did not reply, but followed Pia out. As soon as they were out of earshot of Shen, Katch said: 'Tell Duff he must call a meeting. He must!'

'All right,' Pia said, noting with dismay that even now Katch thought a meeting had to be called by a man.

She related the whole story to Duff and Yana that evening. Duff wanted to call the meeting immediately. 'We've got to show everyone that things have changed for ever here in Farmplace.'

'Slow down,' said Yana. 'Let's not rush into this. Not everyone wants to be told that things have changed for ever.'

'You can't imagine the women want Shen!'

'I'd like to be sure.'

'I can't believe—'

Yana interrupted him. 'Duff, you're surrounded by disobedient women: Pia, me, even your aunt Uda. Think of how much trouble we get into because of what we are. Not all women are like us. Some want a quiet life. It takes a lot to get them to rebel. Let's find out where we stand.'

Duff looked cross. 'Herder women aren't subservient,' he said argumentatively. 'They're like you.'

'But this is a farming community.'

Duff gave in. 'All right.'

Pia made up her mind to be decisive. 'I'm going to dip my toe in the water,' she said. She looked up at the sky. 'There's still a little light. I'll call on Rua. She's independent-minded. Let's see how she feels about Shen.'

Pia circumvented the fields, to avoid trampling the crop, and came to Rua's house. Rua and her son, Eron, had just finished supper. Rua greeted Pia amiably.

Pia addressed Eron. 'How are you getting on working with Liss?'

'It's all right,' said Eron, who had seen thirteen midsummers. 'She gives me nice food.'

Pia turned to Rua. 'And are you managing all right without him for a couple of days a week?'

Rua nodded. 'I have to work harder, of course, but I'm glad we're looking after the lone widows. It's only right.'

'I'll tell Duff. He'll be pleased.' Pia paused, then said: 'Did you hear that Shen is back?'

'Yes,' said Rua. 'Trust him to survive when everyone else was killed. Slippery as an eel.'

So, she doesn't like Shen, thought Pia. But would she support getting rid of him? Pia said: 'I think he wants to take Troon's place and be the Big Man.'

Rua shrugged. 'Someone has to be in charge.'

That was upsetting. Pia said: 'I just remember when Troon made my mother accept his son Stam as partner. Stam was about thirteen midsummers.'

'Well,' said Rua, 'you can't expect to get everything you want in life, can you?'

Pia groaned inwardly. Despite everything, it seemed that Rua had little objection to the return of Shen.

Pia took her leave and returned to her family. She reported her conversation with Rua and said: 'If we call a meeting, I'm just not confident that the women will do what we want.'

'You're right,' said Yana. 'But we have to call it anyway. If we don't, there's a danger that things will drift and Shen will eventually be accepted and become the Big Man just because no one did anything to stop him.'

Duff was horrified. 'Could they really be that dumb?'

'They could really be that cautious.'

Duff shook his head in amazement.

Pia said: 'Duff, you should go around all the farms tomorrow morning and tell them that the meeting is at noon.'

'Where shall we meet?'

That was a conundrum. 'The usual place is outside Troon's house. I'm afraid that might give Shen an aura of authority. But if we hold it anywhere else, that may be taken to signify that we lack authority.'

Duff said: 'Let's hold it where meetings are always held.'

'All right.'

Pia thought they had finished for the day, but just then they heard a child's voice. 'Hello?'

In the dusk they saw a boy of about eleven midsummers. Yana recognized him. 'You're Laine's son, aren't you?'

'Yes, I'm Arp.' He was panting as if he had run there.

He came closer and they saw that his face was red and bruised around his left eye. Yana said gently: 'You'd better tell us what's happened.'

'Shen came to our house,' he said. 'Mamma told him to go away but he wouldn't. Then he wanted to kiss her and everything, and she tried to stop him, but he was too strong. Then I tried to pull him off her and he punched my face. Then I came here. Would you help her, please?'

Pia was so racked by pity for the poor child that she could not speak.

Yana said: 'Of course we'll help her.' She stood up. 'You sit down and Pia will give you a drink of water. I'll go and see your mother. It might be a good idea if the two of you sleep here tonight.'

'Thank you,' he said.

Duff said to Yana: 'Wouldn't it be better if I go?'

'No,' Yana said decisively. 'We don't want another fight.' She left.

Pia got a bowl of water for Arp and he drank it all. Then she sat on the ground beside him. He was at the awkward moment in a boy's life when he is neither child nor man. Right at this moment she guessed he needed mothering. She put her arm around him and hugged him. It was the right decision. He leaned on her and turned his face to her shoulder.

After a moment, he cried.

Everyone in the farmer community was standing outside Katch's house well before noon the next day. Pia listened to the chat. It seemed to her that the women were equally divided. Some wanted Shen thrown out as quickly as possible. Others said the farmer community needed strong male leadership.

No one yet knew what Shen had done yesterday evening.

When the sun was high Shen came out of the house. Katch, behind him, stayed in the doorway.

The crowd went quiet.

Shen stood on the tree stump that Troon had used to make speeches. Duff immediately went and stood beside him. 'What are you doing?' Shen said to him.

Duff said loudly: 'I'm here to make sure no one gets raped, Shen.'

Shen had no answer to that. Quickly, he lifted his head and spoke to the crowd. 'I have come here as your new Big Man,' he said. 'Troon, the greatest man the farmer folk have ever known, died in a battle with the herders, and I was with him. Fate is cruel. I wish, for the sake of Farmplace, that I had been the one to die, and that he had survived to return here. But it was not to be. With his last breath Troon told me to be his successor as ruler of this community. It was his last command, and I am here to obey it.'

A few people applauded.

Duff gently pushed Shen, forcing him to step down from the stump so that Duff could step up. 'I'm not going to say much,' he said. 'Someone else is going to speak now. Arp? Come here.'

Arp stepped out of the store next to the house and walked to Duff.

This had been Pia's idea, and they had planned it last night.

Overnight, Arp's injury had turned into a spectacular black eye, and every woman in the crowd saw it. Pia heard one say: 'Poor child.'

Duff gave Arp his hand and Arp stepped up onto the trunk. Duff said: 'Arp, please tell people how you got that black eye.'

Arp repeated what he had said last night, word for word. Some in the crowd wept quietly.

When Arp finished, Duff said: 'Laine, please come here.'

Laine now came out of the store, and the women gasped. Her pretty face was a mass of bruises and she walked with a limp. Duff and Arp got down and Duff helped Laine stand on the stump.

She said: 'Everything Arp said is true.' She began to cry, and her words came with difficulty. 'I'm so ashamed that my little boy should have seen it.' She gave in to her sobs and got down off the stump.

Duff got up again. 'I have only two things to say. First, if you make me Big Man, every woman will own her land. Second, no woman shall be forced to partner with a man unless she wants to. So . . . just say who you want, Shen or Duff.'

Someone shouted: 'Duff!'

Several others took up the shout.

Pia surveyed the crowd. No one was shouting for Shen, not even quietly.

The noise rose. There could be no doubt. Duff was the Big Man.

A bloodless takeover, Pia thought. She felt proud.

Shen walked to the house.

Katch, standing in the doorway, did not move.

'Get out of my way, woman,' he said.

'No, I won't,' said Katch.

The crowd went silent.

Katch said: 'And if you strike me, those women will tear you to pieces.'

Pia held her breath. So did many other people. For a long moment no one moved.

Then Shen turned aside and walked away.

By spring all ten upright stones were in place in the centre of the Monument, forming an incomplete oval. It was quite a sight, Seft thought proudly. It was easy to imagine that the stones were mighty gods, standing in a ring to discuss the things that concerned gods, thunder and floods, eclipses and earthquakes, plagues.

All their tops were level, a technical achievement that Seft was particularly proud of. Each top had a dome-shaped protrusion in its centre. When the crossbars arrived from Stony Valley, the challenge would be to make sockets in each so that the pegs would fit exactly.

Seft used the priestesses' climbing pole to mount the nearest upright. He was carrying the hide of a large cow and a sharp flint knife. He placed the hide across the upright and its pair, where the crossbar would lie. It was easy to step from one upright to the next: the gap was small.

Tem and Ilian then climbed the pole and stood at the two ends of the hide, keeping it taut and preventing it moving. Next, where the pegs stood up under the hide Seft carefully cut two round holes in the leather, so that the pegs came through. Then he cut the edges of the hide to match the edges of the uprights.

When the crossbar was trimmed to this template, its edge would exactly match the edges of the uprights on which it stood, and there would be a socket exactly over each domed peg.

Seft spent the rest of the morning making a leather template for each of the five pairs of uprights.

It was a good scheme and Seft just hoped it would work.

When he climbed down from the last pair of uprights, he saw two people waiting for him: his brothers, Olf and Cam. 'Oh, no,' he said, and he immediately felt depressed.

This time they did not have to tell him how unlucky they had been. Whatever they had done had ended in a fight and both of them had been injured. Olf had his left arm in an improvised sling made of twisted plant fibres, and Cam had lost his front teeth. They were both filthy.

Seft hated to be reminded so vividly of his childhood: the beatings, the scorn, the practical jokes that were never funny and always cruel. He had escaped from them fourteen midsummers ago, but he could never forget, much as he wished to. He had made himself a new and different life, and he was proud of that, but he still hated the old memories.

Cam looked at the giant stones and said: 'What are they?'

'We're rebuilding the Monument in stone.'

'What for?'

'You wouldn't understand.' Seft sighed. 'Why have you come here?'

'We were attacked by farmers,' Cam said. 'They beat us and took everything we had – food, tools, everything.'

That was unlikely. All able-bodied farmers had died in the stampede almost a year ago. Unless Olf and Cam had been beaten up by women and old men, their story was a lie. But Seft did not challenge it. He did not care what the truth was. He said: 'Why have you come to see me?'

'We're hungry and we have no food and nothing to trade. All our flints were stolen.'

'Come with me,' Seft said reluctantly. He led them out of the Monument and along the track to Riverbend, then showed them a visitors' house. 'You can sleep here,' he said. 'You can eat with my family. But that's all. We eat outside, so you'll have no reason to go into my house.' He was going to ask them what their long-term plan was, but of course they would not have one. They rarely planned beyond suppertime.

He noticed that both of them were barefoot. 'Ani will give you some leather to make shoes.'

Cam said resentfully: 'Why don't you want us in your house?'

'Because you stink. And because with three growing children there's no room for you. Stay here until sundown, then come for supper. And if you want something to do in the meantime, go to the river and bathe.'

He left them and went to his own house to tell Neen that his brothers were back again. 'You sent them away immediately, of course,' she said.

'I put them in a visitors' house.'

She was furious. 'I don't want them anywhere near me or my children.'

'I told them they're not allowed inside our house.'

'Gods, they're liars and thieves and bullies, surely you don't need to be told that?'

'I know, but they're starving. I told them they could eat with us.'

'I really wish you had not done that.'

'I'll make sure they don't bother you.'

'And what will happen on the day after midsummer, when you go to Stony Valley to fetch the crossbars for the Monument?'

Seft was taken aback. 'I hadn't thought of that.'

'Well, think of it now.'

He was inspired. 'I know,' he said. 'I'll make them volunteer.'

Joia had hoped to see Dee at the Autumn Rite, the Midwinter Rite, and the Spring Rite, and each time she had been disappointed. But Dee had promised to return, so surely she would come at midsummer.

Joia had been thinking about what she would say to Dee for the whole of the past year. She realized she had to be prepared to make some sacrifice. After much agonizing she had decided to tell Dee that she would resign from the priesshood soon after the Midsummer Rite, when the five central triliths would have been completed in stone. That would be her legacy, and she would leave Seft and Sary to continue the rebuilding of the rest of the Monument. Joia would go to the North Hills with Dee, and they would be shepherdesses together.

She told herself that this would be idyllic: just the two of them in a little house. Dee would teach her how to care for sheep and nurture the lambs born every spring. They would have no worries. Joia would no longer move giant stones or argue with the elders or cause wars.

She knew she would miss the camaraderie of the priesshood and the excitement and fulfilment of rebuilding the Monument. She had got used to thinking of the Monument as her life's work. But she would have to put that behind her in order to live with the one she loved.

The only problem was that it would break her heart.

She had rehearsed her speech many times, lying awake at night and wishing she was back in Stony Valley with Dee by her side.

As things turned out, she never delivered it.

The traders began to arrive two days before the Midsummer Rite and, to Joia's delight, Dee appeared with a flock of hoggets.

She was even more beautiful than Joia remembered, her hair like a tree in autumn, her smile like the rising sun. They hugged and kissed, and Joia had a feeling that everything was going to be all right.

Dee and her brother tethered their sheep, then Dee and Joia sat on the outside of the earth bank to talk. Dee said: 'I spent the whole winter thinking about the future and our lives together.'

'So did I,' said Joia. She was nervous of what would come next. She knew only too well how Dee could shatter a loving moment with a devastating announcement.

'I know what I want to do,' said Dee, 'and I hope you approve.'

That was ominous. 'Tell me, tell me!'

Dee sighed. 'I want to be a priestess.'

Joia gasped. It was the last thing she had expected. 'But that's wonderful!'

'Is it? Will you let me?'

'Of course! I can't think of anything better!'

'But will I be all right as a priestess, do you think?'

'I know you will. First, all the priestesses like you. Second, you always understand what I'm saying when I talk about the days of the year and the numbers. Most people can't grasp it, and that includes a few priestesses who still can't count properly.'

'I really want to learn all about it. I'm bored with sheep.'

'You will learn, and quickly. Oh, Dee, I can't tell you how happy this makes me. I was ready to come and live with you in the North Hills and be a shepherdess.' Joia became serious for a moment. 'And I would still do that, if you wanted me to. I had really made a resolution.'

'I'm so touched that you would give up everything for me. But it won't be necessary.'

Joia lay flat on her back. It felt like resting after an all-day walk. She realized that she had been tense for a year. This was the first time she had relaxed. The sun on her body was sensual, and she wanted to make love.

She said mischievously: 'Did you know that priestesses have to do what the high priestess tells them?'

Dee grinned. 'I might be a disobedient priestess.'

'No, you won't. You'll be lovely.'

'So we'll be together from now on?'

'For ever and ever.'

'Or at least until we die?'

'Yes. Until we die.'

35

SEFT WOKE HIS brothers at dawn on the day after midsummer.

Cam was the spokesman for the two, Olf not being good at speaking, but Cam always said what Olf wanted him to say. Now he protested: 'It's still dark!'

'Not quite. Get up. Don't argue.'

Cam said: 'We're not going on this stupid mission.'

'In that case you'll have to leave Riverbend.'

'You can't throw your brothers out!'

'It won't be me throwing you out. In Riverbend you have to work if you want to eat. You've been here before, and you've never done a stroke of work. The elders have their eye on you, and they've warned me. If you don't come with me now, you'll be gone from here by midday.'

They got to their feet reluctantly. He noticed that they had ignored his advice to wash.

They joined the stream of people crossing the plain to the Monument. Olf whined: 'I can't work with a bad arm.'

'I'll think of something you can do with your other arm,' said Seft.

When they reached the Monument, the brothers eagerly grabbed slices of salt pork. Seft sought out Joia, and they stood together watching the volunteers arrive. Seft said: 'What do you think?'

'It's fewer than last year,' said Joia.

'Everyone's heard about the battles with the farmers, and some people have been scared off.'

'But we won! And the farmer army was wiped out.'

'And most people know that. But there's still a feeling that the mission can be dangerous.'

'Yes – why do I talk as if people are rational?' Joia said ruefully. 'I spend too much time thinking about the sun and the moon. They always do what we expect them to do.'

They watched the incoming crowd in silence for a while, then Seft said: 'We're going to have enough volunteers. A crossbar is about half the size of an upright, so each one should need only about a hundred people pulling. And we need only five crossbars.'

'So we're all right?'

Seft nodded. 'And I see Dee's here.'

Joia smiled broadly. 'Yes.'

'I'm glad. She makes you happy. Anyone can see it.'

'I'm a lucky woman.'

'So is Dee.'

'Thank you. Now I think it may be time to start.'

'Right. I'll just make sure my brothers don't contrive to get left behind.'

Joia and Dee led the march. Seft found Olf and Cam and herded them out through the entrance and across the plain. They no longer looked so resentful: the salt pork had mollified them.

Seft went ahead to check the condition of the track. He had

surveyed it a month ago and ordered some repair work, and he was pleased to see it was still in good condition.

He returned to the main body of the march and listened to what the volunteers were talking about. Right now they were upbeat. Last summer's mission was spoken of with excitement, not fear. 'Were you here for the stampede?' he heard one young man say. 'It was fantastic.'

This was the third mission, and spirits were higher than ever. The legend was growing. It would continue to survive setbacks and grow more popular, he thought. It had become something that people did every year. That was necessary, for many more years would be needed to finish the task.

The woman flint miner, Bax, came up beside him. 'I noticed you talking to a couple of miners I know – Olf and Cam,' she said. 'I just want to tell you that they're a villainous pair.'

Clearly she did not realize that they were Seft's brothers. He decided not to tell her yet. He wanted to hear the plain truth. Seft said: 'I appreciate the warning, though I do know them. What makes you call them villainous?'

'I saw the fight that gave them those injuries.'

'Ah.' Seft wanted to know more about that. 'They told me they were beaten by farmers and robbed of everything.'

Bax laughed. 'No, they were the robbers. They were trying to steal from another miner, but he caught them, and he and his workmates beat them up.'

Seft sighed. 'I can't say I'm surprised.'

'How do you know them?'

'To my shame, they're my brothers.'

'Oh!' Bax was embarrassed. 'I didn't realize . . .'

'Please don't apologize. I'm grateful to you for telling me the true story.'

When they left Upriver behind, Seft walked with Joia. He had a surprise for her. As they ascended into the hill country, they could see that Seft had extended the embedded-timber track. Originally installed only for the first climb out of Stony Valley, it now replaced the branches-and-earth track on every uphill stretch.

Joia was delighted. 'This will make moving the stones much less difficult,' she exulted.

'It takes a long time to build and uses a lot of timber, but eventually I hope we'll have this type of track all the way,' he said.

'You're looking to the future.'

'If we succeed today, we'll go on to build the outer ring in stone, won't we?'

'I hope so.'

'That will take years. Thirty uprights and thirty crossbars. Are you all right with that?'

'Of course. I'm happy. This has become my life's work.'

Seft nodded. 'Mine, too.'

They reached Stony Valley in good time. The village had grown again, Joia saw, with more houses, a store, and a workshop sheltered from the weather by a canopy. Seft and his family divided their time between here and the Monument, but many of the cleverhands lived here with their families all the year round, only going south for the Rites.

As usual, Seft saw, some of the volunteers regarded this evening as a continuation of the midsummer revel. However, Olf and Cam did not join in: evidently exhausted by the walk, they went to sleep straight after supper.

Next morning they had gone. Seft assumed they would try their luck elsewhere. He was not going to worry about it.

The next day was the least difficult yet. Not only were Seft and the cleverhands experienced in moving stones, they also benefited from the smaller size and lighter weight of the crossbars. And there was no one trying to sabotage their track. In consequence, five crossbars were transported to the Monument in three days.

Still on sleds, the stones were parked just outside the earth bank, in the area that had become the stonemasons' workshop. Each had to be carefully carved, using Seft's leather templates, to match the twin tops of its destination uprights, with two sockets that would fit exactly on the dome-shaped pegs.

The ropes used to pull them were loosened for the carving, then re-tightened when they were ready to be moved into the Monument.

Meanwhile, Neen was furious. Olf and Cam had come back to Riverbend and robbed Seft's house while Neen and the children were at Ani's place. They had taken flints and pots and some of Seft's tools. 'How could you do this to me again?' she raved. 'You know what they're like.'

'You're right,' he said humbly. 'I'm sorry.'

'Please, never let this happen again.'

'I won't.'

'Next time they show up here, you give them no food and nowhere to shelter. And you stay with me until they leave the village.'

'I'll do that.'

'Promise.'

'I promise.'

When all the stones had been painstakingly carved it was time to place them on top of the uprights, where they would remain until the end of time.

Neither Joia nor anyone else could imagine how Seft was going to lift an enormously heavy crossbar to the top of an upright, which was as high as three men standing on each other's shoulders. No one knew what Seft's plan was, and all he would say was that he did not know whether it would work. Everyone was desperate to see him perform a miracle – or fail.

Joia reckoned Seft needed a hundred volunteers, and she recruited more than that with no difficulty from the huge crowd that had gathered to watch.

The two uprights nearest the entrance had been chosen as the first pair to be crowned with a crossbar. Seft had constructed a platform, level with the tops of the uprights. It was made of branches tightly roped together and supported by tree trunks. To reach it he had to scramble up the climbing pole Joia used when she made her speeches.

The first sled was dragged in and parked beside the chosen uprights, with its nose to the outer edge of the near upright. Joia wondered why Seft was going to lift the crossbar up the side of the pair, rather than the front. No doubt the scheme would soon become clear.

Seft had made a timber giant like the one he had constructed at Stony Valley, two tree trunks roped together in a cross shape, with long legs and short arms. This massive frame now leaned against the outer edge of the far upright.

A picture began to emerge. The grab lines of the ropes around the crossbar were now trailed up from the sled, over the tops of the two uprights, through the angle made by the arms of the giant, and all the way down to the ground on the other side.

Joia realized with astonishment that this required the crossbar to be lifted up in the air. This had never been done with the uprights. From the raising of the stone up from the ground in Stony Valley, to sliding it off the sled and into its hole in the ground at the Monument, some part of the stone had always rested on the ground or on the sled. But now the crossbar was to rise straight up.

The volunteers were instructed to take hold of the grab lines. They came eagerly, unsure of what they were doing but proud to be part of the big event.

On Joia's command they pulled the ropes taut, but no harder, while Seft and some of the cleverhands adjusted the position of the giant at the other end.

Seft and Tem went up the pole and stood on the platform. Joia worried about their safety. It was a long way to fall.

There was tension in the air as the big moment approached.

Seft nodded to Joia, and she said: 'Take the strain . . .'

The ropes tightened all along their route. The pointed feet on the ends of the giant's legs sank into the earth.

'And now . . . heave!'

The crossbar rocked on its sled.

'And more . . . heave!'

Joia stared at the bottom of the crossbar. Was it rising?

'And again . . . heave!'

Suddenly Joia could see light between crossbar and sled. 'It's coming!' she yelled. 'Come on, heave!'

With painful slowness the great stone rose. It also swung forward until its front end touched the side of the upright with a deep thud like the sound of a felled tree hitting the ground. Joia wondered whether Seft had foreseen this, and feared that the crossbar might knock over the upright; but the upright was firmly grounded and did not move.

The crowd was silent, rapt. The only sound was the panting of the volunteers. Slowly the crossbar came up until its front end scraped over the edge of the upright.

Now comes the really hard part, Joia thought: letting the crossbar down in exactly the right place.

The great stone inched over the uprights. Seft, on the platform, knelt down to look at the sockets on the underside of the crossbar. If all his calculations were right, the crossbar should sink down with its sockets embracing the domed pegs in a perfect match.

Seft lifted his arm and yelled: 'Stop! Hold position!'

The volunteers relaxed slightly and the crossbar stopped moving.

Seft yelled: 'One more pull!'

They pulled again, and a moment later he yelled: 'Stop!'

The crossbar now lay across the tops of the two uprights. Still peering underneath, Seft shouted: 'Slowly, slowly, ease the ropes.'

The crossbar sank down. There was a scraping sound: the pegs and holes were not exactly in line. But the crossbar jerked sideways by the width of a thumb, and then sank down until it rested flat on the uprights with no gap.

The pegs were in the sockets.

The crossbar lay with its edges perfectly aligned with the edges of the upright stones.

Seft has done it, Joia thought jubilantly. He's triumphed again.

The exhausted volunteers dropped their grab lines and rubbed their sore hands.

The crowd began to cheer.

Seft leaped from his platform onto the crossbar and stood upright, holding his arms up in a victory gesture he had learned from Joia, and the cheering turned into a roar of triumph.

'We did it!' Seft yelled. 'We all did it!'

The crowd went wild, everyone cheering and kissing and hugging. On top of the crossbar, Seft hugged Tem.

Dee kissed Joia. 'You did it,' she said.

'It was a team effort.'

'But you made it happen. I'm so proud of you I think I might burst.'

They stood side by side with their arms around each other and stared at the completed trilith as the cheering went on. 'I can hardly believe it,' said Joia. She thought of the years of effort that had gone into making this massive, simple symbol, and felt a deep sense of satisfaction.

They stared for a long time, and then she said: 'That's just a beautiful, beautiful sight.'

Fifteen more midwinters pass

36

ANI COULD NO longer walk more than a few steps. She did not know how old she was, but Joia knew that this was her sixty-ninth midsummer. Her hair was snowy white, though thick, and her face was lined, but her mind was still lively.

Seft had built her a wooden bed on which she could lie down or sit upright. Before dawn on Midsummer Day a small team came to carry her and her bed to the ceremony of the rising sun. Joia, Neen, Seft and Ilian were the bearers, and as the sky became tinted with first light they joined the stream of villagers and visitors heading for the Monument.

The last crossbar had been raised the year before, so this would be the first Midsummer Rite in the completed Monument. It was a solemn occasion.

On the way Ani exchanged polite words with Jara, Scagga's sister. Scagga was long dead, and Jara had taken his place as the troublesome member of the elders.

Joia had been looking forward to the moment when her mother

saw the completed Monument, with its ring of thirty uprights and thirty crossbars linked in a continuous circle. Now, as they passed through the entrance, Ani's face was the best reward. She was astonished and overjoyed, Joia could see. Joia looked at Seft and they both smiled proudly.

The original oval of five triliths was now completely surrounded by a majestic circle of thirty uprights topped by thirty crossbars, the crossbars forming a continuous ring. Travellers even from unknown lands across the Great Sea were amazed by it, and said there was nothing like it in the known world.

As in the old timber Monument, one upright represented a twelve-day week. The difference was that these could not be burned or knocked over. They would always be there to enable the priestesses, and through them the people of the Great Plain, to know the days of the year. These stones seemed to be eternal.

Today's reverent crowd was the biggest ever, even though this would be the first midsummer for many years when there was no holy mission, no march to Stony Valley, no need to spend days hauling giant stones. Visitors came in their thousands just to see the Monument.

The four bearers set Ani's bed down in a place with a good view. Joia bent to kiss her, and Ani hugged her and said: 'I'm so glad I lived to see this.'

Neen hugged Seft. Joia heard her say: 'You did this, Seft – you and my sister. I'm so proud of you both.'

Joia kissed Ani again, then hurried away to join Dee and the other priestesses in the ceremony.

Pia and Duff brought Pia's son, Olin, to the Rite. He had now seen twenty midsummers, and he was tall, like his long-dead father, Han, with the same massive feet. He was handsome, too, and popular with girls. It was surprising to Pia that he had not yet fathered a child, but it would not be long now.

Olin's fond stepfather, Duff, was different physically, being small and wiry, but Pia was often struck by how Olin had picked up Duff's attitudes and mannerisms. He liked to have his hair cut short, so that it did not bother him, and he had a waving-away hand gesture that was the exact copy of Duff's dismissal of anything boring or irrelevant.

Duff was still the Big Man of Farmplace, and he and Pia made every decision together. Their biggest problem was land. The farmers always needed more. Pia sought out patches of fertile soil and copses that were too small to maintain a tribe of woodlanders. But she always talked to the Riverbend elders before ploughing new land. The elders usually gave their consent, but the asking was important for good relations. If Pia knew anything, it was that war between farmers and herders was disastrous for farmers.

Their relaxation of the rules about women had done nothing but good. The farmer women had worked long, hard days for many years, but gradually their sons had grown tall and strong and had fathered sons of their own, and now men and women shared the ownership and the work of a farm, and no one was forced unwillingly into a partnership. Pia sometimes wondered how the cruel system so beloved of Troon had ever come into being.

The light in the sky brightened, and the crowd quieted. The Rite was about to begin.

The priestesses were ready. Joia had woven oxeye daisies into the curls of Dee's hair, and Dee looked more beautiful than ever.

The priestesshood had become larger as the stone Monument had grown, and now there were a hundred. One of them was Lim, a toddler when her parents were killed by the farmers, now a beautiful young woman.

Joia had taught all the newcomers to sing in unison and dance in formation, and the ceremonies were more spectacular than ever.

Now they came into the Monument, dancing and singing, and the crowd watched in quiet fascination. They danced around the outer circle then the inner oval, honouring each individual stone by naming its number in song. Then they knelt on the ground in pairs, facing north-east, staring at the sky through the trilith that would frame the sun. They sang louder as the heavens turned rose-coloured.

At last the edge of the sun appeared on the horizon. Slowly it went higher, and its light turned the beautiful grey stones pink. Almost all of the red disc was now visible. Then at last the sun broke free of the horizon, and the priestesses fell silent.

The sun was up, and all was well.

THE END

Acknowledgements

My editors on *Circle of Days* were Cassie Browne, Jon Butler, Karen Kosztolnyik and Ben Sevier. Phyllis Grann read the outline and gave me notes.

My historical advisers were Phil Harding and Mike Pitts, plus Heather Sebire and Katy Whitaker of Historic England. I learned a lot from a visit to Butser Ancient Farm in Hampshire, and I thank Rachel Bingham, Trevor Creighton, Andrew Shorter and Joanne Shorter.

Friends and family who read drafts and made helpful comments include Lucy Blythe, Chris Manners, Charlotte Quelch and Jann Turner.

I'm grateful to you all.

About the Author

Ken Follett is one of the world's best-loved authors. More than 198 million copies of the thirty-eight books he has written have been sold in over eighty countries and in forty languages.

He started his career as a reporter, first with his hometown newspaper, the *South Wales Echo*, and then with the London *Evening News*.

Ken's first major success came with the publication of *Eye of the Needle* in 1978, which earned him the 1979 Edgar Award for Best Novel from the Mystery Writers of America.

In 1989, *The Pillars of the Earth*, Ken's epic novel about the building of a medieval cathedral, reached number one on bestseller lists everywhere. It was turned into a major television series produced by Ridley Scott, which aired in 2010.

Ken has been active in numerous literacy charities and was president of Dyslexia Action for ten years. He is also a past chair of the National Year of Reading, a joint initiative between government and business. He lives in Hertfordshire, England, with his wife Barbara. Between them they have five children, six grandchildren and two Labradors.